KATIE WAS FALLING APART. IT WOULDN'T BE LONG NOW....

Kay drew up one knee and crossed the other leg over it. She wondered what Katie was doing right now. She had recognized that tone of voice on the phone. Katie had needed her. But she, Kay, needed Harry. It was just that simple. Dog eat dog. Harry was the lover she knew he would be. It gave her the shivers to think of him. She uncrossed her knees and parted her legs. She would be ready for him when he came. She smiled and softly whistled through her teeth, feeling trickles of perspiration run down her neck.

WITH FRIENDS LIKE THESE...

Liza Fosburgh

PUBLISHED BY POCKET BOOKS NEW YORK

Another *Original* publication of POCKET BOOKS

 POCKET BOOKS, a division of Simon & Schuster, Inc.
1230 Avenue of the Americas, New York, N.Y. 10020

ISBN: 0-671-45258-4

First Pocket Books printing June, 1983

10 9 8 7 6 5 4 3 2 1

POCKET and colophon are registered trademarks of Simon & Schuster, Inc.

Printed in the U.S.A.

*To Great-Aunt Zenith
With Love*

WITH FRIENDS
LIKE THESE...

1

THERE WAS NO SOUND IN THE HOUSE WHERE THE THREE people lay still and quiet. On the second floor, a slender woman, clad only in underwear, napped lightly on the white linen sheets cooled by the late spring breeze that blew in from her open french doors. Above her, to the left on the third floor, in the servants' wing, the white-haired older woman slept soundly, secure that the alarm would get her up in time to prepare dinner. At the opposite end of the third floor, in one of the children's rooms, a fat, dark-haired boy of eight stared sullenly at the ceiling, both hands tied with strips of cloth to the brass railings at the head of his bed. The only movement was his eyes scanning the white blank above him.

Outside the big white house, the once dim sounds of laughter and excited shrieks in the fields below the lawns were growing stronger and finally penetrated the stillness of the second floor. Katie opened her eyes and listened as the noises came through the french doors. She slid her slender white arm back and forth on the sheets, restlessly trying to grasp the noise and crush it into silence. On it came, louder now. Cries of "Look! Look!" and "See that one!" became distinguishable above the merry din.

"Oh, my God," she groaned and sat up, jackknifing her legs, her deep auburn hair falling in waves against her neck as she hugged her knees. "Kite Day." Her head throbbed with the sudden awakening. She had not heard the alarm in Pearl's room nor had she heard Miss Anderson's light footsteps as she went to Freddie's room to untie the pudgy, red-marked wrists. She only heard the laughter and shouts from the fields beyond the long peony hedge.

"Why do they have to make so much racket," Katie mumbled as she swung her long legs sideways and let her feet sink into the deep pile of the carpet. She sat there in her yellow silk bra and matching underpants, feeling nauseated, trying to remember how she had gotten out of Kite Day this year. Slips of memory slowly seeped into her awareness. Last year she had been in the hospital with a liver inflammation. The year before that she had been out of town. But this year . . . how had she managed it?

She had promised Harry she would take the children out into the fields to watch the kites. She had promised Harry she would do it, and she really had meant to do it. Why hadn't she done it?

She shook her head and let her shoulders droop. Why hadn't she done it? And why was her head packed with this close wadding that made her forget so much, so much of the time?

Yes, now she remembered. It had been at lunch, down on the terrace, that she had lost control of her resolve. Kay had come for lunch, to eat with her and to go with her and the children.

Unfortunately, Katie had had four vodka-and-tonics—strong ones—before lunch, then they had some white wine with lunch. Kay was practically a teetotaler, so Katie had drunk the wine almost completely by herself—and that had been her undoing.

She mashed her toes into the carpet and wished the rest of her felt as strong as they did. She was nauseated, her head pulsating with swollen membranes too cramped to ease back where they belonged. And again, for no good reason.

She and Kay had had a mindless lunch, gossiping about school activities and personalities, and she had simply drunk too much wine. That was all. Kay had had only a sip of her wine before Katie refilled her glass, but of course Katie's had always been empty when she refilled it. The children had even behaved during lunch with their beloved Kay, not screaming and fighting as they usually did, so Katie didn't have that as an excuse.

She ran her hand across her forehead. She had failed again. She had promised—not only Harry but the children—and she had failed again. Thank God Kay had been there to help her out . . . Kay and Miss Anderson, of course. She never could have managed without them. She always depended on Miss Anderson to be there, and again Kay had taken Katie's place, as she often did when Katie couldn't manage, when Harry was out of town.

"Katie, you go on upstairs and have a rest. This heat is too much for you," Kay had said after lunch when it was time to go. "Walking across those hot prickly fields won't be good for your health."

"But I promised."

"You only promised the children they would be allowed to go see the kites. You didn't want them out there alone, getting in the way of the students. Does it matter whether you go yourself or not?"

So she had gone to bed. Harry would be disappointed in her. He would frown at her, then she would be angry with him. Damn him. It was his job, not hers. He knew that. He should be the one feeling guilty. It was Saturday and he should have been here to do it.

Still, she had promised him she would do it. And she hadn't.

She stood up and walked across the big room to the french doors and looked out across the balcony, the mountains forming a panorama at every angle. Below her, she could see them grouped at the edge of the terrace: poor fat Freddie, his head set low into his fleshy shoulders, holding tightly to Miss Anderson's hand; chubby little Lavinia trying to be the center of attention, clutching Jewel, the doll that was her constant companion; tall, lean twelve-year-old Joe, so like her own father, his namesake, her first baby, her beautiful Joe. There were two children she didn't recognize, and Kay. Poor homely Kay, her best friend.

She could hear Kay laughing with them, their faces eagerly turned up to listen to her. The children and Kay. It was the only laughter around this house anymore. No question she was wonderful with them.

She had first met Kay three years ago at a tea given for new parents. Kay had made a point of sitting next to her, telling her about the school and town, commenting that she lived right across the street from Katie's new house. When Katie saw her on the road one day, she invited her up for a drink; Harry had not been at home. Nor had he been there the times Katie asked Kay for lunch, tea, afternoon walks and swims. They were always in the afternoon when he was still at the office.

Then Katie got in the habit of asking Kay for dinner when Harry was out of town. Over the years their friendship had grown and cemented. Kay became the friend she needed during her loneliness.

Harry had only met her briefly two or three times at school plays or something like that. Katie couldn't remember anymore just when the occasions had been. But in spirit they certainly knew each other: Katie told Kay about Harry and his life over and over and she told Harry about the things she and Kay did every time he came in. Harry would even ask: "What did you and Kay do when I was away?" Just as if he knew Kay as intimately as Katie and the children did.

Life was very strange.

Katie loved the feel of the warm air blowing freely and luxuriously across her bare skin; it helped her forget how rotten she felt inside. She closed her eyes and listened to the happy sounds, smiling when Joe's voice rose above the others. She wished it were only Joe down there; she would call to him, wave her hand and blow him a kiss. She wished the other two belonged to Kay.

She opened her eyes quickly, ashamed of her thoughts, ashamed as she always was when she thought them, but knowing they were her private truths. Yes, looking down at Kay, she wished that dearest homely dried-up bag-of-bones of a teacher had a husband, and that Lavinia and Freddie were hers.

The motley group headed into the house, the children jabbering among themselves. Katie knew they would be going to the kitchen to get refreshments. Her stomach heaved at the thought of the sweet sticky drinks. She shut her eyes and took a deep breath. This was when she needed a nice cool vodka-and-tonic. Why hadn't she waited until after the kite flying to get bombed? She opened her eyes and looked across the lawn at the spring blooms, the sweep of late narcissus delicately nodding in the same breeze that blew across her skin. Pretty.

She was still looking at the flowers when a child's high

voice called from the other side of the door: "Daddy?" And after a brief pause, again: "Daddy?"

"What do you want, Lavinia?" Katie asked without turning her head.

"Is Daddy there?"

"Why didn't you go to the kitchen with the others to get lemonade? You could have asked Pearl and saved yourself a trip."

"Is he back yet?"

"No, Lavinia, he's not."

"I thought he was back."

"Go to the kitchen, Lavinia! Please!" Katie pressed her hands against her temples. If she got dressed and looked decent, maybe she would feel better.

She went into her big dressing room, with the bathroom beyond, and stepped out of her underwear. She still had that sick feeling inside her; she wished again she hadn't had so much to drink.

She looked at her long slender body in the inner wall of floor-to-ceiling mirrors, turning her head to let the rays of sun light up her hair. Her father had called it "Titian gold" when he saw the sun go through it this way. He would put his hands on her shoulders and smile proudly at her, calling her his "masterpiece with hair of Titian gold." When she moved into the shadows, it turned back to auburn.

Katie stepped over the underwear dropped heedlessly on the floor and opened a closet that held more slacks and blouses than most people had in a lifetime. Looking at them, she came to a quick conclusion: she was definitely going to give some of them to Kay. They were the same height and weight, even if they were built differently. No matter how good and kind Kay was, she was definitely tacky and unattractive—and needlessly so. Anyone had the potential to fix themselves up a bit; Kay just lacked the initiative. And the money—teachers obviously didn't make very much. But Katie could help her out there, on both counts. As the idea grew in her head, she found herself smiling and feeling much better. Of course, there was a possibility Kay wouldn't like hand-me-downs. If not, then she would go out and buy new things for her. But she'd rather try giving her some of her own things first.

Katie put on a pair of cream-colored silk pants and a creamy-white silk blouse, knowing the sensuous feel of silk against her body improved her spirits. Then she opened the top drawer in her dressing table, pushed aside some crumpled bills and loose change and took out a narrow emerald-and-diamond choker and matching bracelet. Next came her makeup. This took longer, especially as the antique mirror was going bad and sometimes she saw herself in opaque duplication. Her hair was no problem, but her face was. She had the right features—high cheekbones, straight nose, brown eyes and shapely mouth—but she had little color. Her eyebrows and eyelashes were golden red, which in hair is fine, but not in eyelashes. She painstakingly brushed green eyeshadow on her lids, tinted her eyebrows and outlined her eyes. The final step was the mascara; her hand shook as she applied this, but she slowly got it done with little smudging. She no longer had that dull colorless look, but had transformed herself into a pale-skinned beauty. Cheek rouge and lipstick completed the "masterpiece," as her father would have said. She looked at the photograph of him watching her from the dressing table and acknowledged his approval with a slight inclination of her head. She had never been a failure to him. He looked at her every day here, his face fixed in time, admiring her, approving of her.

How much she still missed him—after ten years. She wished he could have lived to see this house. He would have liked it here. He liked open country and mountains, mowed meadows and green lawns. He said that was what it was like in Ireland, where he had lived as a boy, before he came to this country to seek his fortune, which he found at an early age. What a man he was. A giant in industry, a man of power and great riches. Young Joe was like him. He would do something with his life. At least one of her children would be a success like her father.

Kay sat on the new-mown grass with the children and Miss Anderson, drinking lemonade and eating chocolate-chip cookies. Joe kept the big plate of cookies close to him and his friends, jerking it away whenever Freddie reached for one. Miss Anderson had already given him two, saying, "Just eat those, Freddie, and don't ask for more."

Joe and the other two boys got up to leave after hastily downing their drinks and cookies. "We're going over to play some ball, Miss Anderson."

"Be back in time to get cleaned up for dinner."

"I will," he called over his shoulder as the three of them raced through the trees toward the road.

"I want to go! I want to go!" Lavinia jumped up, knocking over her glass of lemonade and drenching one leg of her slacks.

Miss Anderson grabbed her arm. "No, Lavinia, you can't go. Joe and his friends don't want you. And look what a mess you've made of yourself."

Lavinia looked down at the stained wet leg and puckered up her chin.

"Now, don't cry. It's not that serious. We'll go right upstairs and change." She clumsily hauled herself up from the grass and took Lavinia's hand. "Will you excuse us, Kay? And Freddie, maybe you'd better come along with us."

"He'll be all right here with me," Kay said. "I'll stay with him until you get back."

"Thank you." She reached toward the cookie plate that sat near an overlooked dandelion.

"Oh," Kay quickly said. "I was just about to have one of those. You aren't taking them away, are you?"

Miss Anderson straightened up her back. "No, of course not." She shot a warning look at Freddie. "Not if you want them left here. Mind what I told you, Freddie." She raised one eyebrow at him, then marched toward the house with Lavinia and her doll.

Kay pulled the plate close to her, pushing it to one side, the side where Freddie sat, so close to him he could smell the sweetness of the round chewy cookies.

"Pearl makes the best chocolate-chip cookies in the world, doesn't she," she commented casually. "I like the chewy kind. Not the crisp ones. These are the kind that are best." She turned her head away to brush a speck of dirt from her shoe, away from the side where Freddie sat, low and rounded like a mushroom. In her side vision she watched him shoot out his hand and stuff a cookie into his mouth. When she turned her head back toward him, he stopped chewing and stared at the ground.

"Too bad you missed Kite Day, Freddie. It was a lot of fun." She knew why he had missed it. He had sprayed a mouthful of water at Lavinia after he had been severely warned by Miss Anderson not to do it unless he were prepared to pay the consequences. "All the children were there. I saw many from your class. They were having so much fun." She looked away again so he could chew. "Did you just decide not to come with us?"

Freddie let his eyes slide to the corners to look at her, but said nothing.

"Well, never mind; it doesn't matter, does it? I'm just sorry you weren't there." She again turned her attention to her shoe that stuck out from the hem of her skirt, and again saw Freddie stuff a cookie into his mouth. "Undoubtedly you had a project of your own that kept you busy," she commented, knowing full well how Miss Anderson had tied him in his room, having gotten it out of Lavinia long ago. She looked back at him and touched a roll of fat on his wrist with her bony finger. "I guess you know how to take care of yourself, don't you? A big boy like you doesn't need to be herded around by a nurse all the time anyway."

Freddie picked at his nose, chewing behind his hand.

"Some day soon," she went on, "you'll have all the freedom Joe has. You'll be able to do exactly what you want to do. You're getting to be such a big boy. I respect children who have minds of their own and do what they want to do. Would you like to have a cookie?"

Freddie looked up at her in disbelief.

"I know Miss Anderson doesn't want you to spoil your dinner, but one won't hurt you. It'll be our secret. Anyway, she simply told you not to ask for more, and you haven't asked. But that doesn't mean I can't offer you one, does it?" She smiled sweetly at him. "One more cookie won't hurt you— and no one but us will know."

Freddie, innocent and greedy, twisted his head toward her, his lips curling upward into a grin as he took a cookie.

"Be sure and lick your fingers good," Kay whispered to him. "Chocolate bits melt, you know, and make all kinds of funny stains when you touch things." She pressed the wrist again. "Want one more? Our secret."

Katie was going toward the back terrace when she happened to glance into the dining room to her left. The table was set for more than two. She stopped abruptly and counted. Six places. My God, had she forgotten a dinner party? She walked quickly through the dining room, the pantry and into the kitchen where Pearl was peeling potatoes.

"Pearl. Why is the table set for six?"

Pearl looked directly at her with one eye, the other one careening out at an angle that saw another side of the room. "Don't you remember, Mrs. Harding?" Her Irish brogue was always accentuated when she had to pointedly remind Katie of things forgotten—reminders that had become more frequent during the fifteen years she had been with the Hardings. "It's the children and Miss Wright that are going to be with you and Mr. Harding. It's to celebrate the Kite Day. Don't you remember telling them at lunchtime before they set off for the fields that you would all have dinner together? That was to make up for your not going with them," she added more quietly, shaking her short white curls. "Sure and you haven't changed your mind, have you?"

"No." Katie vaguely remembered the conversation. "I just forgot. It's all right." This was an unexpected ordeal to face. Maybe a little pick-me-up would help. "Is ice out?"

"Yes. I put a cocktail tray on the terrace. The children are on the side porch now." She didn't add "Not on the terrace." "I only put out peanuts and celery. Will that be enough?"

"Plenty." Katie walked out, glancing at the wall clock as she did. Five o'clock. Harry would be back before too long. She felt fine now, and had time for a drink or two before he came. He was going to frown at her about missing Kite Day; no point in asking for extra frowns with too many drinks while he was watching.

The terrace floor was washed in the pink golds of the late afternoon sun. Katie put a chair in the shadow cast by a big oak, then went to the glass-topped table that held the cocktail tray. She made a weak vodka-and-tonic, dropped in a slice of lemon and went to sit and wait, staring at the blades of grass, dully noting they were the same color from top to bottom.

"There you are."

Katie looked up to see Kay coming out of the house, her peasant skirt swinging around her skinny legs like a flag draped between two thin sticks. The sleeveless white top with the ruffled flounce around the shoulders made Katie think of a balding bird stretching its long skinny neck up from a band of puffed feathers. Kay wasn't what anyone would call ugly, just plain. The cranial structure of her forehead formed the slightest dent above her flat eyes, which gave her a perpetual frown—not markedly so, but a frown all the same.

"Kay. I'm so glad you're still here. You are staying for dinner, aren't you?"

"Certainly. It's part of the big day. How do you feel?"

"I just needed a rest. I should have worn a hat while we were eating in the sun. How was the kite flying?"

"Great. Just great. Some of the kites were fantastic. There was one that was shaped like an eagle with a wing-span of fifteen feet."

"Did it get off the ground?"

Kay giggled in two squeaky spurts. "No. But it was beautiful to see. The smaller ones did more flying."

"Make yourself a drink."

"I'll wait. I've just had lemonade with the children." She sat, back straight and hands in her lap, the sun glistening on her thin hair pulled back into a tight bun, streaks of white scalp showing.

Katie took a big swallow of her drink. "What were some of the other kites like?" Not caring, but trying to sound convincing. Maybe it was Kay's skimpy old-maid's hair that made her head seem too small for her tall body. While Kay babbled about the kites, Katie scrutinized the body sitting two gray-pink flagstones away from her, unkindly thinking what a good scarecrow it would make, arms out to form a cross, hung with tattered peasant skirts in a stark cornfield. When Kay crossed her legs and swung a foot, Katie cringed to see the white vinyl straps on the flat manmade sole. She would have liked to go upstairs that instant and bring down an armload of clothes.

She averted her stare. The silent figure of the new gardener was stooped over the fading hyacinths. What was his name? Franco? Silvio? Paolo? Something Latin.

"The kids had a great time," Kay rambled on more. "Especially Lavinia." She stood up and went to the glass table. "It was a pleasure to see that little face so excited. I think it would have made you happy to see her"—emphasizing the "you" as she took a handful of peanuts from the silver dish and began eating them, methodically chewing one in the left side of her mouth and the next one in the right.

"How about Joe? Did he enjoy himself?" Katie finished her drink, ignoring Kay's last remark. Enrico? Francisco?

"He was farther down, with the other children. I didn't see him," Kay said, "but he was very enthusiastic when he got back here. He said he was going to build a kite bigger and better than any he saw today. Want me to make you a drink while I'm here?"

Katie smiled. He would, too. He could do anything he wanted to do. "Sure." She handed the glass to Kay, who made the drink, brought it to her, then sat down again.

"Thanks," Katie said, taking a swallow. "Wow. Strong."

The gardener stood and moved away, out of sight behind a wall of rhododendron. Riccardo?

Suddenly Lavinia ran through the open door onto the terrace, followed by Freddie, who kept trying to grab her arm. With one hand she held a bowl of goldfish-shaped crackers high in front of her where he couldn't get it; with the other, she dragged her doll by its foot.

"Get away!" she shrieked at him in her high voice. "These are mine! Go get your own!" Her little round stomach was tied with a wide pink sash on her pink dress.

"I want some! Give me some!" Freddie bobbed up and down.

Katie sat up so abruptly she knocked over the glass by her foot. "What is this?! Look what you've made me do!" She stood and stepped away from the puddle. "Look at that!" The glass lay unbroken and empty, having spewed forth ice and lemon with the liquid.

Both children froze and stared wide-eyed at her. Freddie got behind Lavinia, who stuck out her bottom lip.

Katie went over and snatched the bowl from Lavinia's hand. "You shouldn't be eating these anyway. You're both fat as pigs now. All because you stuff up on junk food all day when no one's looking. Miss Anderson can't even go to the bathroom without you sneaking food."

"Lavinia brought them out!" Freddie yelled. "I didn't bring them!"

"You made her knock it over!" Lavinia whined. "You did it! It's all your fault!"

"Stop it! Stop it at once!" Katie towered over them. "Get out of here! Go on!"

Both children started to cry. Katie bent toward them. "Stop that whining and crying this minute! That's no way to behave." She pushed them into the house. "Go to the kitchen and tell Miss Anderson to come speak to me. Please."

They ran from her sight.

Katie leaned against the side of the door. "Dear God. I hope they grow up soon." She tossed the bowl onto the table.

Kay stood up and retrieved Katie's glass from the flagstones. "You shouldn't let them upset you. They're just children. What do you expect from seven- and eight-year-olds?"

"I don't need to be reminded how old they are." Katie spoke as pleasantly as she could, keeping the irritation out of her voice. "I am their mother and I distinctly remember when I had them." She watched Kay pick up the lemon and put it in an ashtray, then lift the glass and examine the rim. Apparently satisfied, Kay went to the bar tray and made Katie another drink.

"You shouldn't let them upset you," Kay repeated as she handed the glass to Katie. "You let your nerves get on edge, and then you lash out. You don't really mean it."

"You're right, of course. I do just that. I fly off the handle for no good reason." She swilled down a third of the drink. "I need someone like you to speak up to me."

They both went back to their chairs, the frankness between them pacifying.

"I'm glad you're going to be here tonight," Katie said. "Dinner with the children is a nightmare for me. I never know what to say to them." She looked into her glass. "It's so easy for you to talk to them."

"I'm with children all day, every day. And I enjoy seeing them more at dinner than in the classroom. I'm especially looking forward to tonight; as much time as I spend up here with you, I barely know Harry. I'm always here when he's away. Does he like to eat with the children?"

"Yes, but he doesn't have to hear them all day."

"True," Kay said mildly. "But then, you don't have to hear them much. Miss Anderson is the one who's with them."

"She is paid to be with them. She stands between me and a nervous breakdown."

"Oh, posh, Katie. What a thing to say." Kay snickered.

"It's absolutely true. I think I hear Harry now." She was feeling much better. She reached for the lemon and threw it into the bushes, then kicked the ice off the terrace with the toe of her sandal.

Just then Harry came through the door onto the terrace, suddenly dominating it as if he were alone there on the warm stones. He was as handsome as he had ever been, his face lean and tanned, his nose straight, mouth wide and ready for a quick smile; he was tall and broad-shouldered, with slim hips and long legs. Katie watched him as he shook hands with Kay, saying how nice it was to see her again. Katie noticed Kay's skinny neck turning red. Then Harry came over to her and kissed her, putting his hand on her shoulder.

"How's it going, Red?" He called her "Red" unless he was angry with her or being stern. Then he called her "Katie" in a deep slow tone of voice.

She reached up and squeezed his hand. "Fine." Maybe he wouldn't remember she had made a promise today. Maybe, but not likely.

"You girls already have a drink? You don't, Kay. Let me get you something."

"Super," she bubbled, "but I'm not sure what to have."

"How about a vodka-and-tonic," he suggested, looking disapprovingly at Katie's glass. "It's sure summer weather already. Got hot today in the woods."

"I'd like to have something summery, but I'm not sure what. Something long and light and cool. We had a hot afternoon in the fields. Let me think."

Katie wished she hadn't mentioned the fields. "Don't forget that other summer delight, the spritzer." She hoped Kay wouldn't tell Harry before she did.

"Oh, dear." Kay coyly pursed her lips. "What shall I have?"

"Harry," Katie said, a little impatiently, "make her a spritzer. It's a wonderful summer drink." It really was so irritating when anyone was indecisive and girlish like this. Especially someone old enough to know better.

"Want a spritzer?" Harry asked.

"Just make her one, s42Katie answered for her.

"Want one?" Harry again asked.

"I can't remember what a spritzer is." Kay looked innocently at him.

"Oh, for God's sake," Katie mumbled and pulled one leg up, crossing it at the ankle over the other knee. She hoped Kay hadn't heard her; she really didn't want to be rude. But it was irritating to see her acting like an ingenue.

"It's white wine and soda water," Harry explained kindly.

"Sounds good," Kay said. "I'll have it."

Katie looked sharply at her. Harry probably could have suggested sewer water with rotten oranges and she would have said it sounded good. Look at her blush, the redness creeping up her neck to her face. Maybe she acted this way around all men. Maybe she was flustered by being with handsome Harry.

Kay asked: "Is it something new?"

"New!" Katie retorted loudly. "It's older than I am. My father used to drink them. How could you get to be thirty-five and not know what—"

"That's enough, Red." Harry opened a bottle of wine.

Katie shut her mouth and watched him make his and Kay's drinks.

He was dressed in khaki pants and a blue cotton shirt with the sleeves rolled up. He wore a tie or jacket only if he had a business meeting or if they had a dinner party. "You do the dressing up," he would say to Katie. "It looks better on you." Sometimes he looked so sexy when he came in like this, with an animal heat emanating from him, that Katie would follow him up the stairs and take off all her clothes and get in the shower with him. Sometimes . . . but not for a long time now. She'd like to do it tonight if Kay weren't here. She wondered if Kay had ever . . . no, no, don't go letting your thoughts run wild.

"Kay took the children to watch the kites today," Katie suddenly said. "It gave me a chance to have a nap." She might as well get it out front right away.

Frowning, Harry looked at her, then at Kay. "How was it?"

"Absolutely wonderful. Poor Katie missed a great day. We had a great time. Or, as Joe would say, we had a blast."

Katie couldn't remember having heard Joe say that. She looked skeptically at Kay.

"The kids are eating with us tonight?" Harry asked.

"Yes. And fortunately Kay will be here, too." Katie sipped on her drink. "To celebrate Kite Day."

Miss Anderson appeared at the door: neat, buxom, a middle-aged woman of medium height, square build and a determined expression. She could have passed for a drill sergeant. She wore, as always, a crisp blouse and dark skirt. "Did you want to see me, Mrs. Harding?"

"Yes, I did. I think the excitement of the day has gotten to both Lavinia and Freddie. They seem in quite high spirits. If they're going to have dinner with us, then I'd prefer it if you were there too. To keep them calm. You know what I mean."

"Certainly, Mrs. Harding. I'll ask Pearl to put another place on the table."

"Where's Carol? She should be the one setting the table."

"Carol's not here today. She wasn't feeling well and didn't come."

"Really?" Katie wondered how she had missed her all day. "She wasn't here for lunch?"

"No, Mrs. Harding. I helped Pearl with lunch."

"That was very good of you, Miss Anderson. Ask the children to help out with the table and in the kitchen, will you? They're old enough to lend a hand when needed."

"Of course. I wonder if we might have dinner at six-thirty

tonight? Seven is a little late for the children. They get hungry before that. We usually eat at six."

"Six-thirty?" Katie looked at her watch. "That's not much time, is it. . . ." She trailed off, trying to think of some positive answer except that she wanted more time to drink.

Harry stood up. "Six-thirty will be fine. I'll go on up and get ready. Won't take me long."

Miss Anderson looked at Katie for confirmation. Katie nodded, almost imperceptibly, but enough for Miss Anderson's trained eye. She left.

"Miss Anderson!" Katie called her back. "The children . . . they didn't do anything wrong when I sent them in. I just wanted them to go."

"I understand. Thank you." Again she left.

As soon as Harry was out of sight, Katie drained her glass and sat staring at it. Six-thirty. Good God. How she hated eating at that hour. Seven was bad enough. It was hardly civilized to eat before seven-thirty or eight.

"This drink is delicious," Kay said. "I'm so glad you suggested it."

"Good." Katie stood and slowly walked across the terrace. She wished she had the strength to put down the glass and not drink anymore. She poured the vodka into the glass, watching it shimmer and swirl, liquid crystal catching the golden pinks of the afternoon glow. Dinners with her father had always been at seven-thirty sharp. He first held her mother's chair, then hers, letting the butler stand idly by, wanting to seat his ladies himself. She added the tonic and sat back down.

"Just look at those narcissus." She pushed her hair back with an emerald-studded wrist. "It's so nice to still have them." Mario. That was the gardener's name. Mario.

2

THE DINING-ROOM WALLS WERE COVERED IN HAND-PAINTED silk murals that Katie's father had brought back from the Orient, scenes of quiet gardens in muted colors. Crystal sconces and a pair of Chippendale mirrors at either end of the room were the only wall adornments. It was a calm, serene room.

Harry had left the table as soon as dinner was over to go make phone calls; Katie had slipped upstairs, murmuring she'd "be right back"; Miss Anderson had ensconced the children in front of a television set with Joe in charge, and now sat at the long table talking quietly to Kay.

"I don't wonder Katie doesn't want to eat with the children." Kay fingered her water goblet. "It's enough to give anyone indigestion."

"If she did it more, they wouldn't be so bad. It's such a novelty for them that they get keyed up and finally hysterical."

"That screaming of Lavinia's is more than just being 'keyed up.' That's practically psychotic."

"Nonsense. You took your child psychology courses too

16

seriously. Since I've known you, you have tended to overstate problems."

"That's ridiculous, Hilda. I know a lot more about children than you do."

Miss Anderson snorted. "All classroom theory. I've lived longer and know what I'm talking about. I have had practical experience. Especially with this family."

"I was glad to see them all together in their natural habitat. Though I've known Katie since the children started school, putting Harry in the right place completes the picture."

"I noticed"—Miss Anderson narrowed her eyes at Kay— "that you were paying quite a lot of attention to Mr. Harding."

"Well, of course; I was sitting next to him." Kay paused. "Isn't it strange, the relationships I have with this family. Katie's my close friend, yet she doesn't know about you and me; the children and I are very close and Lord only knows if they think of my friendship with either one of you; and then I've barely seen Harry at all."

"And what did you think of him?"

"I think he's a saint, just the way Katie called him." Kay repressed a smile; she knew her friend Hilda Anderson constantly was irked that Kay was on first-name terms, while she, the hired nurse, would always have to call them "Mr. and Mrs. Harding." She also knew Hilda resented her insistence that their prior relationship be kept secret from the Hardings. "When Lavinia couldn't get any more dessert and started to sass her mother, I held my breath," Kay said. "I knew something was bound to happen. And when Katie gave her that stern lecture about Freddie and her being so fat, then the screaming started. Her face turned so red I thought she was going to pop."

"Yes. She gets like that. It becomes one long uncontrollable scream that only her father seems to be able to handle. Since she was very small she's done it. He always picks her up and carries her around until she stops."

"What happens when he's not around?"

"She doesn't do it when he's not around."

Kay raised her eyebrows. "You mean she does that number just to get him to hold her?"

"Something like that. She'll outgrow it."

"Interesting."

"She hasn't ever done it at school, has she?" Miss Anderson asked.

"No. Never. You once told me she did it, but what it was never really registered until I heard it myself tonight."

"Well, this was an especially bad night. They had a big day, and plainly were tired out from it. They're easily excited."

"Freddie didn't have such a big day," Kay said pointedly, looking across the table.

"He had a frustrating day. His emotions were pent up and ready to give way in some form."

"Some form is right. Enough to make you throw up."

Freddie had stuffed his mouth full of food, making his cheeks bulge out and the corner slits in his lips dribble juice. His mother had told him how disgusting it was to eat that way, and when he noticed everyone watching him he had simply opened his mouth and let all the food fall back onto his plate.

"I loved your just getting up and taking his repulsive plate to the kitchen, then coming back and calmly beginning to eat again. You're a real master at handling that sort of thing." Kay half smiled.

"It's a matter of practical experience," Miss Anderson answered in a complacent tone.

"Does Katie"—Kay poked a wisp of thin hair back into place—"drink that much all the time when Harry's around? I sort of got the feeling from you that she laid off when he was home."

Miss Anderson frowned. It occurred to her she might have told Kay too much already. "It just depends on how she feels," she said evasively, pushing back her chair and standing up.

"Harry's job sounds real interesting. He was telling me all about getting that contract for lumbering some piece of land around Dorset. I knew he had a big business, but I guess I never realized how important it was. It sounds as if he's in the woods or in his office all the time . . . which accounts for my never seeing him."

"He's gone quite a lot of the time."

Kay neatly folded her napkin and placed it on the table. "Probably the reason she drinks so much."

"I have no idea what causes her to drink. Nor, I believe, do you."

Kay stood up. "No. Of course I don't. As close as we are, I really don't know."

Miss Anderson turned her head to the doorway. "I hear Mrs. Harding coming down the stairs now."

"I think I hear Harry's voice with her." Kay brushed a crumb from the tablecloth into her hand and carefully dropped it onto her napkin. "Time we had coffee."

Miss Anderson pretended not to hear. "I think I'll see how the children are making out."

Katie and Harry appeared at the doorway. "Sorry to have been so long," Katie said. "Oh, Miss Anderson, would you mind checking to see if the children are all right. I don't think we want any more scenes tonight."

"Of course." Miss Anderson walked past them into the hallway.

"How about some coffee, Kay?" Harry asked.

"Sounds wonderful. We were just talking about the children and school." She smiled at Harry. "I've gotten to know Hil . . . Miss Anderson a little during the past few years that she's been bringing the children to school and picking them up."

"She's another saint." Katie leaned against the doorjamb. "You two go ahead to the living room. I'll tell Pearl to bring coffee in there. I think it's a little too cool to go back outside."

When Harry and Kay were across the hall and in the living room, Katie pulled out a chair at the table and sank into it, staring around at the empty glasses, crumpled napkins—except for Kay's—and brightly flickering candles. There was some wine left in the bottle; she decided to drink the rest of it in peace and quiet.

The candlelit dinners of her childhood . . . her thoughts meandered privately and secretively, dipping into quiet eddies of memories, swirling around in vague circles of reminiscences, touching here, there, long-ago pleasures she had shared with her father. But now he was gone—leaving her with Joe to carry on for him. He didn't live to see the other two but how he had adored Joe.

She thought of Joe with his hands and wrists growing faster than his arms, and sticking out of his shirt sleeves. He would be tall—like her father, and like Harry. All her children should have been tall, but only Joe seemed to be showing his heritage.

Freddie and Lavinia. Short, fat, dumpy children. She had asked Harry if he had ever been fat as a child, and he said no. She certainly hadn't been fat, ever in her life. Where did these two fat ones get it? Harry's genes, or hers? Or was it something other than genes?

She hadn't liked being pregnant with either of them; she hadn't wanted to go through it again. That's when she started drinking more, to get through them. Harry had been so happy. And she? A toss of the dice she would get through because she had been taught to accept fate with grace. Grace? Bull. With booze.

First Freddie, then Lavinia. She had tried to be a good mother when they were babies, but she had started to fail even then. They had screamed and cried and took away the time she had wanted to spend with Joe. Each month, each year, she had turned away from them a little more, a little more into her brooding, lonely drinking, until now—now she was no mother at all, to any of them. And it was all Freddie and Lavinia's fault.

She jerked her head up with a start and looked around, feeling her heart constricted in her chest. She hadn't meant that. Not really. It was her fault, not theirs. Tears came to her eyes and she poured the remainder of the wine into her glass.

Poor Freddie, crouched in his chair, tying knots in his napkin, staring at the bare tablecloth where once his dinner plate had been; his fierce ullen look, mouth curving downward, eyes narrowed. What a poor disturbed child of darkness he was. Mingled with her annoyance of him she had felt an overwhelming pity as she watched him. She was glad he had been allowed to have dessert. Angel pie was one of his favorites. He had scraped the spoon over the china, up and down, sideways, across the middle and around the rim, a grating sound that had gotten on Katie's nerves. But she had not said anything.

And Lavinia, shouting about the kites, interrupting everyone (except Harry), screaming when she couldn't have seconds of angel pie, screaming when she was reprimanded for being a pig. Screaming. Screaming.

"You're a saint, Harry," Katie said to him after Miss Anderson had taken the subdued children to watch TV. "How you can go on and on, year after year, picking her up, walking her like that, amazes me. I would have throttled her into silence long ago if I had to handle her alone." Throttle her into silence. She had said it to him, but she hadn't meant it. She hadn't really meant it. But what would she have done if she had had to cope alone? Certainly, any more meals like tonight and she would have an ulcer as well as a tricky liver. Thank God Daddy had left her with enough money so she didn't have to cope alone. Oh, Daddy, why did they turn out to be so awful? Why couldn't they have taken after you, the way Joe did?

She stood up, one hand on the back of the chair, one still

on the table. Those beautiful dinners with her father and mother were like some distant dream; she wished she could bring them back. Someday the dream would slip from her forever, and she would only remember she had once had a dream and would wonder what it was.

She let her eyes wander around the walls, knowing the scene would calm her, soothe her like a soft lullaby. It would give her the vital strength she needed not to drink any more tonight. She had had too much already; she knew before dinner that Harry was watching her, disappointment and regret showing in his eyes when he looked at her. She would not drink anymore, and would be sober and alert and cheerful for Harry. She could feel the calm coursing through her now. The still waters, the low, gently curving bridge, willows bending like ballerinas, beckoning to the regal birds that waded motionlessly for eternity. There she stopped, her eyes drawn to the head of the exotic white bird. She let go of the chair and walked closer to the mural. The bird's eye. What was that on the bird's eye?

"Pearl!" she called, hearing her on the other side of the door in the pantry.

Pearl opened the door. "Yes, Mrs. Harding?"

"Come here, Pearl."

Pearl crossed to where Katie, with outstretched arm, was pointing to the bird. "What is that?"

Pearl cocked her head to make sure her best eye was the one on the spot. "Why, what in the world . . ." She turned her head back and forth a few times, doubly checking that the spot was there when each eye rested on it. "I never saw it before."

"I've never seen it before either." The two women craned their necks forward and stared. "What do you think it is?"

"Well, whatever it is, it wasn't there yesterday, because I myself ran the duster over the murals," Pearl said defensively.

"What is it?"

Pearl gingerly touched the black spot, then brought it back to her nose and sniffed expertly. "Dear sweet mother of Jesus," she muttered.

"What is it?" Katie asked again.

"It smells like chocolate."

"Chocolate!" Katie reeled as if she'd been slapped. Then she said in a low voice, anger sheathing every word, "Report this to Miss Anderson, please, and try to find out which of the children did this."

"I can clean it up all right. Don't worry. This old paper's tougher than you think. I've taken off lots of spots where Mr. Harding splattered the roast-beef juice while carving right over there on the side table, and where fingers touched around the doors. Don't you worry none. I can take it off as sure as I'm standing here."

"Report it anyway. She is to see to it that it never happens again."

"Yes, Mrs. Harding. Yes"—she nodded her head sagely—"it's chocolate all right."

Katie swept past her into the pantry, her sober hopes dissipating like drops of water, her focus on the nearest bottle.

3

KATIE TENTATIVELY TOUCHED THE WALLS OF THE LONG HALL
that ran from the pantry to the central hall between the front
and back terrace doors, pausing frequently to realign herself
with a straight course and to check her fingers for cleanliness.
Chocolate . . . a spot burned into that part of her brain that
didn't forgive. She thought they both knew better. It never
failed: the minute she started feeling sorry for them, they proved
her aloofness to be the correct posture.

Finally at the double living-room doors opposite the dining
room, she paused again and looked across the long room at
Harry and Kay. It was like peering through the windows of a
stranger's house and watching a contented couple relaxing in
comforting blue hues after a satisfying meal. The harmony
would not be broken until someone stepped into the scene
unannounced—someone jarring and out of tune with them.

They were talking quietly and didn't hear her come in, nor
did Katie hear Kay's final remark of "It's a real shame she

can't enjoy the children more" before they saw her approach them.

"We've been waiting for you, Red." Harry watched her closely.

Katie sat opposite Kay, oblivious to the sudden silence that fell with her entrance and the uneasy look on Kay's face. She didn't ask them what they had been talking about, but just leaned her head back with obvious indifference and studied Kay. Kay and Harry began talking again and didn't notice her staring at the peasant skirt, the blouse, the cheap sandals, the plain little pinched face with the mousy hair severely pulled back. A lot of makeup would do wonders. And a new hairdo, or maybe even a wig. Yes, that was it. Katie perked up, almost soberly. A nice, expensive, light brown wig, with soft rolling curls, disguising at least part of the skinny head and neck. But would Kay ever agree to wearing a wig? Maybe. High-necked clothes would be best, collars that stood up and gracefully framed the face. She would have to take her to Elizabeth Arden to get the makeup worked out. Katie felt a flutter of excitement; the challenge was there before her, waiting for her to act. Tomorrow. Tomorrow, first thing, she would figure out how to begin the metamorphosis. Her father had always said: "When you see something that needs changing, change it."

"What?" Katie heard her name being spoken.

"Pearl's here with the coffee. Do you want her to pour?" Harry asked.

She nodded. "Yes. You pour, Pearl."

The black coffee tasted strong, the way she liked it after a meal. It slid down her throat, almost burning it, down through her chest, hot still in her stomach.

She'd had too much to drink again. It had become such a powerful habit now she couldn't fight it. She really didn't want to drink so much—it's just that most of the time, there was nothing else to do. Unless Harry were home with her.

She was never bored with Harry. Angry sometimes, but never bored—unless he talked too much about lumbering. Sometimes that turned her off, like tonight at dinner. And right now. He and Kay were still talking about it. Harry had just mentioned her father. Katie concentrated and listened.

"I wouldn't be in the business I'm in if it weren't for him," Harry was saying. "When I asked Katie to marry me, he wanted to know what my plans were and I told him I wanted to go into the lumbering business. He said that sounded like a good solid future, so he bought me my first mill. I never would have gotten so far without him. If I had had to borrow that money to get started, I may have ended up in a different business, one where I didn't have to get myself so deeply in hock. Who knows."

Darling Harry. He always gave Daddy the credit. She should be more proud that he had such a successful business. The thing she hated was that he was gone so much. He spent more time in the woods than he did at home, more time in his office than in his own house. How nice it would be to have Harry home, and Joe. Just the three of them. Or a vacation together. Just the three of them.

"Harry," she suddenly said, "do you think Lavinia and Freddie ought to go off to camp this summer?"

"Maybe," he said quietly. "It might be a good idea. Certainly something to think about."

"Yes. I think we definitely should think about it."

Katie could see it now, the three of them, having a wonderful summer together. They might take a house at the beach again, the way they had last summer, but with a different cast of characters. Last year, Harry had only come on weekends, and Katie had been stuck with the three children and Miss Anderson; as a result she had spent the mornings in bed, the afternoons at the Club, the evenings either out with long-ago New York friends or in bars. She had barely seen the house. This time it would be different. Joe loved the ocean; he was so daring and brave when he rode in the waves. It would be wonderful. She wouldn't drink so much. She had drunk too much last summer and ended up back in the hospital in the fall.

"Perhaps you could take off some time, Harry."

"What? Take off time? When?"

"This summer, I mean. Perhaps we could have more of a vacation than we had last summer. You barely took any time, except weekends."

"I'll try, Red, I'll try."

Katie shook back her hair and ran a finger around the inside of the emerald-and-diamond choker that sat just at the base of her slender white neck. "Do try." She looked him in the eye. This was something she meant to have, and she wanted him to know how important it was to her.

"I will," he answered.

Kay stood up. "I'm afraid I'll have to go now. All that sun and wind today have made me sleepy. I'm about as tired as Lavinia." She moved toward Katie.

Harry stood up. "I'll walk you home."

Kay protested. "No, no, don't bother to do that. It's hardly as if I had far to go. Thank you so much, Katie, for a really wonderful day." She turned to Harry. "I was here for lunch, too."

"Great," he answered. "Come more often."

"I'm here more than you realize. But thank you." She smiled at Katie. "Katie's wonderful to have me so much. And I'm so glad"—she looked back at Harry—"to have really caught up with you and had an honest-to-God conversation. After three years and three brief handshakes."

Harry threw back his head and laughed. "It's certainly been my loss to have been away the times you've been here. I'll try to do better in the future."

Katie leaned forward. "It's so extraordinary that my best husband and my best friend have barely met. Harry, you must stay home more." But then, she thought, I don't need you here, Kay, when Harry's home. "Goodnight, Kay."

Harry took Kay's elbow. "Sure I can't walk you home?"

"Quite sure. I live in that garage apartment just across from the end of your driveway."

"I know," Harry said as he and Kay walked across the living room. "The children have told me many times where you lived."

"'Night," Kay called back from the doorway.

Katie waved her hand and leaned back in the love seat. Kay was a wonderful person. And what fun it would be to get her all dolled up. "Act on impulse," Daddy had said. "Do what you feel in your gut is right to do."

"Hey, Red," Harry said from the doorway as he flicked a switch that turned off the picture lights. "Ready for bed?"

"Harry, where do you suppose Lavinia gets that terrible temper of hers?"

"You've got the red hair," he said, walking back toward her.

"I suppose so. It's Harrison hair; lots of Harrisons have it. But we've never been out of control. I mean, she gets absolutely wild."

He sat down beside her and took her hand. "Maybe she feels left out or something. I don't know."

"Left out? She could hardly have felt left out tonight, sitting there on the right hand of God." She laughed genuinely. "Isn't it something the way she worships you? How does it feel to be a god, Harry?"

"Just the same as it feels to be a father."

"I don't understand her," Katie continued. "My father came from simple farming people, good, solid, salt-of-the-earth people; his own nature was cheerful, light, happy—unless he was crossed in a business deal. But that was just business. He was full of charm and good will, generous, a loving father and a loving husband. He was like you, Harry, only with a more outgoing nature."

"I know, Red." Harry rubbed her hand indulgently; he had heard Katie go on about her father for many years now. "He was a great man."

Katie smiled at him. "So are you, Harry." She poured herself another cup of coffee. "My mother was a Harrison and she had red hair, but she didn't have that temper."

"It wasn't all that red either."

"No. Not as red as mine, but still red mixed in with the brown." She didn't want the coffee. She wanted a brandy. She would let Harry go upstairs before her and then she would have a brandy. "If you're tired, you go on to bed, Harry. I'm just sitting here mulling things over."

"I'm not that tired."

"My mother's mother . . . you know, a one-m Simons from Charleston . . . I don't know if any of them had red hair."

"Red," Harry said a little impatiently, "what in the hell difference does it make if the Harrisons from Virginia and the one-m Simons from Charleston had red hair or not? We're us, with children of our own, and one of them happens to have had a screaming session at dinner."

Katie pushed her cup across the table with her foot. "We were simply tracing a few blood lines to see where the screw-up happened."

"There's no screw-up, Red. She's just a little girl who got keyed up at dinner, to use Miss Anderson's pet phrase."

Katie looked at Harry, pulling her hand away from his. "And how about all the other times she goes into these 'keyed-up' hysterias, morning, noon and night. Not just at dinner, Harry, but at just about every bloody occasion you can imagine."

"Isn't that an exaggeration?"

"Possibly. But her behavior outbursts are not confined to an occasional keyed-up dinner and, I might add, they usually occur when you're around." Katie's voice swelled with conviction.

"Are you blaming me for doing something wrong?"

"No, I am not. But I am trying to understand it. And that's more than you seem to be doing."

"Good God, Katie! I'm as concerned as you are. It upsets the hell out of me to have her act like that."

"Then you should figure out some way to correct it, instead of just picking her up and coddling her."

"If I could, I would. And you could be more of a mother to them and try to find out what's bothering her."

Katie's eyes flashed. "More of a mother! More of a mother! Do you know what it's like to be stuck in this house with them? Do you know what it's like to have to be around them all day?"

"Don't hand me that crap. Miss Anderson is the one who gets the brunt of them. You manage to escape the whole thing by burying yourself in a bottle of vodka."

They stared into each other's angry eyes.

"You've stopped loving me, haven't you?" Katie finally broke the silence.

"No. No, I haven't. I love you as much as I ever did. But you sure don't make it easy sometimes. You're your own worst enemy." He put his arm around her shoulder and drew her close to him. "I've never loved anyone but you, Red. You know that. I've tried to make you happy. I've tried to be a success in business, the way your father was, so you would give me that unwavering respect and love you gave him. I've tried to be patient with you and understand why you can't cope with your life. I've tried, but I can't understand it. What is it that you want? What is it that's eating you?"

Katie put her hands over her face and sobbed. "I don't know. I just don't know."

"Red, Red. My poor Red. So beautiful, with so much of the world right under your feet, and still so unhappy."

"I'm not unhappy when I'm with you," she cried. "And I love Joe, because he reminds me so much of Daddy. It's everything else I can't handle. If only I could have you and Joe with me all day, then I'd be happy."

"No, you wouldn't. You'd quickly see me as a failure, and once you did that you'd no longer love me." He kissed her wet cheek. "Your father went out into the business world every day and made a fortune so he could treat your mother and you like his queen and princess. If he had sat home doing nothing, you wouldn't have that respect for him that you have now. It would be the same with me. I work very hard to provide you and the children with everything I can."

"We don't need all the money we have. We could just live on mine."

He smiled and brushed her hair back from her damp face. "My dearest Red. I'd lose your respect—and you—so fast it would make me sick with dizziness."

"Oh, Harry, you are so much like Daddy. You're so strong and kind and caring."

"And I love you as much as he loved you."

"I wish he were still alive. He would know what to do to help me."

Harry frowned and looked away.

"He taught me everything. He taught me to dress up for dinner and drink champagne when I was only thirteen. He had the living-room rugs rolled back and taught me to dance. And after mother died, he took me everywhere with him, even to the Stock Exchange to see the seat of power. I miss him so much, Harry."

"I know you do, Red. When I met him . . . from the moment I met him, I wanted to be a man just like him: powerful, rich, successful, generous and independent. He did just what he wanted to do. He was a wonderful man."

"He loved you, too, Harry. I remember when he said to me 'It doesn't matter if Harry is poor now; he'll get to the top just like I did.' He compared you with himself. He saw you were like him."

"Let's go to bed, Red. You're tired."

"But no one ever taught me how to make up a bed or how to boil water. I never had to do anything useful. I never even learned how to sew, though my mother did beautiful needle-point. I never learned how to do anything that would help me cope now."

"Come on, Red. You're tired." He stood up and tried to pull her up.

"I think I'm right, Harry, about Lavinia." She sniffed and cleared her throat, wiping her cheeks with her hands.

"What about her?"

"She's worse when you're around. It never really occurred to me until tonight." When Harry didn't answer, she went on: "That's something to think about. Does she do it just to get you to hold her?"

"I've heard you complain about her screaming when I'm not here."

"It's a different kind of screaming then. Sort of normal screaming. This other is abnormal. Do you think she's some sort of psycho and this is how it's manifesting itself?"

"No. I do nót. Like I said before, she just gets keyed up. That's all." He sat back down beside her.

"That's not all," Katie said. "And Freddie . . . do you think he's the way he is because I was drinking so much when I was pregnant with him?"

She was staring into her lap and didn't see Harry shut his eyes with a pained frown. "No. I certainly do not," he answered evenly.

"Sure? There's an awful lot of publicity on that now."

"I'm sure. That's ridiculous. Don't think such foolish things."

"It would make me feel awful to think I had created him this way—created my very own Frankenstein monster to haunt me."

"You didn't."

"I don't really mean he's a monster. That's the wrong word. But he is a disturbed child. I feel sorry for him. I really do. I know there's something wrong with him. I should love him more and try to help him, but I can't. I can't love either of them the way I should."

"Don't, Red. Don't torture yourself. Put it out of your head. It will all be all right in the long run."

The silence lay heavily between them like a low-lying storm cloud.

"I'm the one who's a monster," she finally said, her voice muffled with tears.

He gently put his hand on her face, brushing the hair back from her puffy cheeks and swollen eyes. "You have never done anything wrong to another person."

"I'm not a nice person. I know I'm not. You deserve better."

"You just need cheering up." His hand slid down her throat while he put his face close to hers, nuzzling the base of her soft hair. "Come to bed."

"Not yet." Just one small sip of brandy was all she needed.

"Come on." He again stood up and tried to pull her to her feet. "It's been some time since I've caught you awake."

"Not quite yet. You go on and I'll be right behind you."

"How long?"

"Not long." Just long enough to get a little brandy.

"In that case, I'll step out for some fresh air. I feel like taking a quick walk. Want to put on some sensible shoes and come with me?"

She smiled and shook her head. "Not tonight. You go ahead, and I'll see you upstairs."

"Promise you won't fall asleep before I get there."

"I promise."

Harry left and she pushed herself forward. Oh, Christ, what to do? Everything was so hard to understand . . . impossible to understand. It was better not to think of anything at all.

She kicked off her shoes and stood up, walking slowly, her aim to have a quick drink and get to bed.

She stole quietly to the pantry and poured brandy into a large glass. She made no pretense of sipping it in a ladylike fashion, but tipped back her head and let it rush down her throat. She rinsed the glass in the sink and put away the bottle.

Family portraits on both sides of the wide hall and on the stair wall looked down at her. She glanced up at the Harrisons, Lockwoods and one-m Simons, and, at the turn in the stairs, into the eyes of her beautiful mother. She stopped at the top of the stairs. She could hear voices on the third floor. She wondered what they were doing now. Joe would probably be watching TV; Miss Anderson might be reading to Freddie and Lavinia. Maybe she was giving them a good lecture about chocolate spots.

Katie knew she should go up and say goodnight to them, kiss them, tell them she loved them. But it would be a lie. She didn't love them, not two of them, not really love them. They were hers, tied to her though the umbilical cord had long been cut; she would always see to their welfare and be responsible for them. But she only truly loved Joe with that gladness that filled the heart. She tried not to admit this, even to herself. She knew she should love them equally. She felt sorry for them, but she didn't want to hold them; she didn't want to wrap her arms around them and blow kisses into their necks. It was possible that if she never saw them again, she might not even miss them. Tears again filled her eyes and she put both hands over her mouth. What a terrible thing to think and worse to admit. She should go to them now and tell them she loved them. Tell them something. Be a part of their lives.

Instead, without hesitation, she walked to her own room, the big bedroom directly across the hall from her. She went in and shut the door behind her, tears falling down her cheeks.

She started unbuttoning her blouse as she crossed to her dressing room. She dropped the blouse on the floor, draped her slacks across the back of the chair, piled her jewelry on the dresser and kicked her underwear to the side of the room. Then she went into the bathroom and turned on the hot water, letting the room quickly steam up.

Freddie or Lavinia? Which was worse? What had happened to them that made them so awful? Watching the water spiral down the drain, she thought of the time Freddie had locked himself in the bathroom, filled the tub to overflowing and calmly waited while the door was broken down to get to the water and him. The plaster ceiling in the study below had fallen and new tiles had to be laid on the bathroom floor. He never said a word; just watched. Lavinia, then aged three, shrieked "Water! Water! Water!" every time she went into the study and looked at the new ceiling. They were both wretched. She hated them for making her feel guilty. If they were only nice. If only she could love them. If.

She took a hot shower, the water washing the tears from her eyes. She had drunk too much and felt sick again. She had to get to bed. She must lie down and rest.

She turned off the shower and dried her hair and her body. With the damp towel wrapped around her shoulders she tried to look into the mirror, veiled with misty steam. She raised one well-manicured finger and wrote on the mirror: I HATE MYSELF.

Then she dropped the towel and went naked to the bed already turned down by Pearl; she slid between the cool sheets, pulling up the blanket, wanting to retreat into her shell where only darkness would surround and protect her. She wanted to forget the children and everything else. She shut her eyes tightly and didn't move, hoping the spinning lights would stand still as she began the warm horizontal withdrawal. Forgive me, Harry, for not waiting for you. Forgive me. I love you.

4

When Katie woke up, Harry was already out of bed. She ran her hands up and down her naked body, feeling the soft warmth. She wished he were here with her. Why was it he was never here when she wanted him, and she was always asleep when he wanted her?

She could hear the distant whirr of a lawn mower—maybe Mario, maybe a neighbor. It was almost nine. She sat up and yawned, stretching her arms out wide; the long sleep had restored her.

Harry had probably gone for the Sunday papers. She pressed the buzzer at the head of the bed to let Pearl know she was awake. She would just go to the bathroom and put on some kind of cover-up, waiting until after she had eaten to take a leisurely bath and get dressed. She was going to try to make it a good day.

She put on a silk taffeta dressing gown of the palest blue, brushed her hair, making it glint in the light, and stepped into blue satin slippers. They were the wrong color blue; she flipped them off her feet, letting them cartwheel across the floor, and found another pair, the right blue. Instead of coffee and toast in bed, she would go down today and read the papers with Harry. Joe would take the sports section; Lavinia and Freddie would share the comics. They would all sit in the living room together. It would be a cheerful domestic scene, one found in every red-blooded American household on a Sunday morning. She would stay sober; she would behave herself and not lose her temper. She would be nice to the children and bask in the gratitude and love in Harry's watchful eyes.

There was a light knocking on her door.

"Come in."

The door opened and Lavinia stepped into the room, timidly inching past the door. Her brown hair softly framed the round face, which was unsmiling and wide-eyed.

"Good morning, Lavinia. What is it?"

"Daddy says for me to tell you to come down and have some french toast with us. He's cooking." She kept one dimpled hand on the side of the door, the other held her doll close to her chest.

"He's cooking! Where's Pearl?"

"She's there, too, but Daddy's cooking."

Oh, Christ. The cheerful domestic scene over the papers was turning into a nightmare already. This meant the children had not already had their breakfast, so they would all be at the table together, drooling over their plates, spilling syrup and fighting over the butter.

"I thought Miss Anderson usually gave you children your breakfast before this. Isn't it late for you?"

"Yes." She shifted from one chubby bare foot to the other. "But Daddy came up early and told her to wait and let him do it."

Katie scrutinized the child's outfit: faded blue denim overalls over a red-checked shirt. The doll was in matching colors.

"Has he gone for the papers?"

"Miss Anderson went down to get them."

My God, this was worse. Miss Anderson wouldn't be there to ride herd. Who was going to remove Freddie's plate when he elected to chuck his breakfast back onto it?

"I'm not really hungry yet." Go, Katie, go. Go be with your children at least one breakfast out of all the ones that roll around. "Well, maybe. Tell Daddy I'll start with coffee. Then I'll see about eating. You look like a little farmer this morning. Cute."

"You know what, Mommy?"

"No. What?"

"You know what Kay said about Daddy?"

"What did Kay say about Daddy?"

"She said Daddy looked like Rock Hudson."

"I bet Rock Hudson wished he looked like Daddy."

A look of bewilderment swept across the child's face.

"Never mind. That was a nice thing for Kay to say, wasn't it?"

"I didn't know who Rock Hudson was. Joe had to tell me."

"Yes, probably. Now you run along and tell Daddy I'll be there soon." Rock Hudson indeed. She smiled at the thought. So that's what Kay thought about Harry. Strange she should have mentioned him to the children when she barely knew him. Actually she wasn't too far off. It was just that Harry was better than Rock Hudson in all ways.

She looked across at the photograph of Harry on her bedside table. Yes, he was definitely better than Rock Hudson.

She wondered what Rock Hudson would be like in bed. She stopped short crossing the room. She wondered if Kay wondered what Harry would be like in bed. Poor dull Kay, plain as a dish cloth, her forehead forever knotted above her small eyes. She probably never had thoughts of sex in her head— maybe even considered it a sin to think of sex. On the other hand, you never could tell about those plain ones.

She swept out of the room, the blue silk rustling like dried delphinium hanging by the stem. Right after breakfast she was going to pull out some clothes for Kay. Not too many at first. She had to be subtle in order to make it work. Just a blouse or two, slacks, a summer suit—yes, that beige Calvin Klein with the mandarin collar and a silk scarf for the neck. That would be a good one. She wasn't sure about shoes; Kay's foot might be wider than hers. She'd have to see about that.

Noise was coming from the kitchen. She paused at the bottom of the stairs and listened, the sharp sounds grating on her nerves and making her insides tighten. Could she face it yet? Could she?

She sat down on a step and stared out the front door that had been left open to let the fresh spring air sweep through the hall. She plucked at tufts of carpeting and looked at the bright sun filtering through the trees. To open the door and walk out into the endless sunlight, not even letting her feet touch the ground, but treading on a long thin ray . . . to wherever it would take her, far away—that's what she'd like to do.

A shout, a scream, Harry's voice calling for quiet. She wearily stood up and walked toward the kitchen. If only they were in the dining room, then she could get some ingredients for a Bloody Mary. Maybe she could still manage it; she might have to skip the Worcestershire and lemon juice. As she stepped onto the spotless linoleum, she had totally forgotten she had decided not to start drinking early today.

Harry was at the stove turning pieces of egg-and-milk-soaked bread on a square griddle. "Morning, Red. You're here just in time to see a master chef at work."

Katie caught the attention of one of Pearl's eyes. "You should have stayed in bed, Pearl."

Pearl was by the counter that divided the cooking area from the eating area. "If I'd known, I would have gone to a later Mass."

The three children were seated at the table. Katie noticed a solid-looking plastic cloth on the table. Freddie had already spilled some orange juice and was now poking his fingers into it.

"How are you this morning, Joe? And you, Freddie?"

Joe was tracing a pattern in the plastic with his fork, his head bent so his hair hid his face. "Okay, Mom. I'm getting hungry though."

"I want the first piece." Freddie jutted out his chin. "I was here first," he said sullenly.

"No, you weren't," Lavinia wailed. "I was here first."

"Hold it!" Harry spoke loudly. "There's plenty to go around. You'll all three get a first piece. There are four pieces almost ready. You three and Mommy can have the first ones."

Katie balked at the thought of eating a piece of soggy toast. "I'd rather wait a little, if you don't mind. I'd like some juice first, then some coffee."

"Here's orange juice right here, Mom," Joe said, looking up through his wavy hair. "There's a pitcher full of it. And there's an extra glass by Lavinia's place."

"I think I might have tomato juice this morning, instead of orange. That is, if we have any. Is there some open, Pearl?"

"Should be." She opened the refrigerator door and peered inside, moving things around.

"If you don't see it, never mind. I can have orange juice." She could slip some vodka into that just as easily. Tomato juice was preferable—not so sweet.

"No, no." Pearl shuffled some more things around. "Should be right here. Aha, here it is. Hidden way in the back." She pulled it out triumphantly.

"I'll get a glass in the pantry." Katie took the bottle from her and walked out of the kitchen.

"Here we go," Harry announced. "Pearl, you pass these plates around, will you?"

Good. A diversion. Katie filled a tall glass about halfway up with tomato juice then quietly opened the lower cupboard where the liquor was kept. She filled the glass three-quarters full with vodka and slowly shut the door. A spoon was lying on the counter top. She stirred the red liquid, careful not to hit the sides of the glass, then put the spoon in the pantry sink. Shouts of "Mine!" and "Hand me the syrup!" and "Stop hogging the butter!" blasted in her ear as she drank about half the glass of laced juice.

"Here's your coffee, Red," Harry called to her.

"Coming." She went into the kitchen and took the cup Pearl handed her. The two little pigs were slurping down their syrupy toast, noisily chewing and drinking juice. Joe ate rapidly, she noticed, but without the disgusting mess of the others. He had never been that messy, not when he was seven and eight. He might need a haircut, but he wasn't messy. "Joe's finished," she said to Harry. "He needs another piece."

"I'm finished, too!" Freddie stuffed a big wad into his cheeks.

"You will have to wait until the next round. Joe is growing faster than you and needs filling up. He's taller, and it takes more fuel to make his engine run." What a revolting simile for her to come out with. She drank another big swallow.

"Mommy's right. Pearl, give this extra piece to Joe. Freddie, your next one is coming right up." Harry flipped the next four pieces.

Freddie watched, glaring, his jaw slack with his tongue spread out between his teeth, while Joe ate. Katie had a terrible feeling he was going to reach over and mash the toast in his hand and stuff it into his mouth. She turned her head away.

"Is Miss Anderson back with the papers?" Katie needed an

excuse to leave the room. She couldn't stand here and watch Freddie and Lavinia anymore.

"No. Not yet." Pearl shot an eye in her direction, while the other remained fixed in its socket. "Sometimes they're ready and you just pick them up; sometimes you have to wait for them to get sorted. You want to sit down?"

"No." She groped behind her for the counter. "I might take my coffee into the library to wait my turn." The pungent aromas were beginning to make her feel sick; she wanted to escape to drink her coffee in peace and quiet.

Harry looked at her, but didn't comment.

Katie took her tomato juice and coffee down the hall. She crossed the central hall where the sun momentarily lit her blue, then went into the next hall that matched the side going to the kitchen, the hall that divided the living room from the library and, beyond that, Harry's study. She entered the library.

She put her feet on the cold marble-topped coffee table, balancing the cup on the arm of the sofa and holding the glass. This was better. Let Harry be the father he wanted to be, but without her. She felt comfortable and safe here within the deep-red walls, the shelves of books, even staring at the inevitable TV. She especially liked the four small oil paintings from the Hudson River School that her father had bought, embracing Americana whenever he could find it. She and Harry had bought so few things together. The house was filled with Homer, Eakins, Bierstadt, Sargent; American antiques and American silver . . . all from her father.

Her reverie was jolted by a scream in the kitchen, followed by loud wailing. Katie wished Miss Anderson would hurry and get back. She was the only one who could control them. She got up and turned on the TV. If she got it loud enough, she wouldn't be able to hear anything else.

The phone rang, jarring her. She knew Pearl would answer it in the kitchen.

Tomorrow she would go to the school and find out about summer camps. They knew about such places. She wanted one that would take Freddie and Lavinia for the whole three months—not just a month or six weeks, but the whole summer. She shuddered. How stinking of her, not to want to be around her own children. No matter how they'd gotten that way, they were hers. She finished her drink. If she could only understand them, but she couldn't. And she couldn't help the way she felt. Maybe they would be more tolerable when they got older.

Maybe. She looked into the bottom of the red-stained glass. She really was awful. How could Harry love her at all?

Harry came in with the coffee pot. "More?"

"Thanks." She put the glass on the floor. "Who was that on the phone?"

He didn't answer, but bent and kissed her forehead. She looked at him expectantly, waiting for an answer, sensing unwanted sentences forming in his head. He seemed to ignore her and watched TV for a few seconds, then said: "The field office in Ontario. They think I ought to get up there for a few days."

"Harry! You promised not to go again so soon!" She had just reached to pick up the cup he had refilled; she sat it back down with a clatter, sloshing coffee into the saucer. "Last time you went, you promised you wouldn't have to go back again for at least a few months! You promised!"

"I'm afraid I was wrong. They need to see me about going in another few miles. As long as we have the roads in as far as we do, we might be able to get farther in and get more timber. But I have to make the deal with the owners."

"No!" She balled her hands into fists and brought them down hard on her legs. "No! I'm tired of being left alone!" She jumped up and turned off the TV.

"I know, Red. But I really have to go. I'll leave as soon as I can get a flight, then I'll get back as soon as I can." Two days in the woods, then a day with Doris, Harry thought to himself. Better say four to be on the safe side.

"You promised to be with me today."

"Can't help it." He watched as she threw herself back onto the sofa. Poor Red. She needed someone with her all the time.

"And what do you expect me to do?" she asked tearfully. "It's gotten so I can't make any plans to have people in—not that I really care about that—but still I can't make plans. I never know when you're going to take off."

He sat down beside her and took her hand. "You really ought to go out and find something to do. Volunteer someplace. The hospital . . ."

"Don't be an ass. You know I can't bear to be around sick people."

"Then go to the museum. I've suggested this many times, but you won't even give it a try. They're always looking for volunteers. I heard it again the other day."

Her brimming eyes pleaded with him to understand her. "I

do not want to be a docent or any other kind of volunteer, dragging snickering school children around and trying to tell them about art when they're not the foggiest bit interested in learning about it. It's a waste, if you ask me."

"You know that's not true. Our kids have learned quite a lot from field trips to the museum."

"Harry, you know and I know that I'm not suited for that kind of work. Groups of children get on my nerves." She reached for a Kleenex from the box on the table and dabbed at her eyes. "You know that. And anyway I don't want to do it and I wish you would stop bringing it up every six months."

He sighed. "There must be something you would like to do. Go to New York and buy some clothes while I'm away."

"I'll go to New York when I want to go to New York, and I don't want to go now."

"Red, there are so many people in this town waiting with open arms for you to call them. And you like people; they stimulate you. Call them, have them for lunch, for dinner, for anything. I don't need to be here for you to entertain."

"I don't like having anyone when you're not here."

"Go out to lunch then. Call Betsy or Margot or Carolyn or June—call all of them and go out to lunch with them. You know you like them."

She stared at him. "It's not what I want to do."

"Why not?"

"I don't feel comfortable around them anymore." She lowered her eyes.

"You've always felt comfortable with Betsy. I bet you haven't even talked to her for a month."

"Wrong. I talked to her last week."

"Really?"

"Really." Katie leaned her head back against the sofa.

"Did you call her?"

"No. She called me."

"Did she suggest some date with you, to do something?"

"Yes, as a matter of fact, she did. She wanted me to bring Freddie and Lavinia around for a tea party. Her sister was there with children the same ages."

Neither of them spoke for a while. Katie stared at the ceiling and Harry looked across the room and out the window, past the driveway and into the woods.

Finally Harry said: "How about you calling her back and asking her to go out to lunch with you?"

"Jesus, Harry! Stop badgering me! I don't want to see her or anyone."

"You enjoyed her and lots of others when we first moved here. You could again."

"I'm not sure about that. Even then I felt they were critical of me." She looked at the vile brown liquid in the saucer.

"Critical? That's not true, and you know it. It's some stupid notion you've gotten in your head just recently."

"Not so recently. They all know each other so much better; I feel like an outsider. They do things I don't want to do, like play bridge and golf, have mini tennis tournaments, plant flowers on the street corners. And I think they think I'm a snob because I don't want to do those things. They're all in a tight little circle and I'm on the outside."

"That's so dumb of you, Red. And it's all in your imagination. Everyone likes you. You've just never tried to be close with them. You had a million friends in New York. You could have close friends here if you'd only try."

"Please don't leave me," Katie pleaded. "I want you here with me. I feel so lost without you."

Harry frowned. "I wish you liked being in the woods and didn't swell up when a black fly bites you; then you could come with me. But you know I have to go when something like this comes up. It's my business. If I sat back and let my competitors win out, I wouldn't be much of a businessman, would I? You know I have to go. It's just like going to Wall Street every day, and keeping up with the stock market. If you have a business, you have to keep up with it. You know that."

She nodded her head and bit her lip.

"How about calling Kay," Harry said. "She sure doesn't seem like the bridge or golf type to me. I can understand now how you've gotten to be so friendly with her. I'm sure she likes coming up here to keep you company. And the kids seem crazy about her. She's a good friend for you to have."

"Yes, she is," Katie agreed. "At least she isn't like all those other mothers who are critical of me for not doing things with our children. As she doesn't have any of her own, she can hardly be in a position to criticize me." She paused and took a deep breath. "And I guess she gives them some of the love I don't seem to be able to give them." She stifled a sob.

Harry held her hand more tightly. "Oh, Red, no one's criticizing you. And it's not the kids I'm worried about right now. It's you. It hurts me to see you alone so much."

"It's not only being without you that's so bad, it's also that I have nothing to do when you aren't here."

"Write. Write again. You did it in college. You were good at it. Try it again. Remember how proud your father was when you were on the yearbook? And later, when you published that article on 'Hidden Treasures in New York'? Remember?"

"I can't write. I can't even write a letter anymore."

"How do you know? At least try."

"Please, Harry, please don't leave me today. You don't know . . . I feel like I'm coming unglued all the time."

He pulled her to him and kissed her. "It's only for a few days, Red. I'll try to get it done in two. Okay? Meanwhile, you call Kay and get her to come up here; you can play backgammon or something."

"Two? Promise?"

"I'll try. I promise I'll try." How could he get it all done in two days? It wasn't possible, but he couldn't bear to hurt her more.

"When we moved up here, you said you'd be home more."

"Dearest Red, I never said I'd be home all the time. I only said I wouldn't be away as much, and that's been true." He hugged her tightly. "Call Kay right away. Sunday is a good day to catch her. Ask her for lunch or dinner or both. It's nice out. You could take a walk with her." He cupped her chin in his hand and looked into her eyes. "Will you call her to come be with you?"

She nodded. "She's hardly going to be a substitute for you. But I'll call her anyway." She blew her nose and wiped the remaining tears from her eyes.

"I want to take a house somewhere, Harry, away from here, away from all this. I want to have a real summer vacation with you."

"I'll be around most of the summer. Pick where you want to go. I can squeeze it in."

"No. Not 'squeeze it in.' I want you to get away from your trees for a while, go away for a real vacation. Can you do it? Please, Harry, before it's too late."

"Sure, Red. Let's make plans. Want more coffee?"

"Promise me, Harry! Promise me!" She felt desperate. "I've got to make you promise!"

He watched her a second before answering. "I promise. Now, want some more coffee?"

"No, thanks. I might have another glass of tomato juice though."

She stood up and took her glass to the pantry. She made another stiff Bloody Mary, then went back to the library. Harry was not there.

Katie went up the stairs and across the hall. She could hear Harry whistling softly in his dressing room, a set-up identical to hers on the opposite side of the bedroom. She put the now half-full glass on her desk and went to his door to watch him. He glanced at her, then went on with his packing, putting wool plaid and blue denim work shirts and work shoes in the bottom of the deep leather bag.

"I still wish you weren't going." She put her hand on the door frame to steady herself; she was feeling warmly dizzy.

"I'll be back soon." He counted out six pairs of socks.

"Six?"

"Never know when you'll get wet feet in the woods."

She unbuttoned the front of her dressing gown and let it fall to the floor. She stepped out of her slippers and walked over to him, putting her arms around him as she pressed her body against his back. He straightened up and rubbed his hands along her bare skin. Katie took him by the shoulders and turned him around. He looked down at her body, put one arm around her and kissed her, the other arm sliding down the front of her. "Don't go," she whispered.

"Jesus," he muttered into her hair, smelling sour traces of alcohol on her breath, but desiring her anyway. "Where were you last night?" Then he picked her up and carried her to the bed. "Jesus, Red, I've got to go. Don't do this to me."

She tried to hold him, tried to cover his mouth with hers to stop him from saying "Can't, Red. Can't." He shook his head. "I've got to go. Oh, my God, I love you so much." He kissed her passionately.

"You can get a later plane," she breathed against his lips. "You said yourself it had been too long for us. I want you, Harry. I want you."

He reluctantly pulled away and stood up. "I want you, too, Red. But I was lucky to get a plane at all." He tucked in his shirt. "I'll be back soon." He returned to his dressing room, leaving her staring after him. He didn't see the yearning, almost frightened, look in her eyes.

A short time later, Harry stood above her, his bag in hand.

"Some body you've got, Red." He lifted her hand and kissed it. "I'd like to be with you the whole damned day. Be ready for me when I get back." He kissed her again while she lay distant and impassive, then shut the door as he left. She heard him running down the stairs. In her mind, a door slammed; the sound of a car. He was gone again.

Katie stayed on the rumpled bed, the covers pushed down to the foot, lying there naked, her nipples firm, her legs at a relaxed angle. She had wanted him; he should have stayed. They never had time to be together. Either he was gone, or— yes, Katie admit it—or she was drunk.

She stared at the ceiling and tried not to think of anything but Harry. She would pretend that he was still there with her. She slowly closed her eyes, the image of his presence close to her. He would be kissing her breasts now, his hand exploring, groping, his mouth on hers. He was gentle and forceful. He knew how to touch her to make her respond. He would slowly envelop her. Katie twisted and moaned. She could feel him; she clutched at the ecstasy and prolonged it, kept the excitement at a pitch, obliterating everything but the intensity of Harry. Yes, Harry, yes. Now. Now.

Suddenly there was a jarring sound. What was it? Startled, Katie opened her eyes and turned her head. There, inside the room, standing by the open door, were Freddie and Lavinia, staring at her, their mouths hanging open. Freddie was holding himself between his legs with both hands.

Katie jumped off the bed and grabbed their arms.

"What are you doing here?! How dare you come sneaking in here and spy on me! How dare you!" She shook them. Lavinia dropped her doll, which fell to the floor with a painted smile.

When they both started to wail, Katie gave the door a slam with her foot. "I'll teach you both a lesson about snooping around, coming in here without knocking!" She threw Lavinia onto the bed and turned her over, spanking her cushioned bottom as hard as she could, infuriated by the screams, half-crazed with the violent power she used on her. After Lavinia was thoroughly spanked, she jerked Freddie against her naked body, pushed him down next to Lavinia, and pounded on him until her hand throbbed.

She stood up straight, panting, her breasts heaving, purged of her imprisoned emotions. "Get out!" She breathed heavily. "Get out and don't ever come snooping in here again!" In wild desperation, she looked at her red hand and said: "Look what you've made me do!" She snapped them both off the bed at the same time and dragged them to the door. "Stop that noise! Stop it, I say, or I'll spank you again!" She clapped her hands over their mouths. She couldn't stand the screaming; they had to be quiet. They stifled their screams, jerking their shoulders, gasping for breath. "Before you go, just tell me what it was you wanted, sneaking in here."

"We were . . ." hiccup from Lavinia ". . . were . . . were looking for . . ." her shoulders shook with hiccups ". . . for Daddy." She trembled and shook. "We thought . . . you were . . . downstairs." She tremulously reached down and picked up her doll.

"Daddy's gone. He won't be back for at least two days. He's gone, do you understand?" Tears welled in her eyes as she turned and walked to where her blue dressing gown lay in a heap. "You know never to enter someone's bedroom without knocking first. Don't you?"

They both nodded their heads, their fat faces red and streaked with tears. They gaped at her body, not her face.

"Now you go find Miss Anderson and you stay with her. I've had enough of you for a while." She went to them, trailing the silk behind her, and pushed them out the door; then she shut it again and leaned back against it, feeling sick and ashamed with her rage and despair. She could hear Miss Anderson's voice in the hallway—she would know what to do with them.

Shaking from the horrible scene, she went into the bathroom and started running a tub of hot water. While it ran, she pulled on her terry bath wrapper and went quickly down to the pantry and made herself a vodka on the rocks. She carried this back up, turned off the water, drank half the drink, leaning against the steamy wall. When she felt calmer, she went back into the dressing room and brushed her hair, almost tearing it from the roots, and finished her drink.

When she went back to get into the hot water to soak, she glanced at the mirror. It had steamed up again, except where she had written the words, and they now stood out for her to read: I HATE MYSELF.

Miss Anderson had heard the shouts and cries from the kitchen where she was putting down the papers. At the first sound, she dropped her handbag and had walked swiftly up the back stairs near the kitchen and headed down the hall to

Mrs. Harding's door. The door was shut and screams were coming from inside the room. She raised her hand to knock, then lowered it. She would wait for them to be sent out. She pinched her lips together and frowned at the door. She wasn't able to sort out the words because of the screams. What had they done now to get Mrs. Harding so upset?

The door opened and she caught sight of Mrs. Harding's thin white body, her red hair disheveled around her face, a patch of red pubic hair level with the children's heads.

As soon as they were through the door, Miss Anderson caught a wrist of each child, "You march right this way," and dragged them down the hallway to the back staircase leading to the third floor. She pulled them up the stairs and turned to the right into the long hall that led to the children's rooms. She passed Joe's room and went into Lavinia's small bedroom.

She pushed Lavinia toward her bed. "You wait here."

She went through the bathroom that connected this room with Freddie's room. She pushed the fat little boy down onto the bed without a word, quickly pulled open the top drawer of his bedside table and took out two long strips of white cloth. She tied these around his wrists, then pushed him flat onto the bed, pulling his arms above his head. She tied the strips to the brass rods on his headboard, then silently left the room, shutting the door behind her. He had not protested in any way.

She stood in the bathroom door. "Come here, Lavinia."

"No!" Lavinia started to scream.

Miss Anderson walked to her, pulled the doll free and tossed it onto the bed, then picked Lavinia up and carried her into the bathroom, shutting the door. She shook her until she stopped screaming.

"Stop that! I'm only going to talk to you now. I'm not going to punish you. Do you understand? I'm not going to punish you."

Lavinia sobbed to a stop and wiped her eyes with her arm, her plump body shaking up and down.

"What did you and Freddie do? I want a straight answer."

"Nothing." Choked sobs muffled the word.

"Well, it must have been something. Your mother was very upset. I could tell even without talking to her." She peered into the red swollen eyes. "Now tell me what happened."

"Nothing, Miss Anderson. We just went to look for Daddy."

Miss Anderson thought about the words. Lavinia was too frightened to be lying. "Where did you look?"

"We went into his room to for him."

"You went into your Daddy and Mother's room?"

Lavinia nodded.

"That's all you did?"

Again the little round head nodded.

"There must have been something more."

Lavinia lowered her eyes.

Miss Anderson pictured the scene. They must have walked in on something, something that upset Mrs. Harding.

"Why did your mother get mad?"

"We didn't knock first."

Ah, so that was it. "What was your mother doing?"

"She was lying on the bed."

"Doing what?"

Lavinia shut her mouth. Miss Anderson looked around the bathroom. This was the place she could get the straight truth. It was the place the children associated with punishment. It was also distant enough to smother Lavinia's screams.

"Tell me what happened, Lavinia." Miss Anderson reached for the short thin tree branch that stood in a glass of water on the windowsill.

Lavinia looked up, frightened. "You said you weren't going to punish me!"

"I won't if you tell me the truth." Miss Anderson hadn't been a children's nurse for thirty-five years for nothing. She had long ago learned that a keen switch straightened them out in a hurry. The fear of the stinging strike across the fleshy backside was far greater than the actual pain itself. "Now tell me exactly what happened."

"We went in the room, and she was lying on the bed with her eyes closed, just moaning and running her hands around."

Miss Anderson's eyes flickered. "Running her hands around? Moaning?" That wasn't a very clear picture. "Running her hands around where?"

Lavinia dropped her eyes. "All over her legs and stomach and all."

Miss Anderson thought of her employer. Idiotic woman— restless, bored, too emotional to be able to control herself, lonely and too weak to do anything about it but drink. And now resorting to masturbating. Disgusting. Well, she was drinking herself to an early grave. How was it Mr. Harding didn't see it? She should never be left alone. But then, Mr. Harding had his business, his lumber company that had grown so big and powerful; he had to be gone a lot of the time, making deals, tramping through deep woods, doing office work. He couldn't stay home and babysit his wife. All that money, and still so unhappy. It really boggled the mind. The decadent rich. No wonder they were called that. Mrs. Harding would have been right in her element in ancient Rome.

"You take a washcloth and run some water on it and wash your face, Lavinia. Then go to your room and brush your hair. It's all over now, but you remember never to go to anyone's bedroom without knocking first. Will you remember that?"

Lavinia nodded. "Yes, Miss Anderson," she said meekly.

Poor little tikes. Miss Anderson opened the door to Lavinia's room. Poor little tikes. What kind of life was this for them? They rarely saw their father, and their mother didn't seem to be able to see them. They needed to be with a mother. Even their mother. They needed her love. They needed a mother a lot more than they needed a nurse. But what did they have instead of a mother? A self-centered lush, that's what.

She opened Freddie's door and went to the bed, looking down at the dark sullen eyes. Here was a disturbed child if she ever saw one, and she had seen plenty. How vividly she remembered the Christmas she had suggested his parents give him an aquarium and an assortment of tropical fish; how fascinated he had been by them, all day, hardly able to take his eyes away from the spectacle of the brilliantly colored specimens. And that night he had taken a big pair of scissors and cut each one of them in half, dropping the halves into the bloody water until they were all dead and he was caught.

Some people might have said he needed to be in the hands of a psychiatrist. She didn't believe that, as she didn't believe in psychiatrists whether they be for the young or the old. What they both needed was love and a normal life. Not that that would cure Freddie, but it would help. But what could she do? She was just a paid member of the household and knew her place. If she complained to Mrs. Harding that the children were with their nurse too much and not with their mother enough, she would be sacked. And she didn't want that. No, indeed not. This was a good job. She might not respect Mrs. Harding in a lot of ways, but she liked working for her; she liked working for her better than anyone she had worked for in the past thirty-five years, since she had been twenty and finished her nurse's training.

In fact, she liked working here so much she was even willing to pretend she hadn't known Kay all her life. Kay wanted to be accepted as a social friend with equal status—as if school teaching were any more high-class than being a children's nurse. But she condescended to Kay's wishes, remembering that fat unhappy child, and was glad Kay had found a niche for herself in the world. Though if truth were admitted, it really was irksome the way Kay put on airs in front of Mrs. Harding, pretending to be a silk purse instead of the bedraggled remains of a sow's ear. Well, what did it matter . . . she gave Mrs. Harding companionship and a certain amount of comfort. And that was something to be thankful for. Miss Anderson wanted someone to help Mrs. Harding . . . especially as long as she worked for her. Yes, it was good work.

Mrs. Harding left you alone. She paid well, better than anyone else; she gave you a long vacation, with pay, and any time off you needed in between (provided you had found someone else to take your place while you were away) and she even paid for your plane tickets. Yes, she was the best person Miss Anderson had ever worked for.

She felt sorry for nurses who worked in big antiseptic institutions, or even in doctors' offices. She had always wanted to be part of a home, feeling part of a family. And she had always wanted to take care of children. Taking a baby and molding it from infancy to adolescence was a real challenge. Of course, this particular household was not exactly a cozy set-up of normal people but she had her established place in it and she felt secure. She felt like somebody.

She untied Freddie's hands, and replaced the cloth strips in the drawer. Then she sat on the side of the bed and looked at him. Poor little fellow. What a mess he was, and always would be. She couldn't leave him alone for five minutes without him getting into trouble. From the time he could walk, he was out in the road, sneaking into neighbors' gardens, destroying anything he saw and didn't like—plucking flowers, breaking pots, crayoning garden statues, mutilating the topiary works (she shuddered every time she remembered that woman at the end of the road having a stroke after Freddie had broken off all the low-growing swan-shaped heads). She finally had resorted to restraining him; it was the only way she could do anything with or about Lavinia or Joe. She disliked seeing him tied like this, she really did. But what could she do? She was fair to the children, doing her best to raise them to be decent citizens. It had been easy with Joe; he had been an easy child. His mother

loved him and had played with him when he was small—until
he was four, until the other two were born. That's when she
turned inward and started drinking heavily. She had never wanted
this child, this male child who was dark and brooding as an
infant and had turned out to be a fat and brooding brat; she
had never wanted the next one, Lavinia, who was precious and
loving as a baby, but then had turned out to be a brat also.
Mrs. Harding had had her tubes tied off right after Lavinia was
born. She had never wanted these two, and now she wanted
nothing to do with them. Poor little tikes. She knew Mrs.
Harding felt guilty about neglecting the children. Yes, she had
seen that. But she was so weak. When Mrs. Harding felt guilty,
she drank more to forget, and then sometimes she drank too
much, so much she couldn't stop and then she got sick. She
was a very weak person.

"Sit up, Freddie, and tell me what happened."

He squeezed his eyes shut in a wrinkled mass and tightened
his mouth.

"Don't do that, Freddie. You'll have to talk to me whether
you like it or not. I'm not going to punish you. But you must
talk to me." She paused. "No? You'll stay on this bed until
you do, no matter how long it takes. Do you understand?
There's no point in going off like that, pretending you can't
hear me. You bring yourself back here and listen. You missed
seeing the kites yesterday because you wouldn't mind me, and
now you'll stay here on this bed and miss lunch and supper.
Is that what you want?"

He slowly relaxed his face and opened his eyes.

"That's better. Now, tell me what happened."

"I heard what Lavinia said. It was like that."

"You have nothing to add?"

He shook his head.

"What have you learned from this?"

"Never enter Mommy's room without knocking first."

"Never enter anyone's bedroom without knocking."

He cut his eyes at her with a cunning look. "No one else
would get so mad."

"A bedroom is a person's private domain. When you intrude
on someone's privacy, you must always knock first." She hoped
he wasn't thinking of plots to sneak into rooms when she wasn't
looking. Any thought that got into his head was apt to get
turned around and cause trouble. "Do you understand that?"

Freddie glared at her sullenly, then nodded reluctantly.

Miss Anderson knew he couldn't be trusted to remember anything the way it was supposed to be remembered. Or he just didn't want to. He was a strange child, deceitful and lying if he thought he could get away with it. He had to be watched, had to be constantly taught the simplest things. Like the chocolate. He knew better than to put his sticky hands on the walls, and to put a spot right in the bird's eye was a pure act of malice. He never admitted doing it, but she knew. So both the children had to get a lecture and miss *The Buck Rogers Show*. She hadn't even bothered to ask Joe; he wouldn't do a thing like that.

She sighed. "Go in and wash up, Freddie. Wash your face and hands, and brush your hair. Then you and Lavinia both put on your shoes. We'll go outside and get some fresh air."

Miss Anderson had been with the Hardings since Joe was two. Ten years. In that time, she had managed to save almost all her salary; she had almost a hundred and fifty thousand saved and invested. By the time she retired—another five years, probably, with the Hardings—she would have about two hundred thousand. At ten percent interest rates, she could live quite comfortably on twenty thousand a year. She had no expenses and her needs were simple. She would be able to travel, see all the places she read about, eat out at restaurants, and, yes, have other people wait on her for a change. She could collect unemployment for a year, then start collecting her social security early. Yes, she would be well fixed. This was a good job and she wasn't going to jeopardize it for anything. She would just do the best she could to raise the children to be decent law-abiding citizens, who knew right from wrong. That's the best she could do. They would have to find love someplace else in their lives.

As Harry turned the jeep out of the driveway, he gestured toward the white garage apartment across the street.

"I suggested to Mom she call Kay and get her to come up and spend some time with her today. I'm glad they hit it off. Mom needs a close friend like Kay."

"Good idea." Joe propped his foot on the car seat and began tying the laces of his running shoes.

"I enjoyed talking with her last night," Harry said. "She's a very interesting person."

"Everybody likes her. She's one of the most popular teachers at school."

"Does everyone call her by her first name?"

"Sure," Joe answered. "She's sort of a dog to look at, but underneath that she's just one of the guys. We all call her Kay."

"Well, I'm thankful to her for Mom's sake. Where do you want to be dropped?"

"Three miles."

Harry checked the odometer. "Okay. Three it'll be."

Joe shifted feet and began tying the other shoe. "Say, Dad . . ." he bent his head, letting his hair fall over his eyes. "I wonder . . . what I mean is . . ."

Harry waited for him to go on.

"I mean, I wish I knew what was the matter with Mom. I don't understand. I wish you'd tell me."

Harry eased his foot up from the accelerator, letting the jeep slow down. "I wish I knew what to tell you. There's a lot I don't understand myself."

"She never wants to do anything, especially with us. I think she would if it were just me. But she gets so mad at Freddie and Lavinia. And then she gets all upset about it."

"I know. I think she feels very guilty about the way she treats them."

"Is that why she drinks so much?" Joe put his foot down and looked over at his father.

Harry turned his head briefly and saw the look of concern in Joe's eyes. "That's part of it. Another part is that she's just bored. Another part is that she can't cope with life. She's a complex person. When she drinks, she forgets all these things and it makes her life more tolerable."

"I don't understand that. Why doesn't she go out and do something—then she wouldn't get so bored."

"I know." There was a long pause while Harry thought of his answer. "You have to understand something about her past in order to understand her. Don't forget she was raised with not only the silver spoon in her mouth, but with a silver platter constantly in front of her handing her everything. Her father had come to this country from Ireland a poor, hungry young man. He was determined your mother would never know any of the deprivations he had known. He married the purest blue-blooded young woman he could find—fortunately it turned out they loved each other—and when your mother was born, he gave her the world. She never even went to the kitchen to get herself a glass of water—it was always brought to her on a tray by the butler. He treated her as if she were made of rare porcelain and might break if she lifted a finger to do anything. I guess she did do her own homework, but that was about all. Everything else was done for her. Everything. He worshipped her. And after her mother died, when Katie was about sixteen, he practically wrapped her up in a cocoon. It's a miracle he let her get married. But he liked me, said I was like him. I was. I had come from a poor family, and my parents died when I was young; I had to work my way up the ladder, too. He admired that. I was working my way through Columbia when I met your mother. What a beauty. I had never seen anyone like her: so poised and elegant, full of high spirits, a grand lady even though she was young. It was love at first sight for both of us."

"She must have been happy then," Joe said.

"Yes, she was. We were happy together; we didn't live too far from the city so she could see her father often; and when you were born . . . ." Harry uttered a short laugh. "Your grandfather was so proud of her he could have burst. Yes, she was happy then."

"When did it all change?"

"It changed slowly. No overnight deal, or anything like that. It was very slow. Your grandfather died. She mourned him so much I thought her heart would break. Then she was pregnant again with Freddie, and instead of being happy, she . . . well, she just never wanted anyone after you. She started drinking. I was gone more and more as the business grew. She drank more and more. It's taken about ten years for her to have gotten where she is now. A little bit more each year."

"I wish there were something to be done for her."

"So do I."

"What do the doctors say? I know that's why she was in the hospital last fall."

"In my experience, doctors have little patience with alcoholics; they prefer trying to cure people with heart disease or cancer."

"Why? Being an alcoholic is just as sick. We've learned that at school."

"It's a lot harder to cure. Did you learn that?" Harry looked at Joe. "The patient has to want to be cured, and most of them won't admit they're sick, or if they do, they think they can handle the problem themselves. Doctors know this. Therefore they have little patience with people who won't take their advice and won't see about getting themselves cured. They look at alcoholics as hopeless cases."

"Hopeless?" Joe looked startled. "You mean, there's nothing to be done for Mom?"

"When she gets physically sick, then she can go to a hospital and they can get her back into good shape. But there's nothing to be done otherwise, except hope."

"Have you talked to doctors about this?"

"Sure I have. Before we came here I talked with the best. I tried to get her to see a psychiatrist, but she said she didn't need one. And here, I've talked with Dr. Ames plenty of times about it. I thought he might persuade her to go to AA or to take a cure someplace. She likes him and I thought she would listen to him. But she told him the same thing . . . that she could handle it herself."

"If you were home more . . . would that help her?"

"Maybe. Maybe not. I don't know. But I can't be home and run a lumber business at the same time. It's taken a lot of hard work to get where I am. I wouldn't be the success I am if I'd stayed home with Mom."

"You do love Mom, don't you?"

Harry looked at Joe, then stared at the road again. "More than anything. Maybe a parent shouldn't say this, but I love her even more than I love you three kids. I love you as much as any parent ever loved a child, but then, Mom did give you three to me, so I guess I love her just a little bit more. Do you understand what I'm saying?"

"I guess so."

"I know it's hard to figure it all out."

"I guess I just don't see what good success is if you lose someone you love."

They drove in silence.

"Let me out up at that driveway, will you?"

Harry slowed to a stop.

"How long will you be gone this time?" Joe asked as he opened the door.

"Not long. No longer than I ever am. Two or three days."

"Okay. See you then." Joe slammed the door and immediately began stretching his leg muscles. By the time Harry drove off, he had begun running back along the highway.

Harry watched him in the rear-view mirror, the long wavy hair swept back by the wind, the blue shoes rhythmically touching the ground. Yes, he was like Katie's father: the same build, the same confidence, the same grace. He hoped Joe had the same strength, too. It wasn't easy growing up these days. It wasn't easy trying to understand why a father had to go out and work to be a big success, and to watch a mother drink herself into inconsolable misery. No, life wasn't easy at all. For any of them.

5

KATIE DIALED KAY'S NUMBER. "WHAT ARE YOU DOING?" SHE asked quickly, as soon as Kay had answered.

"Reading the paper. What's up?"

"Nothing much. Harry's gone to Ontario and . . ."

"Ontario! When?"

"A little while ago." What was it to her? "Anyway, what are you doing for lunch?" Katie jiggled her foot nervously.

"Nothing."

"Want to come on up here?" If Kay turned her down, she wouldn't call her for a week. "We can take a walk, then Pearl will get us a bite to eat."

"Sounds great. Be up shortly."

Katie replaced the phone in its cradle and untwisted the wire from her fingers.

She walked out onto the balcony and looked down at the terrace. Pearl was sweeping the flagstones.

"Pearl." She leaned over the rail. "Miss Wright is coming for lunch. Could you set the table for us down there?"

"Sure." Pearl leaned on the broom handle. "Soup and a salad do?"

"Sounds fine."

"Sure? Miss Wright's a pretty big eater."

"I'm sure it will be plenty." She looked up. The peaceful scene did nothing to cheer her, not the greens, blues and yellows, nor paling pinks. She tried not to look at the peonies that separated the lawn from the fields—the fields where she had not watched the kites, the fields where her absence was yet another failure, for Harry, for herself.

She dressed hurriedly, stepped into linen slacks and pulled a dove-colored silk shirt over her white shoulders, leaving it unbuttoned all the way down to the hook on her bra. She pulled it loosely open at the neck, her eyes traveling down to the rounded mounds that formed a seductive valley disappearing into the gray silk. She put her hand on her throat and decided on a short, single strand of pearls. The emeralds she had worn the night before lay on top of her dressing table. She opened the drawer and swept them into a black-velvet-lined case, pushed it to the back and pulled out a striped silk box that held several strands of pearls. As she selected the shorter strand, she noticed that coins lay in the front of her drawer, but the bills were gone. She bent down and peered farther into the drawer. Harry must have taken them. He knew she always kept emergency money there. Hardly any great amount. She would cash another check and replace it.

She carefully applied her makeup, then stood back and admired herself. A little color worked miracles. Harry always said he didn't care if she wore makeup or not; he liked the plain colorless look. Still, it made her feel better to look her best. Even if he weren't there to see her. Her best almost made her feel like a "masterpiece" again.

Katie went down the stairs and out onto the terrace to wait for Kay. She was going to try not to get drunk today. She'd already had enough to make her feel happy and forget, and that was sufficient. She also would try not to be awful to the children.

When Kay arrived, in another full cotton skirt and a baggy T-shirt with short sleeves, they walked down onto the lawn, circled past the side of the house and the gardener's small cottage hidden in greenery, past the pool, and onto the long gravel driveway that ran through the tree-studded lawn and the uncut woods to East Road. From here the house was out of sight; even the manicured lawns were hidden by growths of saplings and underbrush. The new leaves on the trees hung limp and fresh, almost transparent.

Once on the road, Katie paused and breathed deeply: "Let's go slowly. I've been a little under the weather for a few days."

After walking for some distance, Katie suggested they turn back. The walk had done her good; she had recovered her calm, pushing the scene with the children away from her consciousness, and once again had come to terms with Harry's departure as a necessary disappointment in her life.

As they turned into the driveway, Kay suddenly asked: "Did I tell you my brother's coming? Rather, might come. I'm not going to count on him until I see him."

"Dan?" Katie stopped and looked at her. "How exciting. I'm dying to meet him." She walked on. "I always forget you have a brother. You so rarely speak of him. What an event to have him actually come."

"I hope it won't be a traumatic event." Kay looked solemn.

"What do you mean?" Katie leaned into the subject, delving cautiously, wanting to hear all about him. "Is something wrong with him?"

"Sort of. Oh, you don't want to hear about it."

"Of course I do. Good Lord, I tell you all my troubles. Let's share."

"Well, he does seem to have problems. With his home life, his work, everything."

"I'm sorry to hear that. What sort of problems?"

"For one thing, it's hard for him to keep a job. He drifts from one thing to another. Newspaper work."

"Does he have any family?" Katie had heard almost nothing about him in the three years she had known Kay.

"Yes. He's married and has one teenage son."

"What's his wife like?" Katie pulled a bright green leaf from a young birch and held it up to the light to see the tiny veins.

"She's a . . ." Kay hesitated, a grim expression on her face, and walked on a short distance before she finished the sentence. "Well, frankly, Katie, she's a Jew, and I could have told Dan it wouldn't work right from the beginning. In fact, I did tell him, but he wouldn't listen. You know as well as I know that mixed marriages don't work. He just wouldn't listen to me . . . no matter what I said, or how hard I tried, and God knows I tried. It sort of put some distance between us."

Katie stared at Kay in disbelief. She even thought she hadn't heard her right. "I don't believe I just heard you say that. You, my best friend, and I thought I knew you."

Kay looked startled, dropping her small head to the side like a robin after a worm. "What do you mean?"

"You're against your brother because he married a Jew? A Jew is a normal person, an ordinary, everyday person, who has a different religion, but they do not have two heads and breathe fire. I can't believe I heard you say that."

Kay took a step back. She opened her mouth, but didn't speak.

Katie shook her head angrily, auburn waves undulating in the sun-dappled glow of the tall trees. "Kay, dear God, you're an educated person. How can you be so prejudiced? You talk as if you came out of the last century. I'm really surprised at you. In fact, shocked."

"I'm not against all Jews, Katie," she said defensively. "I have nothing against them at all—"

"Unless your brother happens to marry one? Is that it?"

"Let's drop this, do you mind? I'd rather not talk about it anymore."

Katie felt she had been too harsh with her, even if she was a bigot. If she didn't hurry and throw herself into reverse she'd really say something she'd be sorry about. She slipped her arm through Kay's. "Right. Let's talk about something else. A person has a right to believe whatever she wants to believe." Wait until she told Harry. He would flip when he heard that one. Kay, a teacher of young minds, was a Jew-hater. Well, well, well.

They walked up onto the clipped green square where Mario was planting marigolds in the border by the low stone wall. He looked up at them and nodded.

"Don't you believe in resting on Sunday?" Katie asked him.

He stood up and brushed the dirt from his hands. "I want to get these in before it rains. The radio says it might rain tomorrow."

Katie ran her eyes down his bare chest, which was covered in black curls that matched his hair. His sinewy shoulders glistened with sweat in the sunlight. When she looked back at his face, she saw he had been watching her.

She couldn't resist. She wickedly bent to brush a speck of dirt from her shoe, knowing her breasts would fall forward against the soft silk, knowing he would be able to look down to the fold at her stomach. She uncurled to an upright position and moved toward the terrace. "Don't let us stop you." She had noticed they were about the same height; she might be a touch taller. She could see he thought she was fantastic. She smiled to herself. A little flirting was always titillating. "You know Miss Wright, don't you?"

He nodded at Kay, who walked on without speaking. "I'll finish these up later," he said, lifting the flats of marigolds onto the wall so they wouldn't make marks on the grass. Then he walked off toward his cottage, out of sight from the main house.

Pearl had put the usual cocktail tray on the table.

"Would you like to have a spritzer, now that you know what it is?" Katie teasingly asked.

"I think a little vodka and a lot of tonic would taste good. I don't want much; I still have papers to grade this afternoon."

As Katie made Kay's drink, she forgot she had decided not to drink herself. She made another Bloody Mary, more out of habit than desire.

"Where did you find Mario?" Kay asked.

"Harry found him."

"How on earth does Harry have time to do all he does?" Kay took a dainty swallow.

"What does that mean?"

"Well, he does have that big company, growing all the time and . . ."

"And?"

"And then to find time to locate a gardener as well. That's all I meant."

A cloud swept across the terrace and Katie felt a momentary chill. "Well, Harry didn't actually go out employment-office crawling to find Mario. Mario applied for a job with the company and as it was just when Mr. West had his stroke, Harry asked Mario if he'd like to be a gardener instead of a lumberjack. Very simple."

"As I recall, Mr. West had been here for years and years. He came with the house, didn't he?"

"Yes." Katie watched other clouds sweep swiftly by, racing their shadows across the lawn. "He laid everything out. Mario just keeps up the traditional standards."

"He seems so young."

"Does he? Maybe." Katie stretched her long legs, easing them across the flagstones. How old was he? Twenty-five? Older? Younger? Certainly not a gardener by training, and probably not by birthright. Still, he was good. He would work out fine. Should she tell Kay he was a Jew? That might be fun. A Mexican Jew. Italian sounded too toney, though maybe not for Kay. She could say: "By the way, he's a wetback Jew." Queer, to think you knew someone so well and then have this sort of thing happen.

Katie was on her second drink when Joe came out.

"Joe, sweetheart, come sit with us." Katie held out a hand to him.

"Hi, Kay," Joe said, tossing his head to shake the hair away from his face and neck. "Mom," he said, standing in front of her but not taking her hand. "If it's okay with you, I'd like to have my class over here for a picnic some afternoon after school."

Katie smiled. "Of course you can. What a wonderful idea. How many are there?"

"About twenty."

"Nineteen, to be exact," Kay corrected him.

"Good number," Katie ignored Kay's precision count of Joe's life. "You just name the date, and Pearl and Carol will handle the rest. What fun. I love having your friends here."

"It'll probably be this week." He began to kick an imaginary ball with his foot, dribbling it away from him, then stopping it with the other foot.

"Any day will be fine."

"It'll probably be Friday. Then they can stay out late."

"Fine. Why don't you go call them now and see if they can come then."

"I'll ask them tomorrow at school. It'll be easier than calling." The ball almost got away from him, but he slid and caught it.

"Whatever you say, sweetheart. Want some Coke or ginger ale? Run get it, then come back and talk to us."

"I'm going over to the soccer field now. There's a game going."

"Run along then. Have fun."

He dribbled back into the house and out of sight.

"He is handsome, isn't he?" Katie remarked.

"He sure is," Kay agreed. "Even needing a haircut."

"So like his grandfather . . . my father." She paused. "And there's nothing wrong with his hair. It's smart-looking that way." She gave her glass to Kay, who came over and held out her hand for it.

As Kay handed Katie her filled glass, she saw that vague

detached look on Katie's face and figured she must be thinking about her old man again. She had drunk half of her own drink and now rattled the ice in the glass. "Your father must have really adored you."

Katie didn't hear her. She was remembering the terrifying ordeal of lying in that hospital bed, waiting for her first child to be born—the fear that came with the agonizing pain, not only the fear of her insides being ripped apart, but the awful fear that her father wouldn't like the baby, that it would be a two-headed monster, a Mongolian, something that would make him turn away from her and make him ashamed. That fear had been as intense as waiting for the next excruciating contraction.

Katie's father had wandered in and out of her room during the long labor. Harry had tried to keep him out—he was never sure whether from concern for the older man's health or from jealousy. But her father had insisted on being with her. As the hours wore on, the strain on him seemed almost as hard as it was on Katie. He had held her hands and when she would scream and cry out "No! No! Help me! I can't stand it!" he would cry out with her, damning the doctors, cursing the nurses, raging at them that they were incompetent asses not worth wasting medical training on. When she would sink into a brief exhausted sleep, her father would sit next door in the private room he had taken for his own use, a place to relax and have a drink. A little five-star Hennessy helped to restore his calm. The St. Regis had sent in meals for him, bringing a folding table, linens, crystal, silver, china—everything that was needed to make his respites as pleasant as possible. He had talked to Harry about the effect of the day's Dow Jones pronouncements, expounding on money markets and municipal bonds while eating a little gray caviar and filet mignon. Candles had burned in the silver candlesticks, incongruously casting dancing shadows on the antiseptic walls, sometimes burning all the way down while he was at Katie's side, but replaced before he slipped back to his room. His valet had hovered near him; his chauffeur had waited downstairs. After ten hours, her father had insisted his staff go home, though they were reluctant to leave him. They had come back in six hours, hardly refreshed, but with a little sleep behind them.

Katie had frequently cried out for him to help her: "Daddy, don't leave me! I need you!" Harry felt she needed her father more than she needed him. Especially when she screamed: "If

I'd known it was going to be like this, I never would have had it!"

Joe had been born after a hard thirty-hour labor. Katie, spent and depleted, had been too weak to hold him, merely touching him with wonder as he lay in the nurse's arms. Then Harry had insisted her father take the next turn, before he, the father, held the tiny body. The New York hospital hadn't been too pleased with all this unsanitary handling, but had been warned by the head of the hospital to go along with anything within reason. The baby was perfect and Mr. Lockwood had given five hundred thousand dollars to the hospital.

He had also given Katie a few words of advice. "You were an only child, and you gave us the most perfect pleasure any parents could have. I don't want you to go through this again. You may not be able to stand it. And I'm damned sure I can't. One is enough, Katie. One is enough."

He had been so proud of his grandchild, the hours of trial slipping from his countenance as he announced the news to any stranger he met. The finest champagne had been chilled and waiting for hours; he had insisted the nurses all have some— "Just a sip if you like, to toast his birth"—not allowing them to decline completely with any excuses about being on duty.

To Katie he repeated: "One is enough. Don't you think so, Harry? Of course you do. Especially this perfect child. He'll be tall; he's over twenty inches now. Who do you think he looks like, with that golden-reddish fuzz on his head, such a beautifully shaped head? Who do you think he looks like?"

"You, Daddy, you. I noticed it the first I saw him. Another one would be different, not like you. We couldn't duplicate you two times. You're right, one is enough. Besides, I can't go through that again. My God, how did they ever do it before pain-killers? It's bad enough with them." She had wept then, holding out her hand to her father as Harry had stood in the shadows. "Do you think I'm a coward? Did I act too much like a coward?"

"I think you're the bravest person alive to go through that. Isn't that right, Harry? But don't do it again. It will be your one crowning achievement. When your mother saw you, she said that. She said you were her moment of glory and everything else would be downhill. She was right. You were enough, my beautiful Katie, my masterpiece. And this one, this perfect baby, he'll make you proud. Look at that bone structure. The noble lines, the intelligent eyes. You can tell at a glance how they're going to turn out. You can tell. Never mistrust your instinct. I haven't, and it's paid off every time. What will you name him?"

Harry had answered before Katie had a chance to speak. "Joseph Lockwood Harding." Katie had never loved Harry more than at that moment.

Katie shook her head with a start as she heard Kay's voice. "What?"

"I said, your father must have really adored you," Kay repeated.

Katie tilted her head. "I guess that comes from being an only child." She stared into the glass, not registering that she had yet another full drink. "Isn't it awful that I don't adore all my children? Doesn't that make you despise me?"

"No. I'm sorry for you."

"Sorry?" She uttered one sharp laugh. "Does it sound so wonderful to you to be an adoring mother? To have a great merry brood around you?" She shook her head. "One child is so easy to love. I love Joe that way, the way my father loved me."

It was just as Kay thought. "But you don't do much with him," she commented.

"The other two are always in the way. I can't seem to single him out." She let out a sad heartless sound. "Do all those mothers you see at school . . . do all of them love their children?"

"Certainly they do. Some of them are too busy to do much with their children, and run out of patience. But they love them anyway—the same as you love Lavinia and Freddie."

"I don't love Lavinia and Freddie," Katie said, tipping back her head, her throat a bending arc. "I don't love them. I never have. I never wanted them." The sky was deep blue above the gathering tufts of white clouds.

"Katie! You shouldn't say such terrible things."

"They are terrible, aren't they? I wish I didn't say them, not to you, not even to myself. I don't to anyone else. I certainly don't say them to Harry. He's filled with enough guilt that we don't pay much attention to them. He loves them. Maybe the love of one parent is enough." The shame was there, filling the gaps where love should have been.

"You should both love them. You do both love them."

"I know I should. I feel sorry for them. But that's not the

same as love. Harry wants to be a normal father, but that's not possible either. Our lives as parents have become a jigsaw puzzle with lots of pieces missing, and no matter how hard we look for them, they'll always be missing."

"It would be more complete if you tried harder."

Katie looked at Kay. "I don't want to try harder. It's as simple as that. I would love to do things with Joe, if he were an only child. But Lavinia and Freddie are always getting into trouble and they make me nervous . . . and unhappy." She touched the rim of her glass. "I often wonder if they'll be different when they get older."

"Of course they will. They're just high-strung children now. The day will come when you'll really enjoy them."

"Do you really believe that?"

"Yes. Of course I do."

"You're a fool, Kay. I love you, but you really are a fool. Look, here comes Pearl with our lunch."

Katie and Kay moved to the larger glass-topped table, set with yellow linen place mats and matching napkins. Kay sat primly, rifle straight in her white vinyl-webbed chair, her feet close together as if she were holding an invisible object between her arches, her left hand limp in her lap. In contrast, Katie sat almost sideways, her left forearm resting on the edge of the table, one long leg hooked over the other and swinging limply.

Pearl first served them hot asparagus soup, "Made from those skinny stalks in the garden." She darted one eye around the table as she placed the soup cups in front of them. "Mr. West would have had a fit if he saw me take the fat stalks for soup. Don't know what Mario thinks about it." Soon she returned with two plates, chunks of white crabmeat on a salad on crisp bibb lettuce, and hot blueberry muffins. "I got that crabmeat thinking Mr. Harding would be home today."

As they ate their salad, Pearl returned with a round silver tray holding a small silver pot of hot coffee, two demitasse cups and sugar. "Anything else, Mrs. Harding?" She put the tray on the empty side of the table.

"No, thank you, Pearl. This is all perfect."

It was too much for Katie. She had drunk about half the soup, and now fiddled with her salad and muffin. "All that tomato juice fills me up." She wished she hadn't had so much. It had begun to make her feel queasy again. Her stomach churned, pushing a sick feeling upward in her.

Kay ate everything, including two muffins. Katie watched her, wondering how she could stay so scarecrow skinny when she ate so much.

After coffee, Kay stood, saying she had to get back and finish grading her students' papers.

"You never told me when Dan is coming," Katie stopped her at the door. "And if he is coming alone."

"If he comes at all, it will be Thursday, this week. He'll certainly be alone."

"How long will he stay? If he comes."

"Only one night."

"I'd like to have you both for dinner Thursday night. Will that be all right?" Katie opened the door and they went into the hallway.

"It would be wonderful. Will Harry be back?"

"Yes, indeed. He'll be back soon, probably tomorrow. Is there someone else you'd like for me to ask?"

"No. Just the four of us will be great."

"Good. It will be nice to get a chance to talk to Dan." Katie walked Kay to the front door, then she went upstairs to rest. She was suddenly tired, very tired, her insides an unwanted dead weight that drained her energies. And anyway, she had no other plans.

Kay walked stiffly down the driveway to East Road, across it and to the garage apartment she rented from another big-house owner. She was thoughtful as she mounted the stairs to her small apartment—a medium-sized living room, a small bedroom, bath and a claustrophobic kitchen. It would probably all fit into Katie's bedroom.

She went directly to the bathroom and stuck her finger down her throat and threw up. When she had finished, she washed her face, rinsed out her mouth with cold water, then went into the living room to read. One thing she would never do again was to get fat. Katie thought she had always been thin. Little did Katie know—Kay had once weighed almost two hundred pounds. She sat down at her chipped and peeling veneered desk. Little did Katie know about a lot of things. She was a spoiled, protected creature, who had never had to work, to want, to envy others. She sat around in her gilded cage, acting as if she were the same debutante her father had made such a fuss over almost twenty years ago. No, Katie hadn't seen herself in that antique mirror that was "going hazy" for many years now. Antique mirror, balls! That mirror was just as clear as any brand new mirror. Katie just didn't want to see herself the way others saw her. She would never admit that the years of booze had begun to take their toll: her white skin and perfect face going all red and splotchy and puffy. She just couldn't admit it to herself—not with Daddy right there watching. What a farce. Well, old Daddy perched in his silver frame might not see it, but Kay knew Harry saw it every time he looked at Katie. Oh, Katie did a good job with the makeup all right; she hid all that degenerate disintegration better than most. But it was still there. The youthful bloom was no more and never would be. She still had a good figure though. And she sure still had all that money. Good Lord, just to think of it was enough to make Kay sick.

There had been times when Kay was not only fat and un-attractive, but had been hungry. That was right after her parents died and she found herself with a mediocre education and no job. Fortunately, she had been able to get a job with one of the private schools that didn't require teachers' certification, and had found this apartment. She and Dan had sold their parents' house and split the money. It wasn't much, but it helped. Kay had invested her share and got a couple of thousand a year from it; Dan had spent his on one of his moves. She had enough to live on, modestly. She would never have enough to buy designer clothes and thick lamb chops or enough to pay servants to do all her work. Never. She would be stuck with her dumb job, rubbing elbows with the upper classes, but never being one of them, for all her life. Unless a miracle occurred. Or she could make a miracle occur. Things could be made to happen, with a little bit of luck. And if they did, at least she would have the skinny figure to be able to wear clothes.

She had never been pretty the way Lavinia was pretty—and certainly not spoiled rotten either. No, she had been fat, with a plain pinched face and a tight string of plaited hair extending from her head like a rat's tail. Her mother had often spoken of her looks: "Kay's a sweet, God-fearing child, but she is very plain." Her father had been a stiff, worried man who paid little heed to her or to Dan. They had been great churchgoers, the four of them sitting rigidly on the hard benches, listening to the wages of sin. And after church they would go home to a roast chicken dinner, praying as they always did before meals that God would keep them in his bountiful mercy and grant them salvation.

The children at school had ignored Kay, not so much because of her fat body and unappealing looks, but because she was never allowed to go with them to the drive-in for a soda or to go see a Sunday movie. Dan, being braver, frequently climbed out of the window at night, but Kay had been afraid of her parents' wrath and had never done anything wrong. A dutiful, obedient, ugly Christian child.

At her high-school graduation prom, she had still never had a date with a boy and had wept when her mother insisted she put on her white net dress that made her look like a parachute in full wind and go anyway, being escorted there and back by her father. She had sat on a stiff folding chair the entire evening, staring straight ahead, speaking civilly when the teachers spoke to her, and praying the hour would hurry and come when her father would appear at the door.

She had gone to a nearby state college and roomed with a bosomy boy-crazy girl who talked of nothing but sex. At first Kay had been horrified, ashamed to be listening, fearful her parents would find out and make her come home again. But soon she began to relax and listen, especially when her roommate explained to her in graphic detail about masturbation. It took her a long time to get around to actually doing any of it, but the more she thought about it, the more attractive it sounded. And no bolts of lightning had struck her while she was thinking about it, so she had tentatively touched herself, holding her breath, and again, when she wasn't struck dead, she had gone further and finally became pretty expert at it.

She steeled herself and lost some weight, let her hair hang loose and put on lipstick; she began to seat herself next to boys—not the football heroes, but the pimply faced boys who were having a hard time making out themselves. One of them finally asked her for a date. He had a car. They went to a movie and afterward to some wooded spot by a lake, where he sucked her large breasts and put his fingers inside her panties. She had been afraid, that first time, to do anything more. But he asked her again, and that second time they lay on the back seat and he went all the way. She had cried out in pain as he burst into her, but after that she couldn't get enough of him. They had taken water from the lake and washed the car seat, and he had been nice about it, saying it didn't matter when she shamefully apologized for the mess. She lost some more weight and had seen him several times, thinking she was falling in love, and then he suddenly disappeared without a word. When she asked, she discovered he had transferred to another college. She never heard from him again.

During the four years of college, she had managed to get herself asked out by a few more cast-offs the other girls didn't want, but none of them ever lasted for very long. But she had graduated, as thin as she was now, with her hair pinned back in a knot the way her mother wanted, and had moved back home to read the want ads and look for a job. Then her parents had been killed. Her mother's friend, Hilda Anderson, wrote her about a job opening at the little private day school in the town where Hilda had lived before moving down to Westchester County with her "family." Kay had applied for the job and had gotten it. And she had stayed, now entrenched in the school as solidly as the blackboards and frayed primers.

She had been so pleased when Hilda had called her to tell her they were moving to the town. It wasn't surprising for the Hardings to want to come here: a college town with two museums, a summer theater, year-round activities and sports. If one had to relocate in a place three hours from New York City and three hours from the big timberlands to the north, it was the logical spot. Hilda had been delighted to be coming back to her own home town and Kay had been delighted to have her come. And Hilda had brought with her three children who entered Kay's school; Katie, with her champagne and staff of servants; and Harry. And of the suitable estates that were for sale in the region, Kay had been pleased when the Hardings picked the old Peabody estate directly across the road from her. Such a small world. Especially if there were Hilda Andersons to make sensible suggestions. Odd, how it had all worked out.

And now, here she was, wallowing in the shadow of Katie, who wanted her with her every time Harry was out of town, becoming what one might say an indispensable friend of the family. At first she had been overwhelmed by the riches Katie lavished on everything but as they became more familiar to her, they also became more desirable. Her life in comparison became more tawdry. She became envious, jealous, ungrateful for her own status, which had seemed all right until Katie came into her life. And it irritated her that her mother's old friend lived so much better than she did . . . money-wise. Hilda was still a servant, and always would be. At least she, Kay, was a friend on an equal intellectual footing.

She spread the school papers before her, hiding the cheap

finish of the desk, thinking she should get a colorful cloth to conceal it when she wasn't using it, and picked up a pencil. She couldn't concentrate. She looked around the room, dull, plain, just the way she was: mediocre chairs, second-hand sofa, cheap chintz. No fabulous Chippendale or Hepplewhite, no Winslow Homers or Chinese murals. Some flower prints, a snow scene on a mountain, a Wyeth reproduction of a hay wagon on marshy ground near the water's edge. And the only reason she had that was because Katie had taken her to New York last year to see a Wyeth show, and had raved so about all those old rotten boats and crumbling barns that Kay had bought the first reproduction she could find. It was all right. In fact, it was rather pleasant to look at. Not like having an original though. Not at all.

She walked over to the sofa and stretched out on it, staring at the stain on the ceiling made from a long-ago leak in the roof. Not like Katie's ceilings where any stain would be obliterated overnight. Imagine having all that money. And a husband like Harry on top of that. Katie might be losing her looks, but she knew how to live. Katie had class. How different her own life would be now if she'd grown up like Katie, with city houses and Southern plantations, servants, all that travel, rich-girls' schools, chauffeured limousines. And the clothes! What Kay wouldn't give to have some of those clothes. My God, she must have ten closets full of clothes, by Halston and Dior and Chanel and all those designers. And so many pairs of two-hundred-dollar shoes by Ferragamo and Gucci and whoever those Italians were, it almost made her puke. Just think of it. She could give Kay twenty things and not know they were gone.

She pushed her cheap sandals off her feet and pushed her toes into the worn pillow with feather quills poking through the seams. She would have to be more careful about what she said; it never occurred to her Katie was a champion of the Jews. She just assumed Katie, like all rich gentiles, looked down her nose at Jews. Well, live and learn was what she always said. She would never speak out again about Jews, not in front of anyone. She may not have had that expensive education, but she remembered a lesson when she learned it.

And she'd learned a lot of things from Katie. She understood Katie. Kay really didn't blame Katie for not liking Lavinia and Freddie. They were such sniveling whiners. Small wonder they irritated her. And when they did something really awful, or acted the way they had at dinner, then Katie lost control and instead of trying to help them and calm them, she simply screamed at them and got stinking drunk. That's what upset Harry so much: Katie's impatience with the children, her lack of trying to help them and her weakness that made her drink. All that drinking kept him away from home more. And that made Katie drink more. And that kept Harry away more. On and on, over and over. The true vicious circle. And the children were not only the causes, but also the innocent victims. Hilda Anderson had painted a very clear picture for Kay in the past three years.

Kay pushed her tongue against the back of her teeth and zeroed in on the children. Harry was displeased with Katie for not being a good mother. Kay had seen it with her own eyes this time. Hilda was right when she said Harry got that indignant look when Katie sent Freddie and Lavinia from the room, or sometimes got tears in his eyes when she refused to do something with them and the children were obviously hurt. Apparently he was always upset when she refused to eat with them. Yes, she'd finally seen how Harry felt. His soft spot lay in those kids.

She hooked one bony knee over the other and swung her foot in the air, jabbing out with her big toe to emphasize her thoughts. How wonderful it would be to win Harry's everlasting devotion. She knew how much he appreciated the time she spent with Lavinia and Freddie. Hilda, Katie and the children had made that plain to her. When they ran to take her hand before dinner and babble to her, she had felt the warmth of Harry's eyes on her. Yes, there could be ways to win Harry— Harry and all that money. She stuck her big toe straight out.

She wondered if Lavinia had taken the bait about the money. Standing out there in that hot sun watching those idiotic kites, trying to sound like she was having a wonderful time, an unexpected opening had suddenly presented itself.

"It must cost a lot of money to build those big kites," Miss Anderson had commented. "More than a week's allowance for most of those students." And as soon as Miss Anderson was out of earshot to watch another launching, Kay had said to Lavinia: "I bet those students wish they had just the money your Mommy leaves lying around in her dressing table to use on a kite. Why, if Joe had just the amount from that drawer alone, he could build a kite better than any of these. Look at that one, Lavinia. I think it's the prettiest one we've seen."

She knew Lavinia had taken in every word. She knew Lavinia wanted to curry favor with Joe, her popular older brother. And Lavinia thought if Joe loved her and wanted her around him, then both her father and mother would love her too. Yes, she understood Lavinia too. And Katie would be wild if any of them stole something.

Kay knew she might not be much to look at, and that she had a reputation of being a skinny old maid on top of it. She dropped her legs onto the cushions and stared gloomily at the ceiling. What a life to have to live. It was unfair. Unfair. Unfair and she hated it.

If only she could get Harry to turn to her more . . . if she could be subtle and get him to do it without him realizing he was doing it . . . if she and Harry could talk about more intimate things . . . well, who knows how close they could become. She already knew how much he relied on her friendship to Katie. He was grateful to her for her care and concern of the children. And after one conversation, she realized she knew a damned sight more about his lumber business than Katie did.

It was important that Harry and Katie not know about her past association with "Miss" Anderson—she was always careful to call her that in front of Katie. If they knew she was hobnobbing with the servants, they might start thinking of her in those terms, and might find it awkward to have her for dinner and as an intimate friend. So far she had been able to manage it without Hilda getting sore; if she was going to get in Harry's confidence, too, she would have to be doubly careful.

The ceiling stain seemed to have deepened and grown more loathsome. The sunlight had moved away from the windows and now cast a gloomy shadow on the dingy walls.

Kay sat up and put her bony fingers on her hair. She felt so drab and dingy herself, lifeless to the core, dried-up and spoiling at the center. She stood up. If she fixed herself up a bit, she might feel better.

She went into the bedroom and, purposefully pulling down the shades, took off her skirt and T-shirt—her fifteen-dollar skirt and three-dollar shirt bought on sale years before. Not like any of Katie's clothes. Not like that skimpy black dress that hung straight down like a floor-length slip and had those big white bat sleeves on the top that Katie called "organdy butterfly wings"; not like that one. She had finally gotten it out of Katie how much it cost—five thousand dollars. Five thousand! Anyone who could thread a needle could have made it overnight. Katie said it was special, made for her by famous so-and-so to wear at such-and-such big party in Washington. Five thousand! Unbelievable.

Kay opened her closet door and first put her chenille wrapper on the foot of the bed, just in case someone came to the door. Then she stepped out of her plain white underpants and lifted a pair of black lace bikini panties from a hook near the back of the closet. She pulled these on and then unhooked her sturdy bra. She looked down at herself: She had a lot bigger boobs than Katie; she just kept them mashed in with the foundation garment she had been wearing since her gross days. When she had lost so much weight, she hadn't lost it all up top; she still had her big boobs. She took a black lace bra off the hook and put it on. Going to the bureau, she picked up the brush and slicked her hair flatter against her head. Then she reached under some sweaters in one of the drawers and pulled out a black wig she had bought at a close-out sale. Fitting this over her head, she went into the bathroom and looked in the full-length mirror behind the door. She cradled her breasts in her hands and swayed from side to side as she sauntered back into the bedroom. Lifting the covers up on the side of the bed, she reached beneath the mattress and brought out the latest copies of *Playboy* and *Oui*. Then she lay on the bed happily going over them again for the rest of the afternoon.

6

IT WAS RAINING WHEN KATIE WOKE UP THE FIRST TIME, AND
it was still raining when she woke up the second time. She had
a headache and was depressed. She rang for Pearl and told her
she was going to spend the morning in bed. Pearl brought her
juice, coffee and a piece of toast, which she did not eat. She
got out a sleeveless cotton gown and draped it from her shoulders the way she would hang a coat on a hanger, letting it fall
shapeless and billowy around her body before she settled back
on the bed. She never had liked air conditioning and refused
to have it; her father said it dried the air too much. She found
a mystery book on the bedside table and made herself comfortable—after taking two aspirin and a Librium.

By late morning she was bored, but not as irritable as she
would have been without the tranquilizer. She knew she should
get up and go to the school and try to find out about summer
camps, but she just couldn't bring herself to get going.

The phone rang and she answered it.

"Hi, Red. How're you doing?"

74

"Harry. Where are you? Are you almost home?"

"Sorry, honey, but I have to stay on a few days."

"Few days! You promised me you'd be back! You promised!" She slammed her fist into the pillow.

"I promised I'd try. But I can't do it, Red. I've got to stay and get this deal worked out. There are two brothers who own the property, and I've only talked to one. The other one won't be here until tomorrow. Then, after that, we'll have to work out the details. I think it's going through, though."

"I don't give a damn about it! I want you here!" She picked up the open book and threw it across the room, smashing it into the wall near Harry's dressing room.

"I know you do. I'll be back as soon as I can."

There was a long pause.

"Are you there, Red?"

"Yes," she answered sulkily. "I'm here."

"I'm sorry. I really am. I miss you." No answer from her. "Everything all right there?"

"If you call being cooped up in this house alone 'all right.'"

"What did you do last night?"

"Oh, I had a wonderful time. I read the paper and watched television. I also got drunk. What did you do to amuse yourself?" She felt hot; the damp air oppressed her, coolness coming only when she squeezed the phone between her ear and shoulder and fanned herself with the thin cotton gown, lifting it squarely, a diminutive mainsail catching the breeze she created.

"Listen, Red, you've got to watch it. You've got to cut down on your drinking. You don't want to spend the summer in the hospital, do you? It was only last fall that you were there. . . ."

"I remember when I was there," she cut in.

"Take it easy on the vodka, will you?" Again, no answer. "Will you, Red? You seem to be hitting it a little hard these days. I love you and want you to take care of yourself. Will you do it for me?"

"I'm not doing a goddamn thing for you until you get back here."

"I'll be back soon. Where's Kay? Why didn't she come have dinner with you last night?"

"How should I know? She said she had some papers to correct."

"Call her and see if she can come tonight."

"I will if I feel like it. Her brother . . . you know, Dan,

the one she never talks about . . . is coming this week. I'm having them for dinner. Thursday. I trust you will be here by then." She'd save the Jewish wife until he returned. She was too upset to go into it now.

"Yes, definitely. I'll certainly be home by Thursday."

"To see the brother, or to be with me?"

"To be with you. I'm not planning on going to bed with the brother."

She softened. "I miss you, Harry. I miss you so much. I'm lonely when you're not here." Was there any way to make him understand the depths of that loneliness?

"Take it easy. I'll be back soon. The kids okay?"

"Yes, of course they are. They're all fine. Call me again. Call tonight."

"I'll call tomorrow. Then I'll be more definite about when I'll get back."

"I love you."

"I love you, too."

Katie left her hand lying on top of the phone after she had replaced it in its cradle. Her hopes that he might be back today were gone. She sighed and leaned her head back against the mound of lace-edged pillows.

She felt so desperately lonely, hating her present, afraid of her future. Were there just years and years of being alone, without Harry, waiting out there in time for her? Growing old, afraid of being left again? Losing her beauty, with no one there to notice? Was there nothing but fear and trying to forget ahead of her?

She tried to remember when she had become so dependent on him. Was it from the beginning? After her father died? When? She had met him at a dance, the spring before she graduated from Barnard, and had loved him the minute she saw him. He was in his senior year at Columbia.

She had looked across the weaving heads of dancing couples and met his eyes watching her, paying no attention to his own partner but staring at her. As soon as he was alone, he cut in and put his arm around her waist.

"My name's Harry Harding."

"I'm Katie Lockwood."

It was all he said except "Sorry, she's not free" whenever any other boy tried to dance with her. All night they were together, dancing, finally talking, exchanging addresses, arranging to be together the next day. It had been a mutual love from the beginning. Her father approved, liking Harry's ambitions, his hard work, his determination to make something of himself. So they got married shortly after they both graduated.

Those early dreams of their life together had been filled with promises of happiness. They planned their house and lifestyle around Harry's new lumber business, and around the fulfillment of his drive to be a success and put the world she was accustomed to at her feet. His business hadn't started to expand in those first years and as a result he was rarely away from her except during the working day. And even then she would fill a picnic hamper and rush to his office at noon to be with him. How happy they both were with each other. They even planned the perfect family.

"I want a boy, just like you, Harry."

"With red hair," he had said, gathering her thick luxurious waves in his hands and letting it slide through his fingers.

"No, with dark hair like yours."

"Red," he had answered, "and no arguments."

He was so strong, powerful and determined. Like her father.

Had she started then to want only to be with him? No, she still had friends then, and saw them. It must have been gradual, the fusion of her life with Harry's, very gradual those first two or three years. Then came Joe and the death of her father and finally Harry had become the governing power in her life. Was that how it was?

She looked out the window at the rain. "What pissy weather." She kicked the sheet at the bottom of the bed and sat up.

The rain was still coming down steadily, bouncing onto the balcony, monotonously jamming the muted spring sounds. If it weren't so much effort, she would go down and make herself a long ice-laden drink: a little vodka, tonic, maybe bitter lemon, a slice of lemon and ice, lots of cold, cold ice. In spite of Harry. Harry just didn't understand. Maybe he never would. If he were home, she wouldn't want to go have a drink. If he were home.

There was that quiet panic rising again, the one that made her want to scream and run from the room. She'd have to do something in a hurry to take her mind off it. She could go drown herself in a pool of vodka. But surely there was something else. She looked around, grasping for an idea. Yes, yes. The clothes.

She quickly went to the dressing room, opened all her closet doors and drawers, picturing Kay as she rummaged through them. She pulled out dozens of things, from linen slacks to silk dresses to cashmere sweaters and hand-embroidered over-shirts. Saint Laurent, Mainbocher, Geoffrey Beene and Pucci. A Chanel suit, an Adolfo cocktail dress, Missoni beach paja-mas. She just hoped Kay would accept something. Not too much at once, as she was sure that would offend Kay.

She looked at the pile on the chair. Too much. She sorted through them and ended up with a few pairs of slacks, three shirts, a summer skirt, a slender dress made of Thai silk and the mandarin-collared suit. Just a smattering of assorted things. She carried this batch into the bedroom and tossed it onto her peach-colored chaise. It had made her hot again.

She opened the screens onto the balcony and stepped out. Immediately below her was Mario, bent over the marigolds. He had almost finished planting them. They looked lovely, so neat and orderly. His back looked lovely too, shifting and moving as he worked his arms, lifting, planting, tamping the dirt. Wiry was a good word for him—no fat, strong cords of muscles over a slight frame. How handsome men's bodies were. Katie ran her fingers along the neck edge of her night-gown, admiring the strength and power in those sinews. She wished Harry were here. He might have stayed home today; he might have been making love to her right this minute, com-forting her, caressing her, making her feel important and vital and eternally beloved. A tremor ran through her insides as she lifted her hand to feel her hard nipples. She hoped he would be back tomorrow.

She had been alone last night, alone with TV, the Sunday *Times* and a drink. It would be the same tonight. Kay had already said she'd be busy. Another thrilling evening. But what else was there to do?

The phone rang. She hurried to the bedside and answered it. Maybe it would be Harry again. "Hello?"

"Is this Katie?" A man's voice, but not Harry's.

"Yes."

"This is Bob Crowley at the school. How are you?"

Why was he calling? "Hello, Bob. I'm fine. What's up?"

"Do you think either you or Harry could come over here today and see me? I need to talk to you about something, and I'd rather not discuss it on the phone."

"Is it one of the children?"

"I'm afraid it is. It's something you and I had better talk about."

Katie looked at the clock. "It's eleven now. I can be there in about thirty or forty minutes. Will that do?" Freddie. She bet that's who it was. Probably still resentful of that unfortunate dinner scene and taking it out on a chum—if he had any.

"That'll be fine."

"I wanted to talk to you about summer camps for the children. I was going to come see you anyway."

"Good. We can discuss that too when you get here."

Katie took a fast shower before dressing and looked at herself in the long mirrors. She didn't look her best in this electric light falling on the glaring modern mirrors; the softer light in that antique mirror was kinder.

She went downstairs and along the hallway to the kitchen, pausing long enough in the pantry to pour herself a small shot of liquid courage. As she passed through the kitchen, she stopped and looked at Pearl bending over the sink.

"Isn't Carol back yet?"

Pearl shook the water off her hands and turned to face her. "She called this morning and said the doctor told her to take it easy for a while. I told her we could make out all right until she got back."

"I wish she would change doctors and find out what's wrong with her stomach."

"She had those X-rays like you told her to, but they didn't find anything. Said it was nerves."

"She has too much to do, taking care of an invalid husband and sister and trying to hold down a job."

"That's for sure. A few days' rest won't hurt her a bit."

"Call her back and tell her to take a week or so. Are you sure you can manage without her? We can get in someone to replace her for a while."

"No need. Miss Anderson pitches right in when she has to. We can make out fine."

"If you're sure . . ." Katie shifted her raincoat on her arm. "But if it gets to be too much, get someone else to help you."

"I will. You look too pretty in that outfit to go out in this weather."

"Thanks. I'm going to try to get under cover before I get too wet. I'm going over to the school; shouldn't take too long.

I'll be here for lunch. I only want a cup of cold soup or something like that."

Katie went out the back door that led through a short glassed-in porch to the garage. Rain streamed down the glass and fell in puddles on the grass.

The space where Harry's jeep was kept was empty; her car, a small diesel Cadillac Seville coupe, reigned in the next place. She had sold her Jaguar when the energy crisis came, saying her father would approve of saving as much oil as possible and not being dependent on foreign imports. In the third space was the "family car," the Buick diesel station wagon Miss Anderson used to drive the children around. Katie knew diesel was causing pollution, but pollution seemed preferable to dependency on foreigners.

She started the car, and while it warmed up pressed the electric-eye box that opened the garage door. She backed out, pressed again to close the door, circled down the driveway. The trees with their new leaves hung heavily, dripping onto the car top. She drove fast, peering past the flopping windshield wipers, along East Road toward town. She passed the museum and the rows of expensive houses where friendly people she never saw lived, and came to the center of town where the brick college buildings took over. Passing them, she finally entered the school driveway, spraying water that lay in her path. No one was outside on a day like this. Not even the neighborhood dogs who came daily to pick over the brown bags with their uneaten sandwiches left covertly tucked behind tree trunks and jungle gyms.

Katie had wanted Joe enrolled in this school because the classes were small and she felt he would get more special attention; Harry had wanted the other two here, for the same reason. It was also where they had first gotten to know Kay . . . and that had proved as valuable as a good education.

She slipped on her raincoat and hat, studied the best route around the puddles and made a dash down the walk that cut through the playground to the protection of the small porch outside the main entrance.

The headmaster's office lay just to the right of the entrance hall; from his windows he could see everything that was going on outside. Katie paused at the half-partition that separated the office from the hallway. Neither Bob Crowley nor his secretary noticed her. She backed out of sight, needing a moment longer, and looked toward the coat hooks in the front hall. She pressed herself against the wall as a group of shouting boys surged past her, then stepped over the drying slickers that lay on the floor, having slid off the overladen hooks, and found an empty hook.

She put her hand on the cement wall. It seemed so long ago that they had enrolled Joe in fifth grade, Freddie in first and Lavinia in kindergarten. But it was only three school years before. Sometimes it seemed an eternity since they had moved here, away from the environs of the city, away from the museums, houses and tall buildings.

She took a deep breath and went back to the partition. "Hi," she said.

"Hi, Katie. Glad you could come over."

Katie wasn't, but kept it to herself. She didn't like the serious look on Bob's face. This might be worse than she had expected.

The office wasn't what anyone would call attractive. The old peeling walls had early in their existence been stained by a leaky roof, and no number of students' posters and drawings could hide the prison atmosphere. She always contributed generously to the annual fund drive and always wished they'd spruce things up a bit.

He led her into a small, adjoining conference room and shut the door. She felt trapped at once and sat tensely on the sofa as he sat in the easy chair. He was not one to beat around the bush, so he abruptly said: "We're having some trouble with Joe and I think we'd better nip it in the bud before it gets worse."

Katie felt a roar go through her head. She thought he had said something about Joe, but that wasn't possible. "You're having trouble with . . . ?"

"Joe," he repeated. "I'm afraid he was caught passing marijuana joints around at recess. I don't know whether he was selling them or not. I think he was just passing them out to friends."

"Joe?"

"Yes. I called you at once. It's the sort of thing we can't have going on here."

"Marijuana?"

"I don't know where he got it, but it's not too hard to figure out. I think all the kids his age know they can get it through some of the tougher boys who hang out on Main Street. We don't even approve of them going to Main Street, and try to discourage it. But on the weekends, and at night, we have no way of stopping them."

"Joe had some?"

"Yes. He had about ten joints and was giving them to his buddies when a teacher walked in on them."

"Where were they?" Her hands were clammy and she felt cold. The white-edged stains on the gray walls began to move.

"Down in the basement, behind some of the lockers. And it may be the first time. I have no way of knowing that. But if it is the first time, we can only hope it will be the last time. Ordinarily I would suspend a student who was caught like this. But since it's his first offense here at school, I think we can find an alternative. Especially as school will be out in two weeks. I might recommend you take him home for the rest of the day and keep him home. Maybe Harry could speak to him when he comes in tonight. He needs to be talked to about this."

"Harry's not here." She wiped a trickle of sweat from the side of her forehead. "Harry's gone."

"Well, I'll talk to him, if you want."

"Where is he now?"

"He's in the library."

"No, I'll take him home now." Her head felt dizzy. "Are you going to suspend him?" She didn't hear what he'd said about that over the hum of the gray walls, absorbing sounds and belching them out again.

"No. Not this late in the year. But I don't think it ought to go without some sort of reprimand."

"Reprimand?" Katie's stomach was churning; she wished she could get out. She needed a small drink to calm herself.

"I think if he stays two hours after school lets out, from now to the end of the year, and does some hard work around here, he might get the idea he can't get away with this sort of thing. A little clean-up and garbage detail, something like that, might do him good."

"No." She felt she couldn't breathe. "No. I don't like the sound of that. There must be some other way."

"Can you think of one?"

She shook her head. "No." No, no, no, the walls echoed at her.

"Why don't you let me try it my way. Lots of kids have had the same detail meted out to them when they do something wrong. It often helps."

Katie wavered. "I don't know. . . ."

"Let me just try it. It's for his own good, you know."

His own good, good, good. Katie stood up. She had to get out.

Bob stood. "Will you let me try it my way?"

She nodded. Anything. Anything so she could get out. "Can he come home now?"

"Yes. Take him home and try to talk to him."

She walked stiffly out of the office. "I'll get my coat."

Bob went across the lobby to the library and shortly reappeared with Joe.

Katie mumbled goodbye and walked out, not daring to look at Joe. She didn't know what her reaction would be.

She stood on the porch and slowly put on her coat and hat and walked without speaking to the car. Joe followed silently, the rain pouring through his long hair onto his shoulders, the windbreaker matting against his shirt.

She started the car, turned on the wipers and finally looked at Joe. "Is it true?"

He was looking straight ahead. "Yes. It's true."

She started silently crying, tears slipping down her pale cheeks. She put the car in gear and headed for home, tears falling into her lap.

"Jesus, Mom. Don't do that."

She gripped the wheel and drove silently for a few minutes.

"Why? Why would you do a thing like that?"

Joe ducked his head and stared at his hands.

"Was it for money?" she asked. "I know you don't get much allowance, but if you needed something you could have come to us. Have we ever denied you anything? All you've ever had to do is ask."

"It wasn't for money."

"Then what was it? Certainly not to curry favor. You're one of the most popular boys in school now. Everyone likes you. You don't need to supply friends with . . . with . . ." She couldn't bring herself to say the word. "You don't need to try to win friends."

"That wasn't it."

Katie swallowed hard, trying to sound rational when she really wanted to stop the car and put her head on the steering wheel and sob. "I don't understand. I just don't understand."

Joe didn't answer.

"Can you explain it to me? I'll try to understand and try to help you if you need help. But I can't do it if I don't understand." She wiped her eyes with the back of her hand, smudging the mascara.

"Oh, Mom, I don't know how to say it. Maybe I don't understand it myself."

"Try to talk about it," she urged.

"Everyone's always talking about what a big success Granddaddy was because he was always on top of everything, and everyone's always praising Dad because he's such a big success in his business. Maybe I just wanted to be a success too."

Katie looked over at him. What did he mean? Wanting to be a success like your father was natural, but this was a matter of right and wrong. He knew that. Selling something illegal, doing something against the rules, was wrong. "Joe," she said quietly, "you must know it was wrong, don't you?"

"Yes. I know it was wrong."

"Being a success and doing something wrong are two entirely different things."

"I know. I said I didn't understand it myself. How could you understand it?"

Katie drove in silence the rest of the way home. What did he mean?

Once in the house, she walked through the kitchen without speaking, past the stares of Pearl and Miss Anderson, who were having their lunch. She stopped in the pantry, got out a glass and a bottle of vodka, which she poured halfway up the shaking glass. Not bothering to get an ice cube, she went down the hall. She carefully set the glass on the floor while she hung up her coat and hat, then picked it up and started up the stairs. At the bend in the stairs, where her mother was watching, she looked back down at Joe, wet and miserable, awkwardly watching her.

"When Miss Anderson has finished lunch, Joe, you tell her what's happened. Maybe she'll understand. I'm going to try to myself; I'm going to try very hard. If you want to talk to me about it, I'll be in my room. And Joe, remember above all that we love you and will help you in any way that we can. But we have to understand first."

She went up the stairs and across the hall to her room, shutting the door behind her.

Once inside, she leaned back against the door and put the glass to her lips. She slowly drained it, then reached out her hand and put the empty glass on Harry's bedside table. Then she slid down the door, her back against the supporting wood, and crumpled into a folded sitting position, her head drooped against her chest, tears sliding down her face.

Katie was staring at the thick peach-colored carpet, letting it absorb her like a sponge, her mind a long tedious blank where time had no footing, when a quiet firm knock at her back made her raise her head.

She brought herself up slowly, lifting her chin, trying to bring herself back to where and who she was. "Who is it?"

"Mrs. Harding?"

It was Miss Anderson. Just knowing it was strong Miss Anderson helped Katie; she felt a sort of soggy strength flow back into her. "Yes. Just a minute." She pulled herself across the floor to the bed and managed to get into a sitting position on the side, trying to compose herself, trying to remember all that had happened and what the next step was she must take. "Yes. Come in."

The door opened and Miss Anderson entered, her bearing erect, efficiency unruffled. She shut the door behind her. "I'd like to talk to you, Mrs. Harding."

"Please, pull up that chair." Katie held on to the edge of the bed.

Miss Anderson picked up a straight chair and brought it nearer the bed, nearer her swollen-faced unkempt employer.

"My mother did the crewel work on that chair seat," Katie said absently.

Miss Anderson took a quick look before planting her bottom on it. "Joe has told me what happened. I can't condone it, but I don't think you should let it upset you so much. He's a good boy; we both know that. To err is very easy, especially in this day and age when there's so much pot-smoking and drug-taking going on." She wouldn't mention drinking. "He's made a mistake and he knows it."

"I don't understand," Katie mumbled. "I don't understand." She reached for a Kleenex and blew her nose. "He should be a leader."

"He is a leader." Miss Anderson hoped Mrs. Harding wasn't too drunk to take all this in. She looked pretty foggy. "He was the one who got the joints. He probably was just doing it for his friends; we have no reason to think he smokes them himself." She was up there on that third floor with him every night and there was no way he could be smoking pot in his room without her knowing it. It was her job to be on the alert, and she was.

Katie pushed the stained shoes off her feet, concentrating on that action before she spoke again. "Where did he get the money? I mean, isn't marijuana very expensive? And he doesn't get much of an allowance, as you know."

"He won't say where he got it. But I have a feeling. . . . " she looked stern. "I have a feeling—and, of course, I may be wrong—but I think he may have gotten it from . . . well, I hate to say this because I know it's going to upset you, but he may have gotten it from Lavinia."

"Lavinia?" Katie sat up straight, a shock going through her. All day people had been saying impossible things. "Impossible. She never has any money. You know Mr. Harding doesn't approve of big allowances. Lavinia couldn't possibly get any extra money." She stopped and frowned, a flicker of enlightenment pricking her memory. What was it? Something she had noticed. Something. My God, her jewelry drawer. The bills that were gone.

"Mrs. Harding? Are you all right?" The strange expression on Katie's face, the wide-eyed look, the heightened splotches of color on her forehead and around her puffy eyes made Miss Anderson lean forward and repeat: "Are you all right?"

"Lavinia stole the money from my dressing-table drawer. She must have been the one." Her voice was barely audible, but Miss Anderson heard.

"Have you noticed any missing?"

"Yes. Only yesterday. I thought Mr. Harding must have taken it."

Miss Anderson drew in her breath. "Joe looked so strange when I asked him if he'd gotten it from either Freddie or Lavinia that I just thought she might be the one."

"Lavinia must have stolen it." Katie could hardly believe her own words. "And then given it to Joe."

"I'll question her. Joe certainly won't reveal his source."

"No. No, certainly he wouldn't."

"He was reluctant to tell me anything about it at all. I told him I would help him, and I will, because I want him to trust me." She pursed her lips. "It was just a guess about Lavinia."

"Does he feel awful?" Katie touched the Kleenex to her eyes.

"Yes." Miss Anderson nodded. "He feels foolish and ashamed."

"Poor Joe."

"We must not let it go without some sort of punishment."

"Mr. Crowley wants to keep him at school for two hours every afternoon to do chores . . . garbage and such. What do you think?"

Miss Anderson thought about it. Finally she said: "I think that would be a good thing to do. All he would do at home is get bored. If he is kept busy, he won't have time to get into trouble. He will, of course . . ." she looked down the bridge of her nose at Katie ". . . have to be watched for a while. He shouldn't be allowed too much freedom to wander downtown."

"No. You're right." Katie took another Kleenex and blew her nose again. "Poor Joe. Why do you think he did it?"

"Who knows. I don't think he knows himself. But I do think he feels bad about it. He feels he's let you down, and I guess he's afraid Mr. Harding will be terribly disappointed in him. He's got quite a guilty conscience; he won't forget this any time soon."

"What should we do . . . I mean, say to him? How to treat him?"

"When a child is in trouble, he needs the support of those he loves and respects. We must be careful not to condone his wrongdoings. But we must love him."

"Yes, yes." Katie didn't want this pontificating. She wanted to be alone, to have time to sort it all out in her head. "I think we should still let him have his party."

"If you think so." Miss Anderson would have said no if asked. But she knew when to hold her tongue. "Perhaps the work at school, and the knowledge that he has done wrong will be enough."

"I feel much better." Katie looked up. "But what about Lavinia? Something will have to be done about her."

"We'll have to get at the truth first." Miss Anderson stood up and replaced her chair. "I'll question her. Your mother did a very good job."

"Will she tell you the truth?"

"I hope so."

"Bring her here as soon as you bring them home from school. We'll both question her. We'll show her the drawer and watch her reaction. It may be harder for her to lie when she's staring at the empty space."

"Yes, Mrs. Harding. If that's what you want." She started out.

"And Miss Anderson, I forgot to get the information about summer camps for Freddie and Lavinia. Will you see what they have when you go to pick up the children at school?"

Summer camps? "Of course, Mrs. Harding." She might get a long vacation this summer after all.

The rain was still falling, not so heavily as it had been, but still coming down steadily. Katie's face was a pathetic mixture of regret and longing as she watched it. Why wasn't Harry here to handle this? Why wasn't Harry here to help her?

When she heard the knocking on the door, her stomach almost heaved. She gripped the arms of the chaise, wondering if she would be up to the scene that was bound to follow. Why had she said to bring Lavinia here?

"Come in." She hoped it wouldn't be true; she really hoped Harry had taken it. She didn't want Lavinia to be a thief.

Miss Anderson came in, pulling Lavinia by the hand. Katie noticed she didn't have the ubiquitous doll with her.

"Shut the door, please." She stared at the short plump body dressed in a printed cotton frock. "Come here, Lavinia."

Lavinia hung back, grabbing Miss Anderson's skirt.

"Come here, Lavinia. I won't bite." Katie sat up, tapping the chaise with her forefinger.

Miss Anderson propelled Lavinia over to the chaise.

"Miss Anderson and I have something we'd like to show you." She stood up, dwarfing the child, and took her plump hand. "Please come this way."

Katie went into the dressing room and stood on the far side of the dressing table. Miss Anderson stationed Lavinia directly in front of it.

"Now, Lavinia, I want you to tell us the truth." Katie bent to look into the frightened brown eyes. "You see this drawer?"

Lavinia nodded. Her lips were drawn together, turning down at the corners.

"I am going to open it and show you what's inside." Katie slowly pulled the drawer open as far as it would go. "You see all these cases?"

Again a silent nod.

"Do you know what's in them?"

Lavinia gulped and shook her head.

"Come, come, Lavinia, surely you know what's in them. I keep my jewelry in them. Quite expensive jewelry. It is important that no one open this drawer, for any reason. Do you understand that?"

Another nod.

"I also keep something else in this drawer. Not as valuable, but something I do not want touched. Do you know what that is?"

No reaction.

"Answer me, Lavinia. Either you know or you do not know."

A pudgy hand was timidly raised and pointed at the change that lay in an untidy heap.

"Yes, that's it. Money. You see some change. But the bills are gone. I usually have bills there too. Do you notice that they are gone?"

A nod.

"Do you know what happened to the bills I had here?"

Lavinia took another gulp of air and held it while her face turned red, then she started to cry.

Katie looked at Miss Anderson. "What do you think that means? Guilty or not guilty?"

Miss Anderson shook her head. "I don't know, Mrs. Harding. She just may be frightened." She turned Lavinia to face her. "You must answer truthfully. Do you know anything about the money that is missing?"

Lavinia tried to bury her head in Miss Anderson's skirt, but the older woman held her back. "No. You must answer. Your mother wants an explanation, and so do I. There were some bills there, and only yesterday your mother noticed that they were missing. Did you take them? You must answer me. Yes or no."

Lavinia's face deepened a shade as she started to scream, a high, hysterical scream.

"Stop that, Lavinia!" Katie spoke above the noise. "Can you make her stop?" she appealed to Miss Anderson.

"Lavinia. Lavinia. You must stop that. If you keep screaming, we will have to assume you are guilty. If you do not answer, we will know that you took the money."

The screams became broken. "I did it . . . did it . . . for Joe. He needed the money." She was shaking and sobbing. "For Joe."

Katie involuntarily moved back a step, as if she had been struck. "I can't believe it. I can't believe it. No one in my family has ever been a thief." She looked at the child with horror.

Miss Anderson gripped Lavinia's hand and bent low to make sure she could be heard. "You have committed a sin. It is a sin to steal."

"I didn't steal!" she screamed. "I just took it! For Joe!"

"That is stealing. Now you look at your mother and you tell her you're sorry. And you promise you'll never do it again." Miss Anderson shook Lavinia's fat wrist.

"I'm sorry!" Lavinia shrieked amid her sobs, her face now a deep magenta.

"And you won't do it again." Miss Anderson shook her wrist again.

"No! No!"

Katie felt sick. "What can be done with her?"

Miss Anderson was still on a level with Lavinia. "You will be punished for this, Lavinia. We will go upstairs right this minute, and you will be punished."

Lavinia screamed shrilly and tried to pull away. "No! No!"

Miss Anderson looked at Katie. "We'll go now, if you don't mind. It will be best to punish her right away while the offense is so fresh with her." She began dragging Lavinia from the room.

"No! No! No!" Lavinia's screams echoed through the bedroom and out into the hall. Then, even with the door closed they could be heard slowly receding to the third floor. "No! No!"

Katie sat down at the dressing table. She was shaking. Her hands trembled and she felt sick to her stomach. "Oh, my God. She did steal it." She pushed the drawer shut. "She really did steal it." She was so upset by this additional blow it never occurred to her to wonder what should be done about Lavinia.

"Kay. It's Hilda."

"Good. I was going to call you. How did Katie take the news?"

"It sent her straight to the bottle."

"I thought it would. And what about Joe?"

"That's what I want to find out about from you. I don't understand him doing a thing like that. You've never mentioned any unruly or wrong behavior of his at school. Has there been anything I don't know about?"

"Not a thing. It took me as much by surprise as it has you."

"Do you think he was selling them or passing them around to friends?"

"Oh, I don't think he was selling them. He knows he can get money from his mother any time he needs some. All he has to do is mention a record album, and she whips out a ten-dollar bill for him to buy it. No, I don't think money had anything to do with it."

"What then? I simply don't understand."

"I think he was just proving a point that he could get them any time he wanted to. Sort of a braggart thing."

"But he doesn't need to do that. He's very well-liked."

"No matter how well-liked you are, it's always one more step up the ladder of respect from your peers to be able to do something they can't."

"You think he was just showing off?"

"Possibly. I can't think of any other reason. I'm fairly certain he doesn't smoke pot himself. We've talked about it some, and he seems to think hopheads, as he calls them, are fools."

"No, I don't think he smokes either. Certainly not in his room; I would have smelled it," Miss Anderson explained.

"What are your guesses?" Kay asked.

"I think it has something to do with values and security, but I'm not sure what. I've got to give it some more thought. At the moment I'm a little too upset about everything to get it in perspective."

"Hilda, look at it this way. He's got a father who's driving himself day and night to prove he can be as successful as his late father-in-law. He's got a mother who's a lush, and on top of that could light fires with thousand-dollar bills. His father's rarely at home; his mother rarely goes out. Neither of them seems partic-ularly happy with their lives. Now, if you were a twelve-year-old, what kind of dilemma would you be in about values? What's the point of working so hard and having so much money and being so miserable? On the other hand, he worships his father and adores his mother. So maybe he's trying to do some of what they do, just to be able to try to understand them."

"Dear God. I hope he doesn't start drinking."

"I hope not too." Kay paused before going on. "Look, bring Freddie and Lavinia down here and let's talk about it. They can play in the yard and we can sit and watch them. I'm sure you're upset by this, and you ought to talk to someone about it. And that's me."

"I'm afraid we can't do that. Lavinia's been punished, and has to stay in her room for the rest of the afternoon."

"What did she do?"

"She took some money from her mother's dressing-table drawer."

"No!"

"Yes, I'm afraid she admitted doing it. She said she did it for Joe. I can't imagine whatever put the idea in her head that Joe wanted some money."

"I can't imagine," Kay echoed.

"I'll try to see you tomorrow. Or maybe tonight, after the children have gone to bed. Will you be home?"

"Not tonight. I have that . . ."

"Now I remember. That dinner at school. Well, I'll see you tomorrow. Call me and we'll work out a time. I would like to talk with you some more about this."

7

By four, Katie had had three martinis, a little soup and a half-piece of toast, and had gone back upstairs to try to write a letter.

She sat at the Chippendale desk placed between the french doors and stared at the cream-colored Tiffany stationery with the chocolate-brown monogram on it. Her mind became a blank. Who could she write, and what could she say to them?

She wrote "May 22" before she came to a halt. "Dear who?" she muttered aloud. Who? There must be someone, but she couldn't think who it was.

She wanted to tell someone that she was going to be in New York soon and wanted to have lunch, to hear what was going on, but she couldn't think who she wanted to see. She wanted to say her life here was a hellhole, and that she had to get out among the land of the living again, soon. She wanted to write that Lavinia and Freddie were horrid and that Joe had almost broken her heart. (She might even be honest and add that she wasn't very nice to them either.) She wanted to say that Harry was gone so much, too much. She wanted to say that she was afraid she was drinking herself back into the hospital, and that she couldn't help herself.

She wished she could say all that to someone who would understand and sympathize with her, someone who knew how she felt about the children, someone who would answer "You're right; they're horrid. And no wonder you can't help yourself." But who? She had lost touch with everyone when she had shut herself up in this town—this perfectly nice town with nice decent people—and she was the one who was dumb and boring and a shit. It was her own fault she had no friends she could write to or talk to—except Kay. Yes, there was Kay, of course, but she couldn't keep on using Kay as a sounding board; she had told Kay all this too many times already. If she kept on, Kay would end up hating her too. And then she would have no one.

She shut her eyes and listened to the rain. On it fell, an unbroken pattern of sound. Frogs must like it. Frogs and probably gardeners. If she were a frog, she might be happy, lying in the cool water, bathing on a lily-pad, seeing the world at three-hundred-and-sixty degrees, not trapped with Lavinia and Freddie . . . and, yes, Joe.

She scribbled: "Lavinia is a thief. Freddie is psychotic. I can't love them the way I should. I can't even try to love them. I can't. Can't. I should have been a frog."

She looked down at the page, crumpled it in her hand and threw it into the wastebasket. Then she walked over to the chaise and stretched out on it, staring across the room at the Mary Cassatt drawing above the bed.

Katie stood in the big hallway not knowing which way to turn. She wished she wouldn't get drunk tonight. She had to try to keep in control; there was too much collapsing around her, and no one to help. All the discordant elements of the house began to creep out toward her and the familiar desperation was beginning its slow crawl up her spine.

If she switched to wine, maybe she wouldn't get so bombed. Maybe she would be able to deal with the children, who kept swirling back into her mind, no matter how many barriers she put up against them, like the incoming tide sweeping aside the neat retaining walls of fragile sand.

She went to the kitchen and opened the refrigerator.

Pearl was mincing celery and paused to follow Katie's actions with one wary eye. "You looking for something?"

"Yes. Isn't there any white wine in here?"

"No. The wine's kept in the little icebox in the pantry where we keep all the ice and liquor supplies," she explained in the same tone she would use with the mentally retarded.

Katie shut the door. "What are you making?"

"Stuffing for the roast chicken. The children's bird is already in cooking; they don't like celery and onions or anything like that in their chicken. Is Miss Wright coming to dinner?"

"I don't know. I'll call and ask her. Is there plenty?"

"Plenty." Her eye dropped back to the cutting board.

Katie found the wine, corkscrew and glass. She poured the chilled, pale golden Graves into a big-sized stem glass, replaced the bottle in the refrigerator and went to the library. She dialed Kay's number.

"What are you doing for dinner?" she asked after Kay's hello.

"Tonight's the night of that teachers' dinner."

"Yes. You mentioned it. I'd forgotten." This bitchy day had put everything out of her head. "I thought you were coming by when you got home this afternoon."

"I got hung up at school with some extra work, and I only got home a few minutes ago."

"Come by tomorrow." Katie let the chilled liquid slide down her throat.

"I will. Would you like to have me for dinner tomorrow?"

"Of course. Come early though. Come as soon as you can."

"Will Harry be home?"

Katie pretended she didn't hear this, not wanting to admit the truth, and quickly hung up. She turned to see Joe standing in the doorway. "Joe."

"I'm sorry, Mom, about what happened." He half filled the doorway, one big hand holding a baseball below his outsized wrist.

She put her glass on the table and went to him, putting her arms around him. He was stiff and unyielding to her embrace. "I'm sorry, too." How tall he was getting. Such a combination of Harry and her father. Though neither of them would have stooped to such a low temptation.

"Will you tell Dad?"

She pushed the hair back from his forehead, retrieved her glass and took a sip. "I suppose so."

"What will you tell him?"

"Just what I was told. That's all." What would Harry be saying now if he were home? "I'll also tell him you're sorry and that it was a mistake that won't happen again."

"Thanks, Mom. Can I still have my party?" He tossed the ball in the air and caught it.

"Yes, I suppose so. Just be sure it's not Thursday night. Kay's brother is coming then, and it might be nice if you joined us. Just you."

"Do I have to?" He held the ball between his thumb and forefinger.

"No. Of course not. That probably does tie you down too much. You probably have homework to do. You just be around to say hello. Okay?" She must remember that he wasn't to go downtown alone.

"Sure, Mom. I'll get the party going for Friday night."

"All right. Tell Pearl."

She turned away from him and pressed the "On" button, knowing he wanted to disappear and would; then she sat down to watch a *M.A.S.H.* rerun until the news came on. She felt better. The pill, the wine, the brief talk with Joe—she had handled it all right. It was relatively cool and peaceful, in spite of the hot muggy aftermath of the rain. She had skipped putting on underwear, not wanting to be encumbered with anything unnecessary, and now looked down at her flowing white lounging pajamas printed with palest pink-lined sea shells, so pale they resembled watermarks on fine stationery.

At the first commercial, she returned to the pantry and collected the bottle from the refrigerator. She was almost back at the library door when a voice called her name.

"Mrs. Harding."

She turned to see Mario coming down the hallway from the kitchen with a pot of brilliant pink blooms. When he got nearer, she saw it was a rose-begonia plant.

"This is the first one I've got blooming." He smiled at her. "It's a color of pink I thought you might like." It was a true Latin smile, flashing in his tanned face.

She felt a ripple of pleasure run through her. It was her favorite color. "It's lovely. Bring it into the library where I can see it tonight." She stepped aside to let him pass by her. "Pink is my favorite color."

He placed it on a small table. "Tomorrow I'll put it in the living room. The color will be better there."

"Yes," she murmured. "Did you know it was my favorite color?"

"I guessed." He gestured toward the plant. "Or maybe you'd rather have it in your bedroom?"

Her eyes ran over his face. "It's fine where it is. It's very beautiful."

"Thanks." He started walking away from her, his slim hips molded into the tight jeans.

"Mario."

He turned. "Yes, Mrs. Harding?"

"Thank you. That was very thoughtful."

She watched him disappear down the hall, the fresh scent of soap and shaving lotion lingering in the rich red room.

She sat on the sofa, putting her feet on the table, and drank. With each glass of wine, she relaxed more and stopped thinking about her problems. A warm red-and-pink aura gradually enveloped her, finishing the feeling she had started a short time earlier, and finally completely quelling any disturbances she had felt that day.

Mario was sitting on the porch of the gardener's cottage, breathing the fresh heady air left by the rain in the garden. Some trees still dripped, and tree-frogs sang joyfully in the quiet night air. The rain would be good for the plants he had been putting in; it would save him having to water them right away. Through the trees and rhododendron planted between him and the main house, he could see lights flickering the length of the house, making it look like an ocean liner in that black night.

He would go to bed soon and read the new spy thriller he had bought that day in the drugstore. He had work to do in the morning, hard work moving some bushes, and he was getting tired. He had had two beers, eaten a steak and some salad, and a bowl of peppermint ice cream. Now he was feeling good.

He liked his job. He figured he wouldn't last at it much more than a year or so, but he liked it while he was here. His dad would roll over in his grave if he knew Mario was doing "manual labor"; he always said Mario would grow up to be a man with ambition, a man who would go places, in some important field like banking or business. Mario laughed to himself. Poor Dad. What a hell of a life, running a grocery store in New Jersey, saving and scrimping so his son could go to college and go into some big business. Well, he had lived to see Mario graduate from Syracuse University. And boy, had he been proud. Then he had died that summer, as if he knew his work was done and he could step aside to make room for Mario. His mother had worked herself to death by the time Mario finished high school. How proud they were of him. Thank God he never had to tell them he thought working yourself to death was a half-assed existence and that the business world was full of crooks and bastards who cheated on their wives and income taxes with the same alacrity. The whole suburban scene was enough to make him puke. No sir, it was not for him. He would stay free as long as he could. He would take a job whenever he needed one to save a little bread, then he would move on. He had seen a lot of the West and Alaska since he got out of college six years before; now he wanted to explore the East, New England and on up into Canada and the Maritime Provinces. He would head for them next year.

This was a good job. He liked working with the soil, planting what he wanted to plant. The Hardings were good people to work for. They left you alone. As long as the place looked good, they didn't care how you did it. Just so long as you did it. Some days he would work double time; some days half time. It didn't matter to anyone.

Mario looked up at a sound: the squish of wet leaves. He saw a weaving apparition coming slowly toward him. He quickly stood up and peered at it. On it came, slowly, hesitantly, swaying in muted steps. It came into the dim glow of light from the house.

"Mrs. Harding? Is that you?" He could barely make her out.

"Oh, there you are." She was holding something in her hands. "I see you now." She came onto the porch, one step from the ground. "The ground is very wet," she whispered. "May I come in and take off my shoes?"

"Certainly." He opened the door for her. Christ, it was her house.

He had one small lamp on in the corner of the room—only a faint glow but enough to see her clearly. She had a bottle of white wine in one hand and held two glasses by their stems in the other. She swayed from side to side when she stood inside the room.

"What a charming room." She glanced around at the functional furniture and striped slipcovers.

"Thanks." He wondered if she had ever been in here before.

"Would you like to sit down?" He indicated the sofa that faced the small fireplace.

She walked around the sofa, then turned and held out her hands to him. "Will you take these?"

He took the bottle and glasses from her as she leaned against the arm of the sofa and pushed off her muddied white sandals. Then she stepped to the front of the sofa, onto the sheepskin rug.

"How wonderful this feels," she murmured. "Do you mind if I sit on the rug?"

He shook his head, looking speculatively at her. "Not at all." Some good-looking lush; she walked as if she'd already had plenty of wine. Same as every night, he figured.

She sat down, stretching her legs in front of her, leaning her back against the sofa. Her deep auburn hair fell back from her shoulders.

She turned her head toward him. "Please, bring those around here."

Mario went to the front of the sofa. My God, she was beautiful. He started to sit down in a chair.

"No, no." She held out her hand, the loose sleeve falling back on the slender white arm. "Sit here by me, down here. Then we can share the bottle of wine. I hope you like white wine."

"Yes. I do." He sat beside her and poured wine into the two glasses. Handing her one, he said, "Cheers."

She smiled, caressing the glass in her long fingers. "I'm so glad you were free . . . you are free, aren't you?"

"Free as a bird."

"Good. It's such a bore drinking alone. Don't you think so?"

"Yes, I do." He couldn't help but let his eyes slide down to her breasts, which stood out in rounded points against the loose material. Jesus, she didn't have on a bra. He looked up to see her watching him.

"Are you as bored as I am?" she languidly asked.

"Not right at the moment." If she led him on, should he?

"Would you mind shutting the shades? I don't like anyone to be able to look in on me, no matter what I'm doing."

He got up and pulled down the shades, pushed the door shut, then came back and sat beside her. Jesus. Sweet Jesus.

"Is your father alive?" she asked.

"No."

"Neither is mine. He was a great man. He shouldn't have died so soon."

They drank without speaking for a while. He was afraid to say anything, afraid he might say the wrong thing to her. He didn't know what the fuck she was up to. Just someone to drink with? Or more?

She reached over and touched his arm. "Mario. That's a nice name."

He smiled at her. "Thanks."

As she walked her fingers along his arm, he began to babble, knowing he was doing it and unable to stop. "It was my grandfather's name. Mario. He lived in Palermo. My father was born in Palermo. His name was Rico. Enrico, really, but everyone called him just Rico. He came over here when he was fifteen. My mother was born over here, in Jersey City, but her parents were from Naples. They owned a grocery store in Jersey City. Her parents, that is. Her name was . . ." good God, he couldn't remember his mother's name. The fingers had stopped at his shoulder and were sliding back down now, making his skin tingle, shivers running from his arm all the way to his spine.

"Would you like to touch me?" She smiled and put her glass on the floor. He swallowed hard and kept his mouth shut. Then she took his hand in hers, which was cool and felt smoother than anything he had ever felt, and slowly put it under her loose shirt, pushing it across her breasts. Holy fuck, he was getting a hard-on. He began to gingerly explore her nipples, running his fingers around them, feeling the hardness. She took her hand off his and brought it out from under her shirt, then she started slowly unbuttoning her shirt.

"Would you like to look at me?" she asked softly.

"Jesus," he muttered. He pushed his glass and the bottle out of the way with his free hand.

She unbuttoned the last button and pushed her shirt back against her shoulders. He had never seen anyone like her. Her skin was whiter than he would have believed possible, smooth and firm. He leaned toward her, not knowing whether to put his mouth on her or not. She put her hand around his head and pulled him to her breast. Her skin smelled of jasmine, and tasted sweet. The smoothness against his lips was like kissing a petal; his tongue glided over the nipples. He knew he wouldn't be able to control himself much longer. His breathing quickened, and he could hear her making little cooing sounds. He raised his head and put his mouth over hers.

He spoke against her skin: "I'll probably get fired for this, but what the hell." She seemed not to have heard him. She was twisting her back against the sofa, her eyes closed, little sounds coming from her slender white throat. He pulled the shirt off her and then took off his own. She took his hand and pushed it down beneath the elastic top of her loose pants and into the soft warm mound.

He turned her sideways and slid her flat down on the sheepskin, unzipped his jeans and kicked them off.

"Do you have a bedroom?" she quietly asked as he slid her legs out of the pajamas.

He knew he'd never make it that far. "It's a mess," he answered and climbed on top of her. He didn't know what her husband did, but he knew what he was going to do. Good Christ, what a fucking lay she was.

Later, lying on his back staring at nothing above him, Mario raised his arm and squinted at his watch. After midnight. Christ. She had been here over three hours. They had finished the wine after the first round, then they had gone at it again a few more times before they were spent and exhausted.

The floor was uncomfortable and he wanted to go to bed. He raised himself up on one elbow and looked at her. Jesus Christ, what a body. She lay totally relaxed, one arm above her thick waving hair, the other at her side; her legs were spread slightly apart and her eyes were closed. He feasted himself, staring at every inch of her. He had never known anyone so long and white, with lush growths of red hair. All the girls his age tried to get as tan as they could, and the older women he had encountered had been rumpled and fat. And not only was she good-looking, but what a fucking lay she was. She could give out as well as take. Mr. Harding sure had it made, coming home to this every night. And all that money, too. Wouldn't Dad be proud of him, fucking a goddamn millionaire.

But what to do now? Wake her up and send her home? Or let her stay? He'd like to keep her here about two weeks, to come in to at night and revel in all that red-and-white lusciousness. If she stayed until morning, someone was sure to see her going back into the house and then she'd be mad as hell; he'd heard about that temper of hers.

He put his hand on her shoulder. She immediately opened her eyes. She hadn't been asleep at all. She looked older than when she had come in.

They looked at each other without speaking. Then she stood up, shook out her hair and bent to pick up her two pieces of clothing. She stepped into the pants and pulled on the shirt, carefully buttoning it up. Then she picked up her shoes and walked out without looking back or speaking.

The screen door clicked shut.

Mario sat up and saw the glint of light on the empty bottle and two overturned glasses.

Miss Anderson was feeling restless and a little anxious. She had had a trying day with the children. All three of them. The business with Joe had upset her terribly. How could she have not known what was going on? Was she spending so much time with Freddie and Lavinia that she was neglecting Joe? Was he so insecure and unhappy he would turn to drugs at the age of twelve?

She looked at her clock-radio. It was a little after midnight. She twisted in her bed, then sat up and pushed off the sheet and blanket. She was too hot. Tomorrow she would take the winter blankets off all the beds and replace them with light-weight wool summer blankets. But for now . . .

She got out of bed and went to the window. She breathed deeply, throwing back her shoulders, letting the cool air slowly enter her lungs. Poor Joe. What was he trying to do? Was it just showing off? Was it letting the others know he could get money when they couldn't? Or was he in trouble, real trouble? He was the one who needed to go to camp. It was no good hanging around this town in the summer, where there was so little to do. You could only swim and play baseball so much. He needed guidance that he wasn't getting here. After all, she didn't have time to play ball and referee games and give swimming lessons and teach him to ride and build campfires. She was too busy with the other two.

And Lavinia. Stealing. If that wasn't the limit. One on drugs and one stealing. All in one day. It wasn't as if she didn't pay any attention to them; she watched them like hawks. She was only human and could only do so much. Joe was older and on his own more, so she couldn't keep an eye on him all the time. But Lavinia, why, she watched over her all the time she wasn't at school. Or she thought she did. She'd have to be even more watchful now.

And what a scene that had been, with her screaming through the whole thing. She had checked to make sure Freddie was still tied to his bed, and then had taken Lavinia into the bathroom and pulled her underpants off. Holding her skirt out of the way with the same hand that held her still, she had switched her good, across her fanny and plump thighs, all the while Lavinia screaming and screaming and screaming. And poor little Freddie having to hear it all, tied there helpless. My God, what a scene. By the time it was over, Lavinia had stopped screaming and was making those awful choking sounds; she had left her there in the bathroom, the little thing shaking and sobbing and choking, thin red lines streaking her pale skin. And all the while she'd had to keep talking to her about the sins of stealing. It really had exhausted her. She didn't think she'd recovered from it yet. That was why she couldn't sleep.

She was glad she had made inquiries about camps for all three of them. There was one that sounded good for Joe; it was a hiking-camping-canoeing trip in Canada with nineteen other boys and three counselors, and he fitted into the age bracket of twelve to fifteen. Mr. Crowley seemed to know all about it and thought the spaces weren't filled up yet.

And she had found that there was a space open at a girls' camp in New Hampshire for Lavinia, for two months; she had also located a place for Freddie in a camp for "children with special needs." There were more openings there, and it sounded as if he would get constant supervision. It was expensive, of course—much more than the other two camps. But that's what she would expect from a place that took disturbed and problem children.

She wouldn't have any trouble getting Mrs. Harding to agree to her plans for the children. And not Mr. Harding either. She would talk to Mrs. Harding the first thing tomorrow; there was no time to waste.

She took another long deep breath, and was slowly letting it out when she gasped, almost choking. Someone was walking across the lawn. Someone in white. She stepped nearer the window, concealing herself behind the curtain, and stared into the night, straining her eyes. My God, it was Mrs. Harding! What was she doing out there at this time of night? She was usually passed-out by nine. And where had she been? Her eyes traveled across the lawn in the direction of Mrs. Harding's route. She had come from the area behind those rhododendron. The only thing there was the gardener's cottage. Miss Anderson sucked in her breath. Mario. So that was it. She shook her head in disbelief. Mrs. Harding and Mario? How long had this been going on? How had she not seen it? Was she slipping, becoming unaware of what was happening around her? First Joe, then Lavinia, now Mrs. Harding.

She watched Mrs. Harding walk up the steps to the terrace, her white pajamas flowing around her, and disappear from sight. She shut her eyes and listened. No sound. Well, well, well. Mrs. Harding and Mario. Maybe it was the first time. But first or fiftieth, it disgusted her. That stupid woman, drinking herself to death, and now having to seek diversions from a gardener. What a stupid fool she was, lounging around all day doing nothing, feeling sorry for herself when she had so much. And now risking losing her husband. Mr. Harding should stay home more. He surely saw what a fool she was, drinking and not eating properly. She had a fiery temper and a mind of her own, that was sure, but she couldn't pull herself together to do anything right. Why, she couldn't take care of those children if her life depended on it. She couldn't even boil an egg. It was a good thing she had all that money; she'd never have survived if she didn't.

Miss Anderson turned away from the window, shaking her head. She went to the bureau and opened the middle drawer, reached behind the nightgowns and slips she kept there and brought out a bottle of sleeping pills. Ordinarily she didn't use them, but tonight she would take half of one.

She took the bottle into the bathroom she shared with Pearl and ran the cold water. She shook a capsule into the palm of her hand and pulled it apart, carefully preserving one filled half in a Kleenex. The bottle was getting low. She would have to get a refill. It sometimes took more than one to get Freddie settled in for the night. She always gave him one, dissolved in warm milk laced with honey, but if he were particularly hyper she gave him two. She had been doing it for years. There was no other way she could get a good night's sleep. And as long as no one knew, what harm was there. The doctor assumed that she was taking them herself.

She went back to bed and tried to think of all the places she would like to go this summer. She had never been on a ranch before. They might be too expensive for her, but she would look into them. And England. Yes, she would really like to go to England. Her people had come from England. It was far away, but no farther really than anything in the West what with air travel being what it was. Mrs. Harding would probably pay the plane fare, of course, but she herself would have to pick up the daily tab. Unless she could get on one of those tours and convince Mrs. Harding it was beneficial to her health. Then the fool might pay for the whole thing. She could use a little blackmail and mention Mario. No, no, that would never do; she'd just lose her job.

But where to go? She had cousins in Oregon, and that might be the best place to go. Or to one of those singles resorts in the Catskills. There were lots of places she would consider.

Imagine! Mrs. Harding and Mario. Good Lord—what next?

Miss Anderson quietly opened the doors to the children's rooms and assured herself they were all soundly sleeping before she padded down the back stairs to the kitchen. A rectangle of light surrounded the closed kitchen door. She quietly pushed it open and saw Pearl sitting at the table.

She stepped into the brightly lit room and closed the door behind her. "What are you doing up at this hour?"

"Couldn't sleep." Pearl briefly looked up then continued to stir her tea. "And I might ask the same of you."

"Same. I thought some hot milk might help." She went to the refrigerator and brought out a carton of milk. "Would you like some?"

"I have my tea, thank you."

"Tea will keep you awake. It is a stimulant." She poured a small amount of milk into a saucepan and put it on a burner. "I should have thought you would know that."

"You might know that, but I don't. I have always had a cuppa . . ." dropping back into her brogue ". . . when I couldn't sleep and it's always put me right off like a top. Good black Irish tea, with a goodly helping of sugar, that's the trick for sleeping."

"What rubbish." Miss Anderson stirred the milk.

"Sure it may be rubbish to you, but you're not Irish, are you?"

Miss Anderson didn't answer. When the milk was hot, she poured it into a cup and took it to the table, where she seated herself across from Pearl.

"I got that chocolate off good," Pearl ventured.

"I spoke to Lavinia and Freddie about it. Of course, neither of them admitted doing it, so the only punishment I could give them was to turn off the television."

"Maybe neither one of them did it."

Miss Anderson looked sternly at Pearl. "Of course one of them did it. There's no one else in this house who would do it."

"Maybe we have a poltergeist. I had an uncle who had one in the house and you never heard such carrying-ons: noises and bamming and throwing things. Those of us what witnessed it never forgot it."

"Well, our two poltergeists are upstairs sleeping quietly."

"Still, you never can tell for sure, can you, about these things."

Miss Anderson pulled her wrapper closer about her chest and took a sip of her milk. "Missing a little television never hurt anyone."

"No. I suppose not. And if the poltergeist was watching maybe it taught him a lesson too."

"When I was a child . . ." Miss Anderson began, then paused. She looked across the table at Pearl, who was keenly watching her with one eye. "When I was a child, I was beaten with a wide leather belt when I did something wrong—even the smallest thing. I had to pull down my panties and get it right across the buttocks too. Sometimes it drew blood."

"It's wrong to do that to children. God should look after them better and keep them from people who do things like that."

"Maybe. But it taught me a lesson or two."

"What did it teach you that was worth such a terrible beating?"

"It taught me that strong punishment is not easily forgotten. Strong punishment is remembered and acts as a deterrent to more unruly behavior. Same thing applies to capital punishment: if a criminal knows he's going to get the electric chair, he thinks twice before he kills somebody."

"I don't believe in taking a life."

"It is sometimes necessary."

"I also don't believe in strong punishment. Love is a better teacher."

"I can't remember over the many years of taking care of children that I ever had anyone repeat an offense after getting strong punishment." She looked Pearl straight in the eye, wishing she could catch them both together and then she could really drive home her point. "I never used a leather belt. But a thin keen switch strikes the fear of God in them. It doesn't really matter what kind it is, so long as it makes an impression. That's the key to obedience. Something they won't forget."

"God said we should love little children."

"You are confusing love with direction. Children need direction. They need to be taught right from wrong. It has nothing to do with love." Her thoughts flashed to Joe.

"I never had any soul raise a hand to me. Never a one. And I was a good child." She nodded her white head for emphasis.

"Yes. I'm sure you were," Miss Anderson commented wearily. "You've missed the point." She didn't add "again." "But old or young, a human body responds to certain things the same way. If you touch fire, you get burned, no matter how old or how young you are. Surely you see what I mean."

"It seems wrong to me to be so harsh. To the old or to the young."

"Your cookies were delicious, by the way." Miss Anderson drew herself up in a haughty manner. "In fact, you are a very good cook. You know a lot about cooking. I know nothing about it, really, and certainly wouldn't attempt to cook anything when I'm in a house with someone like yourself who is such an excellent cook."

Pearl stood up and yawned. "Thank you, I'm sure. Well, I'm off to bed. You look wide awake and ready to talk all night, but all that tea has just made me too sleepy to stay up with you."

8

KATIE WOKE UP LATE, FEELING ANGRY WITH HERSELF, ashamed of herself and sore. If Harry came in this minute and wanted to make love to her, she wouldn't want to do it. What a night. She must have been roaring drunk to do that. She could still feel the sheepskin against her back, her frantic passion with Mario, insatiable, wanting him over and over. "Oh, my God," she groaned and rolled over in the bed. "What a shitty bitch I am."

She started to cry, lying naked and messy under the covers, her hair matted against her face. She covered herself with her hands where she was sore and swollen and cried more, the tears soaking into the pillow. "I've got to go wash myself," she spoke into the wet pillow. "I've got to go wash."

She struggled out of bed and groped her way to the bathroom, where she turned on the water, getting it hotter than usual, and stepped in. She soaped herself carefully, over and over, washing her white skin and red hair, covering her breasts with the thick suds, letting the water wash away her mess. But she still had the anger and the shame. What was the matter with her? Why couldn't she handle being alone last night? It was Harry's fault. Damn him. Damn him for not coming back.

She dried herself, rubbing her hair into wild disarray. Oh, shit. What did it matter? Harry would never know. Maybe he was sleeping with some Indian maiden while he was in Canada. She didn't really believe that, but it made her feel a little better just to contemplate it. Well, she would get over it. She had before.

The year they were married, fourteen years ago, she had let her friend Steven screw her at a beach party, right out on the sand, lying on a wet towel, behind a dune where no one could see them. It had been in the darkness of a quarter-moon, quiet and romantic, and she had taken off her bikini bottom and let Steven do what he wanted. She had been ashamed then, too, afterwards. In fact, she had been mortified—until she found out that Harry had been in the house screwing the hostess while Katie had been behind a sand dune. Then she had been enraged.

She almost smiled now, thinking of it. She had found out about Harry, but he had never found out about her. She had screamed at him, making him feel like a rat. Then she had been magnanimous and forgiven him. He seemed to love her even more after that, swearing he would never look at another woman. She hadn't believed that for one minute, but it had been nice to hear him say it.

And then there was another time with Steven, in New York, a couple of years after Joe was born. She had been in town buying new fall clothes and had called Steven and asked him to take her to lunch. After lunch, they went to his apartment and spent the afternoon in bed. She hadn't felt any remorse then at all. She had gone back to Harry as if nothing had happened. There had been a few other men on odd occasions in those early years of marriage, but they had meant nothing.

Then Steven got married, and she didn't see him again until three years ago, when he had suddenly called her and asked if she was coming into town to buy clothes any time soon. She remembered the excitement she had felt, answering yes, arranging a meeting with him, going to New York and spending a whole day with him in his newly divorced loneliness. Then he had gotten married again, and she hadn't seen him since. She knew he was divorced again now, and in the past year had toyed with the idea of calling him when Harry was away in the woods somewhere. But she never had.

And now Mario. One of her own servants. If she could get it in the right perspective, it was almost amusing.

She put on a short-sleeved, red-print wrap dress. As she looked at herself in the mirror, she remembered how much Pearl liked this dress and wondered if Pearl would like to have it. Pearl wouldn't have to wrap it as far around her as Katie did, so it would undoubtedly fit. She could always take up the hem a bit. She touched the soft knitted material and tried to picture Pearl in it. Yes, she would look fine in it.

She didn't bother to spend any extra time with her makeup to cover up the redness around her eyes. She wouldn't be seeing anyone today anyway, so it didn't really matter.

It was almost noon when Katie went into the kitchen where Pearl was paring vegetables.

"Is Miss Anderson around?"

"She's in the laundry room," she answered.

"Pearl, do you still like this dress?"

"That one? Oh, I sure do. I remember when you got it and came down the stairs, sparkling like a rose after a storm, the edges flipping just a little like it was caught in the afterwind."

"When it comes back from the cleaners, you take it."

"Me?"

"Yes. I want you to have it. It will be pretty with your hair."

Before Pearl could speak again, Katie went back through the pantry and to the big laundry room where she found Miss Anderson ironing a dress of Lavinia's.

"Miss Anderson, did you get anything on summer camps yesterday?"

"Yes, Mrs. Harding, I did. I think there are some very good possibilities on the list." She turned off the iron. "I'll get the material right away."

"Go ahead and finish what you're doing. I can wait."

"Where will you be?"

"In the living room. The terrace is still a little damp."

Katie went to the living room, where the first thing she saw was the pink rose-begonia, sitting in splendid solitude on a small round candlestand. She walked over to it and touched one of the delicate petals. She quickly looked away at the soft blue-gray walls, a color repeated in the draperies and upholstery, where touches of apricot broke the monotony of the comfortable sofas and chairs. Deeper blue Oriental ginger jars had been made into lamps that lit up the rich collection of paintings. Katie looked at the room with appreciation mingled with a touch of embarrassment: it was far more opulent than a gardener's cottage. Her eyes went back to the rose-begonia. Maybe that was the most beautiful thing in the room.

She sat on the long sofa to wait for Miss Anderson. She knew Miss Anderson would have studied the material carefully, and probably had already selected the proper places for Freddie and Lavinia. She knew somehow she would be able to get them in, even at this late date. But now she had Joe to worry about; there was the new problem of finding plenty for him to do to keep him busy. They must take a house somewhere, the three of them, and find things to do.

It only took thirty minutes for Miss Anderson to convince Katie of the correct choices for the younger two and also of the advisability of the canoe trip for Joe. Katie was reluctant to give up Joe for so much of the summer, but she saw the wisdom of the trip.

She stood up. "Let me talk to Joe about it when he comes home from school. I'll see if he'll agree to it."

Miss Anderson picked up the brochures and stood.

"And how about this party, Miss Anderson. What do we have to do to get ready for that?"

"You can leave it to us, Mrs. Harding. I think you have enough on your mind now."

"I'd be happy to help. What do they eat?"

"Just leave that to Pearl. She knows the tastes of teenagers. They don't like fancy fare; plain, simple picnic- and barbecue-type foods is what they enjoy. Pearl knows what to fix for them."

"Maybe she could make out a list and I could go do the shopping for her."

"I will handle that. It won't be much trouble. We can get it done in no time."

Katie ran her hand up her other forearm and let it rest on her elbow. "Well, yes . . ." she said pensively, ". . . just let me know if I can help."

"We will. But don't you worry about it." Miss Anderson looked out the window. "The pool is being filled today. You'll be able to swim by tomorrow. This is one of the warmest Mays we have had for some years. It will feel good to go swimming."

"Yes, it will."

Katie first went to the pantry and made herself a Scotch on the rocks, then she went out onto the terrace.

She looked across the sparkling gardens and lush green grass. She wished she could feel as clean and bright and newborn as that; everything shone in virginal splendor. From there, her eyes dropped and she stared into the golden-brown liquid she stirred with her shapely pink nail. That was the color she felt like: brown and unclear, tainted. She suddenly threw the contents of the glass out onto the grass and went back to the pantry to make herself a vodka on the rocks.

Again Katie went into the living room and sat on the sofa. The coffee table in front of her held a variety of magazines. She leafed through *Architectural Digest*, *Audubon* and *Vogue*, then settled back to read *Newsweek*. She let the pages fall open at random, and almost immediately came on a spread of swollen-bellied children, their brown limbs covered in shriveled skin, skin stretched tightly on their skulls, large glazed eyes devoid of hope and childhood pleasures. She wanted to turn the page, but seemed hypnotized by the misery and suffering in front of her. She hated the world that did this to children. She hated Lavinia and Freddie for being so fat. She hated herself for hating Lavinia and Freddie.

She wrenched herself free of the pages of horror and threw the magazine onto the table, then jumped up and walked into the hall that was orderly and prestigious, her forefathers secure in their prosperity. She was comfortable with them. They protected her. If Harry didn't come back soon she'd go mad.

For the next three hours, she wandered, touching chairs and tables, drinking, leaning her head on the windowpanes and looking out at the world, wishing Harry would call and say he was almost home, drinking again and getting a little drunk.

Finally Pearl brought her a grilled-cheese sandwich, half of which she ate, again sitting alone in the living room, sagged against the sofa, staring absently. The sandwich had sobered her up a little. When she felt stronger, she stood and headed for the hall, bumping her leg on the arm of the sofa as she passed it. She steadied herself and made it to the hall, then she bent and pressed her hand on the spot, shut her eyes and waited for the pain to subside. When she opened them, she saw Kay, standing at the front door, looking at her through the screen, her full-skirted dress fanned out above her skinny shins.

"Kay. I'm so glad you've come."

Kay opened the door and stepped into the hall, the crease in her forehead deepening. "Anything wrong?"

"Not a thing. Come on upstairs. I've got something to show you."

"When's Harry coming back?" Kay asked as they climbed the stairs.

"I have no idea. That's another thing that's upset me today; he hasn't called to say when he'll be back." But Kay didn't know about her awful day. "I hope he'll be back tomorrow."

"I hope so too," Kay said in a small voice. "For your sake."

Pearl had neatly folded the clothes Katie had thrown into a pile on the chaise and put them into a large dress box that now sat on a table near the dressing-room door.

"Sit down, Kay, and make yourself comfortable." Katie gestured toward a chair. "I want to show you these clothes."

Kay turned the desk chair sideways and sat, propping her elbow on the satiny mahogany top. She watched Katie attentively, the way a student would pay attention to the details of a laboratory experiment, her eyes darting from Katie's face to her hands to the clothes, not missing any detail.

"These are some things . . ." Katie began, lifting the top mass of rich material from the box and shaking it out in front of her, ". . . like this pair of silk slacks." She held the slacks across her waist, the empty legs resting against her thighs. "They're pretty, aren't they?"

Kay nodded, wondering what Katie was leading up to, beginning to hold her breath with the anticipation.

"And these, too." Katie tossed the first pair onto the bed and shook out more slacks. "The green ones are a wonderful color, aren't they? And these . . ." she carelessly flung the green pants onto the bed and again took out another pair. She repeated this performance, unfolding, shaking, smoothing the slacks, blouses and silk dress until she got down to the beige suit at the bottom of the box, not noticing Kay sitting more rigidly with each display, her elbow no longer relaxing on the desk. Her hands were clenched tightly together in her lap, her narrowed eyes glinting with expectancy.

As Katie held the suit in front of her, pressing it against her body, turning to best show off all the features, right to left, left to right, she finally looked Kay directly in the eye and asked nonchalantly: "Do you like them?"

"Katie. What a question." Kay's jaw stiffened with control.

"You know I have always admired your taste in clothes. And you wear them so well. You look like a million dollars all the time, whether you're in slacks or a dress or a pair of shorts." She leaned slightly forward. "Are these new clothes you wanted me to see?" Kay's voice was arched in guileful innocence, knowing they weren't, recognizing everything, remembering each occasion when she had seen them for the first time and swelled with envy that Katie had yet another new something to wear.

"New? No, but they aren't really old either—not old or worn out or anything like that. They're just . . . it's just that . . . well, frankly, I've barely worn them. They're almost like new. I wondered . . ." she looked at Kay's drab polyester dress ". . . well, I wondered if you . . . you could use them." She watched Kay's face for signs of indignation. There were none. Her face was blank, her lips set in a thin straight line. Perhaps she hadn't understood. "It won't hurt my feelings a bit if you say no. But you and I are the same size; I thought maybe you could use them." She paused. "It's just some slacks and shirts, a dress, a suit. Not much. Do you think you could use them? They're almost like new, and I hate not to have someone enjoy them."

"Katie." Kay stood up and walked to Katie, put her arms around her and kissed her cheek. "How generous of you. I'd love them."

"You would? That's great." They smiled at each other. "Try them on and see if they fit. I'm sure they will. Would you like to try them on?"

Kay nodded, a twisted smile on her lips, her eyes lustfully penetrating the colorful pile with the same look a sleek salamander gives a mound of cooling wet leaves on a blistering hot day. She touched Katie's arm. "They're so beautiful. I'd love to try them on. Though I'm sure they'll fit. Will it bore you if I do try them on?"

"Absolutely not. I'm dying to see you in them. I just know they'll fit perfectly, and you'll make them look even better. Would you like to change in my dressing room?"

Kay smiled at her and began slowly unbuttoning her dress. She wanted to do it here, in the middle of this room, beside this big bed where Katie and Harry slept; she wanted Katie to see her without that cheap dress on, see her breasts and flat stomach, her thin hips. She was sorry she had on that big foundation bra, but even Katie would be able to figure out what was beneath it—even Katie with her small perfect breasts and skimpy underwear. "Right here's fine." Her eyes rested on the far side of the bed, near the night table that held two books on conservation and a square leather-covered clock.

She stepped out of her dress and laid it across the empty box. She leaned over the bed, touching each piece of clothing like an archaeologist touching Macedonian gold. "I'll try this blouse and these slacks first." Kay gently pulled the gray silks from the mound and carefully spread them on the bed. "Yes, these first," lingeringly, seductively, her femininity taking hold from buried depths.

Katie sat down on the end of the chaise and watched, feigning indifference to the body before her. She had never realized before what big breasts Kay had, always hidden by those baggy peasant blouses, and even when she wore a T-shirt they must have been flattened by that awful coarse bra that cut up under her armpits and ended in a wide band above her stomach. Her underpants were of such a heavy material it was impossible to see any immodest dark patch, but a few straggling hairs escaped the banded legs and wickedly tickled her thin white thighs.

Katie had never seen such a happy smile on Kay's face before. Even the dented forehead seemed to unburden as she tried on the clothes, one by one, standing in front of the mirror, looking at the front then the back and then the front again. Kay said nothing; she seemed to be completely absorbed with her image. Katie wondered if Lavinia took such pleasure in dressing that doll of hers, had the same look of single-minded happiness as Kay now had.

"They all look wonderful, Kay. Those colors are perfect for you. Don't you think so?" Katie looked at her watch; they had been at this long enough.

Kay smiled at herself in the mirror, so absorbed she apparently hadn't heard Katie. Or so Katie thought. Kay had heard her, and was thinking of the riches, the power and the beauty that came with these riches, the untold pleasures that riches brought. Kay was thinking how she deserved these riches as much as Katie.

As Kay took off the last of the clothes and put back on her own cheap dress, pulling it over her head like a shroud, Katie almost said, "Why don't you keep on those slacks and that shirt," but caught herself in time and said nothing. It would hurt Kay to tell her to throw out her own dress and never put on anything like it again. She smiled at Kay and watched her fold the clothes and carefully put them back in the box.

Katie was pleased with herself for having brought this off so well. Once Kay got used to these, she would push some more at her. Now for the shoes.

"Try on a pair of my shoes and see if they fit." She kicked off her red sandals.

Kay hesitated before she stepped into them, wriggling her toes past the red straps. "I've never worn sandals with such high heels and tiny straps. I might break my neck."

"Don't walk. Just see if they fit." They fit perfectly. "Oh, Kay, what fun. I'll find the perfect shoes for you, not too high-heeled, to go with these things. I'll do it tomorrow. It's all so exciting." She had better not mention Elizabeth Arden and the wig until Kay got used to accepting clothes. One step at a time. "Well, that's settled, then. Let's go down and have a drink."

They walked down the stairs together, the box under Kay's arm, protected between the two women like an infant in a crowd. Katie was amused by the bright look in Kay's eyes; she assumed it meant happiness. She wished she could find real happiness with something as simple as a box of clothes. She looked sideways at Kay. Was Kay really happy? Was that really a look of deep-down happiness? Or was that just an illusion too?

Katie and Kay were sitting on the terrace waiting for Pearl to bring out the cocktail tray when Joe appeared at the door.

"Hi, Kay. Mom. Miss Anderson said you wanted to see me."

"Come on out, Joe." Katie beckoned to him.

Joe came out and sat in a chair, sprawling, his legs stretched out in front of him. His hands were dirty and his hair tousled.

"How'd it go?" Kay asked. "Pretty dirty?"

"I'll say," he glumly answered. "That place is filthy." He socked one fist into the palm of the other hand.

Katie bit her lip. "Should I say something to Mr. Crowley, Joe?"

"No." He scuffed his heel back and forth on the flagstone in time with the socking. "I'll make it. I'm not the first one who's had to do it." He stopped moving and looked questioningly at her. "What did you want? I'd like to go play some softball before dinner. The guys have got a game going down the road."

Down where on the road? Katie wondered, but didn't ask. Instead she told him about the canoe trip. "You might like to go. If you don't, then you and Daddy and I can go to the beach . . . I thought we'd take a house there for a month or so."

"Where will Lavinia and Freddie be?" Joe asked.

"They'll be going to camp; Miss Anderson will take her vacation."

"When did all this come up?" He rolled his eyes at Kay, then his mother.

"Just recently." Katie lifted the hair off the back of her neck, fanning it. "It's getting hotter every day." She dropped her hair and looked back at Joe. "I can't remember the names of the towns where the camps are, but one is somewhere in New Hampshire and the other is in Vermont."

"I didn't know you had planned this," Kay interrupted, her voice almost accusing. "I mean, made definite plans. You only touched on it the other night. I didn't know you and Harry had made actual plans."

"Really?" Katie answered vaguely, not looking at Kay. "Well, Joe, what do you think? Does it sound like a good idea to you or not? You don't have to be positive right now. I'd just like to know how you feel about the idea. Of course, we can't wait too long if you want to go; we'll have to sign up for it."

"We're not all going anyplace together?" he asked. "The way we usually do?" He looked away from her as a cloud crossed his face.

"No. Not this summer."

"You said you and Dad are taking a house at the beach?"

"Yes. I think so. I mean, Daddy has to get away from his work. But camp sounds like fun, doesn't it? And a canoe trip . . ."

Suddenly Lavinia and Freddie burst onto the terrace. Lavinia was holding her doll by an arm and running away from Freddie, who was reaching out for her, mumbling almost incoherently, mumbling words of "hate" and "screaming."

"No! No!" Katie held her hands out in front of her. "Stop that running!"

They stopped, startled to see anyone there.

Katie narrowed her eyes to focus clearly on them. They remained silent, looking at her as if she were an apparition. Katie was suddenly frightened by their stares. She pulled her skirt together where it had fallen open, brushed the palm of her hand across her cheeks, not knowing it was her lipstick that was smeared. As they stood there, mute and waiting, she saw them as she would new children in the neighborhood.

"What is it you want?" she asked. "I was trying to talk to Joe."

"It's okay, Mom," Joe said. "We can talk later."

"No. It's not okay," Katie said. "I was talking to you and to Kay, and we've been interrupted. What's the matter with you two? You act as if you were on the warpath."

They still stared at her without answering.

Katie leaned forward. Lavinia was really quite attractive looking: round, plump, with soft brown hair; almost a cherubic face, sprinkled with freckles across her nose and cheeks. And Freddie, he wasn't too bad to look at either, though his eyes were a little close together and he seemed to squint, but that may have been the mean sullen look he wore. He certainly was too fat, and his dark hair never looked brushed, though she could tell he was a child who was made to brush his hair frequently. That fat could cover three brown wasting bodies of bones.

She took a deep breath and sat up straighter. Why were they both so fat, especially Freddie? Why? And was it their fatness that she hated? If they were starving, with fleshless limbs and parchment skins, would she hate them, or feel sorry for them and love them? If they had anorexia, instead of just the opposite, would she worry that they were ill? Anorexia was supposed to be the affliction of the rich; when poor children got it they just called it starving to death. Why wasn't rich little Freddie starving with anorexia? Could it be that his compulsive eating was as much of a disease as refusing to eat? Why couldn't she feel sorry for him, feel the aching inside her the way she had when she saw the starving children?

They were both still as motionless as statues, waiting for her next move.

She should reach out and touch them, embrace them with motherly love. She knew they were starved for that. Would it be easier for her to wrap her arms around the decaying flesh of a starving stranger, easier than even touching the round fatness of emotionally starved flesh of her flesh?

"No answer? Then go someplace else." She spoke quietly to them. "Go on the lawn and play, or do whatever Miss Anderson told you to do. Go on." She waved her hand at them as if flicking away specks in the air.

They walked on tiptoe back into the house. In the hall Freddie's voice drifted back to Katie: "I told you not to run from me! I told you! I'll get you anyway!" Lavinia started to wail, her voice rising like a siren.

Katie stood up and started after them.

"Let them go, Katie," Kay said. "They'll find Miss Anderson and whatever it is will get straightened out."

Katie stopped. "Yes. You're right." She sat down again. "I would like to finish talking to you, Joe . . . about the canoe trip I mentioned. Maybe when you get back from your game we could discuss it."

"I like it."

"You like it? Just like that?"

"Yes. I like it. Sign me up." He stood up. "Anything else?"

She studied him a moment, then shook her head. "You run along now." When he was a baby she would reach out to him and he would stumble into her arms. She now would like to feel the rush against her legs, the warm hugs. She now would like to hear him say he never wanted to be parted from her. She and Harry would each take a hand and swing him between them as they walked. She watched him run through the doors and down the hall.

"Well." Katie shaded her eyes with her hand, hiding the tears that glistened there. "That was simple."

Pearl brought out the tray. "Want anything else?"

"No. Oh, Pearl, did I tell you Miss Wright is going to stay for dinner? I hope I did."

"You didn't, but we always have plenty for Miss Wright. Where would you like to eat? In the dining room or out here?"

"I think it would be nice out here. It's such a beautiful day after all that rain yesterday." Katie couldn't remember whether she had looked at herself in the mirror while she was upstairs. She touched her hair; it felt a little messy. "Will it be buggy?"

"No." Pearl stopped at the door. "Mario sprayed this area." She left.

Katie looked at Kay. "Does everyone at school know about Joe?"

"Of course they do. You can't keep a secret in a small place like that."

"What are they saying?"

"If you mean, are they passing judgment, the answer is no. Kids get themselves into trouble. It's only natural." Kay went to the table and made herself a spritzer and a vodka martini for Katie.

"Have you talked to him?" Katie asked as she absently took the drink.

"A little." Kay sat down. "He did a foolish thing, and he's sorry for it."

Katie looked down at her red sandals. She, his own mother, had barely mentioned it to him, and yet Kay had probably had a long talk with him about his problem. Why couldn't she be a real mother to them? "What did he say?"

"Don't worry about it, Katie. He simply said he'd acted like an ass and he deserved to be the janitor. He'll get over it in no time. It's taught him a good lesson." She paused. "Of course, if I were you, I wouldn't give him too much free time for a while. Whoever he bought the stuff from will probably approach him again, and the temptation will be great."

"What can I do? I can't keep him a prisoner here."

"Organize his time for him. Keep him occupied."

"That's easy for you to say." Katie closed her eyes and leaned back her head. "You're used to organizing time for children. You have the whole day set out in thirty-minute or fifty-minute periods. You think in terms of blocks of organization. I don't."

"You could try to."

"Maybe Miss Anderson can come up with something."

"I'll help you if you want." Kay sipped her drink, sitting primly in the white garden chair. "And Harry will think of something."

"Harry!" Katie looked sharply at her. "He's never here. He's always off in the woods someplace, looking at white pine and red maple, counting millions of board feet."

"Come now. That's not true. He does go quite a bit, but he's here most of the time. Unfortunately he's not here for this crisis."

"Or the other ones."

"Have you had more than one?" she asked innocently. "I thought Joe was the only crisis we were going through."

Katie registered the "we." Well, why not—Kay was a best friend to all of them.

"He's number one. But then there's Lavinia, and it turns

out she's a . . ." she couldn't bring herself to say it, even to
Kay. "She's in some trouble herself."

"What did she do?" Kay asked, looking inquisitively over
her glass.

Katie looked at Kay. Was this prying? She drank part of
her martini before answering. "Well, it seems she took some
money out of my dressing-table drawer."

"Oh, no! I can't believe that! A lot?" She hoped she sounded
shocked by the "news."

"Does it matter? A penny or a pound. It amounts to the
same thing—taking something that doesn't belong to you."

"Don't blow it up out of proportion, Katie. She probably
had a reason."

"That's right, she did. She took it to give to Joe so he could
get himself into trouble." She spoke angrily. She felt angry.
She wished she'd get pissy-eyed drunk and not have to think
of any of it.

"Poor Katie. And are you bearing up under it all? If you
don't mind my saying so, you're drinking too much."

"I do mind."

"What are you doing to keep yourself occupied until Harry
gets back?" Kay asked. "You can't just not even try to cope."

"Oh, I'm doing fine. I can cope very well. I have a wonderful time getting drunk and screwing the servants."

Kay laughed. "Katie. You do say such awful things. Look
here, if you want me to do something, I'll take the three children
to see *Gone With The Wind* tomorrow night. We can have an
early dinner and go to the early movie. It won't hurt them to
stay up a little late one night. How about it? It will keep them
occupied for one night anyway."

"*Gone With The Wind?* Is that playing?"

"Right down on Main Street."

"I haven't seen that for twenty years."

"Come with us."

Katie shook her head. An evening out with the children.
The good mother taking her three children to a movie when
daddy was away on business. The theater would be full of
mothers doing that very thing, mothers who had seen it before
and really didn't want to see it again, mothers who went because
the children were too young to go alone and the daddies would
have no part of sitting through anything antebellum again, even
if they weren't away on business. Mothers in pairs or double
pairs, sitting a row behind the children, gossiping, catching

up, comparing notes on colds, teeth, braces, grades and the best kind of running shoes for the growing foot. "No, but it would be nice of you to take them. Maybe Miss Anderson and Pearl would like to go, too." She noticed a quick jerk in Kay's frown.

"I'll ask Miss Anderson," Kay said. "If every day we plan an activity for them, especially for Joe, it will help him not to be bored and be tempted to get himself in trouble."

Katie looked into her glass. "That's very nice of you. It really is."

After dinner—most of which Katie did not eat—she and Kay had strong black coffee, staying on the terrace even though it had begun to get cold. Katie felt a little more sober, even with all the martinis and wine, and thought she might make it through the evening.

"Mario sprayed the terrace this afternoon to help keep the bugs away." No sooner had she said it than she remembered Pearl had already told them before dinner. Why had she said it? She was mad to mention him. Kay might notice something. "I think these wretched-looking wax things he has around the edges help too." What was he doing now? Not getting drunk, that was for sure. Only she got drunk.

She poured herself more coffee.

Finally it was time for Kay to leave. Katie walked her to the front door. Kay carried the large dress box under her arm.

"Kay . . ." she began, "the clothes, I hope you'll . . ." she wanted to say "have the taste to wear them," but instead she said, "be able to use them."

"Of course I will. I'm delighted with them. It was very sweet of you to think of me." She kissed Katie's cheek. "I'll wear them for some special occasion."

As Katie shut the front door, she was already thinking of the other things she would give her. The green chiffon in case she went to a fancy dinner, the black velvet for cocktail parties, lots of Bill Blass dresses for everyday wear, that divine Balenciaga with the big taffeta sleeves . . . no, not that one; it was for a ball or something, and God knows Kay would never be asked to one of those. And shoes. Handbags, scarves, sweaters. And a coat. Yes, a good coat for next winter. If Kay had lots and lots of pretty things, then she would wear them more. If she only had a few, she would save them for a "special occasion," as she had said. She would give Kay lots of pretty things. Then would come the wig and the makeup. She would have her own Pygmalion creation.

Kay walked home without looking to the right or left. She climbed the stairs, opened the door, stepped into the room and closed the door. Then she leaned back against it and let out a loud "Whoopee!" and threw the box into the air. She was so excited she forgot to go into the bathroom and vomit.

She quickly pulled down the shades, then tore her dress off, balled it into a little heap and threw it across the room. She pushed off her pantyhose and fumbled with the hooks on her bra.

"What first?" Her eyes glittered as she looked at the clothes strewn on the floor. She selected the silk dress. Pulling it over her head as she ran to the bathroom, she looked at herself in the full-length mirror, turned, twisted, peered over her shoulder to see the whole effect. She would wear this Thursday night when she and Dan went to dinner there.

Now for the others. She got out the wig and stuck it on her head, then tried everything on, some things two times. She pranced around the room, strutting like a peacock. She had put on the only decent shoes she owned, a pair of medium-heeled navy pumps. But now they looked cheap and shabby. She couldn't remember ever having felt such elation. The excitement, the joy, the pleasure. All her life she had dreamed of owning clothes like these. And now, at the age of thirty-five, she had some. And they wouldn't be the last. Oh, no. She knew that. Katie was too generous not to give her more once she saw how much Kay appreciated them. She would have to be subtle, though; maybe even wear her own clothes most of the time, just putting on one of these for a special occasion and then letting Katie see how she felt. She knew Katie. Katie would give her more.

She touched the wig. It suddenly looked crude and coarse. She would have to save up to get a better one. She'd keep her eyes open for a sale.

And shoes. Katie would give her shoes or go out and buy new ones for her to go with the dresses and slacks. She hugged herself, wrapping her arms tightly across her breasts that rolled beneath the lilac silk shirt; she had on some silk slacks of the same lilac color. She twirled into the living room and turned on the radio. She found some quiet music. Picking up a pillow from the sofa, she held it close to herself, shut her eyes and danced slowly around the room, swaying, undulating her hips and shoulders, humming. How good it felt to be richly dressed. What pleasure.

When the song ended she dropped the pillow and went back to the mirror. She unbuttoned the shirt almost to the waist, her eyes glinting. Wouldn't some man like to get his hands in there—not just young college kids, but a real man.

Someday, some man would hold her and make love to her the way they had to Katie. Oh yes, Katie had told her of the string of men she had before she got married, and she had even hinted at others since. And just tonight, what had she meant by that remark "getting drunk and screwing the servants?" Was that a literal remark? If so, it could only mean one person— that little Wop gardener. But Katie wouldn't stoop that low— or would she? She'd have to keep her eyes and ears open to find out. Hilda might know something.

She hurried to the living room and again took the pillow into her arms. She threw back her head and laughed aloud. "Katie Lockwood Harding, you have just begun my miracle."

After Kay left, Katie walked upstairs, but turned around at the top step and went back down. She simply was not going to go to bed at nine o'clock, nor was she going to watch TV and drink all night, drugging herself into oblivion.

She reached into the closet in the hall and got her handbag. Taking out her wallet, she put the bag back and found a light-weight wool coat. She dropped the wallet into a pocket and went to the kitchen.

"I'm going to go down to Main Street to a movie."

Pearl shifted one eye toward her. "It's *Gone With The Wind*. I'm going to go on my night off."

Katie said, "Miss Wright wants to take Miss Anderson and the children tomorrow night. Why don't you go then, too? You can all eat early and just leave me a plate in the oven. Or a salad in the refrigerator."

"What if Mr. Harding comes home tomorrow?"

"You can leave two plates. Or he can take me out to dinner." Katie walked out. "I'll be back when it's over."

She drove down to Main Street, parked a short distance away from the theater and got in the short line to buy a ticket. The movie started soon after she was seated.

She started to cry at once, even before the halls of Tara bustled with practiced primping, before the thoroughbred-drawn carriages traveled the oak-lined drive, before young men in fawn-colored trousers and tailcoats bent over the lilylike hands of hoop-skirted belles, before any of the grace and beauty of the era that should have been joyful to her . . . before any of this, Katie started to cry. Tears ran down her cheeks and fell into her lap. She stifled her sobs as best she could, but some students in front of her turned to glance at her, whispering, giggling to each other every time she sniffed her dripping nose. Flashes of things to come marred the present, pretty scenes.

She wept for three hours. Then she went home, drank a shot of brandy, took three aspirin and a sleeping pill and went instantly to bed.

Scarlett's face haunted her. She hadn't realized, twenty years before, how really blind Scarlett was. The beautiful face, with its flashing coy eyes, crowned with that magnificent black hair, didn't hide the scheming determination for happiness that would elude her forever. She sought the impossible, never satisfied with what she had, always wanting something she could never have.

Katie pressed her hand into Harry's empty space. What was it she, Katie, wanted? What was it? She had money; she had Harry; she had everything. Except happiness. Yes, she understood Scarlett.

If simple pleasures could have been fully enjoyed, Scarlett would have been happy. Look at Melanie: her simple needs made her completely happy. Look at Kay: a simple box of clothes. Yes, poor Scarlett; how blind she was.

Katie pulled Harry's pillow under her head and succumbed to sleep.

9

KATIE WAS AWAKENED THE NEXT MORNING BY THE RINGING of the phone. She reached over and picked it up, laying the cool plastic next to her cheek.

"Hi, Red. Did I wake you up?"

She looked at the clock. "Harry, it's only eight o'clock."

"I know, but I wanted to catch you before I went out."

"When are you coming home?"

"I have a flight for tomorrow. I'll be there in the afternoon."

"Tomorrow? Thursday?" She sat up, pushing the pillow up behind her back. "Why didn't you call me yesterday? You said you would, and you didn't."

"I know. I just couldn't. We left at six and were in the woods all day. When we got back I stayed for dinner with some of the men, then by the time I got back to the motel I was bushed. I went right to sleep."

"Why can't you come home today?"

"We're tying it all up today. By late afternoon, I'll have it all settled. But there's not a plane out until tomorrow afternoon."

Katie ran her tongue around her lips. They felt dry and sticky at the same time. "I want you here."

"Everything okay?"

Oh, Christ. What a bloody question. She was confronted with thieves and drug addicts and he wanted to know if everything was okay. No, no, that wasn't true; Lavinia wasn't really a thief and Joe certainly was not a drug addict. "About the same," she answered. She'd give him the blow-by-blow details when he came home.

"Take it easy. I'll see you tomorrow."

"All right." She hung up. Another day without him. What would she do? She felt the anger and irritation rising in her. She slid back down into the bed and tried to go back to sleep. But it was no use. She could hear the spring birds singing their sweet ringing notes, and voices from the direction of the pool. The pool; yes, she would be able to swim today. She would swim and have a cool drink in the pool, then she would lie beside it under a big umbrella and read a book. That was what she would do today. All day long, she would do that, from the time she got up until she went to bed. All day long.

She climbed wearily out of bed and crossed the room. She stood at the french doors and looked out. Far below, at the bottom of the lawn near the peonies, she could see Mario. Should she walk out on the terrace just as she was, stark naked, and let him turn to find her there? Should she do that?

She turned and went into the bathroom and turned on the shower.

After she had dried herself and her hair, she dropped the towels on the floor and sat at her dressing table to put on her makeup. All that crying last night hadn't helped the rims of her eyes any. Her lids were swollen, and even in that old mirror she could see a few sags and puffs. "You love me, anyway, Daddy. If I'm just a little off-color today, you won't even notice."

She put on lipstick, then stared at the racks of clothes for a long time, finally deciding on really short shorts, a shirt with short sleeves and some flat tan leather thongs; they would be cool. She hated it when it was this hot in May.

She walked across to Harry's dressing room and looked around at his familiar things: hair brushes, clothes brush, tray with keys and paper clips, a box of cuff links and studs, an old fishing hat hanging on a hook, scraps of paper on a small table in the corner. And photos. All over the place were photos: on the bureau and on the walls, on the back of the closet doors. Photos of herself, going back fourteen years to their wedding picture, then holding Joe in his christening robes, with Joe as a toddler, with Joe and Miss Anderson in the garden, with Joe sitting on the beach, she swollen and gross with Freddie inside her. There were some pictures of her with Freddie and Lavinia at each stage of crawling, walking, running, going to school. What a good mother Harry would have been. Her fingers paused on a baroque silver frame; she lifted it from the bureau and studied it. How long ago that was taken. She and Harry had been married one year, before Joe and anything else that took away from their togetherness. It had been a densely foggy day at Nantucket, while they were waiting for the ferry. A friend had snapped them together, at the end of the pier: Harry with one hand in his pocket, the other draped around her shoulder; she had had on a simple, short-sleeved white wrap dress. Though the picture was in black and white, she could clearly see the gray-white mist around them, Harry in his summer khakis and shirt with the sleeves rolled up, her own hair the one spot of brilliance in their surroundings. How happy they had been. They had spent a week there alone, in a house that overlooked the water. Only a week, but it had been forever to her. They had had the whole world before them then, built on a simple foundation of happiness.

The following year Joe had come. Then her father had died. Harry became wrapped up in his business. Her life became a bore. She started to drink too much. And lastly came Freddie and Lavinia.

She ran her hand over the photo showing them together in gray-white bliss, then replaced it on the bureau. Funny that Harry had kept it. It was such a fuzzy, out-of-focus picture. But then, maybe he remembered it as vividly as she did.

Katie went down the stairs, the photos preying on her thoughts, a kaleidoscope that mostly came up with the children. Harry looked at those bright little faces every morning. Maybe he even thought about how much he loved them every time he opened his bureau drawer. And she? The one thing that was expected of her, and she couldn't do it. She couldn't be a good mother. Such a simple thing.

By the time she reached the bottom step she had decided to try. If she made a real effort, really tried her best—without getting drunk—maybe she could cope with them. It was unnatural to feel the way she did. She was disgusted with herself, ashamed of herself. She hated herself. She would even try to be nice to Lavinia and try to understand her.

She reached the hall where Grandmother Simons' eyes followed her. If she tried a little each day, maybe she would be able to handle it.

She found Miss Anderson in the kitchen making out a grocery list.

"What time do the children get home today?" Katie asked after saying good morning.

"It's Wednesday. They get out at noon."

"What about Joe?"

"I'll go back at three and pick him up."

"It's such a nice day. We can all have lunch on the terrace together."

Pearl threw one eye in Katie's direction. "All? You don't mean you and the children, do you?"

"Yes. I'll have lunch with them out there. Unless, of course, Miss Anderson has made other plans."

"No, I haven't made any other plans." Her pencil was poised in mid-air. "Do you want me to be there?"

"Yes." Good God, yes. "That would be very nice. We can talk about summer camps." Katie looked at Pearl, who was shaking her white curls. "How about some soup they like . . . what do they like?"

Pearl was standing still with a dish cloth in her hands, her mouth slightly opened. Finally she spoke: "I was going to give them hamburgers, but we can have something else."

"No. Hamburgers will be fine. Do they like tomato soup?"

"Yes. That's one of their favorites." Pearl shook her head again, one eye moving with the rhythm.

"Then let's have a cup of tomato soup and some hamburgers. Maybe fruit and cookies for dessert."

"Fine with me," Pearl agreed without enthusiasm.

Katie left them in stunned silence. She might regret it, but at least she was going to try.

She found a good mystery book and read it until about ten-thirty. Then she made a vodka-and-tonic, and read again until noon. She had a second drink to steady her nerves as the lunch hour approached.

She was sitting on the terrace with her book and drink when Pearl came out.

"What time do you want lunch?"

"What time do they usually eat?"

"Now."

"Then let's get started." She put down her book. "I'll be ready whenever you are." She stood up. If she drank this down in a hurry, she would have time for another before the hamburgers were ready.

Katie sat at one end of the large glass-topped table, Miss Anderson at the other end, with Freddie and Lavinia on the sides. Katie had put a big straw hat on her head to shield herself from the sun. She could have asked Mario to put up the big umbrella near the table, but she hesitated to approach him.

"Miss Anderson, tell us about the camps."

"I've already heard it," Lavinia spoke up.

"Do you mind hearing it again?" Katie asked, sipping the hot soup, trying to ignore Lavinia's insolence.

"I guess not."

"How about you, Freddie? Have you heard all you want to hear?"

He had almost finished his soup. He stopped slurping abruptly and rolled his eyes upward without raising his head, the whites forming a half-moon sliver beneath his pupils. "Lavinia hates her name."

Katie put her spoon down. What had brought that on? "Hates her name?" She turned to Lavinia. "Do you hate your name?"

Lavinia screwed up her face at Freddie. "Tattle-tale."

"Well," said Katie, clenching her fist beneath her napkin. "This certainly has nothing to do with camp, but let's talk about this. Do you hate your name, Lavinia?"

Lavinia stuck out her tongue at Freddie.

"Don't do that." Miss Anderson reached over and put her hand on Lavinia's arm. "It's ugly to do that."

Lavinia lowered her eyes.

"You have a lovely name, Lavinia," Katie said. "It was your grandmother's name, my mother. She loved it. Lavinia Harrison Lockwood. There are some things that belonged to my mother before she was married with the initials 'L.H.' on them; these are your initials and someday you'll get these things."

"What are they?" the little girl asked.

"Oh, a gold locket, an embroidered shawl, a few other things."

Lavinia started on her soup again.

"She hates it because she gets called vinegar." Freddie scowled across the table. "Sour vinegar."

"I hate you, I hate you." Lavinia made a face at Freddie.

"That's enough, both of you," Miss Anderson cut in, her bosom pressed against the table. "Behave yourselves." She squared her shoulders military-style and looked sternly at Lavinia.

Katie spoke as pleasantly as she could. "You should be proud of your name. I hope someday you will be." She had eaten half of her soup and put down the spoon. She shifted on the webbing and leaned against the white arm rail, looking at the round freckled face. What a spoiled brat.

Pearl brought in a tray of hamburgers. She removed the soup cups and replaced them each with a plate holding a hamburger, pickles, potato chips, carrot strips and celery. She gave the children and Miss Anderson a glass of milk. "Do you want something to drink?" she asked Katie.

Katie would have liked to say a bottle of red wine, but she shook her head. "Nothing, thank you; doesn't this look good." She still had the remains of her drink.

"We love hamburgers," Lavinia chirped. "We could eat hamburgers all the time."

Freddie had already stuffed his cheeks full, making them round and tight like tiny swollen bellies.

Katie watched him in disgust. At least it kept him from talking.

They all ate in silence for a while, before Katie again broached the subject. "Don't you think camp sounds nice, Lavinia?"

The round face shook up and down. She reached down and touched the top of her doll's head where it was propped against the leg of her chair. "Jewel and I think it sounds like fun. Games and campfires and ponies and everything. But we won't know anyone."

"You'll meet friends your age very quickly." She looked at Jewel, with her large soft body and painted plastic head. She was bigger than a baby, and wore real toddlers' dresses. Harry bought dresses for her whenever Lavinia asked. Jewel's head hung limply to one side.

Katie turned to see Freddie's cheeks puffing in and out as he gulped his food. "Do you like the idea of going to summer camp, too?"

"I don't want to go." Pieces of mashed roll shifted in his mouth.

"Why not? There'll be a lot more to do there than here."

"I don't want to go." He stopped chewing and looked angrily at her.

"Did you go to a camp when you were my age?" Lavinia asked her mother.

"No, I did things with my father." She was sorry she had said it almost as soon as it had slipped out. "I mean, my parents had more free time than parents do now. It was a different world. My father liked to travel in the summers, so we would all go to Europe or someplace."

"I wish we could all go someplace like that." Lavinia took another bite of her hamburger. "We never get to go anywhere."

"We do—and just last summer. Don't you remember?" Katie certainly remembered the god-awful summer, even if they didn't. "We always go someplace in the summer. Last year it was for the whole three months."

"We were at the beach last summer," Miss Anderson reminded the children, "you remember that."

Freddie gulped down all his milk. "But we weren't all there. Daddy never came." Only the carrots and celery remained on his plate.

"Of course he did. You just forget." Miss Anderson frowned at him. He put down his empty glass and started counting his fingers that lay on his lap. She went on. "He was very busy, but he took time off and came almost every weekend. That was a wonderful house, wasn't it? Right on the beach. Eat your carrots and celery, children. The sound of the ocean roaring through the house . . . watching the boats . . . listening to the gulls. That was a wonderful house."

Lavinia tried to shove a carrot into the doll's mouth. "She doesn't like them."

"Then you eat them all." Miss Anderson gestured toward them with her head.

"Make Freddie eat his, too," she said petulantly, sticking out her bottom lip.

"I hate carrots," Freddie said, not raising his head.

Katie moved her hand toward his arm, hesitated, then laid her fingers lightly on the fat wrist, her heart skipping a beat at the moment of contact. "Try eating them, Freddie." She quickly withdrew her hand.

He glared at her. "No."

"Then I'm not going to eat mine," Lavinia whined. "Why

should I eat mine if Freddie doesn't?" She pushed the rest of her hamburger in her mouth.

"Freddie will eat his," Miss Anderson answered evenly, "or he won't get any cookies."

Freddie grabbed the carrots and celery and with both hands shoved them into his mouth, blowing out his cheeks and frowning at Miss Anderson.

Katie jerked his hands away from his face. "That is no way to eat. Now you sit up and eat properly."

Freddie's face became immobile. Katie couldn't tell if he still had the food in his mouth or not. Maybe he had swallowed, but she didn't think he could have.

"Chew that up and swallow it," she said. "And don't you dare spit it out."

The fat cheeks began to work, noisily crunching the carrots. He rolled the food around in his mouth and swallowed it, except for one cube of carrot, which he put between his lips, exposed like a growth on his mouth.

"Stop that! You get that back in your mouth!" Katie slapped his hand.

He sucked it in and frowned at her, his eyes narrow dark slits.

"Behave yourself, Freddie," Miss Anderson said severely. "If you're both good we can go swimming this afternoon."

"Yes," Katie said, thankful to have the subject changed. "The pool is all ready for a swim. I might go in myself."

They all ate so appallingly fast. She left half her hamburger and the potato chips, which she could see Freddie eyeing, but ate her raw vegetables. "Pearl always gives me too much." She did not offer the chips to Freddie.

Suddenly Lavinia screamed, a high shattering scream.

Katie jumped. "What is it?" She looked at Miss Anderson.

"What is it?" Miss Anderson took Lavinia's plump hand in hers.

"Freddie spit the carrot at me."

Miss Anderson folded her napkin. "I think we'd better excuse ourselves." She stood up. "Come along, Freddie; you too, Lavinia." She looked at Katie. "They get restless if they stay too long at the table. They'd better have their cookies and fruit in the kitchen."

"Can we go swimming now?" Lavinia asked.

"Not right away. You have to let your food digest. We'll

read for a while, or do your homework, or go work on Freddie's fort . . ."

"No you won't! That's my fort! You can't work on it." Freddie jumped around in a half-circle, landing with his feet apart, knees bent as if ready for battle.

"It was made plain from the beginning that Lavinia could help you with it. But we won't go into that now. We'd better go in and do your homework anyway; don't forget we're having an early dinner with Miss Wright and going to the movie. Now excuse yourselves nicely and we'll go."

After they had left, Katie wearily shut her eyes. She hadn't enjoyed them one iota. Not a single word they uttered or a thing they did had endeared them to her. They were just as unpleasant as ever. Thank God she wasn't going to the movie with them.

She got up and went into the house to escape the sun. If they were going to go swimming, she would wait. Enough was enough for one day. She had seen all she wanted to see of them. She had tried and she had done it. But that was enough. In fact, too much. What a shitty mother she was.

She sat down on the sofa. She would try again another day. Maybe tomorrow.

She bent forward and buried her head in her hands, the auburn hair falling onto her knees. Why in the hell was it taking Harry so long? She needed him. She didn't want to be alone. She needed him with her. She didn't want to get drunk. She didn't want to think about the misery and torment, hers or anyone's. She just wanted Harry.

10

THE WOODS WERE DEEP AND COOL BENEATH THE VAULTED dome of maple and beech, oak and yellow birch. Harry stopped by a splashing brook, sitting on a log to rest his back against a piece of granite that had been overseer to this piece of sylvan majesty for years counted in milleniums. The clean, cold waters of the brook hurled noisily down the narrow ravine, falling on the dark rocks, slipping into shallows cast with aged yellow shadows as they raced toward the Hudson River.

He took the sandwich out of his worn olive-green L. L. Bean jacket and carefully unwrapped it, putting the paper back into the frayed pocket. He ate slowly, watching the woods for movement. The warblers were already there, singing joyfully, mingling their sweet calls with the melody of the rose-breasted grosbeak and the appealing song of the purple finch. Deeper in, the haunting notes of the hermit thrush echoed toward him. The sharp "tsee" of the redstart was nearby, and then he saw it, flitting nervously from bush to tree and back again, its black body flashing orange wing and tail feathers. Harry watched. They couldn't keep still for a minute.

These were the woods he loved best. He knew every deer path and every manmade trail. He had been coming here since he was a small boy. His father had brought him here to camp and fish, to learn about the woods. His father had had a great respect for nature and had instilled it in Harry.

His father. He wished he could be a father like his father was. He would like to bring his children here, to teach them to hold so still a deer would walk right by, to teach them to recognize the tracks of coyotes and fishers, to respect the bear and leave it alone. He would like to teach them to fish with a fly, deftly casting upstream and letting the weightless hackle dance lightly on the water back to them, passing over a big brookie that was too skeptical to fall for that trick, making them change flies over and over until they finally outwitted the master of the pool. Then he would teach them to gently, carefully, unhook it and hold it back in the water to get its equilibrium, then release it. Unless they wanted to eat it.

Joe should have learned all this by now. He was twelve years old. Freddie and Lavinia should be learning. They should have had a father to teach them. Red wasn't the only one who had failed.

He took another bite of the overstuffed ham-and-cheese on rye. He would never be able to teach Freddie, with the boy's sullen distrust of life, his inability to respect feelings. He wondered, as he had wondered so many times in the past, what he could do to help his children. He didn't have time to give them the attention they needed. Red didn't want to take the time. Miss Anderson was a firm solid influence in their lives, a stabilizing force, but she wasn't a parent. They didn't have the love he had had as a boy. And whose fault was that?

He put the sandwich down on a rock and bent his head to the brook, dipping his mouth into the icy waters, and drank. He sat back, wiping the water from his chin, and picked up the second half of the sandwich.

Harry realized he felt as alone and helpless as Red did. He had buried himself in his work, instead of a bottle, in order to escape the everyday ordeals of family life. He was just as much to blame as she was. He loved her, yet he escaped into the arms of another woman whenever he could. Why? It seemed like a simple reason: he usually found Katie drunk and passed out at night. Was that all there was to it? Or did he feel guilty

when he faced her, seeing his own reflection in her as a failure
of a parent? He didn't know. But it was something he thought
about a lot, and it worried him.

They were both to blame for being failures to Joe, Freddie
and Lavinia, but in the long run he had to admit he was better
off than she was. At least he had his work to fall back on. At
least he had not lost his identity.

Poor Red. She had lost her identity at such an early age,
first to her father, then to her husband. Her whole life had been
swallowed up by them. If he left her or died, she would be
totally lost; she was nothing without him. There probably
wouldn't be enough booze in the country to obliterate her fears
and loneliness then. That was one of the main reasons he liked
to be with Doris so much . . . there wasn't this stranglehold
on him, the oppressive feeling of being manacled to someone
with no escape in sight. Doris made no claims on him, taking
him with pleasure when she saw him and demanding nothing.

Yet he loved Red with all his heart. He had been bewitched
by her the first time he saw her. She was like a rare exotic
creature, one of a kind, that belonged to him alone; it made
him proud to know she was his. There was a magic to her that
defied description. She had an aura about her; she had "It."
There were few women, if any, who could touch her for flair,
beauty, generosity and the ability to please a man. And she
was his. Even with her failures and her suffocating hold on
him, she was his.

There was such peace here, such peace and quiet. It made
all human problems diminish. There was a lot bigger plan in
creation than the mere screams, squabbles and failures of his
family.

He had finished up his deal in Ontario this morning, half a
day ahead of what he had told Red. Instead of trying to get
home, he had hitched a ride on a small plane as far as Lake
Placid and from there had rented a car from a garage he had
used before. He drove southward for an hour, coming here to
this haven to rest and regather his strength before returning
home. Tomorrow he would return the car to the garage and
get another ride to the Albany airport. It had worked out very
conveniently for him. He would like to stay here for longer
than one night, but he had promised Red.

He finished his sandwich, leaned his head back and closed
his eyes. A red squirrel was angrily chattering at him, almost
drowning out the sounds of the distant birds. He especially

liked the lingering call of the white-throated sparrow; it was one of the first bird songs his father had taught him.

After he had rested, Harry walked through the woods cushioned in pine needles and damp spring growth back to where he had left the car on the narrow dirt road. Intermittently, his path was carpeted with the white flowers of bunch-berries in bloom, thick spreads of moss and covers of tall ferns, twinflower and star-flower, all growing in the cool shade of the forest, only occasionally dappled with sunlight that broke through the canopy of tree tops. He wished he could stay.

He started the car and drove back out the bumpy road to the highway, where he progressed a short distance before coming to another dirt road. He took this and drove to a modest yellow clapboard house with a small well-kept front yard. A dirt driveway ran to a small open garage where a Ford pickup waited. He parked by the side of the house and walked to the back door that still had on its storm glass and knocked.

The door was opened by a woman of medium height and build with her hair tied back in a blue kerchief. She had on faded blue jeans and a plaid cotton shirt. She wore no makeup on her sun-colored face, the high cheekbones and large brown eyes giving her natural beauty.

"Harry!" She smiled broadly and opened her arms wide.

They hugged each other, the way old friends do, laughed some, hugged some more and went back into the house with their arms around each other's waists.

"Harry. You should have told me you were coming." She pulled the kerchief off her head. "I would have combed my hair."

"It looks great the way it is. How are you, Doris?" Harry looked with fondness at the woman, her tanned skin showing signs of too much sun, crow's feet around her eyes. She was handsome, with straight white teeth; her blond hair was cut short and had little curl.

"I'm fine, just fine. I was about to clean out the cupboards, but now I've been saved from that." She led him by the hand into the middle of the immaculate, gleaming white kitchen. "How about some coffee?" She gestured toward the big wood stove, brushed clean and radiating warmth.

"Got any made?" He inhaled the rich smells of burning wood, baked bread and fresh coffee.

"Right on the back of the stove." She pulled out a straight chair by the small, square wooden table. "Sit down."

Harry walked around the room, looking at the orderly shelves, pots and pans, large wood stove, smaller gas stove, the dozens of plants that hung at every window and perched on every counter. "Your plants are sure thriving."

"So are you. You look great." She smiled warmly at him. She took two mugs from a shelf, poured coffee into them, added one spoonful of sugar to one cup and put them on the table. "I'll get the cream."

"I'll get it." Harry opened the door of the old Kelvinator and brought out a carton of half-and-half. He poured cream into each mug, then returned the carton to the refrigerator.

Doris gave her mug a quick stir with the spoon, then put it in Harry's mug and pushed it across the table. She sat down and looked at him.

Harry sat down facing her. She reached across the table and took his hand. "I am so glad to see you," she said, drawing out the "soooo." "I've been thinking about you and wondering how you were. Just this morning, I said to myself, 'What do you suppose Harry's up to?' I almost stayed in town to do some shopping." She smiled. "And isn't it lucky I didn't? What if I had missed you?"

"I would have hung around waiting for you to come back."

"I might have stayed for dinner and a movie . . . you never know. It's so lucky. I really do live under some lucky star." She took a sip of coffee with her free hand. "Would you like a bed for the night? Or is this a quick push-through on the way to somewhere?"

"I'd like to stay. I don't have to be home until tomorrow afternoon."

"Where've you been?"

"Ontario. Another parcel of land."

"All signed up?"

"As of this morning. It should bring in a goodly amount. The estimates on the stumpage are pretty high."

"Good for you." She pulled her hand away and picked up her mug, holding it in both hands. They were small but strong hands, browned by the sun, the nails clipped short. "Beat somebody else to it. That's good."

"It's a choice piece. I'm surprised there wasn't more bidding on it. Anyway, the important thing is that I got it."

"You have to be on your toes these days, don't you, Harry? It's dog-eat-dog out there. If you're not right on the spot, someone else gets the contract."

"Jesus, Doris. I wish I could get someone at home to understand that. Red just doesn't understand at all why I have to be gone so much."

Doris looked over her cup rim at him. "How is Katie doing?"

"Not good." He shook his head. "It's beginning to show."

"Drinking a lot?"

He nodded. "She's blind to what it's doing; she can't see the toll it's taking. If she keeps on, she'll lose her looks and her health altogether. It depresses me to watch her doing this to herself. She doesn't want to get interested in anything; she's bored and restless. She can't become a part of the town and won't see any friends. So she drinks." He stirred the sugar in the bottom of the cup absently. "She was the same before we moved, so I don't think another move would change her. It seems as if she's been like this since her father died. Maybe it was when Freddie and Lavinia were born. I just can't remember anymore."

"She might drink even if she weren't bored and restless. It's that way with some people."

"You might be right. But she's not doing herself any favors. I don't seem to be able to help her. I guess if I were home all day with her, she'd be better, but I just can't be."

"Will she see a doctor?"

"No. She won't see anyone . . . she won't even admit it until she hits bottom and gets sick."

"Poor Katie." She sipped her coffee. "And the kids? Are they doing all right?"

"There's another mess. I think Joe's making out all right, but both Freddie and Lavinia seem to be in constant trouble or are screaming and crying. I should do more with them. It eats at my gut the way I neglect them. They don't know any of the things they should know by now. We never do anything together, except an occasional meal, and that's damned infrequent. I've never taught them anything about the woods or fishing or . . ."

She took his hand again. "You can't keep on blaming yourself, Harry. You love them when you're home but you just aren't home that much. Don't blame yourself. Kids have a way of turning out all right. They're a lot tougher than we think."

He looked at her a long time. "I've missed you, Doris. It's been too long."

"It's only been a few months."

"That's too long."

"Hey, want to see my new dog?" She pushed back her chair. "I've got him tied out back because he hasn't quite learned to hang around the house. Got a little wanderlust in him. If I'm out with him he stays right close. But by himself, he wanders. I'll get him."

"What kind of dog is it?"

"A genuine brown-and-white dog."

Harry laughed while Doris went out the back door and soon returned with a hyperactive, bouncing, four-month-old puppy that skittered and slid on the polished linoleum. The dog threw itself onto Harry's lap, then just as fast jumped down and ran scrambling into another room.

Harry laughed again. "Nice. What's his name?"

"You won't laugh at me, will you?" She sat back down.

He shook his head and watched her bright brown eyes.

"I call him Harry. It makes me feel nice and comfortable to have a Harry around the house." She paused. "You aren't laughing."

"No. I'm not laughing." He looked into his mug.

"Hey. Don't look so sad. You know how it is with us. We both know. It's good when you're here, and that's that."

"You should have gotten married again, Doris. You shouldn't have stayed here all alone." He vividly remembered the day, over ten years ago, when Doris' husband had been on a job for Harry and had felled a tree on himself, dying instantly. "You're too good a woman to live alone."

"I'm not alone now. I've got Harry." She smiled at him.

"You've got two Harrys," he said. "In your heart, you've got two Harrys."

"I know," she answered simply.

They looked at each other, then she said: "I've put the seeds in my vegetable garden, and I've got the plants in the cold-frame. Won't be long before the dangers of frost will be gone and I can get them in. Remember all those green beans I had last year? Well, I'm going to have even more this year. I'm going to have to get another freezer." She laughed, tossing back her short blond hair. "I'm really going to be up to my ass in them. I'm also going to have more corn and more zucchini and more peas. I'd better give up meat and just eat vegetables from now on."

"I doubt if you'll ever give up venison." He smiled at her. "How's the store going?"

"Fine. I like only working half a day. The boss says I keep

the books so orderly there's no need to have anyone full-time. I had thought he'd get someone else in for the afternoon when I told him I only wanted to work till noon. But no. So now I do it all in half the time. And half the pay." She laughed. "But I like it better."

"Sure you don't want to stop altogether?"

"I'm sure."

"You'd like to go to some nice warm place in the winter. Think of swimming and sunning and . . ."

"I'd think about my poor empty house the whole time and be miserable." She shook her head. "No, thanks, not for me. I like what I'm doing."

"How much vacation are you taking this summer?"

"Only a week. I like having two weeks in the fall for the deer season."

"What week are you thinking of taking off?"

"Early July. That's when the garden's at an ebb, and there's not much upkeep. The deer don't seem to be able to get in that fence, and there's nothing to can, pickle or freeze then."

"Where would you like to go?"

"I'd like to go to Maine. I've never been in Maine and I thought Harry and I . . . my baby Harry, I mean . . . might go to Maine. We could see the coast and some of those inland lakes I've read so much about."

"Wouldn't you like to take a big trip? Go to Europe or someplace like that?"

"No. I've never had the education to be able to look at all those things properly. I wouldn't know what I was seeing."

"Doris, what nonsense. You may not have gotten past high school but you've got a good mind. You'd know what you were looking at."

She shook her head.

"Then how about going West?" he asked. "You'd sure know the Grand Canyon or a redwood forest when you saw it."

"Harry." She laughed again. "You don't understand. I don't have the urge to travel. I like things that look friendly and comfortable and familiar. I want to go to Maine. Hey, listen, let's change the subject. You know what I was going to do after I'd cleaned the cupboards?"

"What were you going to do?"

"I was going to take my rod and go down to the lake and try to get a nice rainbow for dinner."

"Were you now? I might do the same thing."

"I got the new floating line you sent me. I didn't really need it, you know. It's a kind of expensive gift if you don't really need it."

"You did need it. That old line of yours is rotten. You wouldn't want it snapping when you're hauling in a five-pounder, would you?"

"Five-pounder. Ha! In that lake?"

"You never know. Might be some granddaddy down at the bottom, just sitting there getting fatter and fatter. Shall we go see?"

"You get the rods. Come on, Harry!" She whistled and the puppy came running to her. "That's a good boy." To Harry: "He loves to go out in the canoe."

"Just like his namesake." He stood up. "Come on, we're wasting time."

It was six o'clock and the house was finally quiet. They had all gone to the movies, leaving Katie to her own solitude. She had put on a zip-front terry robe of green, the color of moss on a brick wall.

She made herself a vodka martini and wandered around. When she passed the coffee table in the living room, she put *Newsweek* and *Time* underneath *Town & Country*. She went down the hall past the library and opened the door into Harry's study. It was big and functional and smelled like an office. Bookshelves were filled with volumes on conservation and environment, flora and fauna, fishing encyclopedias and fishing texts. Filing cabinets were neatly arrayed along the inner wall. He had a big modern desk of chrome and glass, and piles of papers were weighted down with pieces of different kinds of rock. Maps and woodland prints were scattered on the walls. She rarely came in here. Actually, neither did Harry. He had another office at the lumber mill and he spent most of his office time there. This room was really a waste. She shrugged. What did it matter? The study filled her mind with Harry and Harry's absence. She walked out and shut the door.

She turned on the TV in the library and sat down to watch the news, during a commercial getting up and making herself another drink.

At seven, she wandered into the kitchen and looked in the refrigerator; Pearl had left her a plate of cold roast beef, sliced tomatoes and cottage cheese. She took it out and put it on the counter. She would have another drink and then eat.

At eight, she was still drinking and had not eaten. She walked unsteadily, having to put her hand out against the wall several times. Auburn locks fell across her forehead and into her eyes, further blurring her vision. She finally got the plate, a knife and fork, and went back to watch TV. After she had eaten a third of the food, she took the plate back to the kitchen and placed it in the sink.

She shook her head, trying to clear her thoughts. What now? She weaved her way to the terrace and looked in the direction of the pool.

Mario finished washing his supper dishes and put them in the dish rack to dry. He wiped his hands on a wad of paper towels, opened another beer and went outside to sit on the steps and enjoy the cool evening air. It had been hot working in the sun today but these spring nights were always cool. He untied his sneakers and kicked them off. Mrs. Harding had been in his mind for the past two days. He had half expected to see her last night, knowing Mr. Harding wasn't back yet. But she hadn't showed. He hadn't even seen her around the yard the way he sometimes did. Maybe she had forgotten the whole thing, with no trace of memory of him or their night.

Katie. Katie. The familiarity of the name challenged him. What if he just up and called her that one day in front of everyone? Or was it better to say "Ready for bed, Mrs. Harding?" What a laugh—to call someone "Mrs. Harding" while you were fucking the shit out of them.

He finished the beer and crushed the can in his hands. As it crackled and bent, he looked up to see her standing by the rhododendron, watching him. Her long green robe blended with the bushes, but the last glows of the sun still in the west caught her red hair, making it look kissed by fire. She stood there with her pale white hands by her side; her pale face above the darkening green was crowned with dying embers. She wasn't coming any nearer; she was just standing there looking at him.

It was quickly becoming dark, that gloaming hour when shapes become vague and a stillness settles over the landscape. It was almost eerie to see her there. He didn't know whether to sit and wait for her to speak, or whether he should stand up and offer her some hospitality. He sat. They looked at each other, the sculptured moment beyond the bounds of time.

They were both so riveted watching each other, they never

heard the minute sound of a snapping twig, nor did they see the stealthy movement in the shadows of the bushes between them and the pool.

He decided to let her make the first move, though it wasn't easy to wait. He was drawn to her like a magnet and the urge to possess her began to throb in him. Jesus Christ. He hoped no one was watching or, worse, came along; he sure didn't want to turn her off now. He swallowed hard and waited, his heart racing.

She raised one hand to the metal zipper pull at her throat, a trailing touch like a falling leaf; with the other hand she barely lifted her skirt off the ground, away from her white ankles and feet. She half turned, as if to walk away from him, then she said, almost timidly, over her shoulder: "Would you like to go swimming? The pool's full."

Harry pulled two bottles of wine from a paper sack, one red and one white. He sat the red on the counter and opened the top freezer compartment of the Kelvinator and found space for the white.

Doris laughed. "You came prepared for any kind of meal, didn't you?"

"Yep. But I was hoping we'd be having the white."

She took the two rainbows out of the net and dropped them into the sink. "Want a beer while we cook?"

"Sure." He pushed her aside and felt the blade of a small knife. "I'll do this while you get the beer."

"Deal."

She poured two beers into tall glasses and watched him clean, rinse and dry the fish. "I even have a lemon."

"Good for you. Got any of those good vegetables left in the freezer?"

"Enough for another month. There are still packages of spinach, beans and also some squash. Let's celebrate and have one of each."

"If you want them, but one's enough."

"I know that. But I want to get the freezer cleaned out before the new crops start coming in."

"Then let's have all three."

"And rice?"

"Sounds good to me. I'm pretty hungry," he admitted.

He sat at the table and watched her getting out the vegetables, putting water on to boil, tossing the fish lightly in flour and melting butter in a big skillet. She then moved the skillet to a cooler part of the stove and sat down across from him.

"Where will you put a new freezer?" He looked around the room.

"In the pantry there. I'm going to move the clothes washer to my bathroom."

"What kind of freezer do you want?"

"Now, listen here, Harry Harding. Don't you go buying me any new freezer."

"Why not?"

"Just because, that's why not."

"You better tell me what kind you want, or I might end up with the wrong one. Of course, you can always exchange it, but that's a nuisance. Might as well get it right the first time."

"Absolutely not, Harry. No."

He laughed. "Give in, kid. I want to do it."

She looked down at her beer sitting in front of her. "You spoil me, Harry. You send me too much."

"Too much? Jesus. A lousy reel of floating line? A bottle of wine? That's too much?"

"That's just what's come in the past month, and you know it. You send me all that money every year as it is, and I can make do without it."

"I know that."

"And the new cultivator . . ."

"That was a year ago."

She was silent for a bit. He watched her, then he reached across the table and took both her hands in his.

"I want to do it, Doris. Just accept that as it is. We've been through this before and I've told you. I want to do it. I've got more money than I can use. I want to do it."

"The lumber business could go sour any time. I know that. You just have kept on top of it so far."

"And I'll continue to keep on top of it. And . . . if I go bankrupt, then we can reconsider things. Meanwhile, let me do it my way."

"Are you tired? You must have had a few busy days in the woods."

"Yes," he said. "I am tired."

She smiled at him. "We'll go to bed right after dinner and I'll give you a good massage."

Harry drove from the Albany airport across the mountains that divided New York from Massachusetts in complete contentment. He had had a successful trip and once more the pleasure of being with Doris. She made him feel satisfied and fulfilled—left him with simple, uncomplicated reward.

The wild pinksters were just beginning to bloom on the mountainside, cascading down the steep slopes to the noxious highway. He should drive Red up here to see them when they reached their height. He was glad he had remembered to dig a plant for her. She loved the wildflowers. He glanced at the roadsides looking for more as he twisted down the mountain into town.

He knew he was lucky to have been able to persuade Red to move. Miss Anderson had suggested they look into the Berkshire area; they had, and had fallen in love with it. It would have been a completely satisfactory life if only Red had found some interest. She said she hated to play bridge and golf and go to chamber-music concerts and that's all anybody did; she said if you went to one cocktail party a year you would see everyone in town, and any more parties were just repetitious. He knew this was Red at her most stubborn, but she seemed to have convinced herself and to have sunk into irrevocable inertia. She had met many people she liked when they first arrived. They still had small groups in for dinner occasionally, but the occasions were further apart this year than they were last year, and those were fewer than the year before. And her inertia was now coupled with a feverish restlessness that seemed to be quelled only with alcohol. The vicious circle: boredom, needing him, desperate without him, anger with the kids, guilt, vodka, passed-out, boredom. He could start it at any one of those and come full circle again. Somewhere in all of it was unhappiness.

When had she become unhappy? When had she not wanted to be where and who she was? He knew she longed for the nearness of New York, saying it was the only civilized city in the world—but he knew she would no longer be happy there either. She was who she was, no matter where she was. Harry suddenly laughed aloud when he thought of her and Boston. He had suggested she get in the habit of going there, as it was closer, but after two trips to Boston she had proclaimed it to be the most pretentious, provincial place she had ever seen, confirming what her father had said about the "proper Bostonians" when they didn't accept an Irish immigrant. She refused to go back. Beautiful Red. So much to offer and give, so generous and no one to give it to. Thank God she had Kay. Kay was pretty dull, but apparently she was loyal and faithful; she certainly was a good friend for Red, and she was wonderful with the kids.

Harry turned his jeep into the driveway, whistling a tune he and Doris had heard that morning on the radio. He hoped Red wouldn't get drunk and that the brother wouldn't want to stay too late.

Katie was tossing clothes out of her closet when Harry came up behind her and put his arms around her. He pulled her thick hair away from her pale neck and put his lips on the smooth cool skin.

Katie grabbed both his arms and held tightly to him, her pink nails digging into his shirt sleeves.

He kissed the other side of her neck. "How've you been?"

"Oh, Harry, everything's a shit-hole."

"That's encouraging to hear. I can hardly wait for the details."

Katie turned around in his arms and put her hands on his shoulders. She smiled at him. "Never mind all that now. You can hear it later. I'll torture you in bed with my tales of woe."

"I'd rather do something else in bed."

"That, too." She kissed him, their lips lingering against each other. Katie wanted to hold him forever, never letting go.

Finally he pushed her away. "What are you doing with these clothes? Planning on a rummage sale?"

"I'm weeding things out for Kay. I've finally gotten her to accept some things; now I want to get more to her before she changes her mind and goes back to those dreary tacky clothes she wears. I'll have to sneak down there and burn all those peasant skirts."

"That's nice of you. I bet she'll be glad to get them. I'm going to take a shower." He glanced at her dressing table and the tall glass with a few melting ice cubes.

"They're coming at six," Katie said, "so we can have a long talk with Dan. We'll just walk in the garden or sit on the terrace until dinner. Dinner's at seven-thirty." She looked down at her beige slacks and shirt. "I want to put on something special for him, but not anything dressy. I probably don't have the right thing."

"You probably do." He lightly swatted her rear. "I brought you a plant."

"What is it?"

"Another pink lady's-slipper. It's in a coffee cup in the car, nice and moist in its forest loam. I'll get it tomorrow."

"You're an angel to me. We'll plant it with the others you've brought. Thank you, my dearest."

"Entirely welcome." He walked out, thankful she was not yet drunk.

Katie picked the clothes up and carried them into the bedroom, dropping them onto the chaise. She hoped Kay would wear one of the things she had given her. She probably would. And if she knew Kay it wouldn't be any of the slacks; Kay wouldn't consider slacks proper for dinner. She would wear the dress. Katie pictured the colors in the Thai-silk dress. Yes, then Katie would wear those watermelon-pink silk pants and top, the ones that were tight at the waist, ankles and wrists, and loose elsewhere. She liked the way the top tied at the waist, showing just a small suggestive triangle of stomach. They weren't too dressy. They would be just right. She wouldn't wear a bra; she would let the fabric lie on her breasts and sway gently when she walked. She would come up behind Harry to ask him a question, leaning into his back, the two pointed mounds pressing against him. He would know. She would keep Harry's attention all night.

She looked at her watch. She didn't have time to get in the shower with Harry—that was something she wouldn't want to rush. But she would hurry and dress and get the plant. She wanted it by her bed tonight. Her heart swelled with her love for Harry.

She had just finished dressing and was leaving the room when the telephone rang. She picked up the receiver. "Hello."

"Katie, this is Kay. Oh, I'm so upset, I don't know what to say to you."

"What is it?"

"It's Dan. I've been waiting for him all afternoon, and he's just called to say he's not coming. It really burns me up. He could have called earlier."

"Oh, Kay. I'm so sorry. I know how much you were looking forward to his coming."

"And now I've let you down about dinner. I know you planned it and . . ."

"Don't be silly. You can still come. Harry's home and the three of us can have dinner. We'll be very sorry not to have Dan, but I hope you told him to come another time soon."

"Yes. I did. He said he would."

"Then it's no big deal. You come ahead, any time you want, and we'll celebrate Harry's return."

"Thanks. I'll be along soon."

Katie opened the door to the jeep and reached down for the white Styrofoam cup wedged between two boots and a tackle box, but her hand stopped short of it when she spied a piece of folded white paper neatly placed in Harry's spot behind the wheel. Letters forming the word "DADDY" had been cut from a magazine and taped on the piece of cheap lined paper torn from a notebook.

She picked up the paper, unfolded it and stared incredulously at the cut-out words clumsily secured with Scotch tape, bold print marring the page. "Mommy went swimming without clothes on with M-A-R-I-O." The last word was pieced together letter by letter. That was all. Some of the words were quite small, from the text part of a slick magazine page; some were large, from ads. "Mommy" was large and printed in red colors. "Clothes" was in detergent blue. Katie sat on the rough worn seat and reread the message several times.

She slowly folded it, over and over, until it was in a piece no bigger than a postage stamp. She unfolded it, read it again, then tore it into tiny pieces that she wadded into her clammy palm. Who had done it? Who? And with so little time. Harry hadn't been home more than half an hour. Someone had seen him drive in and had slipped in here with the message, knowing he would see it tomorrow when he came out to get in the jeep.

Who had seen her last night? The children were at the movies; or were they? Had they already come home, and she had been too drunk to notice? With her free hand she wiped the drops of perspiration from her forehead. She felt sick to her stomach. Who had seen her? And who had had the foresight to get this readied, so the perfect moment would be seized when no one was watching, as soon as Harry arrived? Who had slipped in here and left this for him? Who?

What time had she gone to Mario? Had there been lights on the third floor? She couldn't remember.

If she couldn't determine who was out last night watching

her, at least she could determine who was doing what during the last half hour.

Katie quietly shut the door and went to the outside garbage can, where she lifted up some plastic waste and dropped the damp ball of paper into the midst of the garbage.

Then she walked calmly and quietly into the house and up the back stairs to the third floor. She stopped first at Joe's room and looked through the open door at him, flopped in a chair reading. Not Joe. He couldn't have done it to her. She moved quietly past him toward the voices coming from Lavinia's room.

"Miss Anderson," Katie said from the doorway, looking at Freddie and Lavinia who were sitting at a small table drawing while their nurse knitted in a chair by the window. "I just wanted to say that Miss Wright still is coming for dinner, though her brother's had to cancel his visit. And Mr. Harding's back. It would be nice if we could keep the noise down to a dull roar."

"Of course, Mrs. Harding. I remembered. It's too bad about the brother, but the children are eating early and we'll be up here if we're not outside."

"Yes." Katie walked over to the table. "What are you drawing?"

"I'm making a doll house with lots of rooms. This one is where Jewel will sleep. And this one is where I'll sleep." Lavinia pointed her finger at two lopsided squares on a page of irregular squares, colorfully crayoned to form rooms and furniture.

"That's very nice. It must have taken you a long time to make it."

"No. Not very long. I haven't finished it yet. Jewel likes lots of curtains and they have to all be different colors."

"And what are you drawing, Freddie?"

He looked up at her without speaking, but did turn his page toward her to see.

"That's nice, too," Katie said. "It looks like the ocean, and those are sailboats, and here's the beach, and these must be houses on the beach. Is that it?"

He turned the page back toward him and went on with his work.

"Have you been up here long, Miss Anderson? I mean, these drawings seem to be works that have taken some time to do. But maybe they started them yesterday."

"No. They just started them about half an hour ago." She

looked at her watch. "Yes, we've been here just about half an hour. We were outside playing when Mr. Harding drove in . . . and then we decided to come up here and draw until Pearl called us for dinner." She looked suspiciously at Katie. "Is something wrong, Mrs. Harding?"

"Wrong? No, nothing. I just had a few minutes and thought I'd stop up here. It was really about the change of plans and the noise."

"I understand. Don't worry. The children will be well-behaved. Won't we, children?"

Lavinia nodded, while Freddie squinted his eyes at his picture.

"You've been with them since Mr. Harding returned?"

"Yes, I have. Right here in this room. Neither of them has left my sight for a second." Something must be wrong. Well, it couldn't be blamed on these two. She hadn't left them all day.

Katie felt she was going to faint. If these two had been here with Miss Anderson, that only left Joe. She turned and walked from the room, pulling the door shut behind her. My God, it couldn't be Joe. It just couldn't be. She took a step toward his door, her heart pounding, then stopped. No, it couldn't be. He would have no reason to do anything mean to her; she had always stuck up for him. Even with this marijuana mess, she was supportive of him. She couldn't ask him what he had been doing; it would look as if she were checking up on his movements, and she wanted him to know she trusted him. No. It couldn't be Joe anyway.

She felt light-headed as she slowly walked back down the hall and descended the stairs. "Mommy went swimming without clothes on with Mario." The words burned into her brain. When she shut her eyes, they were searing there, red and blue and tiny black letters.

She went to the pantry and uncorked the brandy bottle, took a swallow, then replaced the cork. She stood quietly in the pantry with her hand on the neck of the bottle until she heard Harry come down the stairs. Then she picked up the bottle and went up the back stairs to their bedroom, shutting the door behind her.

Kay arrived promptly at six. Harry met her at the door, warmly shaking her hand. "Katie's around someplace. It's too bad your brother couldn't make it."

"Yes. But he says he'll come again," she answered, almost blushing at the touch of his hand.

"Good. Come on out to the terrace." He opened the screen doors at the end of the hall. "We've got to keep the screens shut now; bugs, you know."

As he gestured toward a chair, he smiled at her. "You look nice. Very colorful and summery."

Kay was cocooned in smug pleasure. "Thank you." She sat down, smoothing the Thai-silk skirt over her knees. "So do you." He had actually put on a summer jacket and tie for her; she knew from Katie he never dressed up unless it was a special occasion. She must have made a good impression on him the other night.

"What'll you have?" he asked.

"I think one of those wonderful spritzers you made me before. But very light."

As Harry made drinks, Kay pinched her cheeks to bring more color to them and ran her hands over her hair. "Where are the children?" She had heard them coming—and hoped he hadn't.

"I expect they'll show up soon. They've probably been finishing up their dinner."

"Oh?" She raised her eyebrows. "They won't be eating with us?"

Harry paused as he handed her her drink. "No. I doubt it." He sat down just as Lavinia and Freddie came through the door.

Lavinia, holding Jewel tightly to her, ran to her father and took his hand, waving cheerfully at Kay.

"Hello there, princess." He kissed her cheek. "How are you?"

Freddie grabbed his sister by the hand and tried to pull her away.

"No!" She pouted, sticking out her bottom lip. "Leave me alone!" She turned back to Harry. "Did you bring me a present?"

"There's not much to buy in the deep woods. Next time I'll see a store. Come here, Freddie, and give me a kiss." He held out his hand to the sullen child.

Lavinia moved between them. "Did you bring Jewel a present?"

Harry smiled and looked at Kay, including her in the paternal circle. "Sorry, Jewel. Come on, Freddie."

"Did you bring Freddie a present?" Lavinia persisted.

"No. I just have a hug and a kiss for him, and I'd like to give them to him." He gently moved Lavinia to the side and reached for Freddie's hand.

"I was here first!" Lavinia screamed at Freddie.

"No you weren't. I was here first. You pushed in front of me! Get away! Get away!" Freddie jerked Lavinia's arm.

"No! I won't!" She grabbed his shirt and held him away.

Harry tried to quiet them and separate them.

Freddie suddenly stopped fighting and glared furiously at his sister. Then he brought back his foot and kicked her in the leg as hard as he could.

Lavinia started to cry.

Harry lifted Lavinia onto his lap and held her tightly in his arms. "That was not a nice thing to do, Freddie. You apologize to Lavinia."

"She can't hear me with that crying anyway." He jutted out his chin and ducked his head, his eyes sweeping the terrace the way a bull would size up his opponent before the charge.

"Yes, I can." Lavinia abruptly turned off her tears and victoriously nestled her head on Harry's shoulder.

Harry shifted Lavinia to the side and again reached for Freddie. "Come on, Freddie. You can squeeze in here on my other leg. When we have a nice dinner guest like Kay, we shouldn't act like squabbling babies. Come on, Freddie."

"I won't sit by her!" Freddie backed off. "She's trouble."

"Just come give me a kiss." Harry again held out his free arm to the sulky child. "You and Lavinia are here to say hello and then you have to go find Miss Anderson. Let's be friends while you're here." He kissed Lavinia's wet cheek.

Lavinia slid off his lap and edged toward Kay, who put her arms around her and kissed her. Only then did Freddie come near enough for Harry to touch him. Harry leaned forward and kissed his cheek. "How are you? I've missed you the past few days."

"I wish you had brought me a present," Freddie said. "I would have liked something from the woods. You could have brought me a rock or a pine cone or something."

"Next time I will. I did bring Mommy a present that I dug up in the woods."

"Did you have a shovel?" Freddie asked.

"No. I dug it up with my hands."

"What is it?" Lavinia demanded.

"A flower."

"Oh, that." Lavinia turned back to Kay. "We've got lots of flowers."

"I know you do," Kay answered. "You have yards of beautiful flowers. But a single one out of the woods is very special." Kay smiled at the child. "Where is your Mommy?"

Lavinia and Freddie both ignored the question.

Harry looked over at Lavinia. "Why don't you run upstairs and see if Mommy's up there, Lavinia. Tell her Kay is here and we're waiting for her."

Lavinia hesitated.

"Run along and do as Daddy asks, honey." Kay pushed her toward the door.

Lavinia ran into the house.

Harry still had his arm around Freddie. "Does she carry her doll to class with her?" he asked Kay.

"She brings it to school with her, but she keeps it in her storage cubby."

"She's stupid," Freddie muttered.

Harry asked Freddie some questions about his activities at school, getting terse answers.

Lavinia came back out and sat on a chair, her legs swinging in front of her. "You know what, Daddy? We had a picnic at school one day and Jewel got mustard all over her dress. I had to wash it out in the sink."

"Was Mommy upstairs?" he asked.

"I don't know." She dropped her eyes to the plastic skull. "The easiest thing to wash on Jewel is her hair."

Kay laughed and bestowed a warm smile on her.

"What do you mean, you 'don't know'?" Harry asked. "Was she in the bedroom?"

"I don't know. The door was shut."

"Did you go in?"

Lavinia rubbed Jewel's painted hair. "No."

"Well, how about going back up and looking in the room to see if she's there."

She didn't answer.

"Lavinia," Harry spoke gently but firmly. "I asked you to do something. Will you please do it."

"Go ahead," Kay quietly urged.

Lavinia shook her head.

Freddie looked across the lawn toward the pool. "Here comes Joe. Get him to do it."

Harry and Kay both turned to see Joe coming, a towel around his shoulders, his wet hair lying back from his forehead.

"Hi, Dad," he called. "Didn't know you were back. Have a good trip?"

"Sure did."

"Hi, Kay. Where's your brother?"

"He had to cancel his trip at the last minute."

"Too bad. Pool feels great."

"Say, Joe," Harry spoke. "When you go up, see if Mom's upstairs. Tell her we're waiting for her."

"Sure thing." He wiped the towel down his legs and across his feet, then went through the screen doors.

"Swimming's a lot cooler in this weather than all that soccer he plays," Kay commented.

"Sure is." Harry laughed. "But soccer's his game. He'll play it any time he can find some other fools."

"Kay took us to the movie!" Lavinia suddenly blurted out. "Kay and Miss Anderson and Freddie and Jewel and me! And Pearl came too!"

"Wasn't that a nice thing for Kay to do. What did you see?" Harry asked.

The two children looked at each other, then Lavinia said: "I can't remember the name, but it was about fires and burning things down. . . ."

"And people getting their legs cut off," Freddie contributed, talking rapidly: "It was a war and people a long time ago in long dresses and all and then the war came and everything got burnt up and bombed and then this lady, she got married and he built her a big house and she had a big bed and—"

Lavinia's face turned red and she began to scream, that loud piercing high scream on a single note, shaking her head with her eyes wide, screaming so loud it made Harry push Freddie aside and go to her. He picked her up. He held her tightly in one arm and held out the other hand to Freddie. "Come on, Freddie, let's go."

Freddie came and obediently took his hand, and the three of them left.

Harry called over his shoulder. "Be right back, Kay. We'll find Miss Anderson."

As soon as he returned, Kay said: "They're just tired out tonight. And it's spring fever. All the kids at school go wild as the end gets near. Just the thought of summer seems to make them hysterical."

"Yes," Harry said. "I suppose so." He picked up his drink and finished it. "Ready for a refill?"

"No, thanks."

As Harry was making another drink for himself, Joe stuck his head out the door. "Dad." He spoke hesitantly.

Harry looked at him and waited for him to go on.

"I guess . . . I guess you'd better not wait for Mom. She's having a nap."

Harry and Joe looked into each other's eyes. "Okay, Joe. Thanks for checking." Harry stared into his glass for a moment, then said to Kay: "Well, it looks as though it will be just the two of us tonight."

Harry and Kay had finished dinner and were having their coffee at the long, dining-room table, the soft candlelight silently touching the garden scenes and shining on the mahogany surface that spread between them.

"Katie certainly missed a delicious dinner." Kay set her wine glass on the table.

"More wine?"

"Oh. Heavens, no. Everything was just the perfect amount. This coffee is all I need now."

"You don't seem to have any weight problem." He refilled his glass. "I should think you could eat almost anything you want."

"I don't have a weight problem because I'm careful of what I eat and drink."

Harry pushed back his chair and stretched his long legs in front of him. "You and Katie are pretty close friends, so I hope you won't mind if I speak frankly."

"Of course I won't mind. I adore Katie."

"You know she's got this . . . drinking problem."

"Yes, I know. I've tried to help her. Subtly, of course. I mean, if she looks like she wants a drink, I try to suggest we do something else, like take a walk, or drive to town or something like that. Something dumb." She smiled at him.

"That's not dumb. It's very thoughtful of you to try to distract her. I think she probably drinks more when I'm not here. She seems to get so bored. Except when you're around. You don't know how much she's talked about you in the past three years; I know how often you see her and how much time you spend with her. I can't tell you how much I appreciate it."

"It's a pleasure to be with her. I enjoy her company." Kay

began to fold her napkin. "This summer when the children are away at their respective camps, I know you and Katie will be able to take a private vacation together, and that will probably do her a world of good."

"What summer camps? We mentioned them briefly the other night, but I didn't know we'd gone beyond that."

"Oh, dear, don't tell me I've let some cat out of the bag. I just assumed, of course, you knew. I mean, I thought it would be the first thing she'd tell you when you got home today." She looked toward the center of the table where the big bowl of white narcissus complemented the white linen mats with delicate yellow blossoms. "Just forget I said it. She'll tell you in her own good time."

"Why don't you tell me?"

Kay described the two camps for the younger children, just as if she had gotten the information from Katie instead of Hilda Anderson. "And then the canoe trip for Joe . . . well, of course, you know how Katie dotes on Joe and she was reluctant at first to let him go, but after she thought about the trouble . . . well, she saw it would be better if he went away too."

"Trouble? What trouble?" Harry leaned forward and put his forearms on the table, pushing the mat back as he did so.

"Oh, dear. I've done it again. Now I really am not going to say anything about this. It really is up to Katie to tell you." She put her napkin on the table as if it were the period at the end of a sentence.

"I wish you'd tell me." Harry looked deep into her eyes. "I want to know now. I would appreciate it if you would tell me. Katie will understand."

"No. She'll get angry with me. I'd rather not."

"Then I won't tell her how I found out. How about that?"

"Well . . ." Kay slightly arched her back, her breasts molded into the silk of the dress, "I shouldn't do this, but maybe it's best for you to know. It might even help Joe if you talked to him tonight, or early tomorrow morning before he goes to school. Yes, I'll tell you."

11

"WAKE UP, RED. I'VE BROUGHT YOU SOME COFFEE." HARRY gently shook Katie's shoulder. "Come on. You can't sleep all day. It's almost noon."

Katie mumbled an unintelligible expletive and rolled over.

"No, no you don't. Wake up. I've got some cold juice and hot coffee here. Which do you want first?"

Katie barely opened her eyes and looked at him narrowly: "Why are you waking me up?"

"It's late. That's why. I think you should wake up."

"Why? What is there to do?" she asked in a hoarse whisper.

"We can talk about things. Come on now, sit up." He pulled the pillows up behind her.

Katie groaned and pushed herself up in the bed, leaning her head back against the pillows. "What time is it?" She pulled her legs from under the sheet.

"Almost noon."

"Why are you home? Why aren't you at work?"

"I was, earlier. I came home to have lunch with you."

"That was nice of you." She looked down at her watermelon-pink satin outfit. "Did I sleep in this?"

"You sure did." He handed her the coffee. "You slept pretty soundly in it." She had never stirred the night before when Harry took off her shoes and shifted her body so he could pull the sheet over her.

"Halston would have a fit if he knew I'd used this for sleeping. He prided himself on it."

"If I'd known that, I would have taken it off you."

"Did you put me to bed?"

"You put yourself on top of the bed. I only got you under the covers."

She sipped the hot coffee. "Too hot." She tried to put the cup on the bedside table.

"No you don't. You hang on to that until you've drunk it all."

"What's happening today? Why are you here?"

Harry pushed the hair away from her face. "Your mascara ran."

She shoved his hand away. "Then don't look at me," she said grumpily. She took another sip of the coffee. "You haven't answered me."

"Well, I thought it would be nice to be with you today, and since I had little to do at the office, I came home. I hear from Pearl that we're having Joe's class here for supper tonight."

"Is that tonight?"

"It's tonight. They're coming over after Joe gets home at five." He put his hand on her leg. "You should have told me about Joe."

Katie stretched her feet, pulling the toes down and back up, watching the curved pink nails. "When could I?" She licked her lips. "You've been away." Her lips and tongue felt dry and rough.

"You could have mentioned it on the phone."

"I could have, but I didn't." She finished the coffee and handed the cup to Harry. "Who told you?"

"Joe did. I asked him how things were going this morning, and he told me."

She should have asked Joe if she could help with his party. Katie closed one eye, screwing up that side of her face. "I was going to tell you."

"It doesn't matter who told me. The important thing is to talk about it."

"What is there to say? He got caught and he's on garbage detail." She pulled up her knees. "Mommy went swimming . . ." suddenly rushed at her; she froze, not letting it get past the first three words.

Harry stood up and walked to the french doors and looked out. "I think there's more to say than that."

Katie looked at his back, wondering what he was thinking. She swung her legs sideways and sat on the side of the bed, looking down at her hand, the ruby ring catching the morning sun's rays.

"I'm worried about him, Red. I'm really worried about him."

Katie stood up, then sat back down again. She felt awful. Her head felt bunched behind her eyes and there was a heavy dull pain in the pit of her stomach. "Could we talk about this later? I really don't feel very well."

"You probably won't feel well later. So we might as well get it over with."

"What's that supposed to mean?" She stood up and stiffly walked toward her dressing room.

Harry turned around and looked at her. She was disheveled and weak, bent forward, shuffling across the carpet in her crumpled pink outfit, her hair matted in tangles around her head and her makeup smeared, smudges around her eyes. He felt a great sadness watching her. "Why don't you take a shower first, then we'll talk. We can go out in the garden and walk around and talk about it."

"No. No garden. I'll just shower and then I'll be all right. We can talk then." She went through the door.

Soon Harry could hear the water running and see touches of pink littering the floor. He shook his head and went out onto the balcony, looking down at the immaculate terraces and neat borders planted with annuals that would soon give a burst of color across the walls. With a pang he remembered their first spring here, when Mr. West had carefully planted the marigolds in the morning and Freddie had just as carefully pulled them up and broken each one in half in the afternoon. Harry raised his eyes to the fields.

This should be a happy season, the summer soon upon them, the children home playing and swimming, planning vacations they would all take together as a family. That's the way other families did it. But not in this house. They never did anything as a family; if they did, it was chaos. So they avoided any family events. Who was to blame? Any one of them, or all of them? No, he and Red were to blame. He was gone so much of the time; Red couldn't, or wouldn't, cope. Joe was hustling joints; Lavinia and Freddie were screaming and fighting, closeted with a nurse who ruled their lives. It was a hell of a way to raise a family.

Katie came up behind him, fringes of red escaping the towel wrapped around her hair, a terry wrapper tied closely around her thin body.

Harry put his arms around her. "That's better. Much better."

"I'm such a mess, Harry. I've made such a mess of everything."

"No, no you haven't.. We both have done some wrong things. We've got to talk about them before they get worse. Okay?"

Katie nodded her head. She was to blame, though; she knew it. Harry was out doing what he was supposed to be doing, running a business and being successful, the way her father had done. She was the one to blame. But she just couldn't help it. She couldn't be successful with what she was supposed to be doing. She wasn't the right person, the right mother. If she had only had Joe, she might have been able to handle it, but she just couldn't manage with the three of them. Her head still hurt, in spite of the three aspirin she had taken as soon as she went into the bathroom.

"I had lunch with Freddie and Lavinia. . . ." Katie started to cry, tears running down her cheeks. "I had lunch with them one day. It wasn't yesterday, so it must have been the day before. I had lunch with them," she repeated, tears sliding into her mouth. "I tried, Harry. I tried."

"Oh, Red, Red." He held her tightly. "Don't cry." He kissed her wet cheeks. "Don't cry."

"I tried. I really tried." She couldn't stop crying, the flood of tears released by the admission.

"I know you did. Oh, Red, Jesus, it's all so complicated. I know you've tried. I know you have. It should be so simple. So simple. Don't cry." He pulled a handkerchief out of his pants pocket and wiped her face. "We've got to think about Joe now. He needs help." He knew she would listen if they talked about Joe. Get her attention on that, then include the other two. "He told me about the canoe trip, and I think it might be just the answer for him. If he's getting into trouble around here, it's probably because he's bored."

She took the handkerchief and blew her nose. "He should

have talked to us if he was bored and needed help. He should have talked to us."

"I know, but he didn't. Do you know who his friends are? Who he runs around with?"

She shook her head. "Miss Anderson would know, but I don't. Do you hear that? I just don't know. I'm such a failure." She weakly hit Harry's chest with the palms of her hands. "I don't know who he sees or where he goes or what he does. I'm just a failure. If you want things to be so damned simple, then you've got it. I'm a failure. That's very simple."

"Red, Red, you're not a failure to me. I love you."

"How can you? I never cause you anything but trouble."

"That's not true. You never cause any trouble at all, except to yourself. You don't treat yourself very well. And if we don't know who Joe's friends are, I'm as much to blame as you are." He took her face in his hands. "But we'd better start paying attention now. Both of us. We've got to pay attention to what our children are doing."

She nodded. "Yes. Pay attention."

"Pushing marijuana is pretty bad, but it could have been worse. He could be on drugs himself."

"Oh, no!" Katie jerked back.

"I hope not. We've got to see to it that Joe doesn't fall in with a crowd that's a bad influence on him. He may just be mixed-up, confused."

"Joe has nice friends. I'm sure he must." But she didn't know for sure. She didn't even know if he cut out words and constructed notes. Confused! Good God, everything was confusing. Where was Joe? Where had he been yesterday afternoon?

"The ones he brings home are certainly nice enough, but are they the only ones? We don't know who else he sees." He stared vacantly across her head. "Lavinia and Freddie never bring home friends. Maybe that's a worse sign for what lies ahead of them."

"Who would want them for friends? They fight and scream all the time."

"Only with each other. That's fairly natural with siblings so close to the same age. They don't act this way with other children."

"How do you know? We never see them with other children."

He dropped his arms and walked back into the bedroom,

leaving her hugging the wrapper around herself. He said loudly: "Miss Anderson told me about the camps."

Katie's memory was a haze. How did he know to ask about that? She frowned and concentrated, feeling a terrible weight coming down on her. Had she mentioned it to him before she got drunk? Maybe one of the children had mentioned it. My God, just think if she hadn't gone to the jeep. No, don't think of it. She took a deep breath and followed him into the bedroom. "They sound like good places. Miss Anderson would only pick good places for them."

"I would have liked to have been in on the decision. I think both parents ought to make this sort of decision."

"Really, Harry, we mentioned it before you left . . ." she could have said "went for four days," "and then you weren't here, and plans had to be made."

"They couldn't have waited two more days?"

"Four, and no, they couldn't." Katie walked into her dressing room and untied her robe. She sat down and pulled the towel from her head, picked up the brush and began stroking her hair.

Harry stood in the doorway watching her. "Don't get me wrong, Katie. I like the idea. I just wanted to be in on it."

Katie paused in her brushing. He had called her "Katie." He must be angry. Well, so was she. "You should have been here," she said coldly.

He watched her for a few seconds, then turned and walked away.

Katie called after him. "Don't you go blaming me for having to handle all this! I wasn't the one who wanted to be stuck here with them! It was very upsetting for me to find out about Joe, then to have Lavinia turn out to be a thief on top of it was too much! You should have been here!"

Harry came back to the door. "You said Lavinia is a thief?"

"Yes. She stole the money from my dressing table, right here, this drawer . . ." she jerked the drawer open, then slammed it ". . . came sneaking in here and stole it."

"I can't believe that."

"No? Ask Miss Anderson. She got the truth out of her. The little thief admitted it." Her hands trembled so much she had to put down the brush, pressing her fingers against her temples, thinking of Lavinia, trying to make herself remember this was just a little girl, a child, scared, not yet ready to know everything that was expected of her.

"Why would she do a thing like that?"

"To give the money to Joe so he could get himself into trouble."

Harry put his hand over his eyes. "Oh my God." He turned and walked heavily to the chaise and sat down on the foot of it, holding his head in his hand.

Katie watched him through the open door without moving. He lifted his head and looked at her. "Red. She's in trouble. She needs help."

"First you say Joe is in trouble, then you say it about Lavinia. She's not in trouble. She is trouble. And for no reason. She is given everything." Katie dropped the brush and stood up. She walked swiftly in and sat beside Harry, putting her arm around his shoulder. "She has everything. She wants for nothing."

"Except attention."

"Attention?"

Harry nodded. "Can't you see this? She's just trying to get attention. She was trying to win Joe's attention and love by giving him what he wanted. Just the act of taking the money was trying to get attention." He put his hand on her bare knee. "Can't you see it, Red? Can't you really see what's happening?"

"You're taking this too far, Harry. It was a simple act of stealing, that's all. Many people steal." She felt chilled. "I certainly never thought it would be one of our own children, one of my father's grandchildren. With more money than they can ever use, living this way . . ." she waved her hand in the air ". . . having everything. I never thought one of them would turn out to be a thief."

"Stop it, Katie. She needs help."

Katie stood up. "Fine. You stay home and give it to her." She bit her lip, angry with herself. She felt a hot shame swelling over her.

She went into her bathroom and opened the medicine cabinet and shook out two tranquilizers, which she popped into her mouth. She ran a glass of cold water and drank it, leaning her forehead against the cold mirror. Harry shouldn't upset her like this, not when he knew she wasn't feeling well. The past few days had made her ill, especially the discovery of that note. A little piece of folded white paper that would have turned Harry away from her forever. The pink flower fused with the ugly white paper, carefully torn from a child's notebook. Who would do such a terrible thing to her?

She raised her head and looked in the bright bathroom mirror. She looked debauched. She gently touched the little bags beneath her red-rimmed eyes, pressing them into the cheekbones. But they just popped right back. Her hair was frayed and unruly, even though she had brushed it.

She turned quickly away and went to one of her closet doors. She pulled open drawers, yanked out underwear, took the top shirt from a stack of neatly folded ones, not noticing what it was, then jerked a pair of slacks from a hanger. "I'm going to get dressed now. We can talk about this later." Should she let him sit there on the end of the chaise in an enduring silence while she dressed? No, she needed to talk to him. "If you're upset about this, I guess I can't blame you," she called into him. "I was upset too, Harry. I was very upset." She buttoned the shirt front and stopped.

That was not the tone of voice to use with Harry. Not with Harry, who loved her so, who brought lady's-slippers to her. He was right. They had to help their children. She had to spend more time with them. "You're right, Harry. Of course you're right. Will you forgive me? I'm sorry I was so cross. I didn't mean what I said about Lavinia." She stepped into the green linen slacks and zipped up the fly, lost in thought. She faced the open door as she spoke. "I shouldn't have called her a thief. I'm sorry I did. She must have taken the money for some deep reason. You're right. She needs help. We ought to help her." I need help too, Harry. Shall I tell you now while you're here to listen? "Harry, she's not the only one. I need help. I need help and I know it. Will you help me? Will you tell me what to do? I promise I'll do it. I mean, I promise I'll really try. Will you, Harry?"

She walked to the door and looked at the chaise. Harry was gone. The room was empty.

Katie ran through the room and down the stairs to look for Harry. She ran toward the terrace, glancing into the living room and dining room on her way. Not there, and not on the terrace. She went past the library and threw open the door of Harry's study. No Harry.

"Pearl!" Katie called as she walked quickly toward the kitchen. "Have you seen Mr. Harding?"

"He just went out toward the garage."

Katie could feel angry tears coming. He'd walked out on her. She opened a cupboard in the pantry and took out a tall glass. From the little refrigerator in the pantry se got ice. Then she poured vodka over the ice and opened a bottle of tonic. She tossed some tonic into the glass, spilling more on the counter. She brushed the wet spot with her hand, then gave up and walked out, taking a long cool swallow as she went.

She stood by the terrace doors and drank, staring through the screen at the green grass. When she had finished that one, she went back and made another. She took that one outside and sat on the terrace. Her brain was becoming pleasantly anesthetized. Where was Harry? She was ready to talk about everything. She was ready to discuss Lavinia and Freddie without getting mad. Where did Harry go, walking out like that? He must be angry with her.

Why not? She was angry with herself. The tranquilizers definitely had helped. Maybe she would take one more, just to be on the safe side. She wanted to be calm and collected when Harry got back. Where was he?

Harry drove his jeep fast along East Road, bumping and swaying. He was angry with himself, angry and afraid. He was also angry with Red, not even wanting to talk about Lavinia. He was afraid for all three of his children. Up till now, he had fantasized that all was well—rather, reasonably well. He knew Lavinia and Freddie had problems, being pushed out of sight most of the time, but it had only slightly disturbed him. Now he was frightened for them. And Joe—good, solid, dependable Joe, Joe was in trouble, maybe deep trouble.

He turned into the driveway of the school, drove slowly past the field of children playing ball and parked. He threaded his way through the kindergartners who were having an art lesson on the walkway and went into the building.

The school secretary looked up questioningly, her hands poised above the typewriter.

Harry asked: "Bob around?"

"Afraid not. He's gone to a conference today. Be here tomorrow."

Harry felt defeated. He couldn't even get to the batter's box, let alone first base. He needed to talk to someone about Joe, and Lavinia and, yes, Freddie, too. "I'll try to get in tomorrow." He started toward the door.

"Harry! Harry!"

He turned to see Kay walking toward him. "Hi, Kay."

"Fancy seeing you here." She put her hand on his arm. "I had a wonderful time last night, though I am sorry Katie wasn't with us. What are you doing here?"

"I came to talk to Bob, but he's not here."

"What's the matter? You look upset."

Harry looked toward the door. "I guess I am."

"Would you like to talk to me? I'm here."

Harry looked at Kay. She was watching him with such kindhearted interest, such warmth of feeling, he wanted to blurt out all his problems to her right then and there. "Have you had lunch?"

"I was about to take a sandwich out under the trees."

"Can you take off for an hour? We could go to the Corner Restaurant."

"Sure. Let me just tell someone I'm going. Meet you outside."

They went into the dining room to the left of the entrance where the lunchtime crowd gathered, walked past the bar and asked for a table in the corner by the window.

"Would you like a drink?" Harry asked Kay.

"Oh, no, thank you. I'd never get through the afternoon if I did." She looked at him and smiled.

"I'll have a beer," Harry said, picking up the menu and reading down it. "I think the chicken sandwich sounds good. Would you rather have something hot?"

"The chicken sandwich sounds good to me. I'll have it on whole wheat toast."

"Put mine on rye toast." Harry shut the menu and handed it to the waitress. "That was easy."

"What's the matter?" Kay wished she had worn something nicer that day.

"It's all this business about Joe and the other two." As Harry talked about his children, Kay nodded with compassion, touched his hand for encouragement, shook her head at the sorrow of it all. They spoke softly and intimately.

"Poor, poor Harry." She spoke quietly, no longer upset about her clothes as she let her inner light of sympathy shine forth, confident Harry felt its glow.

"No. Poor children."

The sandwiches arrived. They both ate in silence for a while. Finally Kay said, "Harry, is there anything I can do? You know how much I love the children. I'd do anything to help."

"You're wonderful to them all the time, Kay. You're the only one who does things with them."

"I don't do much. I love them, I really do. I enjoy being with them. I have fun with them. And when we're having fun and doing things, no one gets unruly." She dipped her head and smiled again. "But I really don't do much."

He started on the second half of his sandwich. "It's a lot more than anyone else, except Miss Anderson. She's wonderful too. It's only Katie and I who have failed them."

Kay noted he had called her "Katie," and she, too, decided he must be angry. "You're gone so much in your work, Harry. You don't have time to be at home taking care of them. You've got a big business, and you have to be there. You can't blame yourself. You can't be a mother to them, too." She nibbled on a corner of her sandwich.

"But Katie . . ." he began, then stopped, wrapping his hand around the beer glass that had warmed with his frequent touch.

Kay put down her sandwich. "Poor Katie." She must be careful of the tack she took. "She just doesn't realize how fortunate she is. I mean, she has everything: a loving husband, healthy children, the house, servants. She never has to want for anything. Never."

"Don't confuse money with happiness." He continued to stare into the glass. "You can be unhappy whether you're rich or poor."

Kay shifted her approach. "She's not a bad mother at all. She does, really does, care about the children. It's just that she's preoccupied. I do so worry about her drinking, Harry."

"I worry too."

She picked up her sandwich, poking the lettuce back between the bread. "You worry too much about everything. You should take pride in being such a wonderful father. You spend more time with them than most fathers. Believe me, I know; the children tell me. You're better than average."

"I find that hard to believe."

"You are a good father and they know it. I've seen how much they love you. If you weren't a good father, they wouldn't be clamoring over you all the time." She put the uneaten part of the sandwich down and touched the napkin to her lips. "If you weren't a good father, they'd avoid you the way they . . ." she let her voice trail off and picked up the sandwich again, her unfinished words swelling in the silence.

Finally she spoke again. "I worry not only about her drinking and what it's doing to her physical health—and we can all see it affecting her—but I'm afraid it might get to her mentally too."

Harry chewed slowly, listening attentively.

"I mean," Kay leaned forward and lowered her voice, "I've heard of people getting in the state she's in, and then completely losing control of themselves. They start hanging around awful bars when no one's watching, and going off to filthy rooms with all sorts of creeps. Why, just last year there was someone really respected here in this town and she became a drunk and it came out during the divorce that she was sleeping with the handyman every night. Do you remember that? Well, it was so awful. I felt so sorry for her. But she was just a total alcoholic who couldn't control herself. Such a pity."

They finished their lunch without talking any more, both preoccupied with their own thoughts.

Harry paid the check and walked out behind Kay, the back of her head visible to him, not the smile on her face.

Pearl brought a cup of vichyssoise out onto the terrace. "Here, take this, Mrs. Harding. You've got to eat something."

"I'll wait for Mr. Harding, Pearl. He said he would be here for lunch."

"It's two-thirty. If I know Mr. Harding, he's already had lunch someplace. You know he doesn't like to eat late. You take this and try to eat it." She held the cup closer.

Katie looked at the creamy liquid, specks of green floating on top. "I'm not very hungry."

"You've got to eat. You haven't had anything all day. You'll get sick if you don't eat. And you don't want to do that with Joe's party coming up tonight."

Katie took the cup in her shaking hands, causing the spoon to fall into her lap.

Pearl reached down and picked up the spoon. "Let me get you a little table." She went to the corner of the terrace and picked up a small, white wrought-iron table and carried it back to Katie's chair. "Here, you give me the cup. That's it." She put the cup on the table, the spoon in the saucer and the small linen napkin she still had in her hand next to them. "There. Can you reach that? Good. Now you eat it, and see if you don't think it tastes good." One eyelid drooped, closing off that eye altogether.

Katie looked into the visible eye. "Thank you. I'm sure it will be good. You always make good soup." She took a spoonful and put it in her mouth. "Yes. It's perfect."

"Want a cracker or piece of toast with it?"

Katie moved her head from side to side. She took another spoonful of soup.

Pearl watched her a little, then sadly shook her head and left.

Katie managed to eat half of the soup. She must try to do something special for Joe's party. She knew Miss Anderson and Pearl would have it all under control. But she would like to do something too.

She looked down at her flat blue shoes. They were the wrong color with these pants. Slowly, her eyes traveled up her legs, across her lap to the front of her shirt. She had on a lavender cotton shirt with dark purple squiggles on it. She looked up, then back again. This shirt was awful with these green pants. Dear God, suppose she had showed up at the party this way. Joe would have been mortified.

She looked at her hands. The polish on one nail was chipped. She would have to redo them this afternoon. She touched her hair. She could feel it hanging over her face in dry clumps.

Katie pushed back her chair and stood up unsteadily, again feeling sick to her stomach. The green lawn curved upward toward her, then righted itself. She grabbed the arm of the chair. Her face was cold and damp, her hands clammy, another wave of nausea welling up inside her. She shook her head and focused on a bush bunched like a hunchback at the end of the flagstones, watching her, spying on her. She sat back down and leaned forward, letting her head hang between her knees.

"Mrs. Harding?" A hand touched her shoulder. "Mrs. Harding?"

She raised her head to see Mario standing over her.

"Are you all right? You don't look well. Do you feel faint?" She nodded at him.

"Put your head back down for a minute." He gently pushed her head down. "Does that make it better?"

She tried to nod, her chin rubbing the inside of her knees.

"Don't talk. Just stay that way."

Katie could feel his strong hand on her back. She began to breathe more easily and raised her head. "I just felt faint for a minute." She pushed her hair back with both hands, holding them on her forehead.

"You ought to go inside out of the heat, and rest. Let me help you in the house." Mario took her by the arm and helped her to her feet.

"Where did you come from?" Katie asked. "How did you see me?"

"I was working over by those rhododendron, and just happened to see you." He didn't add he'd been watching her for the past two hours, watching her sitting, staring into space and drinking, wondering if he should go talk to her and try to help her. "Come on, let me help you. That's it. You come on in and rest."

Mario opened the screen door and followed Katie in, still holding her by the elbow.

The cool, darkened air felt good. Katie walked over to the Chippendale mirror on the near wall and gasped when she saw herself. She was deathly pale, no color, her eyes dull and lusterless, listless, hair askew and hanging like dyed cotton. The lavender shirt cast an eerie glow on her face.

She turned her head sharply away from Mario and walked away from him toward the stairs.

"Do you need help?" he asked.

"No. No, thank you," she answered, tears slipping from her eyes. Sobbing silently, she tightly grasped the newel post and began pulling herself up the stairs.

Katie took another tranquilizer, turned on the hot water in the tub, then went to the phone and dialed the school.

"Is Kay Wright there?"

"She's outside with the children. Shall I get her?"

"No." She closed her eyes briefly. "It doesn't matter."

"Shall I have her call you?"

"No. Never mind. Thanks."

She sat by the phone and stared at it. She wanted to talk to Kay, even though she would see her at Joe's party shortly. She just needed to talk to her. She needed someone. Harry wasn't here and she didn't even know where he was. She needed someone, someone sane and reassuring. She could always go sit in the kitchen and talk to Pearl, but it would make her uncomfortable. Why had she spurned all those offers of friendship put before her over the past three years? She could call Betsy now or June or someone. They would have talked to her. But it was too late now. No one cared anymore, except Kay.

She sat in the tub, the warm fluid holding her in an ambiotic calm, the steam curling her hair. She was so tired. It would be an effort to get fixed up for Joe's party, but she would do it. She wanted to look perfect. Just slacks and a shirt, but special ones. Yellow? Blue? Green? White? Yes, white. Nice simple white ones, with a strand of pearls and pearl earrings. She looked at her long slender foot sticking out of the water. She would sit by the pool and watch the children swim. She would sit in the cool of the evening and watch Joe and his friends. She and Harry. And Kay.

It couldn't have been Joe who left the note. Not Joe. And she knew it couldn't have been Lavinia. Lavinia might hate her for having "found her out," but she couldn't have left the note without Miss Anderson knowing she was out of her sight. And the same was true of Freddie: God only knew whether he was motivated by jealousy, love, hatred, guilt, resentment or caring—but he certainly hadn't escaped Miss Anderson and left the note. That brought it back to Joe again. No, no, she couldn't let herself believe that.

She climbed out of the tub, trailing water across the bathroom and her dressing room, the great white towel with the blue KLH draped around her shoulders and falling past her knees. She looked wistfully at the photograph of her father. It was the only photo she had in this room. Not even Harry was here. Harry was on her desk and on her bedside table, but not here where the sun caught her hair, bouncing the dazzling golden-red back and forth between the mirrors. "Tell me about your new teacher, Katie. I want to hear what you think of her." "Tell me about that boy I saw you dancing with. Who is he?" Tell me, Katie, tell me anything, everything.

"No," she said aloud, shaking her head. "I've got to stop this nonsense and pull myself together. I've got to think of Joe's party." She turned and looked out the window; it was a perfect day for a party, the newness of the long, hot summer days making it more exciting. It was those first days, after the cold and damp had gone, that gave every child a thrill, that gave forth assurances of fun to come. And not just for children; she and Harry would share that joy. While the children were having their fun at camp, she and Harry would be together. Alone together.

As Katie dried herself, she looked at the stack of clothes

Pearl had folded. Tonight she must remember to suggest a wig. That was going to be difficult. Kay might be insulted by that. She would have to be especially diplomatic to get her to agree to a wig. She hoped she would have the strength to do it.

After she had dressed and carefully applied her makeup, Katie went down to the kitchen. She still felt weak, and walked with her hand out, ready to catch herself.

Pearl was putting the icing on a huge chocolate cake, making waves of chocolate across the top and lapping down the sides.

It almost made Katie ill to look at it. She looked away. "That's beautiful, Pearl. You really are an artist. What else are they having?" She was sorry she'd asked as soon as the words were out of her mouth. Her stomach really was protesting against any connection with food.

"Hamburgers, hot dogs, potato salad . . ."

"Yes," Katie interrupted, hoping Pearl wouldn't continue. "I know you've got everything they want. Do we have lots of Coke and that sort of thing?"

"Plenty." Pearl looked at Katie with one penetrating eye.

"Is there something I can do?"

"Not a thing. It's all set. Will you and Mr. Harding want to have the same thing the children are having?"

"He probably will. I'm not sure about myself. My stomach doesn't feel so hot, to tell you the truth. Maybe I'll have a little soup and toast. But nothing special. I'll see how I feel later."

Katie looked at her watch. It was not quite four o'clock. She must do something to cheer herself up. She wouldn't have a drink, not yet. In fact, she would try not to have one at all. She had to think of something to occupy her.

The house. The house for the summer. She would make herself get on the phone and find a house for the summer. She would call friends, no, agents, and find a house . . . for when? Not June. That was too soon. July? Maybe. Not August; that was too near the end of summer and the children might be coming back from camp then. It had to be July. Cape Cod? Long Island? Harry wouldn't go abroad in the summer—he said he had to be available in case something came up with one of the lumbering operations.

She knew, as she hurried toward the library, that she should cancel the camps and take a big house for all of them. She knew she should try to be with them. They should all be together, happy together, learning to understand each other. Next summer. Not this one. She needed to be alone with Harry.

She got her address book out of a drawer and took it and the telephone to the sofa and sat down. Everything seemed like such a tremendous effort. She felt tight as a wound spring and ready to explode.

Cape Cod was more informal; crowded, but informal. Newport was out. They had taken a house there one summer and Harry had hated it, calling Bailey's Beach a breeding ground of bores. East Hampton might be a happy medium. They could go to the Maidstone Club if they wanted to, but there was plenty to do if they didn't want to go. She knew plenty of members who could sponsor them as guests. She would try East Hampton first.

She felt depleted when she had finished making her calls, but she had been successful. She was just replacing the phone when Harry walked in.

"Harry. Where have you been? I've . . ."

"Hi, Red. I'm going to run up and take a shower before Joe's gang gets here. Seems I'm elected to cook the hamburgers and hot dogs."

"Someone else could do it. . . ."

"No. I want to do it. Maybe I'd better get the charcoal started before I shower."

"Couldn't Mario . . ."

"No. I'll do it." He disappeared down the hall.

He had been so brusque with her. Had there been another note? Another piece of cut-outs waiting for him this morning? She felt her heart pounding.

She looked around the room, reading the titles of books until her head cleared. She hadn't had a chance to tell him about the house in East Hampton. It sounded perfect. A modern creation of glass and wood overlooking the water, and no neighbors nearby. It was expensive—twelve thousand for the month—but so what? She shrugged, her body protesting against even that slight movement. And she had located an agency who would have a couple available to serve them. Just she and Harry, for the whole month, alone together. She wouldn't get drunk while they were there. She would be the wife she was supposed to be for Harry. They would walk on the beach, picnic, build fires, hold each other and maybe occasionally go to the Club for cocktails or something. But only occasionally.

She felt so much better just thinking about it. She would start tonight, trying not to drink so much. She would start right away. How happy Harry would be.

Next year they would all do something together.

At five the crowd arrived *en masse*, spilling into the house with abandon: nineteen twelve-year-olds who raced to the third floor to change into bathing suits, and Kay. Katie, feeling stronger but hardly tip-top, went outside when she heard the commotion. She was using all her inner resources to appear normal.

She went straight to Kay, who was watching Harry poke the burning charcoal around in the grill. "Kay, you look great." She nodded with approval at the blue linen slacks and a blue silk shirt. "Doesn't Kay look great, Harry?"

"She sure does. I've already told her." He backed off. "Whew, that's hot."

"I have another box ready for you," Katie said to Kay. "I've told Pearl to leave it by the front door."

Joe came running out in his trunks. "Hi, Kay. Mom. Coming in, Kay?"

"Not tonight." Kay smiled at Harry.

"Where are the others, Joe?" Katie's heart gave a quick skip.

"The guys are changing in my room . . . here come some of them . . . and the girls are in Lavinia's room." He started running toward the pool. "Come on! Hurry up!" he shouted.

Katie and Kay got out of the way as the door flew open and children of assorted sizes charged past them, laughing, shouting, some dropping towels. The girls came more quietly, smiling and saying hello as they tripped past, watching where they stepped in their bare feet.

"The fire's under control. I'll go over and be the lifeguard." Harry followed the bathers.

Katie touched Kay's arm. "Let's go watch them. Would you like to swim? I have extra suits."

"I'd rather just watch for now. The pool's too crowded for me."

Katie pulled Kay's collar up a little. "If it just stands up a bit, it's softer on the face." She didn't add that it helped hide the scrawny neck. "Would you like a drink to take to the pool?"

Kay shook her head. "I'll wait for you and Harry. Or are you having one now?"

"No." Katie went down the step to the lower terrace. "Not yet."

Harry was running around the lawn, chasing the volleyball that kept getting knocked out of the pool and throwing it back in. Katie and Kay pulled two chairs back, away from the splashing water. They sat and watched in preoccupied silence.

Katie was trying to think of a way to broach the subject of the wig with as little effort as possible; she wasn't up to a harangue. Kay was consumed with curiosity about the new clothes, itching to get her hands on them. She hoped it would be a big haul.

"Kay." Katie laid her white hand with the long tapered fingers on Kay's blue sleeve. "There are times when . . . well, what I mean is, some clothes go better with . . . it seems to bring out the quality of the clothes, make them look better if . . . if the person has long, not really long, but sort of puffed-out, I guess I mean, actually I mean fuller . . . well, a fuller hairdo."

"Good Lord, Katie, I can't possibly have a fuller hairdo." Her frown deepened. "My hair's too thin. It's a curse I've had all my life. What I wouldn't give to have that thick rich hair you've got. But I was born with this thin mess and I'll die with it."

"You can do something about it if you want to." Katie could feel her heart beating faster; she was almost there.

"What can I do? You know all about these things. Just tell me."

"You can always get a . . . a wig." She held her breath and watched Kay's face.

"A wig?" Kay looked puzzled.

"Yes. Some of them are beautiful and they don't look like wigs at all. I don't mean the cheap ones that are so awful. I mean a really good one. Lots of people wear them. All sorts of fancy people."

Kay didn't answer, but just looked at Katie.

Katie spoke rapidly. "I mean a really good one. Go to a professional and get a super one." She paused. "Have I said something awful to you?"

"Not awful at all. But Katie, a really good one probably costs a fortune."

"Yes, they do. I know that. I want to get you one as a present—that is, if you want it."

"I couldn't let you do that." Kay lowered her eyes, looking

at her hands in her lap. "You do so much for me now. That would be too much." She held her breath.

"Oh, Kay, you will agree, won't you? I so want to give you something you really want. Would you like to have a wig? A really good one, the best there is?"

"Yes, I guess so, but . . ."

"No buts." Katie brought her hands together in one satisfied clap. "I'm so glad. I would get one for myself if I had thin hair. But what a pleasure it will be to get one for you."

"A wig." Kay pressed her thin lips together and looked at Katie. She let out a deep breath. "It's just never occurred to me to get one. I've never thought about it at all."

"Of course you haven't. We'll do it right away. We should go to New York to get one. When can you get away?"

"Actually I have to go to Boston very soon to a teachers' conference. Could we get one there?"

"I don't go to Boston myself. Though I guess I could. Actually, you don't need me. There's an Elizabeth Arden in Boston, and you can go there and get them to arrange it all for you. You can charge it to me. While you're there, get one of those divine facials they do . . . you'll love it. I always get one when I'm in New York. You can get them to recommend makeup and things too . . . if you want them to. Just charge it all to me."

"Do you have a charge at the Elizabeth Arden in Boston?"

"I'll call New York tomorrow and have them call the store in Boston and arrange it. You won't have any trouble. I'm a good customer in New York, and they'll clear the way for you in Boston. Just get whatever you want and charge it to me. They'll help you pick out a good color of wig and style and all that. I can't wait for you to go. I'm dying to see you all fixed up. It takes time to make a wig, of course. They'll have to send that to you. But you can get the makeup organized."

"Oh, Katie, you do so much. I wish I could do something for you."

"You do. You're my friend."

"Here comes Harry," Kay said. "Shall we tell him?"

"No, no. Let's surprise him when you get it all done." She leaned back in her chair, the whiteness of her clothes and her pale skin making her auburn hair seem redder than usual.

Harry stood beside Katie's chair, panting slightly. "I'm out of shape from all that running. I think they're deliberately throwing it out to make me chase it. How about a drink, Kay?"

"I'll have a weak gin-and-tonic. Very weak."

"Okay." He hesitated, then patted Katie's shoulder, but he didn't offer to make her a drink.

Katie jabbed her fingernails into the palms of her hands. She wanted a martini, a good strong one; it would help her. But she was going to try not to drink tonight. "Harry, will you get me a glass of ginger ale?" She managed to say it without choking.

"Ginger ale?" Harry looked quizzically at her.

"Yes. I thought that might taste good." She didn't want to tell him she was feeling lousy, her stomach queasy and the queer dull pain still in her gut. She hoped it wasn't her liver again. She hoped it was just something she had eaten, or not eaten. "I might have a drink a little later. But for now, I'll lay off."

Harry bent and whispered in her ear. "Did I tell you how fantastic you look tonight? Like a white goddess."

Katie smiled and put her hand on his. Harry could say things to make her feel so absolutely wonderful. Whoever had left that note . . . whoever . . . nothing would ever stop Harry from loving her. Who was it? Could it really have been . . . ? She put her forearm across her stomach and pressed hard to stop the pain.

"Where are Lavinia and Freddie?" Kay asked.

Harry went to get the drinks. "I'll check in the house."

"I daresay Miss Anderson has them under control to keep them out of Joe's way." It wasn't either of them; that much was certain. The terrible dread of doubting . . . it was coming again, now bringing with it a defiant anger.

"Don't they want to join in the fun?" Kay asked.

"This is Joe's party," Katie answered, watching Joe, the expression on his face, the laughter in his eyes. "She'll bring them out soon, I'm sure."

They watched the merry group in and around the pool, Katie counting heads every now and again, thankful she had had the Librium before coming out.

Harry returned with their drinks and pulled a chair next to Katie's. "Miss Anderson is about to bring them out. She was just giving the others a little time alone."

"I hope she doesn't let them make a nuisance of themselves."

"She won't. And I won't. And you won't." Harry smiled at her.

Katie drank some of her ginger ale. As soon as it hit her

stomach, she began to feel sick again. She set the glass on the flagstones. "That tastes good. I was quite thirsty and it tastes good." It tasted awful. She watched Joe. His long hair was hanging in wet ropes around his neck, hanging there the way doubt sticks in the subconscious.

"Joe ought to get his hair cut," Harry said.

"I know." Katie couldn't go into this now. "He will. Soon." She turned her head, looking through a chink in the shrubbery, to watch Pearl bringing out plastic-wrapped trays of food and putting them on the long table they had set up near the grill.

Miss Anderson passed by them with Freddie and Lavinia, both in bathing suits. Miss Anderson herself had on a matronly one-piece suit of dark blue with a skirt, her ample bosom well covered, the wide straps digging into her square muscular shoulders; her aging arms were lumpy but still firm. She herded her two charges to the shallow end and sat on the side of the pool, her legs dangling in the water. Her hair was tucked under a white rubber cap, with the side flaps turned up, exposing her ears.

"It seems Miss Anderson is ready for any emergency," Harry commented.

"She's a saint." Katie wondered if she should try the ginger ale again. "She may even deserve a raise. I wonder where she'll go when the children go to camp?" She shouldn't have mentioned that; Harry had been so upset earlier about the camp business. She looked over at him. He was smiling, paying attention only to the pool. Instead of a raise, maybe she would pay for Miss Anderson's summer vacation. There must be some nice place she'd like to go and that she couldn't afford. She'd ask her tomorrow.

"When do the children go?" Kay asked.

"Sometime soon," Katie replied vaguely. "I'm not sure when. But it's soon after they get out of school."

"That's two weeks."

"Yes. It's about then."

"How long will they be gone?"

"Joe's trip is for eight weeks. The camps for Lavinia and Freddie are for ten weeks, I think. Something like that."

"Ten weeks? That's a long time." Kay leaned forward ever so slightly and looked at Harry.

"Yes." Katie wanted to change the subject. "When do you go to Boston?"

"As soon as school's out."

"How long will you be gone?"

"Two days. Maybe three now." She smiled at Katie.

Lavinia was trying to get in on the game. The older children kept pushing her away. Miss Anderson must have spoken sharply to her, for she came back and stood in a shallow corner. Freddie had not moved since he got to the side of the pool; he hadn't gone in the water at all, but stayed where he was, his dark eyes narrow slits, watching. His body bulged all over, and rolls of fat hung around his middle. His legs were so chubby it was hard to see his knees.

Joe shouted: "Let's get out and play a game on the lawn!" A great cheer went up. "Hey, Dad! When will the hamburgers be ready?"

"Whenever you want them. The fire's ready to cook them now."

There were some mumbled conferences in the water, then Joe said: "We're going to get dressed now and eat before we start a game. Okay?"

Harry stood up. "Right. You get dressed and I'll start cooking."

"I'll help." Kay stood up. "You stay here and relax, Katie. No need for us all to get in that hot smoke."

Katie sat, watching the children run past, some of the girls shivering as they got out of warm water, the boys gangly and thin, with their hair plastered to their skulls and wet towels around their bony shoulders. Soon they would be tall, taller than the girls who now stood inches above them, filled out and muscular, their arms and legs no longer looking out of proportion and overgrown.

Katie got up and carried her glass of ginger ale to the terrace. She put a chair near the grill, not too near to feel the heat, but near enough to be able to talk to Harry. Kay was busy unwrapping trays and handing hamburgers and hot dogs to Harry.

"No!" Freddie's voice made them all turn and look. He was being dragged by Miss Anderson across the terrace to the door.

"What seems to be the trouble?" Harry asked.

"Lavinia has gone in to get dressed," Miss Anderson answered, not stopping but still tugging Freddie along. "And I want Freddie to do the same."

"I'm not wet!" The dark scowling face was turned away from his nurse.

"I know that. But I have to change and you can't stay by the pool alone."

"Would you like to help me cook, Freddie?" Harry asked. Freddie's face almost became pleasant. "Could I?"

"Sure. If it's all right with Miss Anderson." He looked at the older woman.

"That would be fine. Are you sure he won't be in the way?" She waited for Harry to assure her. "Then I'll just bring you down a shirt when I come back, Freddie. You go help, and mind yourself." She released the fat hand and went into the house.

Katie looked at her ginger ale. It had lost its bubble and looked sickly. She would like to have a real drink now, but she would wait. She wasn't sure if it would help her stomach or not, anyway. She could hold out a little longer; in fact, she probably could hold out all night.

Freddie's eyes were opened wide, looking at all the food. Katie didn't know they could get as big as that. He always seemed to be squinting through slits or to have his eyes squeezed shut or to be looking through lowered lids. "Don't touch the food, Freddie. Wait until your turn comes."

He looked crossly at her, but didn't say anything. He started counting the forks lined up in a row.

"Harry." Katie raised her head and looked into his eyes. "I found a house today. For our vacation, remember? I hope it sounds all right to you."

"Tell me about it. Hand me the salt, will you, Kay?"

"It's a secluded beach house, very modern and quiet, no visible neighbors, just a stretch of sand and the ocean."

"Sounds good. Where is it?"

She crossed her fingers. "East Hampton."

He raised his eyebrows at her. "Does that mean eating at the Club every night?"

"No. It means eating at home. I also found a couple who will be available that month. Pearl can come if she wants to, but she probably would rather have her own vacation."

"Sounds okay, Red. What month do you want to go?"

"July. All of July. We can go down before the big weekend, and stay all month." She felt a glow of happiness that momentarily made her forget her stomach.

Harry flipped the hamburgers. Then he took a long fork and carefully rolled the hot dogs over onto their sides. He waved his hand in front of his face and backed away from the smoke.

"Is it all right, Harry? Does it sound all right?"

"Sounds great. Only I won't be able to go the first week in

July. You can go ahead of me, and I'll come for the last three weeks."

"Why can't you come the first?" The familiar loneliness began to threaten her.

He rolled the hot dogs some more. "I have to go away that first week to look at a stand of beech and white pine. It's a big piece of property."

"For the whole week?" Maybe they could take a house wherever it was he was going.

"Anything over the holiday is slow. You know that."

The smell of the cooking food was making Katie's stomach heave. "Where will you be going?" She didn't care if they went to East Hampton or not. Someplace else would be just as good.

"To Maine," he answered.

"Oh, God," Katie stood up, sickened. "I don't want to go to Maine. The water's too damned cold. And if you're inland looking at trees, it's too buggy in the woods. Oh, God." She really felt sick. She'd better have a small drink to settle her stomach. "I'll go see if I can help Pearl."

In the noise and confusion that followed, no one noticed Katie occasionally leaving for brief periods. The children took plates of food onto the lawn, some sitting on the steps, some on the grass. When they had all stuffed on what seemed to Katie to be an extraordinary amount of food, they ran onto the big lawn to play before having dessert.

Katie had had three small drinks from the vodka bottle in the pantry, but was feeling no better. Harry had cut a hamburger in half for her when she protested at having to eat one at all, and she tried to nibble on it, but didn't get very far. He didn't seem to notice. He and Kay were eating heartily and laughing with the children. Miss Anderson and Lavinia ate on the top step, and Freddie sat on the terrace floor near the food. Katie watched Harry and Kay the most. Kay was acting as if she had a school-girl crush on Harry, tipping her head, smiling coyly. And Harry liked talking to her, no question about that. Good thing she felt secure about Harry, or she might have to keep an eye on Miss Plain Jane Kay. This was a classic case of the frog ogling the prince.

Things were quieting down and Pearl and Miss Anderson began to clear away the scattered remains on the trays when Lavinia started to shriek "Look! Look!" in a loud voice. Katie turned her head to see Lavinia standing by the cake. "Look!"

All the adults stood and went to look at the cake. At one end of the rectangular confection, a handful of cake had been gouged out, fingermarks left in the icing, crumbs spilled onto the table. "Look at what Freddie did!" Lavinia shrieked again.

All eyes turned to Freddie. His mouth was smeared with chocolate, and he had wiped his hand down the front of his gray sweatshirt, leaving dark sticky streaks. When he saw everyone staring at him, he screwed up his face in a tight mass and ran into the house.

"How disgusting." Katie was revolted just having looked at him. The greedy fat pig, ruining the cake. "Pearl, he's ruined your cake."

"It's not ruined," Harry said, taking a knife and cutting a square around the ravaged piece. "The rest will still taste good."

Lavinia ran down the steps. "Joe! Joe! Come see how Freddie ruined your cake!"

Miss Anderson had drawn herself up to her full height. "I'm very sorry this happened. I can't imagine how he did it without my seeing him." Her face was flushed. "I'm very sorry."

"It's not your fault, Miss Anderson." Harry said kindly. "It's just something that happened. It'll still taste good."

"But he was wrong to do this." She clasped her hands in front of her, her knuckles turning white. "Very wrong."

Pearl carried out the trays without commenting.

Katie looked away from the mess. "He really should be punished for this." But you handle it, Harry; let's see how you handle it. Set an example for me.

"It's not as bad as that." Harry put the ragged edges on a paper napkin and threw it into the trash can. "Let's just forget it."

Kay added: "It still looks delicious. He just wanted a taste. A natural thing for a little boy to want. There's nothing wrong with that." She looked at Harry for confirmation.

Katie looked at Miss Anderson. "I think you should reprimand him for this."

"Yes, Mrs. Harding. I'll go see to him right now." Her eyes were fiery with determination. She strode toward the door. "Will Lavinia be all right here?"

"Certainly," Harry answered. "She'll be fine. Don't be too hard on him. Do what you think's best, of course, but don't be too hard on him. He probably couldn't help himself."

Katie avoided looking at Kay. "He did it deliberately. Maybe to just be a pig or maybe to try to ruin Joe's party or . . . maybe to get attention." She added the last more quietly. "Whichever it was, he did something wrong, and he knows it's wrong. We cannot condone uncivilized behavior like this. He'll never be fit to go out in public anyplace." She turned to Miss Anderson who was waiting by the door. "See that he gets it through his head some way so he won't repeat something like this." She was getting a headache and her insides were churning.

Miss Anderson nodded grimly and left.

Katie began to feel so bad she decided to go upstairs and lie down. It was almost dark and the children were finishing up the cake. The still-glowing coals looked like a little pan of hell, and Katie began to feel a panic rising inside her. The Librium had worn off and the vodka hadn't taken effect. She wished the kids would all go home. Their screams and shouts had begun to sound like an unruly mob instead of children at play. Lavinia had been trying to be the center of attention all night, to the point that even Harry finally told her to leave the older children alone.

Harry and Kay were sitting on the top terrace step, watching the game of hide-and-seek, a baby game no one ever quite outgrew. "I see you!" "Behind the tree!" "You're caught!" ricocheting back and forth in the nearing darkness. Katie went inside. No one noticed she was gone.

Suddenly one of the girls ran up and hid behind Harry and Kay, grabbing both their arms and pulling them closer together. "Don't let them see me," the girl whispered.

Kay inched toward Harry, forming a protective shield. "Keep low."

Harry turned his head and grinned at her. "Wonder how long it will take for someone to see her."

"Shhh," Kay whispered.

The girl was one of the last to be found. "Come down from there!" a boy shouted. "I see you!"

Harry and Kay laughed and surrendered the girl. "Well," Harry pronounced happily, "looks like you and I make a pretty good team for hiding people."

Kay could have fainted at the words. Instead, she slid away from him demurely. "I doubt if we'll get away with it again. Smart bunch out there." *"You and I make a pretty good team."* Her heart pounded.

"Hey, Kay," Joe shouted. "That's cheating, you know."

"No, I don't know it," she called back.

"We'll flatten the tires on your bike if you do it again," another said.

"I'll flatten yours right back."

Harry laughed. "You have a great rapport with the kids."

Kay smiled. "Yes. I know I do. I love it, too."

"Do you really have a bike?" he asked.

"Yes. When the weather's right, I ride it to school. Of course that cuts out the winter and most of our slushy wet springs. But I'm using it now." She was nervously running her fingers over her shoe tops. "Did Freddie come back out? This is a game he could play and enjoy."

"I'd like to see him enjoy something." Harry stared across the lawn at the gathered children. "I hope he will in time."

"He will. When he's a little older and realizes that friendship and companionship are fun things he's missing out on, he'll make an effort to get into the midst of things. Give him a little more time. A child with Freddie's personality needs a lot of patience." Kay looked behind her at the empty chairs. "What happened to Katie? I never noticed her leave."

Harry also looked around. "I don't know. Maybe she just went upstairs for a minute."

"I noticed she barely ate any dinner at all," Kay said. "I hope she's feeling all right."

"She's not a very big eater, as you know."

"I know. But tonight she seemed to be eating less than ever." She touched Harry's arm. "Those were delicious hamburgers. There's nothing better than when they're cooked out in the open, either over charcoal or over a bed of wood coals." She had never eaten a hamburger that had been cooked over a wood fire in her life, but she'd read plenty of children's books where that happened. "Hot dogs, too." She took her hand from his arm, and waved to the children, noticing in her side vision that he was looking at her.

Katie leaned against the door as soon as she was in the hallway. Why did she feel so rotten? She needed to get to bed. She went first to the pantry and had a long swallow of the vodka bottle, then she held herself upright against the wall, holding on to it as she went the length of the hallway that led back to the center of the house. She made it to the stairs. Her stomach heaved again. She'd better hurry. She was going to be sick.

She got upstairs and into her bathroom before it hit her.

Leaning over the toilet, she heaved and vomited a thick, dark liquid, so dark she didn't know what it was. It had splashed onto her white silk shirt sleeve and again on the front of her shirt where she was leaning against the cold white bowl. It came to her slowly that she was looking at blood. She stared, unable to think what it meant. She only knew it was blood. Again she vomited, the dark, thick, lumpy blood not pouring out of her as liquid, but welling in a slimy viscous mass that hung in her throat, making her choke, clutching at her neck, before it rolled through her mouth and fell into the waiting ooze. She began to cry, whimpering like an injured animal, not a real cry of pain, but a whine of terror. She wiped her mouth on the other sleeve, smearing blood across the cuff. With shaking fingers she reached the handle and pushed. The bloody water rose toward her, making her cry out and fall back, before it funneled down the drain and became clear again.

Katie crawled on her knees to the tub, trying to pull herself up, finally one leg at a time, rising, hunched over, at last up and holding on to the sink. She stumbled out of the bathroom, felt her way along the dressing-room walls, knocking over the small table that lately had held clothes, and made it into the bedroom. She cried and made little sounds like a beaten child, her hands violently shaking. She got to the foot of the bed and dragged herself to the top, one hand groping in front of her for the bell. Someone come. Someone please be in the kitchen and hear her. Someone please come help her. She kept her finger on the buzzer as long as she could, then she collapsed onto the bed, doubled sideways, holding her stomach, her head spinning. She kept her eyes open, fixed on the open door. Someone had to come.

Pearl stuck her head around the corner of the door. "Mrs. Harding? You rang for . . . Mrs. Harding!" Pearl ran to the side of the bed. "Holy Mother of God, what's happened?" She looked at the bloody shirt.

"Get . . . Harry. Please hurry."

"Yes, yes. Oh, dear God, Mrs. Harding. Yes. I'll get him right away." She ran from the room.

In no time, Katie could hear Harry running up the stairs. He was in the room and beside her. "Red! Red! What's happened?" He tried to put his arm under her head. "Red. What happened?"

"Help me, Harry. Help me. I'm sick."

"My God, that blood . . . Red, what's happened?" His

eyes ran over her body. There was no sign of injury. "What's happened?"

"I threw up," she answered simply.

"Oh, my God, you've been vomiting blood?"

She nodded.

Harry looked over his shoulder at Pearl who was wringing her hands just inside the room. "Go call Dr. Ames. Tell him to meet us at the hospital."

"Should I call an ambulance?" Pearl's eye that watched them was twitching.

"No. I'll drive her there myself. Tell him she's been vomiting blood. I want someone to meet us."

Pearl nodded jerkily. "I'll do it right now."

"And Pearl . . ." he hesitated for only a split second ". . . ask Miss Wright to handle the rest of the party. She'll know what to do. Now go. Come on, Red. I'm going to pick you up. Are you in pain?"

She began to cry. "I don't want to die, Harry. I don't want to die."

He picked her up. "Pearl. Come back here a minute!" He called at the door.

Pearl came running back in.

"Pull a blanket off the bed and wrap it around her.

Pearl jerked off the summer blanket and tucked it around Katie, covering the bloody stains.

Harry carried the limp, whimpering body down the stairs and through the hallway to the kitchen. "Open the door, Pearl. And run ahead of me and open the station-wagon door. The back seat." Katie was crying and moaning, her head buried on his shoulder. "It's all right, Red, it's all right. We'll be there in no time. It's all right."

He got Katie into the back seat, lying down with the blanket around her. Harry opened the garage door and started the car. She sounded so weak and pathetic. My God, vomiting blood.

"I don't want to die, I don't want to die," she kept repeating to his back the entire trip to the hospital. "Help me, Harry. I don't want to die."

12

KATIE WALKED THROUGH THE THICK FOG, HER HANDS IN front of her, moving the way a blind person gropes in the dense unseen. The fog was so thick it felt damp and cool on her face, making her hair curl in moist loops that stuck to her skin. She looked for a shape she could recognize, a familiar sound, a smell that would lead her. "Daddy?" she called timidly. "Daddy? Are you there?" Her heels clicked beneath her, almost drowned out by the beating of her heart. "Daddy?" she tried a whisper, feeling her skin prickle with fear. Somewhere before her, through the fog, she faintly saw a shape, a light. She hastened forward. As she drew nearer, she saw it was a huge deep tunnel, so deep she couldn't see inside at all and the light was just a reflection caught inside the tunnel, a round rim of light, brighter at the outside edge and quickly becoming extinct as it disappeared into the depths. Katie stopped several feet in front of it and tried to see inside. She gingerly stepped a little closer, waving the fog away from her face. "Daddy?" she whispered. "Are you in there?" Her words were swallowed by the massive emptiness as she touched the cold metal rim and tried to find the courage to look inside. "Daddy?"

"Katie, my darling, what is it? You needn't be afraid."

"Oh, Daddy, the tunnel is so long and scary."

"Tunnels have to be long to go under a river, my darling."

"It scares me."

"Even with Daddy here beside you?"

"No, not as long as you're here."

"Would I ever let anything happen to my masterpiece? No, my darling, this is just a tunnel. There's nothing to be afraid of. You must look at the way it's constructed and marvel at the miracle of it."

"It still scares me."

"When I was a boy, a lad about your age, we had a wooden bridge that crossed our stream. I carried bread and fresh eggs over it to town, to help my mother earn enough money to feed us. But that was a long time ago. And look at me now. I'm standing at the entrance of a great tunnel with a fairy princess, and when we tire of looking at it, we have a long black chariot waiting to take us back to our castle. No walking over wooden bridges for my princess."

"A wooden bridge wouldn't be so scary."

"Nor is a tunnel, when you are with me."

"Don't leave me. Don't ever leave me. Don't, Daddy! Don't! I'm afraid! Come back! Daddy! I can't see you!"

"Wake up, Katie, wake up! You're having a dream. Come on, wake up."

Katie opened her eyes and jerked them around the room. Harry was standing over her, his hands on her shoulders.

"That's a girl. You must have been having a nightmare."

"It was that same one, Harry. That same one." She grabbed his hand.

"Don't talk about it."

"It was that same one. The one I had before when I was sick."

"Forget it. Here, sit up and drink some water."

"I want to go home, Harry. Please tell them to let me go home."

"It won't be much longer now. You're much better. Every day."

"I've been here long enough. I'm all right now."

"You're still pretty weak."

"I can get strong at home."

"Soon. Here. Rather have some ginger ale?"

She shook her head and took the water he held for her, sipping through the bent straw. Then she dropped her head back onto the pillow.

"What time is it?"

"Almost noon."

"What day is it?"

"The fifth of June."

"I've been here too long. When I came it was still May."

"That's right. You spent the last week and a half of May here and now we're in the first week of June. But that's only two weeks."

"I want to go home."

"The kids go to their respective camps tomorrow." He changed the subject. "Miss Anderson will take Freddie and Lavinia. They got out of school two days ago." When she didn't comment, he continued: "Joe also goes tomorrow. He'll be in later to say goodbye."

"Tell him not to bother." She wasn't up to confronting him now, not up to peeling off the layers of doubt and finding his attempted betrayal beneath. It was better to try to forget it. "I'm confused about everything. I get too much sleep, then I wake up confused. Some of the early days here are real hazy. I seem to remember being horrible."

He laughed. "That's right. They only kept you in intensive care for one day because you raised such hell about being there, then they brought their equipment up here and gave you a private intensive care. Boy, were you mad about being downstairs in that curtained-off hole in the wall, screaming about the lack of privacy, blasting out at any new face that had the misfortune to look at you." He laughed some more. "I don't think anyone knew you had that much strength; I must say you about used it up complaining."

Katie looked down at her yellow-and-blue bruised arms. The needles were gone and she was once again eating light foods. She had even gotten to like ginger ale. "When can I go home?"

"Probably next week. Early in the week."

"Another week?"

"A few more days anyway. Better to be on the safe side."

"Are you sure?"

"Afraid so."

"There's nothing being done for me here that can't be done at home."

"You only got rid of those needles and tubes yesterday. Give yourself time to get better. Rest and try to make the best of it. If you go home, you'll only want to get up. And you still need to be in bed."

"I've lost weight."

"Probably." He didn't tell her how bone-thin she looked; he figured she must have lost fifteen or twenty pounds.

"I want to have my hair done. It's a mess."

"You're feeling better."

"When's Joe coming?" She needed to be prepared to face him.

"He and Kay will be by later. She's bringing him."

"How's Kay?"

"Fine. She comes up a lot and has dinner with us. The kids like having her."

"She's been in a lot to see me, too."

"I know."

"I can't remember much about her visits, but I do remember that she's been here. She brought me those magazines." She pointed toward a pile on the windowsill. "I remember that."

"She didn't come the first week because you were so sick."

"You came."

"Every day. Many times."

"I love you."

"I love you, too, Red." He lifted her hand and kissed it.

"That's nice of Kay to come eat with you and the children. I assume you all ate together."

"Yep."

"Just what you'd like to do all the time. Eat with the children." She grimaced. "Thank God I wasn't there."

He smiled at her. "You're as impossible as ever. Impossible and bewitching." He rubbed her hand on his cheek.

"You're the only one I want to see, really. I don't care about seeing anyone else. Only you."

"I'm here. I'll be here whenever you want me."

"Will we still go to the beach?"

"Provided I can be alone with you and don't have to play backgammon at the Club every night."

"Just us. No one else." She closed her eyes. "I'm tired now."

"Go to sleep. I'll go home and get some lunch and be back later." He kissed her on the lips and on the forehead, brushing her hair back. "I'll be back later."

Miss Anderson held Lavinia and Freddie tightly by the hand and crossed East Road.

"Will Kay give us something to drink? I'd like to have a Coke."

"Maybe," Miss Anderson replied. "She might not have anything, so don't be pushy and rude if she says that."

"I won't. You'd better tell Freddie, too."

"I was speaking to you both. Did you hear me, Freddie?"

"Yes. I'm not going to ask for one anyway. I don't want an old Coke."

"I see Kay now." Lavinia pointed to a figure on a folding webbed chair behind the garage apartment.

"Well, if she's sunning herself, you just leave her alone. Play in the yard while Kay and I have a quiet talk. Don't get into trouble."

"What will we play?"

"I have a pack of cards in my pocket. You can play Old Maid."

"I hate Old Maid." Freddie scowled at her.

"Try to learn to like it. There's also Slap-Jack."

Freddie grinned. "I'll play that."

"Don't you dare hit my hand so hard, Freddie," Lavinia shrieked at him. "I'll hit you back if you do."

Kay looked up at the voices. "Well, look who's here." She sat up straighter. "I didn't know I was going to have visitors. I would have gotten some cookies."

"We're just here for a minute or two, Kay." Miss Anderson pushed Freddie and Lavinia toward the shade of a nearby tree. "Play over there, and mind your manners."

Lavinia grabbed the cards Miss Anderson held out and they ran to the tree.

"Sunning your legs, I see," Miss Anderson observed, looking at Kay's cotton skirt pushed up high on her thin thighs.

"Yes. Stockings are so boring when it gets hot. Don't they bother you?"

"I'm usually comfortable in all climates. I stay out of the sun on hot days, and dress warmly in the winter."

"Want me to get you a chair?"

"No, thanks. I can sit here on the grass." Miss Anderson settled herself near enough for Kay to hear her easily.

"What's on your mind, Hilda? You look like you've got a bee in your bonnet."

"As a matter of fact, I do. When you and Mr. Harding . . . "she looked sternly at Kay when she said the name " . . . were talking on the terrace last night, I clearly heard you tell him that Mrs. Harding favored Mario. That was a very foolish remark to make."

"Was it? Why?"

"I told you about Mrs. Harding and Mario in the strictest confidence. You have no right to repeat what I told you or even allude to it. You and I have been friends for a long time, and friends do not reveal the confidences of each other."

Kay leaned back her head and closed her eyes. "I think he should know what his precious wife is up to."

"I may have been mistaken about the whole thing. Just because I saw her walking from the direction of his cottage does not mean she has been having any kind of untoward relationship with him."

Kay raised her head and smiled cunningly at the woman on the grass. "You may have been mistaken, but I'm not. I've seen things you don't know about, things between Katie . . . and Mario."

"What things?"

"Oh, you were the one who put me onto them, so you really do deserve the credit for that. But then I decided to watch for myself." She leaned closer. "I saw them go swimming one night, just the two of them."

Miss Anderson sat up straighter.

"Want to know what they did? Sure you do. She had on a long dark robe, and she unzipped it, and let it fall to the ground. Then she slid quietly into the water and floated on her back while he undressed. Got stark as a jay-bird, he did. Then he slid in next to her and they went to the shallow end." Her voice dropped to a whisper. "He kissed her all over her top, then he pushed her against the side of the pool and she wrapped her legs around his waist. Then he held on to the side and really went at her, pushing into her over and over. She would have cried out if his mouth hadn't been on hers all the time."

"Kay!" Miss Anderson gasped. "Were you hiding in the bushes watching?"

Kay leaned back. "Of course I was. How else would I know?" She smiled again. "And wait until you hear what happened next. He floated on his back, with his you-know-what sticking straight up in the air, and she played with it a long time, then she put it in her mouth and . . ."

"Stop it! I'm shocked!"

"Oh, Hilda, don't be such a prude. It's what people do."

Miss Anderson's eyes twitched. "You were wrong to be watching them. I'm shocked you would snoop like that."

"I thought I ought to know what was going on," Kay answered lazily.

"Why? What Mrs. Harding does is her own affair, and certainly not yours."

"I have an interest in her family. Everything about them interests me."

"Ever since that poor woman has been in the hospital, you've been up at the house almost every night, trying to take her place at the table, trying to ingratiate yourself with the children, trying to win the confidence of Mr. Harding."

Kay smiled. "Not 'trying,' dear Miss Anderson. 'Trying' is the wrong word. I've been doing it. The children love me. Harry likes having me there. I fit that chair at the end of the table very well; it could have been made for me, it's so comfortable."

"So that's it. You're trying to steal her husband."

"Is it so obvious?"

"Only to me, I'm afraid. But perhaps others should be put on the alert."

"Others? You mean Harry?"

"Perhaps. I remember you as a fat little girl, so don't go putting on airs with me. We're both from the same side of the tracks. If you try to drive a wedge between the Hardings, I'll tell both of them about you. I'll warn them. Your sainted parents would turn over in their graves if they knew you were trying to be a home-wrecker."

"My 'sainted parents' were ignorant, narrow-minded, unhappy people who would have liked to have kept me an old maid all my life. Not that there's anything wrong with being an old maid, if it's what you want . . . as I gather you do. But it's not what I want."

"I never would have guessed you could be so scheming and conniving."

"Thank you. I take that as a compliment."

"Look at yourself. Take a good look in your mirror. Do you really think Mr. Harding could fall for you?"

"Beauty is only skin deep. I know how to please him and make him happy. Or I believe I do. Actually, I've only just begun."

"I'm shocked at you."

"You just take care of the children and let me take care of my affairs."

"I will not stand idly by and let you break up that marriage, or even try to."

"What will you do? Tell Katie I'm after her husband? Tell Harry I'm too ambitious? You just watch what you say to them. One hint, just one hint, and I'll tell them how you've been giving Freddie all those illegal tranquilizers every night since he was a baby."

They stared at each other. Finally Miss Anderson got to her feet.

"Oh, children," Kay called across the lawn. "Miss Anderson says it's time to go. I do wish you could stay longer. We could run down and buy some Coke and cookies. But we must remember to mind our nurse, mustn't we? A really good children's nurse like dear Miss Anderson is hard to find, so you run along now, and I'll see you later."

Katie slept soundly until she heard her name being called.

"Katie, are you awake?"

She opened her eyes. Kay was standing beside her bed. "Joe and I came for a quick visit." When Katie jumped, startled, Kay added, misinterpreting the look, "He's right there, at the foot of the bed."

Katie turned her head; Joe was watching her with frightened eyes. Frightened or ashamed? Her stomach tightened into a knot.

"You okay, Mom?"

"Sure I am." She didn't smile at him or hold out her hand to him.

"I'm leaving tomorrow to go to Canada."

"How will you get there? Will Miss Anderson take you?" Katie had last seen him at his party, carefree and happy, oblivious of her.

"I'm catching a bus up to Rutland, then I'll be met there by whoever runs this shindig and go with the group from there."

"The bus? Can't someone take you?" He shouldn't be sent alone, not if he couldn't be trusted.

"The bus is all right. I don't mind that. Dad's kind of busy right now, and Miss Anderson has to take Freddie and Lavinia tomorrow. Then early the next morning she leaves for her vacation."

"Oh, yes, now I remember. She came in to tell me." Miss Anderson was going to England, all expenses paid, departing over her protests to Katie that she should stay home and take care of her when she got out of the hospital. "She wanted to give up her trip and take care of me. So good of her." Miss Anderson cared about her.

Kay's lips were set in a thin straight line. "She should have insisted. She should have stayed with you. Granted she needs a vacation, but she could have postponed her trip for a couple of weeks." Her eyes glazed over as she thought of Hilda getting that free vacation. "You would have been more comfortable with her there to take care of you, you're used to her. After all, she is a professional."

"Nonsense. I don't need anyone other than Pearl. And Miss Anderson deserves a good vacation. Let her have the whole time." She looked at Joe standing uneasily at the foot of the bed. "Joe, crank up the head of the bed some. That's it. Thanks." The note preyed on her mind.

"We shouldn't stay too long, Kay," Joe appealed to Kay, shifting from one foot to the other.

Katie watched him squirm.

"Pretty soon," Kay answered.

Joe looked around at the straight chairs. "Okay if I sit down?"

"Sure. Take that one by the window." Was he doubly ill-at-ease, with his conscience and in this room of sickness? "That's where that dumb nurse sits, or I should say, all those dumb nurses used to sit. I let them all go today." Would she ever completely trust him again? Would she ever understand him? She had thought she knew him so well, her golden baby, her joy. "Would either of you like some ginger ale? I can ring for some."

"No, thanks," Kay answered. "We really can't stay long."

Joe just shook his head.

Katie wondered if she would know any of the answers by the time he came home, when she saw him again at the end of summer.

Katie noticed that Kay had on one of her good dresses. It

looked nice. "Have you started teaching summer school yet, Kay?"

"Not yet. I don't do that until after I take that trip to Boston—you remember, the trip we talked about. I go in a few days."

"I hope you have fun. Boston is my idea of a big hole, but there must be something there to do."

"Oh, I'll be kept busy." Kay touched her hair, patting it with her skinny hand. "There'll be plenty for me to do and plenty of people to talk to. And I'll look wonderful, of course, with my new clothes."

Katie smiled weakly, reaching for the glass of ginger ale on the bedside table.

"I'm going to go to the hairdresser and get a soft wave put in my hair before I go, so I'll really look good." Kay's eyes were fixed on Katie's.

Katie almost dropped the glass. "Good Lord. I forgot about your appointment at Arden's. How awful of me. You should have reminded me. Oh, Kay. How awful of me."

"The appointment? What appointment? Oh, you mean about the facial and . . . all. Why, I'd forgotten all about it, too. It went right out of my head when you came in here so sick, and I was worried sick about you. It's a wonder I didn't end up in a bed next door, I was so worried. Oh, that. Pooh. That can wait. We can think about that another time. You're too sick to think about it now."

"I'm no such thing. When do you go?"

"Next week. But don't you worry about it a bit." Kay again touched the thin hair, letting her finger slip to the white scalp.

"I won't worry about it. I'll just call now." Kay reached for the phone. "Wednesday do?"

"Of course, but Katie, you mustn't worry about a silly thing like a facial and . . . hair." Kay glanced at Joe, who was the epitome of boredom. "You must concentrate on getting well."

"This won't take a minute."

Joe stood up. "Mind if I wait in the car?"

Kay touched Katie's hand. "If you insist, then do it after we're gone. I think Joe has some plans for tonight."

What kind of plans? Katie forced a wan smile. "Have a good time, Joe. If you need us, call us. Catch lots of fish or moose or whatever it is one does in the wilds of Canada."

"I will. Hope you'll be okay, Mom. See you in August." He started toward the door. "Ready, Kay?"

"Coming." To Katie: "See you tomorrow. If phoning is too much for you, you just forget it."

"It won't be." Goodbye, Joe. Goodbye. Her heart felt as though it would break.

They left. Katie wept for all the lost innocence that had come about with that note. Would he ever fully realize what he had done? What he had destroyed between them?

To help her forget, she called Elizabeth Arden's and arranged Kay's appointment. The effort exhausted her. Her whole being cried out for Joe walking down the antiseptic corridors. As she fell asleep, she hoped the Canadian woods would be as safe.

"Joe!" She woke up screaming. "Joe!"

"Mrs. Harding! Wake up! You're having another nightmare!"

A white figure, white hair secured beneath the white cap, was leaning over her, breathing into her face.

"Who are you?"

"I'm the floor nurse. I heard you calling."

"Where's my husband?"

"He's not here at the moment, but I'm sure he'll be in soon."

"Is anyone here?"

"Anyone? Who else would you be expecting, dear? Would you like for me to plump up your pillows?"

"No. I'm all right."

"Can I get you anything?"

"No. I'm all right."

"You ring if you need me."

"I won't need you."

"Suit yourself."

Harry stepped into the dimly lit hallway and had turned to lock the front door when a voice startled him.

"Dad."

He whirled around. "Joe! What are you doing sitting here in the dark?"

"Waiting for you. I want to talk to you."

"Fine." Harry turned back and locked the door. "Come on upstairs with me."

They went up the stairs, across the hall and into the bedroom.

Harry sat down on the side of the bed and started taking off his shoes. "What's on your mind? The canoe trip?"

"No, not that." Joe sat beside him. "It's Mom."

Harry held his shoe and looked at Joe. "What about Mom?"

"I don't know. I mean, something's wrong. I don't know what it is."

"This was the first time you've seen her since she went to the hospital. It was probably a shock for you."

"It wasn't that."

"You mean you want to know more about her sickness?"

"No. I figure it's all from . . . from . . . from her drinking. I know she'll get over it again." Tears clouded his eyes.

"What's the matter, Joe? If you're worried about Mom being all right, she will be. She'll be out of the hospital in a few days."

"It's not that."

"Then what is it?" Harry dropped the shoe and put his hand on Joe's arm.

"It's . . . well, she acted so funny with me. She acted like she didn't care whether I was there or not."

"Mom?" Harry couldn't believe this. "Good Lord, if there's anyone in the world she loves first and foremost, it's you."

"Not today."

"Joe. This just isn't true. Mom dotes on you. You know that."

Joe ducked his head and slid his sneaker across the carpet. "She acted like she didn't want to see me or touch me or anything. She didn't say anything to me like she usually does."

Harry frowned, remembering Katie saying "Tell him not to bother." "What happened?"

"Nothing happened. She just acted like she was mad at me or something. Has she said anything to you? Have I done something she's mad about?"

"No. Nothing."

"I know she was upset about the . . . the pot. She cried all the way home from school. But later that afternoon, she hugged me and said it was all right. She seemed to have gotten over it. Do you think she's still mad about that?"

"Not a bit. In fact, I know she's not. She told me you had just made a mistake and she knew it wouldn't happen again."

"What do you think it is then?"

"I think it's because she's feeling so rotten. They only took out her tubes yesterday, and it may even be some chemical reaction. She didn't even ask me to stay with her today," he lied. "You know how it is sometimes when you aren't feeling well. You just don't care about seeing anyone. That's all there could be to it. God knows she loves you more than anyone, more than all of the rest of us put together."

"I don't like going off with her mad at me."

"Joe." Harry put his arm around his shoulder. "Believe me. She's not mad at you. She loves you as much as she ever did. She's just not well. But she will be soon, and she'll be back to her old self. When you get home, you'll see. She'll be her old self again."

Joe nodded, swallowing hard.

"You'll have a great summer up there. I envy you. That's just the sort of thing I like to do."

"Maybe someday we could all go on a trip like this."

"Hey, wouldn't that be great? Right now, you'd better get some sleep. You've got a long day coming up."

"Okay." Joe stood up. "See you in the morning."

After he left, Harry sat staring at the floor for a long time. Joe was right. Something was wrong. She must be having second thoughts about the pot. There couldn't be anything else. Well, she'd get over it; she'd forget about it by the end of the summer.

At the beginning of the third week, Katie woke from a nap to find Mario standing at the foot of her bed. He was holding a large bouquet of flowers, all shades of pink. Katie looked at them a long time and finally said: "Thank you."

"They're your flowers; I just cut them." He smiled at her. They both laughed.

"You should have waited. I'll be home in two days."

"I'll have more then. We've got flowers to spare."

"These are just the colors I like most."

"I thought so."

An awkward silence followed while they looked at each other.

"You doing all right?" Mario finally asked.

"I guess so."

"Do you want to talk about it?"

She shook her head. "I don't like to talk about being sick," she answered, hoping that was what he was referring to. "I'm almost well now. I guess I've gotten pretty weak, so I'll have to do all those boring things like exercise."

"Swimming's not boring."

"No," she answered, "it's not. It's the thing I've always enjoyed."

He nodded. "So have I. By the way, I planted that lady's-slipper in the wildflower garden. It looks real pretty there. You've got a regular spread of them now."

"Thank you. My husband brought all those plants in that garden to me. Once he didn't have any kind of container and came with a muddy wad of cardinal flowers in his hat." She smiled at the thought. "It's the same hat he's still wearing, too."

He smiled at her. "Well, everything's doing very well."

"I only saw it once—in a white cup in the jeep." Her eyes took on a faraway look.

"You take care of yourself." He wasn't sure which one she meant; she seemed so tired. "I'll see you back at the ranch." He smiled again, laying the flowers on the foot of her bed, and tactfully left.

Harry picked her up and brought her home on a hot day in the second week of June. The air was muggy and still, but she wanted to sit on the terrace. "I've had enough of four walls."

Harry helped her to a deep blue chaise with a thick comfortable pad, stretched in a shady spot made cool by the big oak.

"What is this?" Katie looked at the strange chaise.

"It's for you. I thought you'd like to be out here in the afternoons."

"You bought it for me?"

He nodded and gently pushed her down onto it.

"You're an angel to me, Harry. Thank you."

He kissed her before insisting she slide back so she could rest her back; he lifted her legs and put them straight out on the cushion.

"I'm so glad to be home." She looked across the lawn. "The bulbs are all gone. And I've missed the lilacs."

"The iris and the peonies are just about to pop. They'll make quite a show for you."

"I love the lilacs. I wish I hadn't missed them."

"You've got to remember to keep out of hospitals the end of May." Harry pulled a chair near her and sat down, holding her hand.

"I've got to remember to keep out of hospitals, period. I hate them. They're so full of the most awful smells, and the lack of privacy is criminal."

"You've got to take care of yourself, Red. I can't be here with you during the day; you know that. I just can't."

"I know."

"It's when you get so bored and lonely that you start drinking too much. You've got to find something to occupy your time."

"I've gotten to like TV."

"That's not enough."

She sighed and turned her head to look at some pink and purple lupine blooming in a bed lower on the lawn.

"Kay suggested you take up needlepoint. She said she could get you some designs you . . ."

"Dear Lord, Harry. That's such a typical Kay remark. I am not going to sit around here doing sewing all day. I can't think of anything more boring."

"How about gardening? Mario could help you learn about taking care of plants. He does a good job with the flowers."

Katie looked at him thoughtfully, but didn't answer.

"Something to think about," Harry continued. "Some of the best minds in history have taken up gardening as a hobby. And think how you like flowers."

"Did Kay suggest that, too?"

"As a matter of fact, she did. Or sort of. She made the remark that you seemed to be unusually pleased with Mario. And then I got the idea that if that were so, you might like to work with him."

"What made her say a thing like that?"

"I can't remember how it came up. It was during dinner one night, right after the kids had jumped up to go watch some TV program and we were just sitting there having coffee. We were sitting out here, so it must have been the sight of the gardens that prompted her."

"I daresay." Katie frowned, picturing the scene: Harry and Kay at either end of the big glass-topped table, Harry near the wall where he always sat, and Kay at the other end, at her, Katie's, own place, the empty milk and wine glasses, the dessert plates scraped clean, the tangle of napkins and unused silver. A domestic scene, a cheerful domestic scene. Everything as it should be, and no Katie.

"I think I'll watch TV and swim, and leave the gardening

to someone else." She didn't even want to mention his name.

"Swimming will be good for you. But I doubt if you can do it twelve hours a day."

"I like to swim. I'll just swim and watch TV and read for a while. Then we'll go to East Hampton. And when we get back from there I'll find something else to do. I may start going to New York more often, once a month or so while you're away someplace. I miss the theater and my old friends there, and museums and stores, and all those mouth-watering Italian restaurants. Maybe in the fall, when summer is over and the children have all come back, maybe I'll start going there more."

"Good idea. A trip down every month would be good for you. But don't go while I'm here."

"I wouldn't dream of it."

Pearl came out of the screen doors. "You comfortable there?"

Katie nodded at her.

"I thought you might like a little something to drink or eat. I could make you a milkshake . . ." she paused ". . . or maybe it's too hot for that. How about some fruit juice? And a cracker with some cream cheese. That's easy on the insides."

"You keep after her, Pearl," Harry said. "We've got to fatten her up some."

"That sounds good." Katie looked at Pearl. "Do we have any apple juice?"

"Sure do."

"I'll have that and the crackers. Not too much, though. Too much at once turns me off."

Pearl put her hand on the door latch. "Can I get you something, Mr. Harding?"

He would like to have a beer, but wasn't sure about drinking one in front of Katie. "Nothing, thanks."

Katie seemed to read his thoughts. "Have a beer, Harry. It's all right. I don't have any desire to drink. I've got to be around people who drink, and I've got to just say no. We can't run a Moslem establishment here and not offer anyone anything but fruit juice."

"Sure it won't bother you?"

"Pearl, bring Mr. Harding a nice cold beer. And I still want apple juice."

Pearl went into the house.

"I cancelled my trip to Maine." Harry twined his fingers in hers. "We can go to East Hampton for the whole month."

Tears of pleasure rushed to her eyes. "Thank you. Oh, thank

you so much. It's just what I want to do. But I've got to gain a little or my bathing suit will fall off."

"I wouldn't mind that."

She laughed, a ringing laugh filled with joy. "You wouldn't want to see me naked now. I look awful. Everything sticks out or sags. Give me time and I'll look like myself again."

"You will always be the most beautiful person there is."

"I'm dying to see Kay when she gets back from Boston tonight. I hope she'll come around as soon as she gets in. I arranged for her to go to Elizabeth Arden's and get a facial and a new hairdo."

"She's plain, but she's nice. I don't think they're going to be able to transform her too much. But it was thoughtful of you to arrange it."

Pearl returned with a tray and put it on a small table near Katie's chaise.

Harry urged Katie to eat the crackers with cream cheese. She did eat two, to please him and Pearl, then pushed the rest away. She drank her juice.

Satisfied, Pearl left.

"Harry, do you think we have too much?"

"What brought that on?"

"I don't know. I've just been thinking. I mean, so many people are starving and all." She paused and frowned. "And we seem to have so much."

"True. But I don't think we're extravagant. Most people with our income have three or four houses. We have just one. And servants: we have four—when Carol's well enough to be here—compared to fifteen or twenty of other people. We live well, but not in any grandiose manner."

"Do we do enough with our money? Do we help people who don't have anything enough?"

"I think so. Over half of your income is given to charities and educational institutions. Good God, a tenth alone is given for education. And the same with my income; a great deal goes to others. I think it's enough. We live well, but we don't waste."

"I spend too much on clothes."

"Probably. But just think of the pleasure you give others when you pass them on; you give to people who would never to be able to afford such clothes. And when you give them to the thrift shop or some such place, they make a profit on them that helps their financial goals."

"I think I'm not going to buy so many from now on."

Harry smiled at her. "All those designers will be sorry to hear that."

Katie studied her nails. "I don't do enough with my life. I could be doing things to help people."

"I won't argue with that."

"I'm a little tired. Would you mind if I shut my eyes?"

"You go right ahead. I've got some desk work to do anyway." He stood up. "Are you doing it here or at the office?"

"Here. I'll be right here. If you want me, call for Mario; he's around here someplace and will hear you. He'll come get me."

Katie looked at the flowers. Why had Kay told Harry anything about Mario? Had she said something to Kay? Had she let something slip that made Kay suspect her? She couldn't remember. She would try to remember. There were things going on that didn't fit together, but she couldn't tell what they were. She did know that she must try to remember them.

Katie closed her eyes and felt herself slipping away from reality into a semi-dream world, the area between consciousness and unconsciousness, where awareness stands guard against total oblivion.

Harry felt trapped and didn't know what to do about it. He had experienced a sense of purpose while Katie was in the hospital and he had made himself be with the children. It hadn't been easy at times, with Freddie and Lavinia bickering and screaming, and failing to draw Joe out of himself, but he had felt a certain reward at being with them. He felt there was something more to his life than just signing logging contracts and making money. He had actually felt like a father. He knew it was the fear of losing Katie that had scared him into this responsibility, but once in it, he found he liked the role— especially with Kay there to help him. They had cooked out on the grill several times; they had played poker one night, he and Kay letting Freddie and Lavinia win most of the time; they had gone to two movies, all of them together. At meals, Kay would say "Now Freddie, tell Daddy what you and Miss Anderson did yesterday to help Mario in the garden," or "Lavinia, tell Daddy how we helped Pearl make a cake that looked like a bunny." He had seen Kay sitting side by side with Joe in serious conversation; the three of them together had talked about the pros and cons of legalizing marijuana. One day when he came home from the hospital in the afternoon, he and Kay had taken all the children into the fields to look for wild strawberries, each with a small plastic bucket Kay had bought for the occasion. Sometimes Kay would tell Miss Anderson not to bother to be with them, that she and Harry could handle everything themselves and for Miss Anderson to take some time off for herself. He had enjoyed himself those days, before school was out and Freddie and Lavinia were whisked off to camp and before Joe left. He had been part of a real family. It had lessened the screaming and tension and made them all seem like a close family. He wasn't sure he could have pulled it off without Kay.

He wanted to be a good image, a father-figure to his children, to eat with them when he was home, to discuss their problems with them and hear about their fun-times. But he couldn't be here every day, nor was he sure he wanted to be. He didn't want to feel trapped.

And now, again, he felt trapped. If he went north to see Doris, he would be abandoning Katie when she needed him. He knew how dependent she was on him. If he left her for too long, she would start drinking again. Not that he doubted she would start it sooner or later, but he hoped it would be later. It might really kill her if she started too soon. She couldn't lose blood like that, not as weak as she was, and live through it again. No, he couldn't leave her.

Doris had tried to hide the disappointment in her voice, but he could hear it still. When he had told her he could go with her to Maine, she had been as happy as a child with a new toy. It had eaten at his insides to have to call her and tell her it was off. "Don't worry, I've got my other Harry to go with me," she had said, trying to speak lightly. He had felt like a rat.

He had wanted to go with her; he wanted to get away, to go where he didn't have to face his everyday problems. He was a coward and he knew it. He didn't want to feel trapped with Katie. He loved her, but he wanted to be free. Not all the time; just for a little while. Just a week off someplace—Maine, the Adirondacks, Ontario, wherever. Just a week put everything back in perspective. If he couldn't get into the woods periodically to set his mind at peace, he would go nuts. He needed that quiet and remoteness; he needed to be with Doris every few months. Then, in between he could function here as he should, as the loving husband and father. If he couldn't get away, if he would be betraying Katie every time he left, he wouldn't be able to face anything. It was those breathing spaces in his life that kept him level and sane.

Maybe the month at the beach would be all right. If he could keep Katie away from the Club, if they could be alone and live a quiet life, it might be all right. Maybe he would be able to get away and do a little fishing; maybe he would be able to leave her for part of each day. Well, he'd just have to wait and see.

Right now he'd better finish going over these contracts.

Katie and Harry had a quiet dinner, sitting at either end of the long table in the dining room. It had gotten too buggy to be outside after dark; the invisible "punkies" appeared from nowhere and set one's skin to fiery itching.

Pearl had tried hard to think of things that Katie could and would eat and had succeeded.

"This is perfect," Katie said as she ate a piece of poached Dover sole in lemon butter. "It would only be better if we had a glass of chilled white wine with it."

"It's good enough without it," Harry countered, but secretly agreed with her.

After dinner they went into the library to watch TV. Katie tried to call Kay, but there was no answer. "I wish she would hurry and come."

Kay finally did come. She came down the hallway, calling "You there?" and stopped at the library door.

She had on the gray Pierre Cardin dress Katie had bought for a benefit lunch at the Metropolitan. A black lizard bag hung on her shoulder, swinging smartly by her small waist. Her face had been transformed from drab, colorless "plain Jane" to picture-book radiance. Her eyes, cheeks, lips had all been delicately colored, making even the shape of her face different.

"Wow." Harry stood up. "Don't you look stunning."

Katie nodded in agreement. "Kay, you look absolutely fabulous."

Kay's walk was different. She no longer had that hang-dog, stiff-legged gait, but seemed to radiate confidence.

"Do you like it?" She touched her hair that had been softly waved and gathered back in a loose swirling bun. "I feel like the ugly duckling four-fifths of the way there." She laughed. "Just imagine if I really made it to the swan stage."

Harry kissed her cheek. "You look great now. You don't need to do anything more."

"Harry's right." Katie waved her hand at the sofa. "Come sit here and tell me all about it."

"Harry," Kay said, crossing to the sofa. "Do you think I could have a Scotch-and-soda? I'm beat. It's been a long day."

Harry hesitated, frowning slightly at Kay.

Katie looked at him. "Get it for her, Harry. I want to hear about the facial, and it would just bore you to listen. Go on and get Kay a drink. And bring me a cup of coffee, please." It fleetingly crossed her mind that Kay had deliberately asked for a drink to test her. It also crossed her mind that it was an inconsiderate request.

Harry couldn't get over the change in Kay. Even her hair was shining and bright. Katie had sure been right about this; a trip to Elizabeth Arden was just what Kay needed. He had never thought of her as being pretty before, but she really had a nice sweet face. She was exuding a sort of happiness and brightness he had never seen—what would be called "beaming." She had been hiding behind that mask of no makeup, the wrong clothes and no interest in her hair. But all that had been changed. Amazing. She had suddenly come alive, showing herself to be a vibrant, attractive woman.

He listened to Kay and Katie gossip about beauty rituals, silently amused at the importance they now both put on being attractive. Katie was still by far the better looking of the two; she had a unique femininity that didn't come from a jar of cream. If only she were a good mother and took an interest in the children, the way Kay did, what a perfect person she would be.

When it was time for Kay to go home, saying Katie looked tired and needed to get to sleep, Harry said he'd walk her home.

"Oh, please, don't bother," Kay said.

"It's no bother. Besides it's a nice night and the exercise is just what I need. Wait a minute while I help Red upstairs," he said.

"What nonsense." Katie stood up and kissed Kay goodnight. "I'm perfectly capable of getting up the stairs by myself. You go ahead and walk Kay home." She really didn't want Harry to leave her, but he did like to take a walk at night.

"Katie looks so much better," Kay said as soon as they were

outside. "She really looks like her old self again. Too thin, of course, but she'll gain some weight now that she's got Pearl cooking for her."

"I just wish she would find something to do to keep her occupied. She just doesn't seem to be interested in anything."

"If I were Katie, my time would be so full I wouldn't know what to do. If I didn't have to work to earn a living . . . oh, the things I would like to do instead."

"Such as?" The tree-frogs were singing loudly in the marshy area of the woods that lay on their right.

"Well, I'd like to do volunteer work with the new hospice group, and maybe even put in a day at the thrift shop. Then I'd like to sit in on all sorts of courses at the college, art courses and some literature ones. In between, if I had any time left, I'd like to help out at the museum, doing volunteer work in the art library or being a docent. I'm used to handling groups of children and might be very good at that."

Harry linked his arm through hers. "You would be very good at that. It doesn't sound as though you'd leave yourself much free time."

"I'm used to too much free time now. My days are filled, but the evenings and the summers are too free. But I would change all that if I could afford to. There's so much to do in this town; any college town is exciting, but this one is especially so—with the art and theater. Poor Katie, with nothing to do. So much around her—and nothing to do."

They walked in silence to the end of the driveway, the gravel crunching as they stepped in unison.

They stepped into the glow of the street lamp on East Road, and headed toward the neat white garage that housed Kay's apartment.

"Listen to the night sounds, Ka—" Harry caught himself. My God, he had almost called her Katie. He felt a prickle on his neck.

"Aren't they wonderful?" She seemed not to have noticed the cut-off of her name. "I love teaching school, but I also love the peace of the summers. I don't even have to set my alarm clock."

"I thought you were going to teach a course in the summer school."

"I do. But it doesn't start until eleven. That's a lot better than the eight o'clock schedule I meet the rest of the year."

They reached the door at the bottom of the stairs that led

up to her apartment. Kay took out her key and unlocked the door. "Would you like to come up for a drink?"

"Sure," he said, holding the door for her. "I would love a drink. I didn't want to have one in front of Red, this being her first day back in temptation."

"Oh, dear, maybe I shouldn't have asked for that drink." She led the way up the narrow stairs.

"It was all right." He watched her slim buttocks undulate, level with his eyes as he followed three steps behind her. "Red says she wants other people to drink and do whatever they want; she says she's going to resist temptation."

"Maybe she got scared enough this time to really be serious about laying off." She took the key out of her bag.

He watched her unlock the door at the top of the stairs and reach in to turn on a light.

They stepped into the room. "You get out the ice," Kay said, "I'll get the booze. What will you have?"

"Got any Scotch?"

"Yes." She walked to a low cupboard door behind her desk and brought out a bottle. "I seem to have a little of everything." She laughed. "I so rarely entertain . . . it's so small here to do much in . . . that some of this stuff is pretty aged."

"Won't hurt it any. Where do you keep the glasses?" Harry went into the small kitchen and got out a tray of ice.

"Just above the sink." She barely raised her voice, but he heard her.

"You want Scotch, too, I take it," he said.

"Yes, I do. A weak one."

"With water or soda?"

"Soda for me. There's some in the frig."

While Harry made the drinks, Kay looked at herself in the mirror, turning her head to one side then the other, gently fluffing her hair, pinching her cheeks and smiling. She looked to make sure he couldn't see her, then she pressed her hands against the front of her dress, running them from waist to neck. She smiled again.

She went and sat on the sofa. Harry brought out the drinks and also sat on the sofa.

"That tastes good." He stretched out his long legs. "This is very comfortable."

"I guess I have all the room I need. Though sometimes I wish I had more, such as when I'd like to have the children in for an afternoon. It's just too crowded for the three of them, or even two of them, for very long. Lavinia is always wanting to come visit me, and sometimes I do have them in for tea. But they get so restless in such cramped quarters that they don't stay very long. Have you heard from them since they got to camp?"

"No. But it's only been . . . well, almost a week. I wouldn't expect to hear anything so soon."

She smiled at him, tilting her head to what she thought must be an attractive angle.

Harry looked at her, then he sat forward and swilled down his drink. "I've got to get back. Red will be waiting for me. I want to make sure she goes to bed and gets a good sleep." He stood up.

Kay took his glass and put it and hers on a small table at the end of the sofa. She stood up and walked to the door. "Thanks for seeing me home." She was facing him, so close to him that she knew she must seize the opportunity and be bold. She put her arms around his neck, resting her forearms on his shoulders and locking her fingers behind his head. If he rebuffed her, this could be no more than a gesture of friendship. If he felt any desire . . .

Harry searched her face with his eyes. "You're very pretty." He put his hand on her face, touching it with his fingertips. Then he put both arms around her and drew her to him, closing his mouth over hers. Kay pressed hard against him, moving slightly from side to side, such a small motion, but she knew he felt it.

Harry pulled back. He frowned and looked away. "I've got to go." He quickly opened the door and left, closing the door behind him.

Kay put her arms up in the air and slowly turned in a circle. She smiled and pushed her loose coil of hair up with both hands. If she prayed, prayed real hard, maybe he would come back. Tonight or some other night soon. Just in case, she must be ready. She went into the bathroom and ran a hot bath.

Harry walked quickly home, surprised and disturbed. Something had happened he never had dreamed of happening. He couldn't understand his feelings. He wasn't angry or sorry or happy or anything. He was upset, but he didn't really know why. Was it because he had betrayed Red? But he had betrayed her often before. It had never really bothered him too much—

she was the one he loved. He just thought of it as being a part of some grand scheme of nature. And she was no saint. She didn't know he knew about Steven, but he did. He knew she had been in that sand dune even though she became so indignant when she found out about him and tried to pretend she was a wounded innocent. He knew she probably had seen Steven on other occasions. And there probably had been others; he just didn't happen to know who they were. But it didn't matter, because he knew he was the one she loved. The others were just diversions.

He had been pretty faithful to her, all things considered. He hadn't slept with anyone other than Doris for years. Before he met Doris and got to know her in her bereavement, he had slept with an occasional barmaid or innkeeper's wife when he was traveling. But there hadn't been too many of them, and none of them meant anything to him. Until Doris. Doris was different. She was a very special person.

But Kay! What had happened there? It really baffled him. Was he overcome by her new appearance? Or was he lonely again? Was it because he had had to call Doris and cancel the Maine trip that he was feeling a little sorry for himself, feeling like a man who needed to be coddled? He didn't know. He walked up the driveway to the front door, all the way without knowing, wondering what was happening.

There was no one like Red. She had a body that was not to be believed. And she enjoyed it so much, reveled in the ecstasy he brought to her. He felt like he was really doing something big when he made it with Red, and she made him feel like some goddamn hero, someone really special, someone bigger than life.

But he hadn't had Red for a long long time. When he got to bed at night, she was asleep—passed out, if he were being honest. And then she slept later than he did in the mornings. And the last three weeks had added to the number of nights without her. He hadn't made love to her for at least three months, maybe four. Maybe more. He couldn't even remember when they had last done it, it had been so long ago.

He thought of that luxurious red hair, flowing against the pillow, her long delicate hands trailing over his body, then her own body, guiding his hands, caressing him, the red ready and waiting for him. He would like to have her right now. He wanted to hold her, smell her, taste the sweetness of her body and enter her. He wanted to feel bigger than life. Right now.

He turned out the lights and went upstairs. Their bedroom door was ajar, a faint light glowed from within.

She was half under the covers, one arm up across the top of the pillow, the other arm lying limply by her side. The short puffed sleeves of the summer nightgown hid her white shoulders. She looked so frail and thin. She slept soundly, not moving when he sat on her side of the bed. He gently touched her hand. It felt cold and almost lifeless. He couldn't wake her up. She was too fragile to make love to him, as fragile as a doll made of white flower petals, her skin as transparent as tissue paper. He drew back his hand and slowly stood up, not wanting to disturb her sleep. She needed her sleep.

Harry walked softly out of the room and back down the stairs. He unlocked the screen door to the terrace and went out and sat in the cooling evening air. The tree-frogs could be heard from here too, but not as ringing as when he and Kay had walked past them on the driveway.

Harry sat alone for a very long time. Finally he got up and went back inside, carefully locking the screen doors. He then walked the length of the hallway and went out the front door, closing it softly behind him. He walked down the drive, listening to the rhythmic crunch of his steps, to the road, and turned toward the white garage where a light burned upstairs.

With her heart racing, Kay listened to Harry's steps. At his knock, she opened the door and took his hand, leading him into the darkened living room. He put his mouth over hers and held her tightly to him. When they pulled apart, she led him to the bedroom, feeling almost faint with the weighty anticipation. The light from the bathroom shone in a wide strip across the floor, defining a path to the foot of the bed. Kay again put her arms around his neck; she could feel him responding, his body tensing, an urgency in his desire consuming her thoughts. She slid her hand to his shirt, her fingertips touching the hair on his chest for the first time. He kissed her mouth, her eyes, her neck, and put his hand on her firm breasts where her nipples pressed forward, straining against the silk.

As he released her and began to take off his clothes, she first pulled the pins that held the wavy bun at the back of her head and shook out her long hair, letting it trail over her shoulders. Then she stepped out of her thin robe and went to the bed to wait for him, the palms of her hands damp with nervousness, her fingers trembling with long-starved appetite. She prayed she would know what to do; she had rehearsed it so many times in her mind, remembering every detail she had learned from those smelly, pimply-faced boys who had sweated over her body fifteen years before. She had seen the explicit acts of sex in magazine pages and at the few X-rated movies she had attended. Now those limited experiences, plus her unwavering belief in her instincts, would have to carry her through. If she failed him tonight, it would be the end. She must be as careful and as delicate as a flamingo choosing its mate. She must excite and satisfy him the way Katie did . . . or had. If she had to, she would fake an orgasm; Masters and Johnson had clued her in on that.

Harry lay beside her and began to stroke her long hair. Kay held her breath and gently touched his shoulders with her hands, leaning over him so her breasts would press into his chest. Dear God, let her know what to do; don't let her fail now; give rein to that inborn knowledge stored in her libido. She gasped and held her breath, waiting for him to take her.

At her gasp, Harry swiveled their bodies and put his mouth on her sweet-smelling breast, sucking her ripe, swollen nipple. She writhed with pleasure as his hand went to her legs, pushing them apart, stroking the insides of her thighs. He rubbed her gently, then forcefully, hoarsely voicing his pleasure at her moistness. She lightly ran her hands up and down his body, moaning softly as she felt his throbbing hardness.

When he spread her legs farther apart and kneeled between them, his lips on her abdomen, asking "Do you mind?" her heart began to pound, not knowing what to expect, but knowing she must answer "No, no, I don't mind." She encircled his head with her hands and stroked it, her hips arched in ecstasy as his tongue touched her. It was beyond belief. She had no idea it would be so exciting.

His mouth finally came back to hers, his body covering her; she bowed her legs and raised her knees, no longer fearful of ignorance, but rejoicing in her seductive responses. As he gently thrust himself into her, time stood still for her, the past gone and the future holding in abeyance, letting her have the prolonged awaited period of rapture without interruption.

The gripping orgasm came easily, making her heart contract with bliss. Like waves on the beach, one bursting explosion followed the previous one for them both, and after he had withdrawn from her, he entered her once more. Still the night had not moved forward as they silently and hungrily made love.

Spent for a brief period in each other's arm, their hands still intimately exploring, they soon felt another surging wave of sensation. He rolled onto his back and Kay gently moved her head down his torso, down toward his slim hips and muscular thighs. She knew what she was supposed to do, and prayed she could do it. After a moment's panic and hesitation, she quickly learned the depths to go. As she felt his power and tasted the sweet beauty of it, she relaxed. It was going to be all right.

"My God," he muttered, "what you're doing to me . . . " his voice broke off as he pushed himself farther into her mouth.

When he pulled her head up and again rolled on top of her, she heard herself crying out with a pleasure she never knew was possible. Nothing had prepared her for this exquisite sensation, nor the intoxicating headiness at the moment of supreme climax. As once more the pulsation against him ebbed, she let a past memory intrude and was thankful for that dingy back seat that held the mess in her mind; now the sheet beneath them was blessed with nothing but the wet sweet smell of sex.

Kay clung to Harry, knowing she could never give him up now. No matter what she had to do, she could never give him up.

13

DURING THE NEXT TWO WEEKS KATIE IMPROVED. SHE SWAM a little more every morning, ate regular meals, though still small ones, turned on the TV less and less and began reading books. Along with weight, she regained some of the vitality she had once had. She enjoyed the morning laps in the pool and looked forward to them as soon as she woke up. She took Valium several times a day to control the craving for alcohol.

By evening she was tired and went to bed early, exhausted. During this period of recovery she did not dream, sleeping without worries like a small child, aided by two sleeping pills when she got into bed.

She organized her clothes, selecting the things she would need for the month at the beach. She counted the days until July, lovingly advancing her desk calendar one small square further each morning, racing with the numbers to be well enough by then to do all the things with Harry that she longed to do. The thoughts were tonic to her.

She daily fought the desire to have a drink in spite of the

Valium. Sometimes the struggle was so great she almost suc- cumbed. Sometimes, lonely and bored, when she would be on the verge of giving in and sneaking to the pantry, she would pop another pill in her mouth, hastily put on a bathing suit and plunge into the pool, stroking the length, up and down, until she was exhausted and had no desire for anything. She was proud of herself for being so strong. Once she was back to her normal self, then she would consider the possibility of con- trolled drinking—a little wine with meals, a light drink before dinner. But for now, she wasn't going to allow anything to get in her way of getting well. She needed Harry; he must need her by now too. She wished she weren't so exhausted at night. But never mind, she would say to herself, in just another week I'll be as fit as the Katie Harry once knew and we'll be away by ourselves at the beach. She would save herself for him until then, and once there, they would revel in all the pleasures they both knew how to revive. They would spread towels behind sand dunes and turn back the clock.

Kay came almost every day to see her. Katie no longer noted the Geoffrey Beene or Calvin Klein or Adolfo; she began to accept Kay as a fairly attractive well-dressed woman. Even the thin hair no longer bothered her.

It was her own looks that she cared about now, not Kay's. She saw herself clearly in the antique mirror, and though her face was a little thin, the puffiness had gone from her cheeks and jowls and the redness from her eyes. Almost every morning she picked up the photograph of her father and hugged it to her, smiling, knowing what he was thinking.

Harry was happy with her progress. "You're doing great, Red. I'm proud of you."

"I still get so tired at night. I can hardly wait for dinner to be over so I can go to bed. It's not very fair to you."

"Don't worry about it. Better not to rush things when you've been so sick. In no time you'll feel like your old self again."

"I don't have any desire for sex now. Is that awful to admit?"

"Red, honey, you forget how sick you were. It will come back."

"Can you keep on waiting for me?"

Harry put his arms around her, his face into the back of her neck. "We'll be on vacation next week. I'll give you good odds you'll feel like it then."

"You have to be alone every night. Poor Harry."

"It's the other way around. I wish I didn't have to leave

you so much at night. But there are a lot of loose ends to tie up before we go away."

"You've been wonderful to be here so much during the day with me."

"Sure you don't mind my going out at night?"

"Not a bit. I go to sleep thinking of all the nights we'll be together in July."

One morning Katie was lying on her chaise under the shade of the oak, reading a novel. She had been swimming and her hair was still wet in the back, though the front had dried and rose up in uncontrolled curls around her face. Her skimpy bikini was the only thing cool enough to wear in the oppressive late-June heat. She had orange juice in a tall glass, floating with ice cubes, within reach of her hand. She longed to be at the ocean where there was a breeze off the sea.

Harry came out onto the terrace, letting the door glide shut behind him. Katie could tell by his face that something had happened, something bad.

She folded the book shut, alarmed. "What's the matter?"

"I just got a call at the office . . ." he looked into the distance with his jaw set.

Katie sat forward. "Go on. About what?"

"It's not good." He shook his head and came to sit on the end of the chaise, pushing against her bare feet. Suddenly he reached for her hand.

"My God, Harry. What is it?" Katie felt frightened. She grasped his hand tightly.

"It was Lavinia's camp. The director. He called to say . . ." he pulled his hand away, putting the heels of both hands against his forehead ". . . he says Lavinia's in trouble. She won't stop screaming. Two days now she's been screaming . . . and she won't stop. He says . . . he says we should come get her and take her out of camp."

Katie slumped back, the muscles tightening in her neck. "Take her out?" She had only been there two and a half weeks.

He nodded.

"You mean bring her home?"

Again he nodded.

"For how long?" It was almost July.

"For good. He says they can't have her there." Harry leaned forward with his elbows on his knees, his head still in his hands. "I'll go up and get her."

"Go up and get her?" Katie couldn't believe she was hearing this correctly.

"Yes. I said I'd be there as soon as I could. It's about a five-hour drive. Maybe more."

"Harry, we paid for the whole summer."

"He says he'll send us a refund."

"Good Christ. Who cares about the money? We paid to have her kept there for the summer. They're breaking their contract."

"Red. She's got to come home." He turned his head sideways and looked sadly at her.

Katie looked wildly around her, then back at him. "What happened? What did she do?"

"She didn't do anything. It's what the other girls did to her. They . . . oh, God . . . they hung her doll by the neck from the rafters. When she saw it she started to scream and . . . can't stop. Oh, my God. Poor Lavinia."

The grisly scene hung in front of Katie, the doll swinging limply, the smiling plastic face rigid above the rope, Lavinia screaming. "She must have done something to have made the girls do that," she said. "It doesn't take much imagination to see her being the pest and show-off that she is, butting in, being obnoxious, having to have things her way, acting as if—"

"Stop that, Katie. She's a little girl who's been hurt and needs help. That's all we have to know for now."

There was a long pause, a wave of heat drifting across them as a few trees trembled in the hot air.

"What will we do? Miss Anderson's in England." Katie felt her hands beginning to shake.

"Is there someone else we can get in to be with her?"

"I don't know of anyone. Miss Anderson is the one who handles all that."

"Maybe we could call her and find out. Meanwhile, we have Pearl to help out with her."

"Pearl is not paid to be a nurse to Lavinia. She has all her other duties."

"This is an emergency of sorts. She'll have to help out until we can get someone else." He looked questioningly at her. "Do you think you feel up to spending some time with her? She'd love to swim with you in the mornings and play here on the terrace while you're reading."

"Harry. We're going away in a week. We won't be here." And no matter how much she hated herself for saying it, she wasn't going to give in to Lavinia and let her ruin this new-found health.

"I'd better go get ready and drive on up there."

"Wait, Harry. Call the director back, say you're coming up to see her and calm her down. You can always calm her down when she's like this. Say you'll come talk to her, then maybe she can stay on."

He shook his head. "It won't work. I already suggested I come up and talk to her. He says they want her to leave. She's just not fitting in."

Katie threw her book across the flagstones and looked quickly toward the lawn, her eyes traveling past the beds of blue iris to the long row of peonies in full bloom, their heavy heads hanging low in white conformity.

"It can't be helped, Red. She's got to come home."

"I can't believe that she's really going to spoil our summer. Do you think she has been awful deliberately just so she would be sent home?" Even as she said it, she knew that wasn't true; Lavinia had liked the idea of going to camp. "Why has she done this? Why? Why couldn't she have tried to get along with the others?"

"She's just a little girl. There aren't any easy answers."

"We'll have to find someone fast. I will not allow her to ruin my vacation at the beach with you. I don't want you down there worrying about her the whole time. Christ, why did this have to happen?"

Harry stood up. "Take it easy, Red. It'll be all right. Even if we can't get off right on the first, we'll go as soon as we get Lavinia settled with a new nurse."

Katie looked at him suspiciously. "Are you sure?"

"I'm sure. But her mental health is more important than our vacation, and we'll have to see about that first."

Katie closed her eyes and leaned back her head, her fists clenched by her side. She heard Harry walk across the hot stones and open the door, then the soft whish as the door closed again. Good God. Why did this have to happen? Why?

As soon as Harry left to go to New Hampshire, Katie called Kay.

"What are you doing?"

"Nothing much. Want some company?"

"Yes. Come up and swim with me. This sweet summer day has just turned sour."

"What's happened?"

"Harry just left to go get Lavinia. To get Lavinia and bring her home."

"No! Why?"

"God only knows what she did, but it's not hard to imagine. Whatever it was must have riled the other little girls, because they . . ." even Katie found it hard to repeat the mean cruel act against Lavinia.

"They what?"

"They took that stupid doll of hers and hanged it."

"Hanged it?"

"Yes. Hanged it. By the neck, from the rafters in the cabin. I must say it's very crude of them."

"I think 'crude' is too nice a word."

"Of course you do." Katie felt it was, too, but didn't want to admit it to Kay. "You're always so hung up with kids and their problems, you'd like to make this into some Shakespearean tragedy. Anyway, enough of that. Would you like to come up and swim?"

"I can't right away. But I'll be up in an hour or so."

"Fine. I may still be in." Katie hung up, irritated with herself. Pill time again. She had already taken two Valium, but they hadn't started to have any effect yet. Another one probably wouldn't either. What she really needed was a good stiff drink.

She ran to the door, past the Harrisons and one-m Simons, across the terrace, her bare feet sinking into the soft grass below it, ran to the pool and took a running dive into the cool water. She swam up and down, up and down until she was gasping for air. She dragged herself out and lay on the hot concrete, gulping air, breasts heaving. Her closed eyelids blazed red and yellow with brilliant streaks and dots. The hot sun began to dry her skin. Soon she would be roasting and wet with perspiration. She must move into the shade. But it was so much effort. So very much effort. How tired she was.

How long did Harry say it would take him to get there? Five hours? Then five hours back. And probably an hour there to talk to the director and counselors. Eleven hours. He wouldn't be back until very late, not much before midnight. She had to call Miss Anderson in England. What else did she have to do? She would like to have a cool drink.

Katie sat up and slid back into the water.

* * *

Miss Anderson boarded the plane in Gatwick ten hours after Mrs. Harding had called. It hadn't been easy to make the air arrangements so quickly, but she finally had done it. She had been summoned to the phone, right in the middle of her slab bacon, fried egg, fried toast and fried tomato, leaving her tea to get cold. It hadn't surprised her to hear Mrs. Harding's voice, apologizing, hoping she had figured out the time change correctly, and was not waking anyone up.

She carried a small travel bag into the first-class cabin and found her seat—fortunately by the window—and took out a John le Carré she had bought in the airport. She buckled her seat belt and began to read. It would help take her mind off the abrupt change of plans.

Poor Mrs. Harding. She had sounded so upset and apologetic, but clearly unable to handle this crisis herself. She had said she only needed the name of someone else to call, but when Miss Anderson had said, "I'd better come back myself," she had sounded greatly relieved. Who knows? This might mean a bonus. And after only two weeks, she had decided England wasn't the end-all answer anyway. Everything was too expensive and she missed Pearl's cooking.

They left England and climbed high above the Atlantic. Miss Anderson leaned forward slightly and scanned the heavens: nothing. They were alone in the sky, one metal body filled with flesh and blood in that whole blue universe, and nothing, no one else.

She sighed and shut her eyes. What bad luck. Lavinia should have been able to get along. If it had been Freddie sent home, then she could understand it. In fact, she had been half expecting it, and was therefore not really shocked when she heard Mrs. Harding's voice. But to be told it was Lavinia was indeed a surprise. She must have done something really horrid to those other girls; she must have been a real pest.

Lavinia's round face with the freckles across the bridge of her nose and her cheeks dominated her thoughts. She had a sweet laugh, sparkling mischievous eyes that could be endearing. Could be. If only she weren't so difficult, wanting attention, starved for love, screaming when she couldn't get her way.

But she did all right at school. She was hardly the most popular child in her class, but she was no worse than most of those runny-nosed unruly boys. Other girls seemed to cluster together, leaving Lavinia on the edges. If they played jump-rope, she was never asked to turn, and even if she yelled that she wanted to do it, they pretended not to hear her and got someone else.

She tried too hard, Lavinia did. She demanded too much. She wanted to be included, but ended up excluded because she pushed too hard too obviously, too demanding to be the center of attention. Poor child. She would never get the love she was looking for—not as a child, and not as an adult. She'd never get it in a hundred years. When your own mother doesn't love you, you can never accept any other love freely.

She hoped this wouldn't turn Mrs. Harding back to the bottle. She had talked to Pearl once before leaving London and learned that Mrs. Harding was behaving herself, eating well, exercising and not drinking. This might be just the thing to change all that. She hoped not. Mrs. Harding needed to take care of herself. She wouldn't be able to survive another bad hemorrhaging like that, not unless she were a lot stronger than she was—and maybe not then. She and Mr. Harding needed to get away. He, as much as she.

In fact, especially he. He didn't know what kind of sneaky designs Kay had on him. At first, when Mrs. Harding was in the hospital and he seemed to be paying a lot of attention to Kay, Miss Anderson had thought it was just because Kay was trying to help him with the children and was really concerned about Mrs. Harding. Then little things started to come out, leading to suspicious undercurrents. The fancy ways, sticking her little finger out when she drank tea, telling the children it wasn't proper to put the milk carton on the table—the kitchen table at that—and asking for a plate for the cookies when Joe brought them out in a box. Just the sort of things a real lady like Mrs. Harding wouldn't give two hoots about.

Yes, Kay had even fooled her at first. Miss Anderson had even laughed to herself about Kay, the likes of her, putting on all those airs just because she finally got herself some expensive clothes. Well, Kay might not know it, but you can't make a silk purse out of a sow's ear, and there was no point in her trying. Or so Miss Anderson had thought at first. Then Kay started to show her true intentions, referring to her old friend as "Miss Anderson" in front of Mr. Harding. Ha! As if she hadn't known her for thirty-five years. And inching her way into Mrs. Harding's place, sitting at the head of the table, oohing and aahing over every word the children uttered. And Mr. Harding eating it all up, smiling and laughing and never noticing he had a viper in silk at his table. Miss Anderson had seen Kay worming her way into his confidence, acting like a damned fool. But the real revelation had come that night she leaned toward him and hintingly confided that Mrs. Harding had a special fondness for Mario. Fortunately Mr. Harding hadn't seen the vile intentions beneath that remark. But Miss Anderson had.

Men were such fools. Having a little flattery and a good listener and God-knows-what-all turn their heads so. It was one thing to be attracted to some beautiful movie star, but to start paying attention to some plain old-maid school teacher was ridiculous. Not that Mr. Harding was making moon-eyes over her or anything like that, but it was easy to see he was fond of Kay and liked being with her. What a fool he was. Such a nice man, but what a fool.

And that was all two weeks ago. What had Kay been up to while Miss Anderson had been in England? But surely she would be back in her proper place now; with Mrs. Harding's release from the hospital, it was impossible to imagine Kay acting so uppity in that house. Mrs. Harding would cut her down to size in one sentence. But if Kay were capable of sneaking around in bushes spying on people, she was capable of any kind of lowdown trick. Well, she'd find out as soon as she got home. It wouldn't be hard to tell. Not for her. Now that she was on the alert, she'd soon see what Kay was doing.

Kay had felt hot and sticky all day. She lay flat on her back on her bed without any clothes on, her breasts tilting toward the sides of her thin chest. She frequently fondled them, running her fingers around the nipples until they hardened. She had planned on being with Harry tonight. He should have called her to tell her he would be away. He must have been upset about Lavinia to have forgotten. He hadn't been here with her last night, staying home to be with Katie. Kay wondered if he had gone to bed with Katie last night and made love to her. He hadn't up till then; she had asked him and he had told her. Katie had been home two weeks and he had not screwed her once. Kay smiled. He hadn't needed Katie because he could get it from Kay any time he wanted to get it. He could just walk up those steps, open the door and unzip his fly. She would be on the bed waiting for him any time he wanted her.

The thought of him being away from her for a whole month tortured her. Katie would be well by then, and they would be together all the time. There was no point in trying to fool herself into thinking he would want her when Katie was ready and willing to let him be with her; there was no point in believing in a make-believe world that she was better in any way than Katie. No point at all. Katie was better at everything—when she wanted to be.

A grand plan had begun to form in Kay's mind that morning when Katie called and told her about Lavinia. Maybe, just maybe, when Lavinia came home Katie would be so upset she would start to drink again and then she would end up in the hospital again, out of the way. Maybe they wouldn't go to the beach. Maybe. She knew Katie had wanted her to come up and be with her today, and God knows she sure had wanted to be in that big expensive pool cooling off. But it had crossed her mind that if Katie were alone all day, bored and upset about Lavinia, it might just push things along. And once Lavinia was home, acting like a wretched spoiled brat, then Katie would really be pushed to the brink. And just suppose a bottle of vodka, here and there, out of the way, out of sight to everyone but Katie . . . just suppose . . .

Kay drew up one knee and crossed the other leg over it. She wondered what Katie was doing right now. She had recognized that tone of voice on the phone. Katie had needed her. But she, Kay, needed Harry. It was just that simple. Dog eat dog. Harry was the lover she knew he would be. It gave her the shivers to think of him. She uncrossed her knees and parted her legs. She would be ready for him when he came. She smiled and softly whistled through her teeth, feeling trickles of perspiration run down her neck.

Katie was awake early the next morning. She raised her head and looked at Harry's side of the bed. The pillow was dented and the sheet rumpled. She had never heard him come in or get up. She dropped her head back onto her own pillow. How could she sleep so soundly? And so much? It was all those bloody tranquilizers and sleeping pills. As soon as they got to East Hampton she would stop taking sleeping pills. For the whole month. She would be awake at night and awake in the morning for Harry.

She sat up and pushed the sheet down, looking at her white nightgown made of the thinnest handkerchief lawn. She couldn't remember when she had started sleeping in nightgowns all the time. It must have been while she was in the hospital. But now she was almost well, and she would discard them.

Today she would have to face the ordeal of Lavinia. She put her hands over her face. No, no, she mustn't think of it as an ordeal. She must try to show her some love. She must make an effort to be calm and welcoming. No matter how wretched Lavinia was, she had just been through a terrible trauma. Yes, she would be nice to her. Then Harry wouldn't feel so bad about leaving her when they went away.

Katie took a shower, put on shorts and a halter, stepped into flat sandals, brushed her hair and applied just the right amount of makeup for a hot summer day. Then she went downstairs to look for Harry.

She could hear his voice in the kitchen and knew by the tone he was talking to Lavinia. Katie took a deep breath and walked down the hallway to the kitchen, passing the pantry that held such welcoming temptation for her.

They were both sitting at the kitchen table, Harry drinking coffee, Lavinia eating a bowl of cereal.

"There you are." Katie walked to Harry and kissed the top of his head. "I never heard you get up."

"Doesn't Mommy look pretty and summery." Harry smiled at her.

Katie went to Lavinia and kissed the top of her head too. "I haven't seen you for a long time, Lavinia. How are you?"

"I'm all right now. Daddy came and got me and Jewel and I'm all right. I hated it there." She scooped cereal onto the spoon and shoved it into her mouth.

"Yes. So I gather. Well, that's too bad. Summer's not very exciting around here, but I'm sure you'll find things to do. Have you eaten?" she asked Harry.

He nodded at her.

Katie went to the stove and poured herself a cup of coffee. "Where's Pearl?"

"She's around here somewhere. I told her to go on and do whatever she had to do; I'd get Lavinia's breakfast."

Katie took the cup to the table and sat down. She looked at the puffy round cheeks rapidly chewing. "Miss Anderson is coming home to be with you." The chewing stopped and the small brown eyes looked at Katie in a frightened manner. "Isn't that nice?"

Harry said: "Did you ask her to come back?"

"No. I didn't. I asked her the name of someone to call, but

she wouldn't hear of anyone else coming. Said she'd come home herself."

"That's being a little overconscientious, don't you think?" Harry asked.

Katie sipped the coffee and ignored the question. "Isn't that nice of her, Lavinia?"

"Will she be mad at me?"

"Mad? Of course not. She was very sorry to hear you had . . . had difficulty." Katie glanced at the doll by the child's chubby bare feet.

Lavinia began eating again. When she had finished, she looked at Harry. "Can I have some more?"

"May I have some more, please," Katie corrected.

"Sure you can." Harry got up and went to a cupboard and brought out a box of Sugar Smacks. He poured some into the bowl, then got milk out of the refrigerator and poured that onto it. "Enough?"

She nodded and began eating.

"Isn't that one of those sweet cereals children aren't supposed to eat?" Katie looked at him.

"It won't hurt her once in a while." Harry put the cereal and milk away.

Katie watched him with interest. She would never have known where the cereal was kept. What a good parent Harry was.

"Does Miss Anderson let you eat those sweet cereals? Or is this just a Daddy treat?" Katie asked Lavinia.

Lavinia tucked the cereal into her cheek. "Sometimes she does. She says it's a treat for us sometimes."

"Well," Katie shrugged, "she certainly knows best." She looked at Harry. "I'm not sure what time Miss Anderson will be back. I get mixed up on the times."

"She can't be here much before tonight at the earliest. With luck she could get a late afternoon or night flight out and that would put her here . . . I'm as bad as you. Would it be early this morning? Anyway, it should be sometime today."

Katie felt a surge of relief. If Miss Anderson was getting in today, maybe even by midday, then maybe she could handle a little time with Lavinia. She got up and refilled her cup.

"Want me to fix you some breakfast, Red?"

"No, thanks, Harry dear. I'll have some yogurt." She opened the refrigerator door and brought out the orange juice and a container of yogurt. "Anyone else want any?"

"I hate it." Lavinia pushed her empty bowl away from her. "Jewel hates it too. They had it at camp and we hated it. It's yucky-tasting."

"You don't have to eat it then." Katie finally found the drawer with spoons. "I happen to like it."

"If you've finished, sweetie, why don't you run up and watch TV for a little, while Mommy and I get a few things settled about today. Give me a kiss first." Harry held out his arms to the round body; she quickly hugged him, then grabbed her doll and ran from the room.

Katie sat back down. "What is it we have to discuss about today?"

"I'm worried about Freddie."

"Freddie?" The spoon slipped from Katie's hand onto the table. "What brought that on? Have you gotten a call about him?"

"No. No call."

"Then what is it?"

"I want to see him."

"Oh, Harry, for God's sake. Just because Lavinia has been sent home does not mean that Freddie is also in trouble. We have had no word from his camp, and you know what they say about 'no news.'" She picked up the spoon and looked around the big, bright modern kitchen. She had never eaten in the kitchen before. It was rather pleasant.

"I'm worried about him, Red. I called the camp a little while ago to see how he was making out."

"And?"

"Said he was fine. No problems."

"There. You see what I mean. No problems." She took a spoonful of the yogurt.

"They didn't tell us Lavinia was in trouble until she had a crisis situation. She apparently had been at odds with the other girls in her cabin from the beginning, but no one told us. If they had told us before this happened, I might have been able to spare her. . . ."

"Harry, really. I'm sure the director and counselors would have called if they had foreseen this. It certainly was unfortunate."

"It was worse than unfortunate, Red. That was very upsetting to Lavinia."

Katie ate in silence, not saying that Lavinia seemed perfectly all right to her.

"I'd like to go up and see Freddie, see for myself he's all right."

"Go." She drank the coffee, draining the cup.

"I'd like to go today."

"Today! Before Miss Anderson gets back?" Katie suddenly felt deeply threatened.

"Yes. I thought about it all night. I can't get it out of my head. I want to go right away."

"What about me? Are you just going off and leaving me with Lavinia?" That was the wrong thing to say.

Harry looked at her in disgust. "It won't hurt you to be with her today. You're almost well, and plenty strong enough to handle that. And after all, Pearl will be here to help."

"Don't go, Harry. I want you here."

"I'm worried, I tell you. I want to see for myself he's all right."

"You were gone all day yesterday."

"Jesus, Red, I know you're lonely. I try to be here as much as I can during the day."

"You're gone a lot at night, too," she complained for the first time.

Harry didn't want to add it made little difference, as she went to bed so early and almost instantly fell asleep. He looked at her. She was looking much better, but she still wasn't very strong—she tired so easily. He would have to be patient to be with her. "I know." He took her hand. "We'll be away soon. It'll all be all right then."

Katie bent her head over his hand and kissed it. "I love you. I've never loved anyone but you. Maybe that's my trouble. If I could love a bunch of other people, then I wouldn't miss you so much."

"I love you, too, Red. No one but you. And the kids." He stroked her head.

Pearl came into the kitchen. "Oh, Mrs. Harding. I didn't know you were up. Shall I get you some breakfast?"

Katie straightened her back. "I've had juice and coffee and yogurt. That's enough."

"You didn't eat much of the yogurt." Pearl lowered an eye toward the container. "Would you rather have something else?"

"No. I'll finish this. I'm just being slow."

Harry pushed back his chair and stood up. "I'm going to go on up there. I'll be back in time for dinner."

Pearl raised an eyebrow, pulling her eye up with it, and looked at him questioningly.

Katie started in on the yogurt again. "All right. If it makes you feel better."

"Pearl," Harry turned to her. "Can you keep an eye on Lavinia today until Miss Anderson returns? Whenever that may be."

"Sure, sure. No trouble at all."

"She can swim with me this morning," Katie reluctantly said. "It's when I have to rest that she'll need watching."

"Don't worry about her." Pearl took the empty cups from the table. "She'll be fine with me. I'll watch out for her."

Harry left.

Katie put down her spoon. "I've had enough of this. Do you think you could get some shrimp for dinner? I feel like having some."

"Certainly I can. Do you want them hot, or do you want a shrimp salad?"

"Cold, I think. I don't know what time Mr. Harding will be back . . . he's going up to see Freddie for the day. Have them cold and they'll be ready whenever he gets back."

"Just you and Mr. Harding?"

"Yes." Katie stood up and went to the door. "Just the two of us. Miss Anderson should be back by tonight, and if not, then Lavinia can eat here with you."

Katie had just made up her mind that she wasn't going to take any more sleeping pills, starting this very night. She also wasn't going to get herself too tired out during the day. "I'll swim with Lavinia in an hour or so, then we'll have some soup and a sandwich for lunch. Then I'll rest. This hot weather is so tiring."

"It sure is. That pool feels good."

The pool was reserved for the help from three to four every afternoon; that didn't interfere with the midday or late afternoon swimming for her and Harry if he got home early enough before dinnertime. If no one was home, the help could use it any time they wanted. It seemed to be an agreeable arrangement.

Katie stepped into the pantry just as Pearl said: "Did that camp call to say for him to come see Freddie?" It was a deliberately offhand tone.

"No. He just wants to see him, to make sure he's all right. I wish Joe would call."

"No news is good news."
"That's just what I said about Freddie."

Harry drove up Route 7, through Bennington, Shaftsbury, Manchester and into the Green Mountains of Vermont. It wasn't like going through New Hampshire, which he had done only the day before, with the deep-hued lakes ringed with thick growths of evergreens. Here the valleys stretched across farmland and woodland to the mountains, spectacular views and distant hills. There was a bit of both, the lakes and mountains of yesterday, and the stretches of pastures and mountains of today, that reminded him of the Adirondacks.

He wondered what Doris was doing. She would be going to Maine next week with Harry. He would have to call her before then. Right now she would be at the store, keeping books and riding herd. Then she would come home and she and Harry would romp in the yard. She would heat herself some soup, probably made from vegetables left in the freezer, and eat it with a piece of toasted homemade bread. This afternoon, she would fuss around in the garden, then go to the lake to fish, she and the puppy, gliding across the still waters, watching a loon nervously guarding his nesting site, quietly coming up on the beaver house to see if there was any new activity. She would probably catch a fish; if it was a good size, she would keep it. Her hands weren't very big, but she could grasp a fish by the upper jaw and swiftly bend its head back to break the spine, putting it quickly out of its misery. She hated suffering. She would toss it in the bottom of the canoe, then she would paddle slowly around the lake, looking for nesting birds, listening to the songs of the warblers, noting any wildflowers that had bloomed since she last looked. Her short hair would be blown by the wind, her unpainted face tanned by the sun. She would smell of Cutter's and put a hat on her head as soon as she got back on shore to keep the bugs away.

Harry tapped the palms of his hands on the steering wheel of the Cadillac. As soon as they got back from East Hampton, he would go to the Adirondacks for a week. He missed her. He had talked to her while Red was in the hospital, but that didn't take the place of seeing her.

He hoped, for all their sakes, he found Freddie in good spirits. He didn't know why it had bothered him so much last night—the worry about Freddie. He couldn't get it out of his mind. Probably because he was so accustomed to seeing Freddie and Lavinia together, that when one was in trouble he automatically assumed the other one was too. He was sure it was nonsense. But he wanted to check and put his mind at rest. He'd never be able to go away for a month without knowing Freddie was all right.

He passed so many cars with the windows down, the passengers looking hot and miserable, while he sat here in the comfort of air conditioning. He felt a twinge of guilt when he saw the cars with hot air rushing through them, children panting in the back seat, dogs hanging their heads out. No question he enjoyed the good life. Red's father had made it possible for him to have everything he needed and wanted to enjoy the pleasures of the privileged class.

It made his mind cloud over to think of the life he was leading. Not just his life with Red—but with Doris and now with Kay. My God, he didn't even know how that one had happened. But it had, and he was enjoying it. He knew it was a reaction to Red's sickness, her frailty and inability to make love now. If Red had been well and sober and waiting for him with open arms every night, he never would have gone to Kay. But Red hadn't been able to do any of that. Not for a long time now. He had just drifted to Kay the way jetsam comes in on a wave, effortlessly and without a fixed plan. It wasn't hurting Red—so long as she didn't know—and it wasn't hurting him. He would call a halt to it when they got back from East Hampton. But for now, Kay was a refuge for him, a respite in his troubles. He needed someone to hold and love, to help him forget about contracts and troubled children. He needed Red, but . . . And Kay was so much like her. Funny he had never noticed before. Not only in figure and looks, but in actions. They were both positive and determined, wanting their way. They both knew how to satisfy a man.

And then there was Doris.

Harry turned into the narrow dirt road with the modest sign "Camp Bear Run" and drove slowly across the potholes, looking at the stands of timber on both sides of him, unconsciously appraising the value. He came into a clearing dotted with trees, where a half-dozen small log cabins on his right sloped down the mountain side; to his left there was a bigger cabin, apparently the main lodge, with "Office" over the door. He looked around. It was the kind of place he liked: rustic, orderly, unpretentious. This was a good place to learn about nature.

He parked in front of the main lodge behind a truck, stepped out into the hot air and walked to the door. Before he could knock, a short round man with rimless glasses opened the door and smiled at him.

"Can I help you?"

"I'm Harry Harding. Freddie's father."

"Oh! How nice." A look of surprise registered in the pink-rimmed eyes behind the glasses as the man stuck out his hand. "I'm Bill Babcock, the director. Do come in. This is quite a surprise. You didn't say anything about coming up when I talked to you. We weren't expecting you." He had a flabby handshake, weak, with skin soft as a young girl's.

Harry didn't feel the welcome was exactly heartfelt. "Have I come at a bad time?"

"No, no, of course not. Usually . . . well, it's just that we like to have a little warning. Some of the children get hyperactive if a parent shows up unexpectedly. If we have time to prepare them for the visit, they take it more calmly. Come in." He led the way into a modest room with a desk, filing cabinet, a few slat chairs with cushions in them and woven Indian rugs hanging on the walls.

"Nice," Harry said, looking around. "No, I won't sit down. I've been sitting for hours. I wanted to have a look at things and see Freddie. We're going away next week, and I just wanted to see him before we went. Has he been all right?"

"Oh, yes, yes, fine. Just fine." He took off his glasses and wiped them with a red handkerchief he pulled from his pants pocket. "He gets along with the other children, and he causes no trouble with the counselors. We have a pretty small group here, as I'm sure you can appreciate. There are three campers and a counselor in each cabin. The counselors are trained to handle children with special problems. If one of the children needs extra attention—more than that one counselor can give him—then we have an additional staff member to handle that. He's a nifty young man who has a great many duties, but he finds time to take on a child if he needs special attention. Very bright, conscientious fellow."

Harry began to get an uneasy feeling about the man he was talking to. He didn't know what it was, but he made Harry uncomfortable. His hands were too white, not the kind of hands an outdoorsman would have. Harry cleared his throat and glanced at the rugs again.

The director went on: "Freddie is like a lot of children we've had. He's right on the verge. He doesn't need medication to keep him calm; yet he can't be left alone to be by himself. Some of our children . . . well, Mr. Harding, some of our children are very difficult and we have to use stronger methods with them. But not with Freddie."

"What do you mean by 'stronger methods'?"

"Medication mostly. Of course, they usually come with their own prescriptions from their doctors, and we wouldn't do anything to uspet that. If we have to increase the dosage, we always call their doctors to get the approval on it. If that fails, then the young man I just mentioned takes them into a small cabin all by himself, and he sits with them and disciplines them if necessary, and holds them and keeps at it until he's conquered whatever devil they have in them."

"Devil?" A cold shiver went up Harry's spine.

"Just an expression. It's a controversial handling of these cases, I know; there are two sides to this. It's recognized by many child psychiatrists and denounced by others. But we have seen amazing results, and we have a lot of backing in the world of psychiatry. Don't you want to sit?"

Harry shook his head. "You go ahead."

"I will. We had a long hike this morning and it pooped me." Director Babcock sat down, crossing his legs in front of him; above the socks, his skin was white and shiny. "We have a lot of successes leave here, Mr. Harding. A lot of successes. Some of the children—we have boys only, but I suppose you know that—come in here hating the world, ready to tear everyone apart. Most of them leave happy, well-adjusted, finding it easier to face the real world back home." He smiled benignly. "We wouldn't be able to do it if we didn't keep them all summer, you know. A shorter term just wouldn't work. It takes half the summer to just get their confidence. But at the end of eight weeks, we've molded them into new boys."

Harry felt the hackles rise on his neck. He hadn't sent Freddie here to be molded. He had sent Freddie to have a good time.

"Do the children enjoy themselves? I mean, do they do things that are fun?" Harry asked.

"Yes, yes, of course they do. We swim, have cook-outs and sit around the campfire singing songs and telling stories. We hike in the woods and learn about nature, and a little later we'll go on a big all-day hay-ride. They all love doing it. Of course we have fun. That's what camp's all about, isn't it?" He cocked his head and peered over his glasses at Harry, again smiling.

"I'd like to see Freddie now, if I could. Or if he's out doing something, I could just watch him for a bit until he's finished."

"Certainly. Certainly. I'm not quite sure where he'd be just now." He stood up. "If you'll excuse me a minute, I'll go find out." He started for the door.

"I'll come with you."

The director looked at him in a puzzled manner with pursed lips. "If you wish."

They went back out into the clearing, dotted with tall evergreens and maples shading the cabins.

"Jim! Jim!" the director called. He pointed to the other end of the main lodge. "That's the dining room, if you'd care to see it. And just beyond that is the rec room, with pingpong, games, you know, rainy-day doings. Jim!"

Just across the dirt track a door opened in the nearest small cabin and a young man stepped out. "Yeah?"

"Would you come here, please?"

The young man was dressed in blue jeans and a T-shirt with a smiling-bear logo across the front. His hair was longish, falling onto his neck in the back. He walked quickly in sneakers, a light, cautious step as if he were crossing a field of marbles.

"Jim, this is Mr. Harding, Freddie's father. This is Jim. We don't use last names with the counselors; it's better to keep everything informal."

Harry shook hands with the young man. "I'd like to see Freddie, if you tell me where he is."

The director and Jim looked at each other. Jim spoke: "Sure thing. I'll have to think for a minute where he is."

"Well, Mr. Harding, I'll leave you to Jim. If you have any questions, I'll be in the office."

Harry had decided he didn't like the director and was glad to be rid of him. He looked around the woods and buildings. He also didn't like the way they had looked at each other. He got the distinct impression they didn't want him to see Freddie.

"I assume all the counselors are male, since this is a boys' camp," Harry commented as they crossed the track, heading toward the woods.

"Yes, sir, they are." Jim paused every now and again to look around, as if to get his bearings. "Freddie could be out on a hike or at the lake. Of course, he might even be in the showers now," he added nonchalantly. "We could look at the lake first."

"All right, let's go." Harry was determined not to leave his side, and he figured Jim knew it. If Jim was trying to think of some excuse for not taking him to Freddie, he wasn't buying it. "I'll just follow you until we find him."

Jim looked at him with his eyes cut sideways. "Sure you don't want to wait under a shady tree?"

"No, thanks. I'll go with you."

Jim veered his course. "Then we might as well go straight to the showers."

The building was tucked behind a dense spruce growth, almost out of sight from the other buildings. It was bigger than the sleeping cabins, but not as big as the main lodge. It was made of the same wooden slab siding as the others.

Jim walked ahead of him. "You know some of our boys are on a lot of medication. . . ."

"So Mr. Babcock told me."

"Yes? Well, maybe he mentioned some of our treatment methods to you also." He waited for an answer, but got none. "Some of the kids respond to just a regular routine, working with the same people every day, keeping a tight schedule. Other kids have to be kept on these drugs to keep them calm. And then others . . ." they were almost at the entrance of the building. It had no door; the opening faced a wooden wall, forming a sort of short corridor. Harry could hear water running and even out here could smell that musty odor of damp wood that never got to dry out.

"This is where the showers are," Jim said unnecessarily, pausing at the entrance. "Sometimes, we find that a shower will calm a kid down no end. Not taking them at a regular time or anything like that. No kind of routine to it. But it's just that sometimes we find if a kid gets out of hand, the best thing to do is let him stand under the shower for a few minutes. Water has a very soothing effect. We could let them go swimming, of course, but that tends to get them excited. That seems like a time to get excited and splash around. But a shower . . . now, that's different. It has the effect of water, but it's not stimulating. Know what I mean?" He turned to look at Harry.

Harry listened to the water running in the building. He jerked his head slightly, indicating to Jim he wanted to go in.

Inside, another young man, dressed in tight blue jeans and

a smiling-bear T-shirt, was reading a magazine, his chair tipped back against the wall. He raised his head and looked questioningly at Jim.

"Hi," Jim said. "This is Luke. Luke, this is Mr. Harding. Freddie's father."

Luke let his chair drop back to the floor. He snapped his head toward the sound of the running water, then stood up. "Hi."

Harry nodded at him and walked past him, past the pegs on the walls to one where a towel hung, to the stall near the end of the row of stalls. There were no curtains on the stalls; the metal compartments were small and bare with only a water fixture high up in the compartment and one knob to turn on the water. That was also high up, out of reach of a small child.

Harry stopped in front of the stall where water splashed out onto the soggy wooden slatted floor. Inside, standing directly under the stream of water, was Freddie, his arms hanging at his sides, his dark hair running in thin streams down his forehead, his head shaking from side to side, his fat, softly bulging body trembling, his mouth moving with chattering teeth. He was muttering something so softly Harry couldn't hear what it was, not over the sound of the teeth, muttering and shaking. His eyes were glazed and lifeless. He seemed not to see Harry.

"Freddie." Harry sank down into a squat, putting himself eye-level with the shaking child. "Freddie." His voice was low and quiet. "Freddie, can you hear me?" Nothing but the shaking and mumbling.

Harry stood up straight and reached into the water to turn off the tap. The water was icy cold, colder than any water he ever remembered feeling. He turned the handle to "Off." His heart had turned cold and his veins felt as if they were running with that same icy water.

"Freddie. It's Daddy. Can you hear me, Freddie?"

The body shook, not just blotched white or blue-white, but mottled with a great searing redness as if he had been burned with ice. Harry took Freddie's hand. The nails were blue, the fingers shriveled and frozen. When he touched the skin on his shoulder, it was like touching a pale red balloon packed with snow. "Freddie." He reached behind him and pulled the towel off the peg. He gently wrapped the towel around the icy body, the mumbling sounds now becoming distinct in the noiseless building.

"Ninety-eight. Ninety-nine. One hundred. One hundred and one. One hundred and two. One . . ."

Harry looked fiercely at the two young men who had not moved. They were just standing there watching him. "Where are his clothes?"

"In his cabin," the one called Luke answered.

"Get them."

Jim and Luke looked at each other, then Jim nodded. Luke dropped the magazine in the chair and went out.

Harry picked Freddie up and carried him out of the damp building into the sunlight.

"Now Mr. Harding . . ." Jim ran behind him.

Harry walked up the pine-needle path toward the Cadillac, past the stately trees and low-growing scrub.

"I'd better get Mr. Babcock to come talk to you," Jim said.

Harry never looked at him as he grimly cradled his burden.

"He'll tell you some of these methods are controversial, but . . ."

Harry reached the car and opened the front door on the passenger side. He sat Freddie down on the seat and looked back at Jim. "Get his clothes."

"They're coming now. See. Here comes Luke." He ran toward the main lodge. "Bill! Bill! Come here!"

Luke handed the clothes to Harry, who carefully dressed Freddie in his T-shirt and blue jeans. He pulled the socks over his icy feet and dropped the sneakers onto the floor. He then reached into the back seat for his own jacket and wrapped it around Freddie's still-shaking shoulders.

"A hundred and twenty. A hundred and twenty-one. A hundred and twenty-two. A hundred . . ."

"Mr. Harding! Mr. Harding! What's the meaning of this? You can't come in here and take the children out." The fat director came running heavily across the rough-cut grass.

Harry shut the door and walked around the car to the driver's side. He looked briefly from the director to each of the young men. Then he got into the car and started the engine, turning off the air conditioner.

"Some methods are bound to surprise you, but . . ." the director shouted through the car window.

Harry saw the wet towel on the car seat. He picked it up, opened the door and threw the towel out into the dirt. Then he turned the car around and drove out the narrow dirt road.

"A hundred and thirty-three. A hundred and thirty-four. A . . ."

About halfway home, Harry was roasting, sweat pouring down his face, his shirt sticking to the leather car seat. He had opened the windows in the back to let in some air, but still he sweated. He stopped in front of a store.

"You wait here, Freddie. I'll get us a Coke."

The shaking had stopped; the teeth no longer chattered; some of the redness had disappeared; the dark hair had dried—but the same dead look was in Freddie's eyes. And he was still counting.

Harry clenched his fists and got out, his shoulders hunched like an old man's, and went into the store. He bought two Cokes, a bag of the potato chips and a box of Oreos. When he got back to the car, he opened the potato chips and handed them to Freddie. Freddie slowly lowered his head and put his pudgy hand around the bag of chips and began to eat them, starting over at "One." Harry held the Coke out to him, but he ignored it. Harry wedged it on the seat between them. He opened the window on his side and slowly drank his Coke, the fury in him still throbbing at a peak. He couldn't remember when he had ever felt such deep anger and so sick at heart.

He watched Freddie eat the chips, not pushing them into his mouth the way he once had, but taking them one by one, counting them as he ate them. He counted during the entire drive home. Sometimes he went past a thousand; sometimes when he got there he started over again at one; sometimes he just stopped in the middle of a sequence and started over. It made no sense to Harry, but somewhere in the dark cold reaches of Freddie's mind there must be a scheme of counting.

Freddie had finished the potato chips and let the bag fall to the floor. Harry handed him the box of Oreos. "Want me to open that for you?"

Freddie didn't answer, but took it. "Forty-three. Forty-four. Forty-five." He began to open the box. When he got out the first cookie, he said "One" and counted, eating, the whole box. "Two. Three. Four."

Harry drove again, in silence, the rage in him controlled like a bull ready to burst out of a box.

Kay never came and Katie was furious. She was damned if she would call her again.

She took the glass of tonic and sat on the terrace to watch the shadows lengthen on the darkening grass. She hadn't seen Mario since she had been home. Maybe he was spending his time in the vegetable garden; maybe he was weeding the other side of the peonies; maybe he was untangling the thickets in the wilds by the road. She didn't have any urge to see him anyway—even though Harry seemed to be gone most nights, and in spite of what she had told him, she was lonely.

It was when she had a few drinks that she wanted to be with someone. All those experts were wrong when they said alcohol dampened sexual desire. A few drinks just whetted the appetite. Not getting really bombed, of course—that did shut down the libido—but a few drinks took away all those inhibitions and stirred up the juices.

She looked at the tonic. It did nothing for you at all. It wasn't even a good thirst quencher. She hated the bland, plain, dull taste of everything she drank. She wished she could have a drink, a real drink. Just as soon as she was strong and well again, she was going to work out a proper plan for drinking; just a little, enough; but not too much.

How was she going to be able to manage, even for a week, having Lavinia back home, screaming, crying, climbing over Harry when he was here, interrupting, getting in the way? How was she going to be able to take it without a good stiff drink? Thank God Miss Anderson said she would come home at once. She'd better give her a bonus.

Katie looked again at the glass of tonic, then suddenly hurled the clear liquid over the edge of the terrace. She stood up and went into the house. She could watch TV for a while, then go to bed.

14

KATIE SAT ON THE TOILET SEAT, TRYING TO GET THE TOP off the bottle, pressing and turning with clammy fingers, until finally she made it. The pills rattled as she shook two into her hand and slapped them into her mouth. She reached for the glass of water she had ready and waiting, then leaned against the cool porcelain back. She wiped her eyes with her fingers, letting her thoughts roll around explosively, trying to keep them from settling on a focal point. By hunching forward she could reach the washcloth she had already wet and left on the sink. She ran it over her face and neck, breathing deeply, consciously taking as deep breaths as she could. If Harry didn't come soon, she wouldn't be able to make it.

She breathed deeply again and pressed her hands into her stomach to stop the churning. She wished she could stay this way, hugging her despair to her like a tight ball.

Time passed and she began to feel the effects of the pills. She stood up and walked stiffly to her dressing table, where she sat and looked at herself. She was a mess, not only from so much swimming, but from everything else. She had never wanted a drink more in her life. Not in all the years could she remember so desperately wanting a drink. The bloody pills were just pills; they didn't take the place of a drink sliding down the throat to still the churning of her insides.

She picked up the hairbrush and watched her face as she slowly brushed, stroking over and over. The mascara had run below her eyes and spread over the pinks with harsh strokes. She took a Kleenex with her free hand and wiped around her eyes and down her cheeks. She would have to start over. Everything was so awful: her face, her life, everything. She was ashamed that she had hated being with Lavinia all day and she blamed Harry for leaving her for some ridiculous whim. And Joe. If only she had talked to Joe and tried to understand him before he went away from her.

She put down the brush. What had happened to her? Her father's masterpiece, with hair of Titian gold, what had happened to that make-believe girl who had everything and ended up with so much misery? She looked at her father's photograph on the table. Why had he had to die? Why had that ruddy Irish complexion gone the color of wet granite?

With effort, she applied a sketchy makeup job, found a pair of slacks and shirt she thought would be cool and stepped out of her shorts and halter. She was a failure as a mother, a failure as a person. Her whole life had just reflected the achievements of others. She had been her father's daughter, basking in his success, doing nothing to make herself a notable child; she then became Harry's wife, the wife of the big lumberman, living his life in this town because he wanted to; she was the mother of Joe, the straight-A student who kicked more goals in soccer and batted in more runs than any of his teammates; yes, she was even the mother of Freddie and Lavinia and remembered for their horridness. There was nothing in her life she could claim as her own.

She had definitely made a real effort today to be with Lavinia. She had sat on the sofa with her and Jewel, and read them a book about a wild stallion. Then she had taken her in for a swim, where Lavinia refused to try to learn anything. Katie had discovered she could float, and had tried to tell her that if you could float you could swim. But Lavinia would scream and raise her head out of the water every time Katie tried to get her arms moving forward in a simple crawl. Then Katie tried the backstroke, which was likewise a failure. After an hour of this Katie was exasperated, shouting at her angrily and telling her what a bad sport she was not to even try, and then Lavinia had started screaming and crying. Pearl had had to come take her out of the pool and back into the house.

Then they had tried lunch together. Katie asked Pearl to bring two trays onto the terrace, with soup and sandwiches and iced tea. Lavinia had tasted her soup and pushed it away, saying she hated pea soup. Katie had pointed out it was not pea, but watercress and that she would like it. Lavinia announced she hated watercress soup without trying it again. Katie had insisted she try it, and in pushing it farther away from her, Lavinia had pushed it off the tray, off the little wrought-iron table onto the floor, where the soup cup crashed into myriad pieces, the creamy green running into the crevices between the flagstones. Fortunately Pearl had not yet left, so Katie had not gotten up and hit Lavinia. She had simply gone into the house to take another Valium. By the time she returned, Pearl had cleaned up the mess and Lavinia was happily stuffing the sandwich into her mouth. Katie had eaten slowly, hoping they could drag out the meal; once it was over, she didn't know what she was going to do with this child she was saddled with for the day.

By the time they had finished lunch, with Lavinia eating an enormous piece of pound cake, Katie was given a reprieve when Pearl had come out and asked Lavinia if she wanted to help make cookies.

"Cookies! Yea! Can I, Mommy?"

"Yes. Yes, by all means." She hadn't asked Pearl to do that, so she didn't feel mean about pushing Lavinia off on her.

She had then stretched out in the shade, hoping to fall asleep so she would be able to stay awake tonight. She hoped Harry had satisfied himself about Freddie and was on his way home now.

She brushed her hair some more. Yes, the swimming and lunch had been bad, but she hadn't felt the need of a drink so much after them. It was what happened next that had kicked any complacency out of her.

She had been almost asleep when Pearl had come to the door. "Sorry to bother you, but you're wanted on the phone. It's Miss Wright. She asked for either you or Mr. Harding. I told her he had gone for the day, so she asked for you. She sounds upset."

Katie jumped up and walked quickly into the house. Kay upset? It wasn't like Kay to get upset.

"Kay?" She had picked up the phone with apprehension. "What's happened?"

"Oh, Katie, something terrible has happened. I can't even bring myself to say it." Her voice had a muted funeral-parlor tone.

"Kay. What is it? Do you want me to come there? I'll come right down."

"No. Yes, I mean. I want you to come. But I want to tell you now." She had paused. "Give me time."

"Take your time, Kay. Take a deep breath. It will help. Are you sitting down?"

"Yes."

"Take your time."

"Katie, it's . . . it's Dan . . . you know . . ."

"Yes, Dan, your brother. What's happened to him?" Katie, now brushing her hair, again felt the sudden fear that had rushed through her. "Has something happened to Dan?"

"Yes."

"Kay, don't say any more. Let me come right down."

"No! I want you to know first! Just listen!"

"I'm here. Take your time." Katie remembered speaking calmly then, but now her knees again felt weak as she stepped into the slacks and her hands began to tremble. She had known he was dead, but she had to let Kay say it.

"Dan's dead," Kay had blurted out.

"Kay, oh poor Kay." She gripped the phone. "How did it happen? Was there an accident?"

Katie stopped and looked out the window of her dressing room. A chill pricked at her back as it had when Kay answered, snorting a vicious laugh at the other end of the line.

"Yes, there was an accident! He had the accident all by himself."

"I don't understand what you're saying."

"He killed himself! That's what I'm saying! He killed himself! I'm so ashamed. I wouldn't be able to say it to anyone else." Her voice had caught in her throat, clipping off the last word.

"My God." Katie had sunk to the floor, holding tightly to the phone with both hands as if it were a lifeline. "Poor Dan." Her heart now pounded again. She was afraid of death, even the death of someone she never got a chance to meet. Death was so final, robbing those left behind of so much love still left in them to give.

Katie was afraid she was going to cry again; she went back into the bathroom and drank a glass of cold water. If she could have one drink before she went down to Kay's, she would be able to face it better. Just one drink was all she needed—and how she needed that.

She leaned her forehead on the doorjamb. She wouldn't do it. She just couldn't. She would have to be strong, for as long as she possibly could.

Kay had been so angry when Barbara called to tell her about Dan that it was all she could do not to slam the phone down on her. How dare he do such a thing! And to fool them into thinking nothing was wrong. Nothing wrong, indeed! Something had been wrong with him for about twenty years now. It had all started when he met Barbara. That peace-marching idealist who told him to do whatever he wanted to do, had practically encouraged him to be a drifter. She thought nothing of picking up lock, stock and barrel and traipsing off to another town and starting over, finding out where the Democratic headquarters were and getting to know the local politicians. Stupid bleeding heart. She even organized a picket once around the sheriff's office when she heard he had arrested a black man for loitering in a white neighborhood. As if it were any of her business. Meddling do-gooder, saying it didn't matter to her where they lived; there was always plenty to do in any town to keep her busy. Just dragging along behind Dan, cooking barbecued spare ribs for him and his cronies and turning his collars when they began to fray. That boy, Jake—Jacob they had to name him, as if it weren't going to be obvious enough what kind of blood he had—he would never amount to anything, not with the nomadic life he had been raised in. Well, it was too late to do anything about him now. The twig was bent.

And what had Barbara said? "He didn't give any explanation. He just left a note saying he was sorry. That was all." He had fooled her too, apparently. She hadn't been so damned smart after all.

Well, at least he had been thorough and neat about it. He had driven to a remote dead-end lane, hooked a hose to the exhaust and brought it in the window, stuffed towels around the opening to make a tight seal and that was it. Very neat. Not what you'd call classy, but neat.

Kay had stormed back and forth between the two rooms,

kicking the chair legs, throwing pillows across the room and looking blacker by the minute. How dare he do that? That sort of thing was bound to get around, especially in a small town like this, and everyone would know. She wouldn't be able to hold her head up. If the children at school found out—and someone was bound to tell one of them and there it would go—they would snicker and point at her behind her back. "Her brother committed suicide." "Isn't it a shame?" He might as well have been a murderer. Murder and suicide were the same sin. She had always been taught that and Dan knew it too.

Kay kicked the bed pillow again. She would have to tell Katie, and dear God, Katie would have to tell Harry. What would Harry think, going to bed with the sister of a suicide? Would he keep his distance from her now, as if she also were tainted? Would he avoid meeting her eyes, afraid of giving himself away? Would he start making excuses about not being able to be with her?

Damn him! Even if he was her brother. Damn him! Why did he have to go mess up her life, just when she thought she had it under control. Kay wept, not from grief, but from anger. She tasted the bitter tears of self-denigration, and choked on the hopes she saw drifting away from her. If he had spoiled everything for her, she would curse him until the day she died.

She blew her nose and went to the phone. She might as well call Katie and get it over with.

When she hung up she felt much better. Just the way Katie had said "Poor Dan" gave her a flicker of relief. Maybe she wouldn't be so humiliated after all. It was a shameful filthy trick to have played, but maybe Katie—and of course Harry, since he seemed to think just the way Katie thought—maybe Katie wouldn't look at it that way. Katie had peculiar notions. All that money had really given her distorted values. Not exactly un-American, but close to it.

Katie was a bleeding heart herself. If she had been born poor and a kike, but still smart, she probably would have turned out like Barbara, getting up petitions, marching, picketing, door-to-door do-gooding. Yes, they were a lot alike. They both had these queer notions about people. Not alike in looks, of course; she couldn't imagine Katie with black hair and a hooked nose with a little bulb on the end. But they both were the same kind of champions of people. Dear God, just look at the way Katie treated her servants. If one of them asked for a Rolls Royce, she probably would go out and buy it. And the idea of

giving the imperious Hilda the whole summer off! Two weeks
was all she deserved, like any other worker. But Katie not only
gave her the whole summer, but she paid for her plane tickets
and tour tickets to boot. God, what a fool Katie was. She was
glad the old biddy's vacation had been cut short and she was
coming back. Hilda made about twice as much as a teacher.
That glorious father Katie was always talking about wouldn't
have done anything stupid like that. If he'd given away all his
money like that, Katie wouldn't be sitting in the cat-bird seat
she was in now.

Kay began picking up the room. She wouldn't do anything
about the red eyes that gave her a facsimile of grief, but she
would straighten up a bit. Katie wouldn't be moving too fast.
This kind of thing upset her no end, and she would be having
a hard time getting herself up and out the door. She was probably dying to have a drink, and fighting it like crazy.

A drink? Well, why not? Why not have a drink, Katie? It
will make you feel so much better. And there's no time like
the present.

A sudden elation made Kay stop in the middle of the room
and thoughtfully raise both eyebrows. She looked down at her
hand with the short fingernails accustomed to hard work and
washing dishes. She hated those short nails. They didn't go
with her new clothes or her new makeup. It would be nice to
have long tapered fingernails like Katie's. Very nice.

Kay first went into the tiny kitchen and got out a dust cloth.
Then she went to the cupboard in the living room where she
kept the whisky. She opened the cupboard and looked at the
four bottles. Scotch, Bourbon, gin and vodka, all opened and
in varying degrees of fullness. She carefully arranged space on
the top of her desk near this cupboard, then sat the four bottles
out onto the end of the desk. She made sure the doors were
open wide, exposing the bare shelf. She dropped the dust cloth
onto the shelf so it hung over the edge, clearly visible.

Next she got a tray and emptied the contents of the neigh-
boring cupboard onto it: scraps of string, wire, flashlight bat-
teries, a hammer, a sack of nails, a screwdriver, vacuum-
cleaner bags and shoe polish. She sat this tray on the floor
under the open cupboard. Then she stepped back and nodded
in grim satisfaction.

All she had to do now was sit down and wait for Katie.

* * *

Kay heard Katie lightly running up the steps. She had left the downstairs door unlocked, anticipating the appropriateness of meeting her in the gloom of the living room, where she had lowered the shades halfway down. As soon as Kay heard her at the top she threw open the door and gave her best look of anguish.

Katie put her arms around Kay and hugged her tightly. She kissed Kay's cheeks, leaving a smear of wet tears.

"Kay, it's so awful." With her arm still around Kay's shoulders she led her to the sofa. "Come sit here. You must be just shattered by this."

"Yes," Kay spoke in a low voice, not looking at Katie's whiter-than-usual face that betrayed how upset she was. "I am. I can't believe it. I just can't believe it. He sounded so well when I talked to him. He never mentioned any problem. I just can't believe it."

They sat on the sofa, Katie holding the bony shoulders and making cooing sounds—"there, there now" and "poor Kay" and "go ahead and say it"—whispering the words softly the way most mothers would have to a child.

Kay finally disentangled herself and leaned back. "I just can't believe it," she repeated, noticing the desperate haunted look in Katie's eyes. "And poor Barbara, and Jake . . . that's his son."

Katie squeezed the sofa cushion by her leg. "So awful for them. Will there be a service?" She was on the verge of tears and trying to think of something constructive.

"Not much of one. She said she was going to have the body cremated, which was what he wanted, then just have a grave-side service. I can't imagine there'll be much of that even. He wasn't very religious." She didn't add that Barbara had said the rabbi would simply read the burial service. Imagine, some-one in a skullcap saying the last rites over her brother, the only son of two dyed-in-the-wool Methodists.

"Will you go?" Katie was watching her with an intensity that made Kay pull back. She hastily added: "Of course you'll go. What a stupid thing for me to say. I don't know why I did."

"Yes. I'll go. Just for the day. I'll fly out and go to the service, then fly right back home."

"Doesn't she want you to stay?"

"Oh, sure she does. But I really don't want to go to the

house. She and I have never been very close." She glanced at Katie's reaction to that; it was touchy to get near the subject of the wife being a Jew. "It's nothing to do with her or anything. It's just that it's so upsetting for me . . ." she let her voice dwindle.

Katie put her trembling hand over Kay's. Kay looked at the flawless white skin and shapely nails painted a perfect shell pink.

"It was so selfish of him," Kay suddenly said loudly. "He fooled me. He fooled me, letting me think there was nothing wrong. It's so awful and I'm so ashamed. I don't know what to do. You won't hate me, will you, Katie? You won't blame me for this, will you?" She had to find out how things stood.

Katie's lips parted. She looked at Kay in astonishment. "Hate you? Whatever would I hate you for? You haven't done anything."

"I've got the same blood as he did. Suicide is a sin. You do know that, don't you? Suicide is a sin."

"That's ridiculous. I never heard anything so ridiculous." Katie drew her hand away angrily.

Kay looked at her friend. Katie never said anything she didn't mean. "Don't you think suicide is a sin?"

"Of course not. What a perfectly ridiculous thing to say."

"But he fooled me and lied to me. I can't help it, but I feel so ashamed—even in front of you."

"Kay, I'm shocked. You're sounding like a total ass. You make it sound as if you were the wounded party. Dan didn't do anything to you. What he did, he did to himself. For whatever reason he may have had. But it has nothing to do with you." Katie's voice became breathless as she fought to control her feelings. "I'm surprised to hear you say such stupid things. You might feel grief, and to feel anger is an honest reaction, but to feel ashamed is just plain stupid. Where are your senses? I hope Barbara doesn't feel that way."

Kay shook her head. "No. She's simply in mourning."

"And that's all you should feel. Just the loss, nothing more. You have nothing to feel ashamed of at all." Katie was reacting strongly to all this, feeling even more upset than she had before. She thought she knew Kay pretty well, but this really shocked her.

"I'm glad you could come down." Kay switched the emphasis, carefully registering Katie's reaction, which would be Harry's. "I was feeling pretty awful."

"Of course you were. You mustn't stay here alone. You must come home with me and stay there until you're feeling better."

"I couldn't do that." My God, how would she ever find a place to be alone with Harry in that house? "I'd better stay here. I've got to get used to this. It was just the first shock that upset me so. I'll be all right." At least here, even small and cheap as it was, it was private. She could walk around all day with no clothes on if she felt like it. She could do any damned thing she wanted to do. "I'll be all right. I just wanted you here with me now."

Katie nodded and let her eyes travel around the room. Kay noticed them pause on the desk. "If you want to come stay with us, you come. Any time. You know that. Harry and I would love to have you. If you change your mind in the middle of the night, you just come on up. All right?"

"Thanks, Katie. You're always so generous and thoughtful." She raised her head and looked toward the cupboards. "Look at that mess. I had just started cleaning out the cupboards when . . . when Barbara called and told me. I had just started, and of course I couldn't go on. I'm afraid everything is sort of chaotic."

"Not at all." Katie patted her hand. "Everything looks fine. You mustn't worry about straightening up when you're feeling like this."

Now was the time to make her move. Kay said: "I would like to call back, call Barbara now, if you wouldn't mind being alone for a minute. I was in such a state of shock, I'm afraid I wasn't very coherent when I talked to her. Would you mind if I left you to go call her?"

"Of course not. You go right ahead and do whatever you want to do. I'll just hang around and try to help you until you want me to go."

Kay stood up and straightened the front of her expensive slacks. "I won't be long. I'll have to talk a little while, though, to go over the plans again. I might call the airlines while I'm at it. Do you mind?"

"Don't ask that again. Take your time."

"Death is so awful . . . losing someone so close to you. There were just the two of us, you know. Now I'm all alone. It's not easy. No matter how it comes, death is . . . well, death." She walked out on that morbid note.

Katie bit her lip and fought for control. She wanted to jump up and run, run down the roads and across the fields until she was panting for breath. She was stifling with the thought of death; she wept for those strangers, his wife and son. And Kay . . . the stupidity of being ashamed, stupid and unreal. Why did people kill themselves? If Dan needed help, he should have called for it. He should have cried out in his desperation, cried out for help. Someone would have heard him. No one cried out to totally deaf ears. Did they?

Katie stood up and circled the room, passing the desk, the partially opened door to the bedroom where Kay's voice rang out, circled past the sofa, chairs, dreary prints and slipcovers, back past the desk. The smell of booze wafted into her nostrils from the closed bottles.

She clutched her hands together as if they held the key to life, fighting panic and trying to keep up her courage. The knuckles on her hands stood out in bony skeletal knots. She tried not to look at the four bottles beckoning to her. Kay's voice didn't sound so upset to her, didn't have that wounded tone that comes with great sadness. Kay should show what she felt, not try to fight it and act so nonchalant on the phone. There wasn't any point in trying to fight it. There wasn't any point in trying to fight anything, really. Two were brown and two clear, alternating their appeal to her, guilelessly waiting for her.

She hesitantly reached out her hand and touched the bottle of vodka. It didn't burn her hand or strike dread into her heart. It just felt like glass. Who would ever know if she had that one little drink to help her? Who would ever know? This was the first time she had been alone in a room with a bottle since she had been sick. It didn't look like the poison she had begun to think it was. It looked as innocent as any liquid in her parched need. It looked easy, and it would be easy. Just one small swallow to give her the courage and calm she needed to help Kay. Life was too short to be so complicated. Life should be simple.

By the time Kay returned, Katie was sitting calmly on the end of the sofa, her face composed.

"Well, it's all set. I have a reservation, and Barbara will meet me at the airport. It's all set." Kay looked with narrowed eyes at Katie. "Could I get you something? A cup of tea?"

"Nothing, thanks." Katie stood up, unbending her long body gracefully. "I wish you'd come home with me. We really want to take care of you."

"No, thank you, I won't. I feel all right now that I've had a chance to talk to you about it. I just needed someone to talk to. You know how it is."

Katie nodded. "I think I'd better go, unless you want me to stay. Harry should be home soon. Do you want me to stay?"

"No. I'm all right now. You go ahead. I may drop by later. I want to finish those cupboards now; I feel like tackling something physical and grubby. You go ahead."

Katie walked home, thankful she was better able to face ordeals. She felt fine and was not as troubled by Dan's death and Kay's strange reaction as she had been. She wished she had met Dan, and his wife. Barbara must feel very lonely now.

Katie went first to the kitchen, which was empty. Pearl must either be napping or swimming. She glanced at the diamond watch on her wrist. It was a little after four. Harry should be home any minute now. She had to tell him about the sad news, but other than that she felt fine. She wanted to kiss him and maybe get into the shower with him. She felt better than she had for days. It was all that swimming; she felt toned up and relaxed. A drop of vodka had helped too; no question about that.

In the pantry, she took out a bottle of vodka and carried it up the stairs to her dressing room, where she hid it behind all those lace and silk nightgowns she never wore. Pearl wouldn't open that drawer and find it. She wore thin cotton nightgowns now that it was so hot, and they were in another drawer altogether. And after tonight, she wasn't even going to wear those.

She heard noises in the kitchen and went to tell Pearl she was back. It seemed there was more noise than just Pearl and Lavinia.

Katie stopped in the pantry doorway. "Miss Anderson! How wonderful!" She smiled broadly and looked at Lavinia hugging the older woman around the thighs. "Did you have a good flight?"

"Very easy, thank you. You look well, Mrs. Harding."

"Thank you. I feel well."

"You must have been taking care of yourself." Miss Anderson traveled in gray, this time a two-piece gray poplin suit with a small gray hat perched on the side of her head, anchored no doubt with gray pins. "Doesn't your mother look wonderful, Lavinia?"

Lavinia kept her eyes on the gray and nodded.

"Doesn't she just though," Pearl turned an appreciative eye to Katie. "Every day she looks better. And you should see her eat now."

They all laughed.

"Well, I am truly delighted to see you," Katie said and certainly meant it. "It's too bad your vacation was cut short, but perhaps you can plan another one in the fall after the children go back to school. I can see that Lavinia is glad to see you."

Miss Anderson patted the little brown head. "And I'm glad to see her." She smiled kindly at Lavinia, who hugged her even tighter.

"Lavinia," Katie said, "you mustn't tire Miss Anderson tonight. She has had a long flight from England. You just let her rest tonight, and tomorrow we'll all talk about some plans for the rest of the summer. Maybe we can think of something interesting for the two of you to do."

"I'm sure Lavinia and I will be quite happy right here. We have that beautiful pool and we'll find plenty to do while you and Mr. Harding are away. Don't you worry about us, Mrs. Harding. We'll be fine."

Pearl began chopping an onion. "Well, I for one am glad to have some activity around here. I wasn't looking forward to being in this big empty house all by myself."

Katie laughed. She turned and started through the pantry. "I'll be on the terrace. Mr. Harding should be here soon. Do you want to swim now, Miss Anderson? No one's using the pool."

"I think I'll just take a hot bath, and save the swimming for tomorrow. Would you like to stay here and help Pearl while I bathe and change, Lavinia?"

Katie didn't listen to any of the rest. Things were looking up again. Everything was under control here, and she and Harry could leave on schedule.

Harry pushed the back door open with his foot and carried Freddie into the kitchen, pausing to shake his head at Pearl, who opened her mouth to exclaim something.

"He's asleep," Harry said softly. "I'll carry him upstairs."

Pearl wiped her hands on her apron. "Is he sick?" she whispered.

Harry nodded. "He's had a rough time."

Pearl dropped the lid over one eye and shot the other at Harry. "Miss Anderson's back. She's upstairs. Lavinia's just gone up there to be with her."

Harry nodded and walked on.

He deposited his burden onto the bed with the brass rods at the top, then quietly left the room, pulling the door shut behind him. He knocked on Lavinia's door, then opened it.

"Daddy, Daddy, look what Miss Anderson's doing! She's putting my hair in pigtails!"

Miss Anderson looked up at him from the side of the bed where she sat in her seersucker wrapper. "Hello, Mr. Harding. How are you? Did you find Freddie all right? Pearl told me you had gone up to see him."

"I brought him home with me. He's had a bad time. Very bad. I'll tell you about it later." He indicated Lavinia with a motion of his head. "Right now he's asleep. I suggest you let him sleep as long as he wants. He can get something to eat whenever he wakes up, which may not be before morning."

An uneasy look swept across Miss Anderson's face.

"Your pigtails are nice. I like them." Harry winked at Lavinia. "See you downstairs."

"Wait, wait, wait for me," Lavinia squealed. "I want to go down too."

Harry and Lavinia went down the stairs hand in hand. In the big central hall, Lavinia broke away from him and ran to the terrace door.

"Mommy, Mommy, Mommy!" She shouted through the screen. "Guess what! Daddy's home and he brought Freddie back with him! Freddie's back!" Then she ran back toward the kitchen hallway.

Harry walked out onto the terrace. Katie was sitting bolt upright on the chaise looking as if she'd been kicked in the stomach.

"Hi, Red. How are you?" He went over and bent to kiss her.

Katie put up her hand and stopped him. "What did Lavinia just say? Freddie's home?"

Harry nodded. "I need a drink. Mind if I have one?"

She shook her head.

"Let me make myself one and I'll tell you all about it. Want anything?"

"Bring me a glass of tonic."

When Harry returned with their drinks, Katie was standing

at the top step, looking out over the lawn. He paused at the doorway and looked at the rich auburn hair tumbling onto her upturned collar. Her back was straight, the shoulder blades slightly protruding. She looked as beautiful as she had fifteen years before.

He handed her the glass of tonic, then put his arm around her. The disbelief in her face gave way to pity and finally dismay and anger as he told her about Freddie.

"My God, Harry. Thank God you went. What were they thinking of, treating a child that way. It's barbaric. Something ought to be done about those people. We should sue them, get them in court where they can be exposed."

"I thought of all those things driving down . . . suing them, getting the sheriff, calling some newspaper to expose them. But I don't think any of it would do any good. We knew from the beginning it was a place for problem children; their methods are probably accepted in many psychiatric circles. I daresay they have their tracks well covered, or they wouldn't be doing it. They're not stupid people."

"Why would the school recommend such a place to Miss Anderson?"

"Reputation."

"There's nothing we can do?"

"I'll tell Bob Crowley, and he can at least stop giving out the name to other parents. I wanted to turn around and go back and knock them all down. But one thing was for sure: I wasn't going to let Freddie ever see the inside of that wooded area again."

Katie sipped the tonic. "It's providence that brought Miss Anderson back. No substitute would be able to handle all this."

"But now we have the problem of the summer. It's not even the end of June."

"Do you think Joe's all right?" Again that mixture of doubt and love pierced her.

"Yes. A canoe trip is a lot different than being in the hands of psychotic therapists."

"But we thought Lavinia and Freddie were all right. Maybe we should try to get in touch with Joe."

"I feel certain Joe is fine. We're talking about a different child. He doesn't have the emotional problems the other two seem to have."

Emotional problems? Katie wondered what kind of emotional problems drove someone to leave a note about their mother's secret life.

They stood silently, side by side on the step.

Harry was glad Red was taking this so calmly and acting like a mature, thinking mother. He had expected a scene.

Katie was fighting the turmoil that was rising in her, gritting her teeth and trying to figure out how she could get upstairs and have a drink. She was not going to let any of this ruin her vacation with Harry. But between now and then, she had to manage the days somehow. Nothing had gone the way it was supposed to go.

"I've got some more bad news," she said. "Kay's brother killed himself."

"Kay's brother?"

"Yes. He's dead."

"Oh, my God. Poor Kay. How is she taking it?"

"Surprisingly well. I went down and stayed with her some this afternoon. She was upset, of course, but collected. She's so rational anyway. She would be able to handle it."

"How did it happen?"

Katie told him the details.

"I'd better go in and call her."

"Yes. Good idea. You do that and I'll just run upstairs for a minute."

Harry had two more drinks before they ate. He was so absorbed by his own thoughts, he never noticed that Katie began to take on an old familiar glow.

Katie ate two shrimp and pushed the rest around on her plate, hiding one under the watercress, another behind a slice of tomato and more under the lettuce. She watched Harry eat all of his plus three popovers. They had rhubarb pie for dessert. Katie didn't take any, and between that and coffee she excused herself again and went upstairs.

She was feeling warm and slightly euphoric. She had ceased to dwell on Dan's death and Freddie's return, letting them slip to some inner niche in her mind.

"You're awfully quiet," Harry commented, looking at her over the rim of the demitasse cup.

"Just thinking," she murmured somewhat dreamily, shrugging her elegant shoulder.

"Care to let me in on it?"

She smiled at him and shook her head, stretching her legs out in front of her.

"I must confess I'm pretty tired. I guess wrapped up in my own thoughts too. I can't get Freddie out of my head."

"Just try not to think of him."

"Afraid I can't do that. We've got to think of something for them to do the rest of the summer. They ought not to just sit here. They need to get away too. A change will help him; it might help pull him out of this . . . this counting."

"Ask Miss Anderson. She might have a suggestion."

"Actually I have one myself."

"Yes? What is it?"

"Why don't we send them, Miss Anderson and the kids, to the beach?"

"Fine. What beach did you have in mind?"

"You're not going to like this, but I'll say it anyway."

Katie could feel that warm glow waning, going fast, while a cold fear began to take over. She put down her cup and waited.

"Why don't we let them go to the house in East Hampton. It's all set and ready for them in four days. I think the sooner we get Freddie away the better off he'll be. If we have to wait until something else can be found, he may be worse." He watched her. "I can see you're not happy with this. And I'm not either. I was looking forward to that month with you. But we've got to put his health first."

Katie's face drained of color. "You're not serious."

"Red. Think of it. Think of the kids first, then us. We've got to see about them first. You and I can find someplace else to go. . . ."

"At this late date? Everything decent's taken."

"We can find something. We can stay at an inn and eat at restaurants. Miss Anderson can't do that with them. She has to have a house, and she has to have someone to help her with cooking and all. You do see that, don't you?"

Katie stood up and walked across the terrace into the house. She didn't bother to go upstairs, but went directly to the pantry. She got out a glass and put ice in it, then filled it with vodka. Pearl came in from the kitchen and followed Katie's movements with a roving eye.

Finally Pearl spoke up. "Are you feeling all right? You didn't eat much dinner."

"I'm fine." Katie saw the concern on Pearl's face. "It's all right. I'm well now. It's all right."

She carried the drink back onto the terrace and dropped onto the chaise.

"What have you got there, Red?"

"This?" She held up the glass. "This is vodka on the rocks. Straight vodka. No water and no vermouth."

"For Christ's sake, Katie! What kind of fool are you?!" It was hardly a question. "You shouldn't be having that!"

"Says who?" She put the glass to her lips.

"Jesus." Harry stood up. "You can't do this. You're just going to get sick again."

She looked at him but didn't answer.

"I can't stand by and watch you do this."

"Don't." Katie said in an offhand manner. "You go ahead to East Hampton with Miss Anderson and Freddie and Lavinia, and I'll stay here. Then you won't have to watch me."

"Jesus Christ." Harry left, jerking the door open and disappearing down the hall.

15

HARRY LAY IN THE NARROW BED AND LOOKED AT THE ceiling, barely illuminated by the sheet of light from the crack in the bathroom door. A great stillness enveloped him, the coupling of nothingness and nowhere in his mind; the fury and worry about Red and about Freddie that had almost blocked out his rationality had subsided. In their place, a resolve of what to do had settled in.

The warm body that lay in the crook of his arm stirred and he looked down.

"Feeling better?" Kay asked.

"Much." He kissed her cheek, letting his lips brush the soft skin.

"Good. It'll be all right. You'll see." She curled the hair on his chest around her fingers. "You mustn't worry. You did the right thing. And you've made the right decision."

"You mean about the kids?"

"Of course. The two of them and Miss Anderson should go to East Hampton. You and Katie will have to work out something else. She might not even mind spending the summer here; I mean, she does have that beautiful pool, and some people would kill to be in the Berkshires, so it must have something to offer."

"No. We'll have to go somewhere. She needs to get away."

"Too bad she doesn't think of the children first, the way you do. But it's a good thing you do. They need help. Especially Freddie. You have to think of him first."

"I know." He wished Red had said that. "You're so understanding. You always think of others first."

"My training as a schoolmarm."

Harry laughed. "Some schoolmarm."

"I'll miss you, of course." When he didn't answer, she went on: "You've given me a lot of pleasure—plain, simple pleasure." His arm tightened around her approvingly.

"I wish I could help you, Kay. Today . . . tonight, we both had our problems, and you've helped me with mine. You almost made them go away. Have I helped you any?"

"You've given me comfort. I was feeling so alone, so . . . so sad about Dan, wondering why I hadn't known he needed help. I would have helped him any way I could."

"Of course you would have. But no one can see into another person's head if they've got it wrapped up so tightly. No one could see he needed help. You've got to be grateful he called you and kept in touch with you; that showed he loved you."

"It must have taken a lot of courage to do what he did."

Harry gently touched her face. "A lot. He must have been a fine person."

"Yes. He certainly was." Kay rubbed her cheek against his shoulder that pillowed her head. "So are you."

They lay in their silence, each carefully guarding the moment to make it last. Without disturbing the silent bond between them, Kay raised herself on an elbow and pressed closer against him, her breasts cradling his rib cage. She ran her tongue across his lips, and kissed him, then whispered in his ear. "Give me your hand. Here, put it here."

Harry rolled toward her. "You never cease to amaze me."

When Harry got home he first went to the third floor and looked in Freddie's room. He saw that Miss Anderson had put him into summer pajamas; she probably had given him something to eat and drink too. Harry stood by the bed and looked at the pudgy body sprawled in deep sleep, the dark hair mashed against the soft pillow, the lips finally still, the counting over for the night. He wanted to touch him, but was afraid Freddie might wake up. He silently stood and watched, then glanced around the room, with its orderly array of story-book water-colors—Peter Rabbit, Johnny Chuck, Sammy Jay; Alice playing croquet with the Duchess; Winnie-the-Pooh, Kanga and Roo; pictures Red had had painted from book illustrations— the chair, table, bookshelves, shelves of games and model tanks. A nice room for a little boy. A safe room, with familiar and reliable pleasures. Red had cared enough to give him a nice room.

He quietly closed the door and took a few steps to his right, then opened the door to Lavinia's room. The light from the hallway fell across her bare legs sticking out from the hiked-up nightgown; one arm lay across the lifeless Jewel, whose head was resting on the pillow beside Lavinia's, her open eyes watching Harry above the frozen plastic smile. Harry shut the door and went back downstairs. No need to look in Joe's room, the edges stuffed with tennis racket, baseball bat, hockey stick, soccer balls and footballs; the walls hung with science-fiction posters; the twin beds covered in bright Indian spreads. He could see it in his mind.

He went down the second-floor hall, flicked off the lights and opened the bedroom door.

A light had been left on. Harry walked to the bed and stared at Katie. She lay in a pale mint-green heap, her arms and legs angling out from her untucked shirt and crumpled slacks, her hair not quite covering the makeup smeared across her pale face. Harry sat down on his side of the bed, put his head in his hands and silently cried, tears sliding down the palms of his hands onto his wrists, his shoulders hunched and shaking. It was the first time he had cried since Katie's father had died and left him with the terrible knowledge that he would never measure up to what Katie's father had been for her.

Harry was swimming the length of the pool, over and over, his head parting the mist that rose from the warm water in the cool dawn air. In the bedroom Katie sat up with a start. The room was bathed in pale, gray morning light from the open french doors. The clock on her desk said five-thirty. She reached out her hand for Harry, but it fell on the empty space. The mashed pillow and creased sheets told her he had been there beside her. Where could he be at this hour? She looked down at her clothes and moaned.

Christ. What a stupid fool she was to have gotten drunk. It had been okay to have had a drink or two to calm her nerves. But to have gotten drunk was stupid. Harry must be disgusted with her. No wonder he had gotten up and left.

By six, she couldn't stand it any longer and got up. She went into the bathroom and finally emerged cocooned in a white silk kimono, her neck and hair curved into the soft collar. She had taken two pills to be on the safe side. She wanted to be calm and relaxed when she found Harry. She stood in the room and stared at the floor, waiting.

When she got downstairs she saw the door to the terrace open, and realized he must be swimming. But when she got to the pool, it was empty, only his wet footprints left as evidence. Katie searched the lawn and gardens with her eyes trying to think where he could have gone. She wished she had gotten up at five; she could have been swimming with him. They could have made love with the cool water swirling around their legs, lapping at their shoulders, the way they had done the first summer here. No one would have been up at that hour—not even Mario. Her gaze went beneath the surface of the water to the blue tiles, enlarged and distorted by the moving water.

Katie looked in the living room, dining room, kitchen, library and finally Harry's study.

He was sitting behind his desk, his chair swiveled toward the window, and didn't hear her open the door. Katie ached at the sight of the broad shoulders wrapped in the brown terry robe. He was lost in thought, absorbed in some distant idea from which she was excluded.

"Harry?"

He turned his chair toward her. "Hi, Red. What are you doing up at this hour?"

Katie crossed the room and sat on his lap, her legs sideways across him, and put her arms around his neck, burying her face there. He held her close.

"I'm so sorry. I'm so sorry." She whispered so softly he almost didn't understand her.

"It's all right."

"No, it's not. I'm really sorry. It was just such a shitty day, what with Lavinia, then Dan—that upset me so much—and then Freddie. I just couldn't be strong anymore."

"I know."

"I've tried so hard. I really have."

"I know you have."

"And then I just couldn't do it anymore. I didn't even want to try."

"When did you start?"

Katie raised her head and wiped her eyes with the flat of her hand. "I can't remember. Oh, yes . . . I do now . . . it was . . ."

"Don't try to remember. It doesn't matter when it was. It happened. You've been very strong, and I know how hard you've tried. You'll do it again." He kissed her cheek. "You've got to, Red. You can't go getting sick again."

"I know that. I know I can't. I want to be well. For you."

"It's going to be all right. We've just got to sit down and make some new plans about a vacation. That's all. Either for us or for the kids. And we both know it would be best to replan our vacation."

Katie took a deep breath. "Yes. You're right. It will be best. It's just that I was so looking forward . . ."

"I know you were. Don't you think I saw you counting the days off on the calendar? Don't you think I feel lousy about it too? But we have to think of Freddie and Lavinia first. That's all there is to it."

"Yes. You're right. If only they could have stayed at camp." She could feel him tighten beneath her. "But they couldn't, so that's that."

Harry pushed back her hair with his hand. "I'll go down to that travel agent on Spring Street today and see if they have anything that sounds interesting. Okay?"

Katie nodded and looked out the window. "It will be all right staying here for a little while longer. We've got the pool, and I've always got Kay to talk to during the day. Poor Kay. What a terrible time for her. Did you know she's only going to be gone that one day for the funeral? Queer she doesn't stay longer."

Harry suddenly buried his head against her breast and tightened his arms around her.

"I love you so much, Harry. I don't know what I'd do if anything happened to you."

He shook his head slowly. Katie knew he was reassuring her; he wouldn't let anything happen to himself. She knew he loved her.

"I wish you had woken me up early to go swimming with you."

He raised his head and with a flicker of a smile said: "Next time I will."

It was mid-morning when Katie first encountered Freddie. Miss Anderson was leading him by the hand across the lawn just below the terrace. Even from where she sat, Katie could distinguish the "Eighty-eight. Eighty-nine. Ninety. Ninety- . . ." She stared in horror at the lumpy shapeless body in his too-tight shorts and T-shirt being led by the brisk Miss Anderson, neatly dressed in a white blouse and dark cotton skirt, stockings and washed sneakers on her feet. She couldn't take her eyes off them, marching evenly to the beat of the counting.

"Miss Anderson." Katie stood and walked down to the lawn. "I just wanted to know what you think . . ." she stopped and stared at Freddie.

"A hundred and ten. A hundred and eleven. A . . ."

"Good God, what did they do to him?" Her eyes were riveted to Freddie's mouth.

Miss Anderson shook her head grimly. "It will take some time to get him over this. Time and patience."

"Did Mr. Harding tell you about the beach?"

His lips never stopped moving.

"Yes, he did. I know how disappointed you must be. But frankly, it will be the best thing in the world for Freddie. He needs a complete change."

"Yes. Lavinia will have to go, too, you know."

On and on he went.

"I know. She'll be good for him. They like doing things togethe."

"Yes, well, I won't stop you. You go ahead with whatever you were doing."

His dull eyes had never even blinked. Only the lips moved.

"We're walking around. That's all. Just walking around."

Katie stepped back and they started off.

"A hundred and twenty-nine. A hundred and thirty. A hundred and thirty-one. A hundred and thirty-two."

She turned and walked quickly into the house and up the stairs to the bedroom. She took the bottle of vodka from the folds of pleated silk and took a good long swallow. Then she carefully screwed the top back on and lifted up the soft materials and laid the bottle among them the way a baby was laid to rest.

She pushed the drawer shut and went into the bathroom and drank a glass of water. Not sure if that would control her nerves, she took another Valium.

Harry had gone to his office, promising he would be back for lunch. She decided to wait and swim with him when he returned. On a hot day like this, he surely would want a swim before lunch. It must be ninety already. Katie looked down at the shorts and halter she had on. This was about as cool as she could get without going totally bare. If they were at the beach there would be a breeze off the ocean. But here, the air sat in between the mountains and didn't stir.

If they were at the beach. Katie walked over to the calendar on her desk and touched the geometric promises of good times to come, each square a step on her yellow brick road. With a savage grasp, she ripped out June and threw it into the trash basket.

She went back downstairs determined to tell Harry that she was planning on having one small drink before lunch and a couple of light ones before dinner; not enough to get a buzz on even, but enough to help her relax. The bloody pills simply did not give her that little lift; all they did was sit on the nervous system and make her depressed. She would tell Harry that she was going to be strong and controlled about it, and would not let herself get carried away and get bombed. He could help keep a check on her. Also she was going to throw out the Valium and go back to Librium; they weren't such depressants.

Having resolved all that, she felt better and went back out on the terrace to read. Hot as it was even in the shade of the oak, it was better than being cooped up in the house alone.

Harry sat at his desk in his small, bare, functional office and tried to concentrate on the contract still opened to the first page. He was so absorbed with his home life he could barely grasp the meaning of the columns of figures.

Once Miss Anderson and the kids got off to East Hampton maybe he would be able to straighten out the rest. He did need to get away with Red.

And what was he going to do about Kay? She was wonderful to be with, so understanding and compassionate . . . as well as passionate. He never would have thought she would have been like that; not until he found himself with her that first time. He had gone to her blindly. He knew that kiss had been a welcome sign to him, and when he went back, she never said anything; she just led him by the hand to the bedroom and began unbuttoning his shirt. And it was so easy to talk to her afterward. She knew how he felt about the kids, and the problems he had with Red. She loved the kids and she loved and understood Red.

Harry pushed aside the contract and stood up, walking to the door then back again to the desk. There wasn't much floor space, but he had covered it several times, his hands sunk into his pockets, head lowered, when the phone rang.

He opened the door and stuck out his head. "I'll get it." He closed the door and crossed back to the desk. "Hello?"

"Harry?"

"Doris. How are you?" A smile immediately spread across his face as he went around the desk and sat down. "It's good to hear your voice. How are you?" he repeated.

"I'm all right. I just wanted to talk to you before I left."

"When do you go?"

"Tomorrow. I snitched a couple of extra days from the office. How are you?"

"Okay, I guess. Better, hearing from you."

"You don't sound too sure of yourself."

"I've had some problems at home."

"Such as?"

He told her about Lavinia and Freddie.

"What an awful story. How's Katie taking it?"

"Not too well. It's started her back drinking again. Hey, enough of that. I want to hear about you. God, it's good to hear your voice. How's the other Harry?"

She laughed. "Frisky. He's looking forward to the trip."

"I would be too."

"Harry. I want you to know something. I couldn't go without you knowing."

Harry picked up a pencil. "Tell me."

"Well . . . this isn't easy for me."

"Tell me anyway."

"I am. What I want to say is, well, what I want you to know is . . . Harry, I'm not going alone."

"I know. You're going with the other Harry."

"There'll be three of us."

He gripped the pencil. "Three? Anyone I know?"

"No. It's one of the guys from town. I've known him for some time and he's . . . well, he's pretty keen on me, I guess. I've never given him too much thought, but lately, well . . . lately, he's been around more and . . . Harry? You're not saying anything."

"What do you want me to say? I'm just listening. Go on."

"Well, anyway, he wanted me, and Harry, to go off with him for my vacation. Then, as I really had my heart set on Maine, he suggested he come along with us. And I said all right."

"Are you sorry you said it?" His nails dug into the palms of his hand as he squeezed the pencil.

There was a long pause before she answered. "No. I'm not." She waited for him to say something, but he didn't. "I know this comes as a surprise, and I probably should have mentioned it to you before now, but I really wasn't too serious about him . . . then. I guess I am now. He's real nice. You'd like him."

"Are you going to marry him?"

"I don't know. I just don't know."

He knew. He broke the pencil in half.

"Harry?"

"I'm here. I just can't think of anything to say."

"Nothing may come of it, you know. He might decide he's sick of me after a solid week of me. Who knows? Anyway, I wanted you to know. I wouldn't have felt right about going without you knowing."

"I'm glad you're not going alone, Doris." Why wasn't he the one going?

"That's nice of you."

"Call me when you get back."

"I will. And Harry . . . I'm sorry. I really am." She hung up.

Harry held the phone for a long time, then he put it down and threw the pencil across the room. "Shit!"

Harry ran up the steps, calling "Kay? You home?"

Before he got to the top, she had opened the door. "Harry! What's the matter?"

He walked past her into the living room. "Nothing. I just wanted to see you."

"In the middle of the morning? I thought only the nights had committed themselves to my pleasure."

He put his arms around her and kissed the top of her head, holding her tightly to him. "I felt lonely, and wanted to see you. That's all."

"Is something wrong?"

"No. Nothing," he repeated. "Nothing. Can you spare me some time now?"

"Of course I can." She pulled back and smiled at him. "I can spare time for you whenever you want it."

He looked down at her bare feet. "Got any shoes you can take a hike in?"

"A hike?"

"I'd like to go for a walk in the woods. I thought you might go with me."

"Oh, Harry. I'd love it. But only if you promise to tell me about the wildflowers and the names of the trees. I have a lot to learn about the woods."

"I'll tell you anything you want to know. I'll walk along with one arm around you and the other pointing out the flora and fauna."

She kissed him. "You're so wonderful to me."

"Get some shoes on before I get too distracted and we end up staying here."

By four Katie was frantic with worry about Harry. She had called the office at one and been told he'd left at least three hours before. He had promised to be home for lunch with her and he hadn't shown up or called. Was he upset with her and had simply decided to ignore her? She twisted her fingers together.

She had been so awful. Small wonder if he never came back. She knew she was being silly. He probably just went into the woods for something and couldn't get back in time.

Ordinarily she wouldn't have given it a second thought. But she was so nervous. She had taken too many tranquilizers, trying not to get hysterical with the counting; she had had a small drink or two to help her. The whole household was under such a strain: Freddie counting; Lavinia shrieking and being obnoxious; Harry not showing up. She worried about Joe. He had been gone over three weeks and no word from him. Guilt flooded into her when she recalled how she hadn't kissed him goodbye when he left; she still felt sick when she thought of the note.

Only ten minutes had passed since she last had looked at her watch. She went upstairs and put on her bathing suit. If she swam, it would take her mind off the time.

But when she got back to the pool, she hesitated. She didn't want to go in without Harry. She didn't want to call Kay and ask her to come up, then be turned down. Nor did she want her with them for dinner. She wanted to be alone with Harry.

Katie looked at her watch again. She could feel pricks of hysteria collecting. She sat down, then jumped up again. She would just have to have another drink, a small one, while she waited for Harry.

Quietly, like an amateur thief, Katie checked the kitchen area for Pearl before opening the pantry cupboard. She felt ashamed as she noiselessly lifted the bottle from the shelf and unscrewed the cap. How foolish of her to feel this way, in her own house. She lifted the bottle to her parted lips and drank until she was satisfied, then, again silently, returned it to its place as the magical potion began to disperse in her body. The entire action took less than sixty seconds. The full effect of the results would take longer—but not too much longer. She raised her shoulders smugly and smiled.

Katie lay on her back in the center of the big bed to wait, briefly frowning as she extended her arms out straight to the sides of the bed and wondered if numbing the nerve ends helped ease the agony of crucifixion, or was it brain waves that needed to be knocked out. She shook her head. Not given to frequent or serious thoughts of religion and certainly not wanting to think of pain, she quickly tried to remember what statues she had seen posed in this position, the sculptors, the museums, the countries. If she concentrated hard, it would absorb most of her mind and make the time pass more quickly.

By five, she was calm and detached. She got up from the bed and went downstairs where she openly made herself a vodka-and-tonic. By the time she finished it, she had managed to put everything out of her mind except Harry when he arrived.

"Harry! Where have you been? You said you'd be home for lunch." She looked at the muddy work shoes and wet cuffs of his khaki pants.

"Sorry, Red. I got tied up." He looked at the empty glass in her hand. "I'm going to run up and take a shower. Be right back." He disappeared before she could say anything.

Katie's slight anxiety now gave way to anger. He thought nothing of going off into the woods without telling her, letting her sit and wait, not knowing when he would be home. A drop of water slid off the bottom of her glass and hit her bare stomach. She watched it trickle into her navel. Why was she still in her bathing suit? Harry didn't want to swim with her. She'd been waiting for him, and he'd just gone off without caring that she'd been waiting. He never even gave her a chance to ask if he wanted to swim. What the hell. She might as well go get dressed. To hell with swimming. To hell with him. To hell with everything. She needed another drink.

They were halfway through the smoked salmon when Katie remembered she had forgotten her makeup. She put her hand to her face. And what did she have on? She looked down at the brown slacks and blue shirt that were wrong together, and farther down to high-heeled sandals that only went with dresses. She shrugged. It didn't really matter. No one gave a shit anymore. She sure didn't.

She sipped her chilled wine and ate another bite of salmon. Harry finished his and sat staring at the empty plate. She reached for the small leather case that held the buzzer.

"Aren't you going to eat more?" he asked, looking at her, seeing the early warning signs: sloppy dressing, unbrushed hair, no makeup.

"No." She ran her fingers around the glass. "There'll be more coming."

Harry shifted in his chair and looked vacantly across the lawn.

"Did you get to the travel agent?" she asked.

He shook his head. "Didn't have time. I'll do it tomorrow."

"Where were you all day?"

"In the woods."

Pearl came out with a tray of covered dishes. The eye supervising the presentation of the platter half closed with satisfaction. "Sure and this will please you; it's Chicken Kiev."

Katie looked at the golden-brown cylinders, knowing all that butter trapped inside would make a greasy mess, probably hardening in waxy lumps.

"Don't forget to take a lemon wedge," Pearl said. When she got to Harry: "You can have all you want. I've got some flattened breasts out there ready to cook up if anybody wants more."

Flattened chicken breasts. Katie tried not to picture them.

"This is about the end of the asparagus," Pearl commented.

"Then I'm going to make a pig of myself," Harry responded.

"Take it all," Pearl urged. "There's some left for me in the kitchen."

Katie looked at the chicken and green spears, fearing she would be sick.

"Why don't we have a dog?" she asked with a worried frown.

Harry stopped his fork in front of his mouth. "A dog? Because you never wanted one. That's why."

"Why didn't I?"

"You didn't want one barking or sitting on the furniture or sleeping with the kids. That's why."

"I'd forgotten. Was it all my fault we never got one?"

Harry ate for a bit before he answered. "No one's fault. We just never got one. I was away in the woods and couldn't be home to train it; you didn't want to do that. So that was that."

"I seem to remember . . ."—she spoke slowly ". . . now I think of it, I seem to remember it was something to do with Freddie. He wasn't nice with dogs, even when he was two or so."

"We didn't have one before he was born because you didn't want one."

"Are you sorry?"

He thought of the frisky puppy scampering through the kitchen, jumping into the canoe. "Not especially. I like dogs, but I am gone a lot."

"Yes. You are." Katie clumsily cut into the chicken, the butter spurting out onto the plate. "I don't like cats. No one in my family ever liked cats."

"What have the kids been doing today?" Harry ate hungrily.

"Counting and screaming," Katie said matter-of-factly.

"Think we ought to get in touch with a psychiatrist?"

"I don't think Miss Anderson approves of psychiatrists. She may or may not be right. I have no idea. We'll see how he is at the end of July."

"Would you like to drive north? Maybe go to Nova Scotia?"

Katie looked over the rim of her glass at him. "What's there?"

"The ocean, the coast, fishing villages, that sort of thing."

She put down her knife and fork. "Please pass the wine."

"Not such a good idea?"

"I don't know. I can't get a picture of it. Get some literature on it."

Harry passed the decanter to her. "Take it easy, will you."

"Definitely. I will." She poured wine to the top of her glass and pushed the decanter back toward him.

A wood thrush was singing below the garden. Katie leaned back in her chair and looked into the trees. "Listen to that, Harry. Just listen." She sipped her wine and stared into the long shadows that spread across the distant mountainside while Harry ate.

"You'd better eat while it's still hot." He was almost finished.

"I've had enough," she answered thickly.

"That's not much, Red. You've got to keep up your strength. You're getting ahead and you've got to keep going."

"Why?" She dropped her eyes to his.

Harry shook his head and took the last bite of asparagus. After he finished his wine, he wiped his mouth, dropped the napkin into his lap and pushed back his chair. "Boy, that was good. When Pearl retires she can start a cooking school."

"I would have eaten lunch," she mumbled and pressed the buzzer. "But you weren't here."

While Pearl was clearing away the plates and dishes, Miss Anderson came out with Freddie and Lavinia.

"Would it be all right if the children played out on the lawn for a while? They seem pretty calm," she added. "Or would that disturb you?"

"Certainly not," Harry answered before Katie could protest. He held out his arms to the fat little bodies.

"Eighteen. Nineteen. Twenty." Freddie hung at the edges, just out of reach of Harry's hand, still holding on to Miss Anderson.

"Eighteen! Nineteen! Twenty!" Lavinia mimicked, leaning against Harry's legs.

"That's not nice, Lavinia," Harry reprimanded her. "You mustn't make fun of Freddie."

"Twenty-one! Twenty-two! Twenty-three!" Lavinia echoed, giggling in between.

"No, Lavinia!" Harry took her arm and turned her to face him.

Miss Anderson said sharply: "That's enough of that, Lavinia! I'm sorry, Mrs. Harding, I thought they would behave. I'll get them down on the lawn."

Katie wanted to get up and slap Lavinia, but she didn't have the energy.

Freddie counted on, undeterred by his sister. "Twenty-eight. Twenty-nine. Thirty. Thirty-one."

Lavinia pulled away from Harry's hold and ran to put her face right in front of Freddie's. "Twenty-eight! Twenty-nine! Thirty!"

"Stop that at once!" Miss Anderson reached for her, but Lavinia ducked and ran to the steps that led to the garden.

"Thirty-one! Thirty-two! Thirty-three!" She shrieked, then when she saw Harry stand up she took a deep breath, her face turning red, and started to scream.

"She's just trying to get attention, Harry! Remember?" Katie said fiercely.

Harry stopped and looked at Lavinia. "I'm ashamed of you, Lavinia!" he said loud enough for her to hear. "If it's attention you want, you've got it! But the worst kind! You make me and Mommy ashamed of you!"

Lavinia stopped abruptly and stared at him across the terrace, then she again started to scream the high piercing scream.

Katie stood up. "Don't pick her up! Don't do it! Can't you see that's just what she's trying to get you to do?" She leaned on the table top. "Ignore her!" Her head throbbed. She clutched the edge of the table. "Don't do it, Harry!"

Miss Anderson had tried to make a dash for Lavinia, but Freddie was dragging on her hand, holding her back. "Thirty-nine. Forty. Forty-one."

Lavinia screamed a solid, long ear-splitting scream, her eyes wide open and her head shaking from side to side, gasping for more breath and screaming.

Harry went to her and picked her up. He carried her out onto the lawn and walked her until she stopped.

Katie sank back down into her chair. "She just does that to get him to hold her."

"I think you're right," Miss Anderson agreed. "But it does stop her. I think it's something she'll outgrow."

"If we can stand it in the meantime."

"Fifty-two. Fifty-three. Fifty-four. Fifty-five."

"All right, Freddie." Miss Anderson led him down the steps. "We'll go for a walk. Maybe we'll go down and see how Mario's vegetable garden is coming along. Or we can look for wild strawberries in the field."

Katie poured another glass of wine. That wasn't going to be enough. She'd better get upstairs and take a pill.

Pearl brought out a bowl of strawberries and a pitcher of cream. "Shall I leave these on the table for you and Mr. Harding to help yourselves?" She obviously had heard the screaming and knew where Harry was.

"Yes. Just put it here." Katie waved her hand toward the bare spot on the table.

Pearl put a dessert plate, fork and spoon in front of Katie and another set at Harry's plate. "Shall I bring out coffee or shall I wait?"

"Bring it out. He'll be back soon," Katie said wearily, her voice sounding old. How many days was it until the children went? Four? Something like that. All she had to do was control herself until then. After that, she could relax again. Dear God, what horrible children. Where had they gotten those genes? She'd just get upstairs and pop a pill before Harry got back. Or a quicks42drink.

Harry was piling strawberries on his plate when Katie returned, holding on to the screen door for support, not really feeling drunk, simply weak.

"Everything quiet now?" she asked, weaving her way to her chair.

"Want this one?" He held up the plate.

"No. That's too many. Give me about three or four." She watched him as he carefully counted out four berries and put them on her plate. She wasn't amused. "No cream." She took the plate from him. She didn't even want these.

They ate in silence. Katie concentrated as she lifted the coffee pot, watching it, carefully tipping it, and managed to pour two cups of coffee. She slowly pushed one toward Harry, and with another effort gave the sugar bowl a nudge. She was feeling calmer now. Still pretty wretched, but at least calmer. She looked at her hands. They weren't trembling quite as much.

"Will you be here tonight?" she asked, not looking at Harry but at the black coffee.

"As a matter of fact, I won't. I've got to see the forester this evening."

Katie turned her eyes back to him. "Oh?"

"Yes. But I won't be late. Why don't you go to a movie? I could drop you off, then come back and get you. Or if I finish up in a hurry, come join you."

"You won't finish in a hurry." A little brandy in the coffee would just hit the spot, but she didn't have the courage to ask for it.

"You're probably right. But I could certainly come back and pick you up."

"If I go, I'll drive myself."

"Wouldn't it be easier if I took you?"

"No. It wouldn't. I'll drive myself. What's playing?"

"I don't know, but they're usually pretty good."

"How do you know? I haven't noticed you going to the movies so much."

"True. But I read about them in the local paper."

A movie. Yes, she thought, that was a good idea. It would at least get her out of the house and into a quiet theater where she could lose herself in someone else's life. Anything was preferable to staying here tonight, alone. "I'll go to the nine o'clock showing. That was very thoughtful of you, Harry, to suggest I go to a movie."

She stood up and walked into the house, leaving three strawberries on her plate.

16

At nine-thirty Katie got up and walked out of *The Tin Drum*. It was too upsetting. The midget entertainers reminded her of freakish children; the sexual innuendos got mixed up in her head with her longing for Harry; and on top of it all there was the war. She had enough screaming and fighting at home.

She drove home and put the car in the garage, looking with regret at the jeep's empty space.

In the kitchen, Miss Anderson was seated at the table drinking a cup of warm milk.

"I do not recommend that movie, Miss Anderson. It's very depressing."

"I read the reviews and had already decided not to go. Can I fix you something? I'm having warm milk. It works wonders for a good night's sleep."

"I think I'll have a drink. After that ordeal, I need something stronger than milk." She went into the pantry and made herself a strong Scotch-and-soda, which she carried back to the kitchen. "Do you mind if I sit with you a minute?"

"Certainly not." Miss Anderson did not look at the drink.
"The children are asleep. It will be good to get Freddie to the
beach; I think a complete change will help him a lot."

"Poor Freddie."

"Yes. It's a terrible thing. But he's very fond of the beach;
he likes playing in the sand and watching the waves rush up
to his feet. It will be good for him."

"I hope so." Katie sipped her drink. "So many awful things
have happened lately, haven't they?"

"An unusual number, I would say."

"Of course I never met Miss Wright's brother, but even so
it upset me a great deal. The suicide of someone so young . . ."
she twisted the glass in a circle on the table.

"He was a very fine person." Miss Anderson emptied her
cup and pushed it neatly to the side.

"You knew him?" Katie looked at her questioningly.

"Certainly I knew him. I've known Kay and Dan since they
were very young. I knew their parents. Their mother was a
grand person. I first met her through a church function many
years ago. I was still in nurses' training then. Both the parents
were very religious people, with a strict sense of morals, and
they lived by a religious code of ethics. Very nice people."

"You knew Miss . . . Kay?" Katie looked at her with
disbelief.

"Yes. From the time she was a child."

"But . . . but why have I never known this?"

Miss Anderson looked at her empty cup. "I don't really
know. Of course, as I said, it was her mother who was my
friend." She looked at Katie. "I was the one who got Kay the
job at the school. I heard through local friends that they were
looking for a teacher, and I got in touch with Kay—at the
time, I was near the city with you—but Kay's parents had
recently died, and I got in touch with her and told her to apply
for the job. She got it, and has been there since."

"But . . ." Katie brushed her hair back with her hand. "I'm
absolutely dumbfounded. I just assumed you knew her through
picking up the children at school; I mean, that you had gotten
to know her the same way I had."

"No. Not at all." Miss Anderson looked at her with un-
blinking eyes, catching every slight expression on Katie's face.

"But why haven't you ever told me this?"

"It didn't seem important for you to know. You and Kay

became friends on one level; Kay and I were friends on another level."

"But I don't understand why Kay didn't mention it to me. It makes me feel very stupid to have been referring to her as 'Miss Wright' to you for three years when you've known her a lot longer than I have."

Miss Anderson smiled kindly at her. "Don't let that bother you. It is not the sort of thing that bothers me."

"But didn't it make you feel I was being . . . well, superior or something?"

"Not a bit. You and I respect each other in our roles in this family; anything like that does not affect our relationship to each other, nor to my job here."

"But why wouldn't Kay have mentioned it?"

Miss Anderson knew why Kay hadn't mentioned it; she also knew Mrs. Harding would figure it out herself very soon.

"Kay had a difficult childhood. I don't believe she was ever happy until she got with the school. She likes teaching, and she seems to enjoy children." She noticed Mrs. Harding hadn't had any more of her drink. "Dan was a very fine person, but he and Kay were never close. Of course it was a shock for her when he killed himself, but one she will get over quickly. Kay never liked his wife, and I don't even know that she ever has met the son. I must remember to ask her. The wife, Barbara, is a wonderful person, too. She and Dan were made for each other. This will be a great loss for her, and of course she will always worry that she didn't see he needed help. She's a great girl."

The Jewish wife was a great girl? Katie remembered she had never told Harry about Kay and that awful remark. "Someday you must tell me about them both, and the son. I would like to understand this better."

"Yes. I will."

"But Kay . . . not letting me know she knew you. And she never has called you by your first name in front of me, or not that I can remember."

Miss Anderson saw that Mrs. Harding was grasping the entire picture. A few hints would help her along. "I daresay she didn't want you to know she was friends with one of your staff. Perhaps she's insecure, and was afraid you wouldn't be quite so friendly with her if you knew. Or something like that. Of course, I know that sort of thing would never stand in your way of being friends with someone, but I guess she was afraid of losing your friendship. It's certainly the only explanation I can come up with."

"Yes. Maybe you're right. I'd like to talk to her right now, to get this straight. I don't like it. There's something wrong here."

"Plus, she may have needed the children as a sort of surrogate family. And then, Mr. Harding . . ." Miss Anderson stood up and took her cup to the sink to wash it out.

"She's never known my husband very well. As you know, I usually have her up here when he's away."

"Yes, I know. But when you were in the hospital . . . well, I believe she got to know him quite well."

A chill ran up Katie's spine. She stared into her glass; she had barely touched her drink.

"I believe I'll turn in, if you'll excuse me," Miss Anderson said. "I have a lot of packing to do tomorrow and want to get up early and get at it before Freddie gets up."

"Of course, you go ahead. I'll turn out the lights."

"Thank you. Goodnight, Mrs. Harding."

"Goodnight, Miss Anderson," Katie murmured, still staring into the glass.

At last, Katie stood up, locked the back door, turned out the kitchen lights, leaving her Scotch-and-soda on the table and walked down the hall. She put a key in her pocket, let herself out the front door and started down the drive in her high-heeled sandals that twisted and turned every time she stepped on a rock or in a hole in the gravel. She struggled on in her sandals, twisting and stumbling, holding her arms slightly in front of her to ward off any branches that might be in the way or the ground if she went down to meet it. It was beautiful out, the first quick flickers of fireflies dotting the black night. Overhead the waxing moon cast a soft light on the trees and deeply shadowed driveway. It was very hard to see where she was going. She walked gingerly, picking her way along the gravel.

When she reached East Road, she took off her shoes, then looked to make sure lights were on at Kay's apartment. There were. She followed them to the neat white garage building, the asphalt soothing to her feet. As she turned the corner that led to the back of the garage and Kay's downstairs door, she stopped short. There was a jeep. In fact, Harry's jeep. She reached out her hand, dangling her sandals, and touched a nearby tree. What was Harry doing here?

But of course. He had finished his meeting with the forester, and he thought she was at the movie. So he had stopped here to pass the time until she got home. He would figure Kay was still upset about Dan and needed company. They had become close when she was in the hospital. Should she turn around and go home? No, she would go on upstairs and get a ride home. She began to feel frightened.

Katie tried the downstairs door. It was unlocked. She glanced up at the apartment. A light was on in the living room, but not in the bedroom. There was another small light, there at the end, yes, in the bathroom. Well, they would be in the living room, probably having a drink. She wondered if Harry knew about Kay's friendship with Miss Anderson.

She climbed the stairs, making no noise in her bare feet, and raised her hand to knock, but before she did she listened. They weren't talking. She leaned her head close to the door. No sound at all. She put her hand on the doorknob and tried to turn it, but it was locked. She listened some more. There was a faint sound of laughter—Harry's—far off someplace. She could just barely hear it. Certainly it was not coming from the living room.

Katie stepped back as the cold sensation swept from her head down her body. Beads of perspiration formed on her forehead and upper lip and she almost dropped the sandals. With her hands trembling she clutched them to her chest and opened and shut her eyes a few times. This wasn't a dream. She slowly sank down onto the top step and bent double as the blood drained from her face. She fought the urge to faint, fought it by dropping her head lower. When she again felt the blood in her head, she slowly raised it and stared down the long narrow flight of steps to the door. Then she stood up, holding the wall for support, and eased herself down to the door. Once outside she took a deep breath and walked slowly to the jeep. She opened the door on the passenger side and sat down, staring straight ahead of her. She never moved for almost an hour.

She could hear him coming down the stairs, quietly shutting the door, then opening the door to the jeep. He was in the seat and pulling the door shut when he suddenly turned his head and jumped.

"Red!"

She didn't look at him.

"Jesus, Red, what are you doing here?"

Still she didn't answer.

Harry reached over to take her hand. It felt like ice and pulled away from his touch. He withdrew his hand, saying nothing, and started the car. He switched on the headlights, shooting beams into the black night, and quickly drove the short distance home. He left the jeep in front of the house.

Katie got out, pulled the key out of her pocket and opened the door. She dropped her sandals on the hall floor and walked down the side hall toward the kitchen.

Harry caught up with her and took her arm, stopping her. "Red. You've got to talk to me."

She turned her eyes on him, narrow and cold, then jerked her arm free and continued on her way. In the pantry she took a full bottle of vodka out of the cupboard, started to reach for a glass, then changed her mind. She brushed past Harry and carried the bottle to the central hall, past the ancestral faces to the terrace door. She unlocked it, went out and walked down the steps onto the lawn, unscrewing the cap as she went.

Harry followed her to the terrace and stopped at the door, watching her fade out of sight into the darkness. He slapped his fist downward, hitting his thigh. "Shit." He turned back and went upstairs.

Through many dark hours of the night, Katie stumbled across the lawn, sobbing, openly weeping, stopping to drink from the bottle, occasionally crying out like a wounded bird. She wept and walked with her head tipped back, staring blindly at the elusive half moon that over and over hid behind the windswept clouds. There was so much sky above her, spreading endlessly; beneath it, she seemed so small and diminishing. She felt so alone.

Her arms hung limply at her sides, trailing the bottle like a weighty wing, while her bare feet pressed the wet grass. Once she screamed loudly: "Why did you leave me? Why?!" Other times there were only whimpering sounds.

She didn't know that three people watched her agony. Still dressed in his blue shirt and khaki pants, Harry watched from the upstairs balcony; on the floor above him, the ramrod position of the gray-haired watcher never relaxed or moved; in the darkened shadows of the garden, the other one sat on the porch step and followed her every move, by sight and by sound.

Finally she stumbled and fell to the ground. She knelt, doubled forward, and unscrewed the cap for the last time. Unsteadily, she raised her head and shook the last drop of liquid into her mouth. Then she let the bottle fall from her hand and sagged to the ground, putting her face on the soft grass. There was one last dying murmur before silence fell beneath the trees.

The watcher in the garden, alerted by the sudden silence, quickly stood up and sprang forward. He scanned the grounds from the shadow of a tree, taking in the scene. But before he could move, a tall figure could be seen running from the terrace. Obscured by the tree, Mario stood where he was while the tall man knelt by the collapsed body, lifted it in his arms and carried it back into the house.

On the third floor, a shade was pulled down.

Mario went back to bed. It was three o'clock in the morning.

The hot summer light brightened one side of the bedroom; the other side, where Katie lay on the bed, was in shadow. When Harry saw her eyes open, he crossed the room and sat on the side of the bed, taking her hand in his. Katie clutched it in a desperate squeeze and shut her eyes again.

Harry wanted to get up and open the heavy brocade curtains of the french doors to let in the light, but he couldn't release her hand. Instead he leaned across her and pressed the buzzer.

Presently Pearl called from the other side of the door, knocking softly. "You want me?"

"Yes," Harry answered. "Come in." And when she was in the room: "Open those curtains, will you? Let's get some light in this place."

Pearl pulled the cord and the curtains parted, letting the light sweep into the room and across the bed. "Anything else?" she asked anxiously, looking at Katie.

"Why don't you run Mrs. Harding a bath. Not too hot. It's going to be a scorcher today."

Katie lay still without moving. She could hear the water running in the bathroom. She stared at the ceiling and listened.

"All ready any time she wants it," Pearl called.

"Thanks," Harry answered.

"Glad to do it," Pearl replied. "Now here's a fresh nightie for you to put on when you get out of the tub. I'll just leave it here on the foot of the bed. Now you be sure and ring for me when you get in the tub and I'll come straighten up the bed." She stopped by the door. "Feel like some juice and a cup of tea?"

Katie shook her head.

"Maybe later then." Pearl went out and closed the door.

"Why don't you sit up and I'll help you get to the tub. It'll make you feel better." Harry tried to pull his hand away, but Katie squeezed tighter. "I'm not going anyplace, Red. I'll be right here with you. Let's just get you in the tub. You're hot and sticky now." He managed to loosen her fingers, while not taking his eyes from hers. "Sit up and I'll help you."

Katie allowed herself to be pulled to a sitting position on the bed. Harry unbuttoned her wrinkled shirt and dropped it on the floor. He then pushed her back down, the top half of her bare and fragile as a china doll, and unzipped her slacks, pulling them off her in a touching maternal gesture. He slid her skimpy silk underpants off and tossed them aside, then he picked her up and carried her into the bathroom.

While she sat in the tub, Harry again pressed the buzzer for Pearl. When she appeared he said, "You can straighten up now. Then bring her up some juice, coffee or tea and a piece of toast. Got any of those strawberries left?"

"Sure do."

"Bring a few of those. Not too much of anything."

"I know."

Harry went back into the bathroom and sat on the small chair in the corner and watched her slowly soap and rinse herself. He helped her out of the tub and wrapped a large towel around her; he turned her around and rubbed her back. Then he went to the bedroom, crossed it and went to his own bathroom where he splashed cold water on his face. He dried his face, hung the towel on the peg and went back to get the white nightgown. This he took to Katie and pulled it over her head while she stood stiffly, staring into space.

"Come lie back down, Red. Come lie down and rest."

She let herself be led by him.

Pearl had just finished putting clean linen sheets on the bed and was turning back the top sheet. "There we are. You just lie down here." She propped two pillows against the headboard.

Harry steered Katie to the bed and onto the cool pillows. He picked up her legs and swung them onto the bed. "Now Pearl's going to bring you something to eat." He pulled the sheet all the way to the foot of the bed and loosely folded it there. Then he sat back down beside her.

Katie closed her eyes, again curling her fingers around Harry's hand. There was no movement or talk until Pearl returned with a tray.

"Just put it over here where I can reach it," Harry said. "Want to try a little juice?"

Katie finally looked directly at him, watching his eyes as he put the glass to her lips. She took a small swallow, then pulled back.

"Maybe something hot. What is it?" he asked Pearl.

"Tea. That seems to sit better on the stomach, I think. Leastways, it does on mine."

"Good. We'll try some of that."

"You want me to get something else?" Pearl asked.

"No. That's all for now. I'll ring if we need you."

When he and Katie were alone, Harry tried to coax her to drink some tea. It wasn't easy to hold the cup with one hand, but she wouldn't turn loose the other one. "There we go, Red. Just a swallow or two. You'll feel better then." He replaced the cup and lifted the toast triangle to her mouth. "Just take one bite. Just one." She shook her head. "Okay. Maybe later." He saw the tears fill her eyes before she shut them.

He sat for the rest of the morning, leaving his hand in her tight grasp. When she seemed hot and restless, he rang for Pearl and asked her to bring him a cool wet washcloth. He wiped her face, neck and arms with this, then patted her dry with a soft linen towel.

They sat alone, not speaking. Summer sounds drifted through the screens of both open double doors, and the air, though hot, was not oppressive.

The time had passed so quickly, Harry couldn't tell how long he had been there on the side of the bed. Occasionally he looked at the clock on her desk. She had been awake at nine. Ten came. Then eleven.

"We'd better go for a swim later. Think you'll feel up to it?" He touched the unruly mass of auburn hair that spread across the pillow. "Maybe we ought to call the air-conditioner man after all."

"I hate air conditioning." It was the first thing she had said.

"Stubborn, that's what you are." He bent and kissed the tip of her nose.

Katie shut her eyes again and tears slipped past the closed lids at the corners. "Why?" was all she asked.

"Jesus, Red. I don't know. I'm half crazy with it. I've been about to go out of my mind, all night and this morning. I don't know. I just don't know."

She choked back a sob.

"Oh God, Red. I'd give anything to have it to do over again. I never wanted to hurt you. Never."

"Why, Harry, why?" She wiped her eyes with the back of her thin white hand, opened them and looked at him.

He bowed his head. "I don't know. I just don't know. Can you ever forgive me?"

"I hope so." Her head felt ready to burst with the terror swelling there. "I'll have to. You're all I've got. Oh God, I wish I knew what to do."

He bent and put his arm around her and held her close to him. "You're the only one I've ever loved. No one else."

"I trusted you, Harry. I trusted you." Her trust for him had never wavered the way it had for Joe. "I was so wrong both times."

He didn't know what she was saying. "Jesus, I never wanted to hurt you. I'd rather kill myself than hurt you. I should have killed myself before I did this to you."

"No. I need you." She took a deep rattling breath. She knew now it had been Kay who had put the note in the jeep. Kay had done it. She had failed then in her treachery, but now she had succeeded. It had not been Joe. How could she have been so blind? How could she have ever doubted Joe and turned away from him most. "I have to talk to Joe." She reached across the bed, frantically clawing at the edge to get to the phone.

Harry pulled her back. "Joe? You can't telephone him, Red. You know that."

"I have to. I have to tell him I love him." She tried to fight Harry away from her. "I have to."

"Lie still, Red. Joe knows you love him."

"No. You don't know."

"That's one thing I'm sure of. Joe knows you love him."

"Oh, Harry, you don't understand."

"Lie back and rest." He pushed her down onto the pillows. She seemed so frail and small, as if she had shrunk overnight. He wanted to get out of the room and breathe fresh air, to escape for a little. Instead he leaned over her and spoke softly. "You're the only one I love. Only you."

"How could you have done it?"

"I don't know. I just don't know."

"You must never do it again, not as long as I'm alive."

"No, no. I won't." He kissed her cheeks and eyes.

"You must promise me. Not as long as I'm alive will you do that again."

"I promise." His mind could reject Kay as easily as it had accepted her.

"Are you just saying that, or do you really mean it?"

"I really mean it."

"You swear?"

"I swear. I love you, Red. I'll never hurt you again."

"I wish I could talk to Joe. Are you sure we can't find him?"

"He's all right. Nothing's happened to him. And he knows you love him."

Katie closed her eyes. "I never understood." She tried to think of nothing but the summer sounds: birds, distant voices, the faint dull roar of cars on the road. She tightened her hold on Harry's hand and tried to sleep. If she could sleep, if only for a little while, she wouldn't remember anything then—not last night, not Kay, not the note, not Joe. Sleep would release her from the world for a little while. Sleep, with no dreams.

Katie slept just deeply enough to relieve her mind, but not so deeply she didn't hear the faint knocking on the door.

"Come in." She turned her head on the pillows.

The door opened and Mario came in, his clean blue jeans and blue workshirt with sleeves rolled to the elbow, looking wholesome and refreshing. It made Katie smile to see him, a faint wan smile, but a smile nevertheless.

"Come on in," she said.

He walked into the middle of the room, leaving the door open. "How are you?"

"Fine."

"I heard you were sick."

"I guess so." She looked down at herself in the long white nightgown. Her feet and ankles lay on top of the sheet across the bottom of the bed. "I guess I was just tired."

"Yeah, probably. It's nice in here though. Real hot outside." He looked around the room, taking in everything.

Katie watched him.

"I left flowers downstairs. Pearl said she'd put them in a vase and bring some up to you."

"Thanks. How's the garden going?"

"Everything's doing fine. This hot weather is good for things.

And the dews at night are still heavy, and that's good, too. We need a little rain. I guess we'll get it soon."

"Probably." She pointed toward her desk chair. "Will you sit down?"

"No thanks. I really wanted . . . well, I really wanted to come in and say goodbye."

"Goodbye? Where are you going?" Katie raised herself more onto the pillows.

"I'm leaving. That's all. I'm leaving." He looked uneasily around the room again. He did not let his eyes rest on her for long.

"Leaving? I don't understand. Why are you leaving?"

"It's time for me to move along."

"I thought you were happy here and would stay for a while."

"I thought so, too. But I've changed my mind."

Katie put both her hands together in a prayerlike position under her chin. "Has anyone . . . anyone said . . . said anything to you? To make you leave, I mean?"

"No. Nothing." He turned and walked to the french doors that opened onto the balcony. "The garden looks nice from up here."

"Have I done anything to offend you?"

"Good God, no. You couldn't offend anyone." He continued to stare out the window.

"A better job? Is that it?"

"No. No job. I'll look for one after I get farther north. I think I'll wander a little first though." He turned his head and smiled at her. "You pay pretty well, you know, and I've been able to save up some money. I can coast for a while before I have to look for another job."

"Something must be wrong. You must tell me what it is." She dropped her hands to her lap. "The summer's the nicest time around here. I think you'd enjoy it."

He turned and walked to the foot of the bed and looked down at her. "I'm leaving because of you."

Katie looked at him questioningly.

"I can't stand by and watch you destroy yourself, with no one to stop you or even help you much. I see you sitting on that terrace alone, all day, reading and staring into space. Swimming until you're exhausted because it's all you've got. Standing out there," he motioned with his head, "on that balcony staring into some distance that only you can see and maybe not even you. I see you. You're destroying yourself. I can't step forward and help you myself. If I did, I'd be out on my ear. I'd be out if I even said anything like this to anyone but you." He reached down and touched the linen, then put his hand back on his hip, arms akimbo. "I can't stay here and not step forward and try to do something. So, if I'm going to be out, I'd rather go on my own steam." He paused to let this sink in. "It's as simple as that. You understand."

Katie lowered her eyes and nodded. "I'm sorry."

"Jesus, lady, I'm the one who's sorry. But I can't stay here and watch you."

Tears gathered in Katie's eyes. She bit her lip and looked up at him. "I'm sorry," was all she repeated.

"Yeah. Well, take it easy. It was really something for me to have known you." He walked to the door. "So long."

"Mario." Katie stopped him.

He looked at her.

"Thanks." Tears fell down her cheeks.

He jerked his head sideways in resignation. "Yeah, sure. Any time." He left, closing the door after him.

"Where have you been?" Katie asked Harry when he came back and sat beside her.

"Having lunch with the kids."

She clutched his hand. "How's everything?" She felt so weak.

"Everything's fine. Miss Anderson is getting ready to take the kids away. They're all excited about that."

"Tell her to take the Cadillac. It will be more comfortable for her to drive than the station wagon."

"I think she's got the wagon half packed by now. She's not one to wait until the last minute. Besides, I think you and I should take a drive someplace, and you'll be more comfortable in the Cadillac too."

Katie looked vacantly across the room. "We won't go anyplace," she said wearily.

"Don't say that. Sure we will. We can go as soon as you get out of bed and get dressed. We can go today if you want."

"I don't feel like it."

"Then tomorrow. The minute you feel like it, we'll pick up and go."

"Maybe."

"Feel like a little soup? Pearl made some delicious gazpacho."

"I don't want anything red."

He laughed at her. "What color would you like?"

"I don't know." She closed her eyes. "What about Kay? What'll I do about Kay?"

She felt Harry's hand tighten. "I don't know. Maybe we won't have to worry about it for a while. She won't be up today, and tomorrow she goes to Dan's funeral, and maybe we'll be gone after that."

"We'll be back sometime. Then what will I do about her?"

"Try to forgive her."

Katie opened her eyes and stared coldly at him. "Why?"

"Because she's your friend. And because you're a very forgiving person."

"I may not be anymore," she answered bitterly.

"Joe made a mistake and we sure didn't hold it against him."

"That was different." How could she ever have mistrusted Joe?

"You know yourself how easy it is to slip up once in a while."

"What do you mean?" Did he know about Mario?

"Just that."

"It's one thing to slip up with someone who doesn't matter. That doesn't mean anything. It's a different matter with friends. Best friends. She was my best friend."

"Don't put all the blame on her."

"I don't." She paused to watch him, noting the words had hit him deep. "But I forgive you. I love you."

"This will all pass, Red. You'll see."

"I love you enough to forgive you anything. You're my life. You slipped away from me when I wasn't looking, when I wasn't trying to understand. You needed someone and you didn't have me. But she was my best friend. She doesn't have any good excuse."

"It's over with. You'll see, it's over and done with. You'll forget and forgive."

"I'll never trust her again. I never want to see her again. You see to it that she stays away from here. Do you hear me, Harry?"

Harry brought her hand to his lips. "It will be all right. You'll see."

Katie wondered if her father had ever deceived her mother.

Probably not. He adored her. He worshipped her like a goddess. After she was dead, maybe. But not before.

"I love you, Red."

Later that afternoon Katie woke up from a nap feeling very sick. Harry said it was because she hadn't eaten for so long. He had Pearl bring her more tea and a piece of toast. Katie went to the bathroom and took two tranquilizers. She had a few bites of toast and felt worse. Harry wanted to call Dr. Ames, but she wouldn't let him. She said she was just tired.

She knew she was depressed. She enumerated to herself all the reasons for her depression. She had almost lost Harry. She had been betrayed by her best friend. But neither of those was as bad as her own betrayal of Joe; she had doubted him, believed him to be guilty. She hadn't had the brains to ask him about it. Instead she assumed his guilt and sent him off, not loving him, not kissing him, nor touching him the way she always had. And all because of Kay. The depths of her hatred for Kay grew with each hour. There would never be a boundary where that growing hatred would be halted. Never, until death.

And on top of all that, she hated hearing the noises of Lavinia and Freddie. Once when the incessant counting drifted over her like a smothering shroud, she began to scream: "For God's sake, someone shut the windows!" Harry had called to Miss Anderson to take the children to the pool and keep them there.

Harry had pulled an armchair to the side of the bed to ease the strain on his back while he held her hand. He faced it toward her so he could watch her while she slept and she could see him when she awakened.

"It's almost six," he said, looking at the cold tea and toast. "I'm going to go see what kind of soup Pearl made for dinner." He eased his hand from her grip. "Be right back."

"Don't go." Katie was frantic he would leave her and not return.

"Don't worry, Red. I'll be back."

Harry returned with a soup cup and a tea cup on a small bed-tray. "It's carrot. She made it especially for you." He put it on the bedside table and pulled up the pillows behind her. "You've got to eat. And hot tea."

"All right. I'll try."

He pulled out the legs under the tray and straddled it over her. "Eat it all, Red. You'll feel better."

"Where will you be?"

"If you don't mind, I'd like to have a quick swim. Then I'll bring my dinner tray up here and eat with you. You have that finished by the time I get back." He went into his dressing room and soon came back in his trunks. "How're you doing?"

"I'm eating it. Don't rush me."

"Good girl. Be back soon."

When he left, Katie moved the tray to the side and got out of bed. She stood at the french doors and watched for him. When she saw him cross the terrace alone and head for the pool, she breathed easier. She waited until she heard the splash.

Katie took the soup cup into the bathroom and poured half of it down the toilet. She got the vodka bottle out from under the silks and carried it to the bedroom and poured a good shot into her tea. Then she replaced the bottle and got back into bed. She drank the tea and ate the small amount of soup in the cup.

Harry came back with his towel wrapped around him and his hair wet. "How's that sitting in your stomach?"

"It's all right. I feel better. You were right. I must have just been too empty."

"Want to try coming downstairs? A change of scenery might cheer you up."

"Where are the children?"

"They're eating their dessert on the lawn right now. Miss Anderson can take them off to play someplace else if you want to lie on the terrace."

"Mario left, you know."

"Yes. Too bad. Did he come up here?"

"Yes. He came to say goodbye."

"Short notice, but that's the way it is with these young boys. At least he found a temporary replacement until I could get hold of someone else. That was decent of him."

"Yes. Very decent."

Harry stepped out of his wet trunks. It had been a long time since Katie had seen him naked. He walked into the dressing room. His back was a deep tan above his lean white buttocks. His legs were light tan. "You need to get your legs in the sun more," she called after him. She wondered what Kay thought of that strong muscular body, lean and brown with the wide white band around him. Kay. She buried her face in her hands, with her thumbs in her ears.

Before Harry could come back, she had been in the bath-room, taking a small drink from the bottle, and had put on a gossamer cotton negligee. She didn't bother to look at herself in the mirror, but she did run the hairbrush through the front of her hair leaving the back a matted damp magenta.

"I think I will go down." She felt dizzy and put out her hand to Harry.

He caught it. "Are you okay? Feeling a little faint?"

"I'm all right." She straightened up.

"Want me to carry you down?"

She waved the thought away with her fingertips. "No. You'll have a heart attack if you keep hauling me around."

"You don't weigh very much."

She let that pass and walked out the door, holding on to Harry's arm for support.

Two sleeping pills and a little more vodka had allowed Katie to get a good night's sleep. But when she woke up the next morning and tried to get out of bed, she felt worse. The nausea swelled up from the pit of her stomach and hung in her chest. She was dizzy and began to get that cold clammy feeling again. Harry was gone. She lay there awhile, then tried again. Struggling out of bed, holding on to the table and the back of the chair that Harry had sat in the day before, she managed to get across the room and into the bathroom. There she sat on the toilet, breathing heavily from the exertion.

She was afraid she would fall if she got in the shower. She took off her nightgown and wet a washcloth, running it around her face and up the length of her arms. She managed to get a summer negligee around herself and buttoned up the front. Then she went back and sat on the side of the bed until her head felt clearer.

It was after nine. Harry would have gone to the office by now. If she called him, to hear his voice and reassure herself, he might think she was checking up on his whereabouts. She couldn't do that. He had to feel that she trusted him. She did trust him. Now. He had promised her he would never do it again. She trusted him, but a quiet rage overcame her when she thought of Kay.

She got to the head of the bed and pressed the buzzer for someone.

Pearl soon came. "How are you feeling today? You're looking better."

Katie knew that was a lie. "Has Mr. Harding gone to the office?"

Pearl nodded. "But he said to call him if you needed him. He wasn't going off into the woods, and could come home in a hurry. Do you want him?"

"No. I'm all right."

"Feel like some breakfast?"

"No. I want to go lie on the terrace. Maybe something cool to drink. That's all."

"Don't you think you ought to just lie right here? It's terrible hot outside, but it's real nice in here."

"You may be right. Could you bring me up that little portable TV, the one Mr. Harding uses to watch the news at breakfast?"

"Sure thing. And what kind of cool drink? Orange juice, apple, grapefruit?"

"Grapefruit."

While Katie waited for Pearl to come back, she tried to remember the name of the vodka-and-grapefruit concoction. Not orange blossom. Sea something? Sea breeze? Was that it? She wasn't sure and there wasn't anyone she could ask. She could call someone in New York and ask, but she couldn't ask anyone in this household, even if she thought they'd know.

Call someone in New York? It would be nice to talk to Steven. Just to talk to him. He made her feel attractive and desirable. Over the phone, he couldn't see the way she looked. She wondered if he ever thought of her anymore.

After Pearl had straightened up the bed and gotten Katie back in, with the grapefruit juice by her side and the TV on a small table where she could reach it, she left, closing the door.

Katie reached for the phone and dialed Steven's apartment number. It was an easy number to remember, though she hadn't thought of it for a long time.

"Hello?"

Katie closed her eyes at the sound of his voice.

"Hello?" he repeated. "Hello?"

Katie felt so tired. She let the heavy curved instrument fall onto the pillow, the voice coming from it now a faint crackling "Hello?" Taking the receiver with both hands, she noisily replaced it in its cradle. She didn't have anything to say to him anyway. She turned on the TV and sipped some of the juice.

Not only did she feel nauseated, but she had a fluttery shallow feeling as if her heart were filled with dying butterflies. She went back to the bathroom, took a Librium and pulled out the vodka bottle. It was getting low. Enough for the grapefruit juice, enough for now, but she would have to replace it soon.

A half-hour later she felt calmer and tried to concentrate on the TV, but Kay's face kept appearing on the screen: Kay in men's clothes, Kay in other women's bodies, Kay's face, over and over. It angered and sickened her to think of Kay. She wished she would never think of her again, but she knew she would not get off that easily. Kay would torture her for the rest of her life. Even if she never came face to face with her, she would be there, every day, popping up in her mind. Katie knew she would start to analyze everything Kay had done or said for the past three years, unraveling, remembering a word, a gesture, a simple action that had seemed so innocent but was really Kay going after Harry. She would never be able to escape it. It would be with her daily, driving her mad that she was forgetting something.

She went back to the bathroom and drank the last of the bottle. The only way to escape Kay was to obliterate everything.

As Kay drove to the diner on the outskirts of town, Harry's words flashed in her brain, over and over: "Katie's beside herself with despair; I don't know what to do. But I've got to see you and talk to you." "Beside herself." That almost certainly meant she would start hitting the bottle again to drown that despair—hitting it hard. And if she did that, if she got blotto enough and churned up her insides enough, then it would be back to the hospital for her. Maybe for longer. And Harry would be hers again. It almost made her have an orgasm just thinking of him, holding her, caressing her; Harry on top of her pushing into her; she straddled across him and riding him like a wild animal; kneeling, her face in the pillow, as he mounted her from behind.

What infuriating luck for Katie to have found out. Katie had everything; she couldn't even let Kay have a little bit of happiness. At first when Harry called, Kay had been furious, furious to have been discovered, and furious when he said he couldn't see her anymore. But the more she thought about it, the more she decided to behave rationally and analyze her next moves as carefully as a chess player at match point. Maybe all wasn't lost, not by a long shot. But she had to be very careful— very, very careful.

Harry was waiting for her at a booth in the rear. He stood up and took her hand briefly before she sat down across from him.

"I ordered two coffees. That all right with you?"

Kay nodded. "Tell me what's going on."

When he had finished, Kay absently stirred her coffee. "Harry, I want you to know," she paused and looked at him, "I'll do whatever you feel we must do to help Katie. We can't let her drink herself to death. As much as I would hate . . . giving you up, I know you have to think of her health first. And . . ."

"Kay."

"Wait. Let me finish. This isn't easy for me to say. Be patient and listen. Even if we can never be together again . . ." she reached across the table and put her hand over his ". . . you have given me something rare and wonderful, and in my mind and in my heart it will never end. I will think of you always, and be happy with the memories I have. The happiness we have shared can't be destroyed. It's probably a lot more than many people get in a lifetime. Maybe a brief period of perfect happiness is enough for anyone."

"Oh God, Kay. You were there when I needed you. You've become a part of me now. Jesus. I don't know what to do."

"Don't do anything except what you have to do. Especially don't worry about it now. You go home and take care of Katie and get her well. That and your lumber business should be enough to occupy your mind for a while. You don't need me now. Maybe you'll never need me again and don't worry about that. I will always know that once the most wonderful man in the world wanted me and needed me and loved me. Even for a brief while—and that will be with me for eternity." She pulled back her hand. "There's nothing more to say now. Go back to the office before you're called and someone discovers you're not there. I'll be all right."

"Kay. I promised Katie I'd never see you again. As you can see, I haven't been able to keep that promise for twenty-four hours."

"Harry, stop fretting about this. Things will straighten out. Who knows? Maybe we'll all get to be friends again." She smiled. "Fate has strange ways of arranging things. Don't fight them. Just get through each day as best you can. Do what's right, Harry." She stood up. "Call me if you need me."

He watched her leave, a heavy depression settling over him.

17

With the wail of the ambulance still careening in his head, Harry followed the stretcher into the emergency room and waited helplessly while Katie was whisked into a cubicle, with white-frocked nurses and interns rushing back and forth, equipment, bottles of clear and dark liquids, the loudspeaker monotonously paging Dr. Ames, Dr. Ames, Dr. Ames. And Katie, her nightgown spattered with blood, limp and motionless, white as the sheet that covered her inert body.

"I don't know," Harry answered. "I don't know how long she was there. The cook found her and I got there the same time as the ambulance. I don't know."

The intern nodded and wrote something on his chart. Dr. Ames came and told Harry to wait outside.

"No. I'll wait here."

Dr. Ames shrugged and went into conference with the staff who had started to work on her.

"She's stable now," the nurse finally said to Harry. "We'll

move her to intensive care. You'd better sit down yourself. You look a bit under the weather."

Harry looked at the clock on the pale green cement wall. The hour had passed so quickly he hadn't realized it. He hadn't thought of anything, time, people, anything, as he kept out of the way and watched all these strangers jab, stick needles into and hook wires around Katie. He thought he recognized a few of the faces from his vigil here a month ago. A month? Five weeks? How long had it been? And here they were again.

He followed the stretcher into intensive care and waited again, never taking his eyes off her.

When Dr. Ames came, Harry said: "I want her put in a private room as soon as possible. She won't like it when she wakes up."

"We can put her in one as soon as we locate some private nurses. Everything that's wrong with her can be handled from a room. She needs transfusions and needs to be monitored."

"Is someone trying to find nurses?"

The doctor nodded. He took off his glasses and wiped them on a clean handkerchief he pulled from his top jacket pocket. "Any way of knowing what set her off again? She was doing so well. I thought she'd be able to stick it out."

"No." Harry almost gagged on the lie. "No, I have no idea. I thought she was doing fine, too. She was exercising, eating, not drinking. Until now."

"She must have been having a little more alcohol, more often than you realize. However, it wouldn't take too much to get her in this condition again. She probably wasn't completely healed."

"Will she pull out of it the way she did before?"

"I don't know, Harry. I really don't know. There's just so much abuse the human body can take before it gives out. We'll do our best. That's all I can say."

"What are you saying?"

Dr. Ames put his hand on Harry's arm. "She's a very sick person, Harry. She's weak. She's lost a lot of blood. Those ruptured veins might not heal again. Or not in time. I'm not sure. Try to understand the problem in its fullest, and worst, aspects. The major blood vessels coming from the intestines go through the liver, which is like a river. Her liver has already been badly scarred; this scar tissue has a constricting effect on blood vessels going into it. These blood vessels become dammed up and in turn they become like lakes; all the little feeder streams going into the river then back up, become engorged, and tend to overflow their banks. This backing up goes all the way into the esophagus, and the delicate walls holding the esophageal veins rupture. That's why she vomits the blood." He put his glasses on. "It wasn't very long ago that the same thing happened. I just don't know, Harry. I have to be honest with you. Internal bleeding . . ." he shook his head. "I just don't know."

"Oh, my God." Harry turned his back on the doctor and walked to the window. What had he done to her? What had he done?

Katie came to before they got her to a room. Harry could tell by the frightened look in her eyes that she was pleading with him to get her out of this curtained cubicle opened at the end to the bustling comings-and-goings of white-coated strangers who peered at her and made clucking noises with their tongues when they read her chart. The beep, beep of the monitor frightened her. The thin red tubes dangling above her arms frightened her. Her inability to make him hear her was the worst of all.

"Don't try to talk, Red. Don't try to talk."

She moved her lips, the swollen tongue trying to push the words out between her teeth, but there were no sounds.

"It's all right." Harry held her hand. "You'll be out of here soon. They've found some nurses, and they'll move you and all your paraphernalia . . ." he indicated the bottles and machines ". . . to a room. Any minute now. It'll be better."

He stayed by her side until she was moved, the entire insides of her cubicle moving as a unit down the corridors smelling of Lysol and death, to a quiet, dimly lit room.

Her nurse checked all her vital signs again, then went to sit in the corner while Harry pulled a chair up beside her and held her hand until she went to sleep.

Harry hadn't prayed for a long time, but he prayed that night after he got into bed. For the first time he was really scared. Her previous hospital bouts had meant drying out and letting things get back to normal, building up her strength again. It had just been a matter of time to get everything working again. But now . . . this time, he was scared.

The big bed was lonely without her. Even if she were passed out, at least she was there. But now he was lonely. He couldn't call Doris; she was gone, gone with another man, someone who might take a permanent place by her side. He had lost Kay—though that wasn't as much of a loss as Doris. Still, Kay meant something to him.

He was sorry about Kay and Red. Right now was the time Red needed a friend. Kay was always so good about being with her when she needed someone. And it was all his fault. Maybe he could get Red to forgive and forget. Well, forgive. Maybe she would see the need of having her friend back when she was feeling so sick. She needed someone besides just him, and Joe wasn't here. If he convinced her that Kay meant nothing to him, then maybe Red would see her and take her back as a friend.

But that wasn't the real reason, if he were honest with himself. He needed to have Red do this because he needed to be forgiven. The burden of what he had done to her was too great for him. He was overwhelmed with guilt.

He finally sank into an exhausted sleep.

The next morning before he went to the hospital Harry called Kay and told her the latest news of Red.

"I know it won't be easy, for either one of you. But she really needs you. And I need you to do it; I feel guilty as hell. Do you think you could bring yourself to go see her? Or would it be too embarrassing for you?"

There was a long pause at the other end of the phone. "It won't be easy. I'll think about it. First you have to make sure she will see me. I don't want to go in there and be thrown out. I know that temper of hers."

"She doesn't have much fight in her right at the moment."

"I told you to call if you needed me. I'll think about it."

"Thanks, Kay. I think you'll see a way to do it. I knew I could count on you."

He hung up thinking what a good person Kay really was. She was one of a kind. Understanding and dependable. He might have promised Red he wouldn't go to bed with her again but he hadn't said anything about not keeping her for a friend. And she would be Red's friend again. Kay would do the right thing, and get Red to forgive her. She knew how to handle Red.

Kay hung up and looked at the polish on her nails. Harry needed her again. In a different way, but he needed her. It was nice; a real Katie pink. If she played her cards right, she could win him back. If she didn't . . . she shrugged. At least the funeral was over and she could put all of that out of her mind, forget the jabbering rabbi and tragic-looking Barbara, forget the strange motley group of unkempt women and seedy men who were an embarrassment just to look at, and who the fuck cared whether they were writers or editors or union organizers that Barbara seemed to extol, hugging them and weeping with them. God. What a day. Thank the Lord there was a plane right back and she had gotten on it.

She ran her hand over the sleek telephone. Well, if Harry'd get in there and pave the way, which she knew he would, then she would confront Katie and see what happened. She wasn't such a coward that she couldn't try. Especially for Harry. She couldn't give him up, not now. Nor did she want to give up his and Katie's life. They might be vicarious rewards for her—always on the fringes of the rich lifebasking in the reflections of their pleasures, accepting the charities that Katie doled out, enjoying the wines and foods that only Katie could afford, riding in Cadillacs and staying at the Carlyle in New York for weekends—it might be enjoying someone else's life, but she did enjoy it. No, she couldn't give that up, not without a fight, and go back to a circle of humdrum mediocrity. She patted her hair and went in to look at her clothes.

"Can you hear me, Red?" Harry bent close to her face, the smell of aftershave lotion mingling with the antiseptic odors that bathed the room. "Can you hear me?"

Katie's eyes felt so heavy she could hardly open them. She tried, and through the haze saw Harry's face. It was out of focus, but she could see his dark eyes, the dark hair, the tan all before her, saying something to her. What was he saying? She parted her lips and touched them with her tongue. She tried to move them, to tell him something.

"I'm right here. Don't try to talk. You're doing fine. Much better."

Katie closed her eyes, faint lights of yellow in lengthening streaks breaking up the dark. She was so tired. She would sleep. Sleep. He was talking again. Again she tried to look at him. He was saying something about coming back later. Later. A great drowsiness overcame her and shut out the rest.

She could hear voices as she drifted back in again. She

wanted to listen. She wanted to open her eyes. It was such an effort. She tried and looked. A great white blur was bending over her, a darker blur nearby.

"Are you waking up, Katie?" She didn't know the deep voice. She narrowed her eyes and tried as hard as she could to concentrate. The dark blur became clearer and she recognized Dr. Ames. "Feeling any better?" She turned her head and looked around the room. The deep voice said: "If you're looking for Harry, he'll be back soon."

"Where am I?" she asked weakly, but she at least was able to talk.

"You're in the hospital."

"I thought I had gotten out."

"What's that? I can't quite hear you."

What was this great heaviness that held her down? She tried to lift her arm, but it was too much for her. She gave up on it, and tried to raise her head, but she couldn't lift that either.

As she lay there she felt a paltry strength flow back into her. Not enough to help her lift anything, but enough for her to concentrate on the room and to speak.

"Why am I here?"

"Why? Because you had another bad spell with hemorrhaging, the way you did before."

"No, no," she moaned. "Not again."

"Afraid so. But you be patient and we'll get you back right again. This is your nurse, Miss Carothers. She'll take good care of you during the day. There are two others, but you don't have to think about them yet."

Miss Carothers smiled kindly at her. She looked strong and efficient, the way nurses were supposed to look.

"Where's Harry?" Katie asked Dr. Ames. "I've got to see him."

"He'll be back soon. He just ran down to the office for a minute. He'll be back soon. I'll drop in on you later."

She watched him go.

The nurse took her hand and patted it. "Would you like for me to wash your face and arms? You might feel better."

She didn't care. She looked at the bottles hanging above her and the connecting tubes like long strands of spaghetti. The nurse was saying something.

"What?"

"Would you like a sip of water?"

"No." She tried to shake her head, but it barely moved. "Is my husband back?"

"Not yet. Very soon, though. Here, let me undo that gown."

After being wiped clean and rubbed dry, Katie didn't feel any better than she had before.

"Now. Isn't that much better?"

"No," Katie answered. She hoped this woman wasn't going to hang over her. She looked at her and after two tries managed to ask: "Do you have something to read?"

"I have my knitting. I'm making a coat for my little granddaughter. Would you like to see it?"

"No, thanks. Little girls' clothes don't interest me." Lavinia in her blue overalls, screaming, sobbing, "I was looking for Daddy." "Just sit over there and knit. I'll be fine." She closed her eyes. She didn't want to see her, white-stockinged, white-dressed, white-capped, the wrinkled white face of efficiency. Neither did she want Lavinia in her mind's eye. "If I need . . . I'll call you." It was Harry that she needed. She had to tell him. She needed Joe.

"All right, dear. You rest now."

Rest. How peaceful that sounded. She would rest and wait for Harry.

It was Harry's attentiveness that brought Katie around, that magnetic pull that sucked her out of the depths of sleep and brought her to reality. She knew he was there even before she opened her eyes.

He leaned past the tubes and kissed her lightly on the forehead.

"I need some water."

Harry leaned closer to her. "What did you say, Red?"

"Water." Why couldn't he understand her?

"Try to say it, Red."

She waited until she felt some strength gathering. "I want some water."

"Water. You got it." Harry put his hand under her head and lightly raised it, while putting the end of the straw in her mouth.

"Not too much, Mr. Harding."

Katie drank, then looked in the direction of the strange voice. Then she remembered the nurse.

"You're much better tonight." Harry pulled a chair close to the bed.

Her mouth felt better. She moved her eyes around the room.

Nothing looked familiar. How long had she been here? She couldn't remember anything for a long, long way back. It was all in some gray fuzz. That wasn't even the right nurse.

"How long have I been here?"

Harry had leaned close to her mouth when she started to speak. "Since yesterday."

"Who is that?"

"Your nurse."

"That's not the nurse."

"Yes. It's the night one. The other one has gone for the day."

"Is it night?" She wanted to touch his face, so close to hers, but she couldn't raise her arm.

"Yes." He put his hand on her shoulder. "You're much better. You've been asleep most of the time since you've been here, and that's helped." He didn't tell her they'd kept her knocked out to keep her quiet.

"When can I go home?"

"When you get well."

"Have you had dinner?"

"Don't worry about me. I can get something downstairs."

"That food's inedible," she said feebly. "You should go home and eat."

He smiled at her. "I will when I'm hungry."

Katie closed her eyes and tried to remember why she was here. "What happened?"

"I don't know. I guess you fainted or something. Pearl called me and called an ambulance. That's all I know."

"I was at home in bed. I think I was feeling sick to my stomach. But I can't remember."

"It doesn't matter. Try to rest. It's what you need."

"I want to go home."

"You will soon."

"I miss you."

"I miss you, too, Red. It's pretty lonely around there, with you and the kids gone."

Joe. That was it. "Harry, please try to find Joe. You can do it if you try."

"Red, honey. I can't phone Joe. You know that."

"You can phone the director and find out where he is. He may be someplace where there's a phone."

"Why do you need to talk to him? Can't it wait?"

"Please don't argue with me." Her eyes filled with tears.

"All right. I'll try." A little lie wouldn't hurt anything; it would even make her feel better. "Miss Anderson has taken the other two to the beach. They just left today. I called last night and the house was all ready, so they left early this morning."

"Where have they gone?" She felt herself sinking again.

"To East Hampton. Remember?"

She remembered. She remembered it now. Lavinia and her doll, Freddie counting, Miss Anderson coming home, the vacation with Harry spoiled because of the children. They had spoiled so much of her life, without meaning to, without knowing what they were doing. At least they were out of the house and wouldn't be there when she got home. She couldn't take any more of the screaming and counting. If only she could talk to Joe and tell him how much she loved him and trusted him.

"Will you try to find Joe?"

"Yes. Sure I will."

"Will we go anyplace, Harry? Will we go away anyplace?"

"Sure thing, Red. Just as soon as you feel up to it."

"Sure?"

"Sure."

She closed her eyes, easing into the calm darkness, away from lights and sounds. She wished she didn't feel so heavy. She wished she could move her arms.

Harry called Kay again the next morning. "It's pretty bad, Kay. She started hemorrhaging again during the night. I don't know if . . ." he couldn't go on.

"Harry. Are you at the hospital?"

"Yes."

"Have you been there all night?"

"Since they called me at the crack of dawn."

"Is she conscious?"

"In and out. When she comes to, they come get me. She just can't seem to fight it. She's so weak. She can't talk anymore."

"She never really recovered from the last bout."

"I know." Harry's voice broke.

"I'll be right there. You need someone with you. I'll be right there."

The nurse came out and got Harry. "She's awake now."

"Hi, Red." He bent low and brushed her cheek with his

lips. "You're looking better. What did you say? What? Me? I'm fine. I miss you, but other than that I'm fine. I love you, Red. You know that." He raised her hand and kissed it. She was so pale. His guilt mounted as Red sank. He hoped to God Kay could make it right between them.

She tried to clutch his collar. He hadn't understood her. "Did you find Joe?" she repeated in voiceless words.

"What's that, honey? Try to say it again."

"Did you find Joe?"

Harry shook his head and eased her hand back to the bed. "Don't try to talk. If you rest now, you'll be better later. You can tell me then."

"Joe. Joe." She knew he didn't understand her. It was so frustrating, trying, and no one hearing. Not even Harry.

"There's someone coming to see you soon, Red. Now don't blow up about it. It's Kay. She feels bad about what happened and she wants to make up and ask your forgiveness. You'll do that, won't you? You tell her you forgive her. You may not forget it, but at least forgive her. Do it for me, Red. For me. Think you're up to it? Think so?"

Katie opened her mouth and tried to tell him she didn't want to see Kay. Ever again. No. No. Don't let her in here. Tell her to go to hell. She tried to say it, but he couldn't hear her. She would hold his hand and not let him go get her. No. No.

"I'll be back shortly. I'm going to run down for some coffee." To the nurse, he said: "If her friend Miss Wright comes, let her in, will you? And give them a little time alone."

Katie was so tired, watching wearily as Harry crossed the room and opened the door.

Before he returned, Kay came in, walking past the nurse with a nod, walking up to Katie.

Harry. Harry. Katie tried to cry out for him. She watched the white nurse leave the room. Then she looked back at the pinched face above hers, the skimpy hair hidden under a silk scarf Katie had given her. Katie suddenly thought of Dan and remembered she had never told Harry about the Jewish wife.

"You're pretty sick, Katie. But I guess you know that."

Katie hated her and wanted to tell her how much she hated her.

Kay bent lower toward her. "You may not make it this time. What are you trying to say? How dare I? How dare I come here? It's what you'd like to say, isn't it?" Kay put her mouth against Katie's ear. "I dared come . . ." she hissed ". . .

because I wanted to thank you. Yes, thank you. I needed a miracle and you gave it to me. I can smell death around you, Katie. Harry can't; he doesn't believe it. He can't bring himself to face the fact that you're going to die. But I can. This is the end. Unless, of course, you get a miracle, too. If you do, then I'll think of something else. Now I want to show you something." She straightened up. "I hope it will amuse you. Don't forget you wanted to spruce me up like a goose for the gander, to be attractive the way you are."

Katie felt a stabbing constriction in her heart as she watched Kay go to the mirror and, letting the scarf flutter to the floor, she pulled the pins out of the bun at the back of her head and ran her fingers through her hair, fluffing it out like a preening bird.

"Like it?" Kay asked, with a twisted half-smile, her eyes watchful as she went back to stand over Katie.

Katie looked at the deep auburn hair, rich waves of luxurious hair tumbling in soft curls around Kay's face, hiding the scrawny long neck and ears that stuck out too far. Anger and hatred sapped her sparse strength.

"I thought you'd like it." Kay again bent to speak close to Katie's face. "You were very clever to have suggested I get my hair fixed. I thought about the wig you wanted, but then I decided to have a good dye job and a body wave instead. Just got it yesterday afternoon. Isn't it amazing what they can do with skimpy hair nowadays? Mine looks as full and rich as yours. And now I've perfected my makeup. Every day I look as good as you do when you're all dolled up." Kay ran her eyes down the thin body under the white sheet, then back to the drawn, graying face.

"Right now," Kay went on, "I look considerably better. Do you know how much I envied you? Do you know? Have you any idea? You had everything, everything. You had the beauty and the brains and the money . . . oh, so much money you could buy anything you ever wanted: houses, servants, yachts, vacations, clothes—fabulous clothes you finally got bored with and handed down to me. I never dreamed anyone could spend so much on clothes—thousands of dollars for a dress, three, four, ten thousand—it meant nothing to you. This dress. Remember it?" She swept her fingers down the white linen wrap dress. "Remember this one? A simple little Ralph Lauren that cost more than I make in two weeks, and this is one of your cheaper ones. Yes, you had everything." She glanced at the door. "But in the end, you couldn't hang on to your husband and you never had the love of your children. Too bad money couldn't buy those for you. Was all that money worth this? Worth dying just the way the poor die? Money might buy you a private room, but it won't buy you any extra time. Was it really worth it?" She raised her head and stood erect by the bed. "You're too far gone to be able to answer me, aren't you? Well, maybe, not for sure, but maybe, someday I'll know the answer to that. When I have everything, the way you did. When I'm in your place. I have half your name now; I doubt if it'll be too difficult to get the other half."

A choked, rasping rattle came from Katie's throat as she tried to raise her head and speak.

"Strange, isn't it, about the name." Kay smiled. "The same name, and the same clothes, and now the same hair. We're almost clones. Isn't life strange?" She backed to the foot of the bed. "I had to come thank you. Don't you see? It wasn't to taunt you. It's just good manners."

The door opened and Harry came in. He stopped when he saw Kay. "Look at that, will you!"

"Oh, Harry," Kay said quickly. "Katie thought it up some time ago. I just got the courage to do it yesterday." She smiled at the stricken figure on the bed. "Katie especially wanted me to have her exact same color. We both thought it was a great joke and would amuse you."

He laughed. "You're a funny one, Red—to talk Kay into getting a hairdo exactly like your own. It looks nice, Kay." He looked from Kay to Katie anxiously.

"It's all right, Harry," Kay said reassuringly. "Katie and I understand each other. It's all right now."

He smiled broadly, letting out a deep breath, and draped his arm around Kay's shoulder. "I'm glad. Really glad. How about that, Red?"

Katie tried to cry out a warning to him: Watch out, Harry. Watch out. But the words were silent. She looked through the fog at the two of them: Harry with one hand in his pocket and the other around Kay; Kay in her white wrap dress, her rich auburn hair the one bright spot in the picture; standing side by side smiling at the camera through the Nantucket mist.

The fog thickened and Katie saw the dense round mouth of the tunnel coming closer. She blinked once, as the brilliant white rim of light passed her by and she went deeper into the darkness.